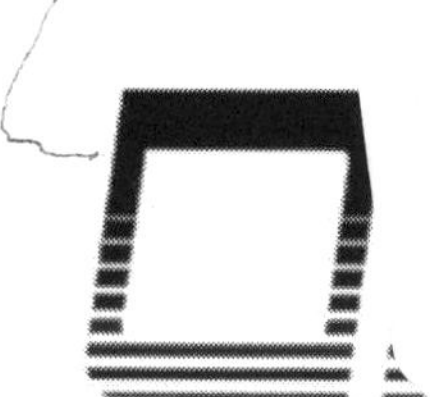

# AGAINST

**ACES HIGH, JOKERS WILD BOOK 7**

**O. E. TEARMANN**

This is a work of fiction. All of the characters, organizations, and events portrayed in this novel are either products of the author's imagination or are used fictitiously.

ODDS AGAINST



Amphibian Press

13820 NE Airport Way
Suite #K471902
Portland, OR
97251-1158
United States

ISBN: 978-1-949693-49-2

www.amphibianpress.online
www.oetearmann.com

Printed in the United States of America

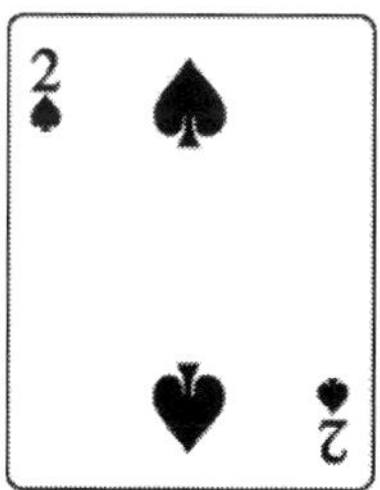

*The activist's first task is to make sure the pillars are shaken.*
*-Srdja Popovic*

## Reader Advisement

Themes of police brutality, injustice and abuse are explored in this volume. Included are romantic and sexual scenes between people whose genders may not fit your expectations. If this offends you, consider yourself warned.

If you want to be involved in the kinds of communities discussed in this story, there are resources for the real world in the back of this book and at www.oetearmann.com.

Buckle up for the ride.

# Table of Contents

## Event File 01
## File Tag: Adaptability Test
## 07:20-06-05-2161

A jaundiced pall hung over the Dust. Smoke insinuated itself through the garage door as it rumbled open.

Kevin pulled off his respirator, packed it, and slid on his riding helmet, weak morning light playing over his hands. A cough doubled him over on his seat as the helmet's air circulation kicked in, and he felt his ribs creak. Damn these summer fires. Maybe he should have listened to Damian and stayed indoors. But *someone* had to teach Inyoni the ropes of requisitions work on the Grid.

The boy had done an exemplary job on requisitions in the Dust since he'd joined up, but any requisitions personnel worth their salt needed Grid training. Kevin needed to introduce him to their on-Grid contacts and get him trained up, and he couldn't entrust that responsibility to anyone else. He'd already run the logistical algebra: yes, he was a hot commodity on the Grid these days, and if he'd had his way he'd continue to make his runs alone and ask someone else to do these trainings. But that wasn't an option.

Of his available base mates with requisitions training, Blake was too old these days, Yvonne wasn't a good choice for escorting a trainee—whatever she said on the subject—and she had her own Grid assignment as well, God help them all. With Blake in the office and Yvonne bouncing around the Grid with her wife like ping-pong balls full of nitro, Kevin *knew* he was the most logical choice to train their newest requisitions specialist in the most dangerous of his duties. And if Kevin ever wanted to breathe normally again, he *had* to go pick up the shipment they'd requisitioned. Damian and his ribs would just have to hold their peace.

"You sure about this, man?" Inyoni asked dubiously. "Ain't good, that cough."

"Give it up, Inyoni," Dozer offered with a chuckle. "Kev's got a stubborn streak big as the West."

"You wound, Dozer," Kevin called over to their senior transport man, using the exterior speakers on his helmet as he ran checks on the paraphernalia of the disguise he'd be using today and the bike itself. "I always listen to sensible advice."

"Yeah? Since when?" Topher called back from under the chassis of their biggest truck. Kevin didn't dignify that with an answer. He switched the exterior speakers on his helmet off, speaking to Inyoni alone once the other man slid on the custom helmet Topher had designed with decorative fins on either side to accommodate his long Gamma ears.

"We're all set. Are you ready?"

"Yeah," Inyoni agreed, though his tone was anything but.

"Right then," Kevin agreed, and kicked his bike into life. No sense giving the boy any more time to ruminate.

They entered Denver through a new route: riding I-70 down to the potholed mess of 287, the chips on their bikes spoofing the automatic toll-chargers built into the concrete dividers of the road. Eventually, they were on the Colfax Expressway, one of the few roads in town that permitted manually operated vehicles. ArgusCo charged anyone riding manual a staggering fee for a Manual Vehicle Operation License on their roads, of course, but that was what spoofing broadcasters were for.

"How are you doing?" Kevin asked into his mic. Inyoni's voice was gruff in reply. "'M fine. Gonna be fine."

"Yes, you are," Kevin reassured. "This is nerve-wracking, but trust me: it's never as dangerous as your nerves are telling you it will be. Keep breathing. Remember, this is routine for us."

"Sure," Inyoni agreed, the tension in his voice wound tight. Kevin could imagine how the younger man was feeling just now. He remembered that jittery paranoia that Inyoni must be experiencing all too well; the emotional whiplash of a former corporate citizen whose old haunts were now enemy territory. There was a unique terror for someone returning to a comfortable milieu now rendered inimical by a personal change of allegiances; a shivering, sick dread of the familiar turning on you. He'd been younger than Inyoni when Blake had begun his own training for Grid runs, and he made a mental note to be aware of that. He'd need to be careful not to copy Blake's training techniques for a teenager too closely, lest he inadvertently patronize this fellow.

Their first stop was a maintenance closet in the underground parking garage of the Cavanaugh Campus Anschutz, down in a corner where a sloppy contractor had failed to install a camera. They slipped into the maintenance closet, Kevin pulling off his riding helmet and setting up a portable mirror. Inyoni hefted the bag full of the disguise du jour, passing it to him. It still galled Kevin that on-Grid runs were so *inconvenient* these days. Everything took so much *time* now that he had to create elaborate personae each time he sallied out. But, given the alternative, it was worth the effort.

Sliding out of his riding gear, Kevin stripped down to his boxers, the costume bag open in front of him. He looked himself over in the mirror, considering today's disguise. The people who'd tailored his genome had intended him to stand out and be noticed, and they'd given him all the features for it: bright red hair, skim-milk skin, an aquiline face and a slim, patrician build. These days, his project was to hide every inch of that in public. He was incredibly grateful for the training he'd been given in disguise since the corporation who thought they owned him had started hunting him in earnest. He'd decided to take advantage of the fact that he and Inyoni were roughly the same height for this disguise; they'd present themselves as a frail old father and a protective son.

"This may take a bit," he offered over his shoulder.

Inyoni shrugged in the mirror. "'S'okay, I got a book."

Kevin nodded, pulling out the first element of his costume: a prosthetic pot belly. He'd be in close proximity to a number of people today, so holomasks wouldn't cut it. He'd have to go all out in order to interact closely with the number of people he'd see. The contacts that gave his eyes the desired hue, among other things, came next: those allowed him to see everything else he was doing. The contacts were followed by a tight cap over his hair, then the carefully painted and prepared silicone prosthetics to cover his head and shoulders. He pasted everything into place meticulously with spirit gum, ensuring that the facial attachments moved naturally. Wherever there was a gap that showed his own skin, a little makeup ameliorated the shortfall. Then it was time for the silicone gloves inlaid with synthetic skin, the genome in the printed cells linked to a falsified set of credentials that would fool the security readers. Eventually, he pulled out the clothes and water-cooled chill-vest that he'd picked up at a few second-hand stores, fumbling his way into them with fingers hampered by the gloves. Finally, he checked himself over in the mirror.

An elderly Black man looked back at him, rheumy brown eyes with yellowing sclera meeting his in the mirror. Arthritic, walnut-knuckled hands hung loosely at the character's sides. Kevin studied the effect. Not bad. He wasn't really comfortable switching races in his disguise work—the history of European Americans dressing as African Americans was abominable, and it still seemed disrespectful—but Inyoni was Black, so he needed to appear Black too. *Needs must when the Devil drives*, he told himself, interrogating his appearance with narrowed eyes. Something was still off.

The posture, that was it. Kevin dropped his shoulders and changed his body language a bit, adjusting his stance. Much better. He'd have to keep the adjustment in mind; if he got sloppy and reverted to his natural posture, it wouldn't do them any favors.

"What do you think, Inyoni?" He asked over his shoulder.

In the mirror, Inyoni stared at him.

"Y'know, the way you change up your looks…that's spooky."

Kevin laughed. "I'll take that as a compliment. Now—" he considered it for a moment, adjusting and reshaping the way he pronounced words in accord with his character—"come on son, we got errands."

"Okay, now it's really fucking spooky," Inyoni stood. The boy had his own features in need of disguise: the long goat-like ears that marked the results of shoddy gene splicing in his family line would get him killed out here as surely as Kevin's own peculiarities, if for different reasons. But Inyoni's approach to disguise was routine; he simply tapped the holographic emitter implanted in the side of his neck. Now he had human ears and violently blue hair. He'd gotten his riding gear off, and the coolant-inlaid backpack and jacket that hid his tattoos were unremarkable.

Kevin nodded. "Perfect. Once more into the breach, then."

Heading upstairs, they walked into the Cavanaugh Supply Center and made the purchases that Kevin had set up ahead of time. He was glad he had too, in spite of the slight risk; it allowed them to bypass a ridiculously long line.

Four packages were pushed across the desk to him. Kevin checked his tab as any good delivery man should, feeling his heart sink into his boots.

"Clinic delivery sheet says there's supposed to be pulmonary nanites in this order? Looks like it's just dental-care nanites here." He mumbled in today's voice, working to sound as disinterested as any old man running delivery gigs should. The clerk behind the desk shrugged, eyes opaque.

"Those're on back order."

Kevin cursed inside his head. No pulmonary nanites. Damian wouldn't be happy with him about that.

"Thanks," Kevin sighed, stowing what they were able to get in a courier bag and shuffling into the street with Inyoni at his side. The heat was well into the triple digits when they stepped out, and the sidewalks were nearly empty under the billowing shade cloths meant to reflect harsh sun off the walkways. The occasional car shushed past, but people were indoors if they could be.

The pavement sizzled in the heat. Kevin wished the persona he'd taken could be seen wearing a better class of chill-vest; he was sweating under the silicone.

"C'mon boy," he offered in his old-man rasp. "Don't want to be out in the heat too long."

Kevin took care to limp at a fraction of his natural pace; the small rubber balls he'd put in his shoes helped him unconsciously change his gait to avoid any flagging of his body mechanics in surveillance data. He knew from experience that he'd loathe and despise the things by the end of the day, despite their usefulness.

When they reached it, the cool air of the TechoCo wholesale supply center washed over them like a benediction. The warehouse was blessedly dim as well, giving them a break from the oppressive sear of June sun.

"Got a PO number?" the man behind the wholesale center's counter asked.

"We're here for Ernest's handbag," Kevin stated. His contact blinked. Quietly, the sandy-bearded man reached under his station, flicking what Kevin knew was a concealed sound-wave emitter.

"Hey," the man greeted once it was safe to speak. "We haven't met before, I think. Andy."

"We have met before, actually," Kevin offered, reverting to his natural tones and straightening his spine. Andy blinked. "Wait…who?"

"It's Kevin."

Andy stared for a moment, absolutely goggle-eyed. Then he barked out a laugh. "Holy fuck. Nice work man."

"Thanks," Kevin acknowledged with a smile. "I'm pretty pleased with it. Andy, I'd like you to meet Inyoni. He's the newest requisitions man on the crew. He'll be coming over for pickups now and again."

"Good to meet ya, man," Andy offered, reaching out to shake Inyoni's hand. "You need coolant or the good plastic for the printers, you come here."

"I'll remember it," Inyoni agreed with a smile that bordered on shy.

"Do we have today's shipment ready to go?" Kevin asked.

Andy nodded. "Yup. Got it all set." He hefted a box onto the counter. "Try not to keep this outside too long when it goes over a hundred an' ten," he cautioned Inyoni. "Three or four hours tops, otherwise it starts going bad."

"Thanks for the tip," Inyoni acknowledged, pulling off his backpack and carefully stowing the box in its cool interior. "You got paid already, yeah?"

"All taken care of," Andy acknowledged with a nod for Kevin. "Only client who always pre-pays, you guys."

"Good money for good supplies," Kevin quipped, smiling. "We have to keep moving, Andy. Good seeing you." Digging in his pack, he passed over a sealed box. "That's strawberries to take home to the polycule. Give your fellow and your ladies my regards."

Now Andy really smiled. "Thanks pal."

"Any time. Keep your head down in the storm," Kevin replied with a smile. Turning, he readjusted himself into the stance of an old man, and walked.

"Hey uh, it okay to ask something?" Inyoni asked as they paced under the weight of heat.

"Sure," Kevin agreed in the voice of today's persona. "Shoot."

"Something about…y'know, work?" The younger man tacked on.

"What would make that a bad idea right now?" Kevin asked, hoping the boy would take it as encouragement to think through the puzzle and not as something sarcastic. He'd been practicing, but it was still tricky to hold an unnatural speech pattern and inflect as he intended simultaneously. Luckily, they'd done enough of these coaching sessions that Inyoni knew the drill. He considered for a moment.

"Uh, we're on a street on the Grid?"

"And what's around us?"

"Warehouses, supply centers, some bars and stuff up ahead?"

Moving through the heat like a man wading through molasses, Kevin continued the thought exercise. "What around here has tech capable of zeroing in on specific conversations?"

Inyoni considered for a moment. "I guess…some bars might, but not out to more'n fifty feet past their doors."

"So, is it safe to talk?" Kevin asked, quietly throwing the ball back into Inyoni's court.

Slowly, Inyoni nodded. "Yeah, I guess, unless somebody walks by."

"And if they do, you…" Kevin prompted.

Inyoni gave him a quick smile. "I don't just stop talking, I switch the topic to something like the heat. Regular stuff. People notice it more if you shut down, yeah?"

"Exactly right," Kevin agreed, giving the other man a quick smile. "Well done. So what's your question?"

Inyoni's eyes were anxious and hopeful in equal measure when he glanced Kevin's way. "This's the second grid run I done with you, an' you talk to everybody like you're all old buddies. You friends with everyone you work with?"

Kevin snorted, thinking of all the people he barely managed to be civil with; Blucifer, that bastard Schultz, the requisitions man from Base 1491 who'd felt up Sarah once and still harbored a grudge over getting punched for it. "I should be so lucky. Nobody authentic is friends with everybody."

"Oh." Inyoni shoved his hands in his pockets, lowering his head.

They walked in silence for a moment.

"What makes you ask?" Kevin queried. Inyoni shrugged. "Just wanted to know…how long it took, I guess. To get to be friends with everybody. Do this like it weren't no thing."

Ah. That was it. Kevin reached over and gave Inyoni's arm a quick squeeze. "Don't worry about that. I've been at this for years. You get to know people and build up contacts in time. It's slow, because people are careful. We have to be, given our work. We can't afford to be too trusting; the corporations will take every chance to destroy us if we let our guard down. But once you're introduced and start showing up, you'll have some friendly contacts in no time. Wait and see."

Inyoni flashed him a grin. "Thanks man. I guess I…nevermind."

They walked in companionable silence for, quite literally, a hot minute.

"Hey ah," Inyoni began, "one other thing."

"Shoot."

"Is this like, a weird number of trips we been doin'? Seems like we're gettin' more stuff than the other base rosters I was lookin' through for that training simulation you had me do."

*Clever fellow, he caught on,* Kevin thought to himself. *Shame I'll have to put him off the scent of that for now.*

"Not really," he demurred, watching himself lest he lose his voice modulation. "Better to have a supply surplus and not need it than—" In his pocket, Kevin's tab buzzed an alert.

"Hold that thought, Inyoni." Reaching into his pocket and quietly cursing the silicone gloves that made his fingers clumsy, he pulled out the tab and read the alert. His heart froze in his chest.

"Inyoni," he stated, feeling ice grip his innards, "we've been tracked. Our location is going out on an EagleCorp alert."

"The fuck?!" Inyoni whispered, voice tight. "How?!"

"It's the Sleepwalker. Again. We'll have to hit pause on the rest of this run." Kevin nodded in the direction of an alley. "Come on. We need to get out of sight and out of signal range. There's a bar I know that runs GPS spoofers in the background. Follow me."

Now he cursed the gait-changing accouterments he wore in earnest for the way they hobbled him. He needed to *move*, but he was chained to a snail's pace by today's disguise. And this bloody cough that kept doubling him over would slow him down too. Damn the smoke. Damn the scarring in his lungs. Damn, damn, damn this entire situation to Hell!

Well, no sense fretting about it. Contracted bounty hunters would, of course, be headed his way, followed by Peacekeepers. But they couldn't get here in less than twenty minutes. In that time, hopefully, they'd be undercover.

In the back of his mind, his thoughts spun like gears hooked to an overactive dynamo. How?! How had this Sleepwalker prick gotten a lock on him so quickly?! It defied everything in his training. He knew what a valuable bounty he was. Cavanaugh Corporation wanted his head on a plate, and they were paying very well to get it. He'd planned meticulously with that fact in mind. Unless he'd ended up with a micro-tag under his skin—and he knew for a fact *that* hadn't happened, Damian checked him over weekly and he ran his own checks too— then a GPS lock happening this fast was impossible.

And yet it had happened. He needed to know *how*.

Had Cavanaugh figured out how to re-activate the key-codes on the nanoids housed in his bones and joints, and tracked the GPS on those? No, as far as he knew that was impossible to do remotely.

As far as he knew, of course, was the worryingly operative clause in that sentence.

Damn it, he'd been *so careful*!

"Down this way," he murmured, sidling down an alley. From now on, he told himself, they'd carry GPS spoofers on their persons, not just in their vehicles. They'd have to remember to turn them off before they stepped into corporate stores and set off the security systems, and the range would have to be restricted to a three-foot diameter; otherwise the

GPS scrambling they'd cause in the population at large would leave a trail any moron could follow.

Yes, that would help in the future.

That left the nastier question: what the hell were they going to do about *now*?

Step one: go to ground. Once they were under cover, they could plan.

"Down this way," he murmured, and Inyoni followed him down into the sunken stairwell that led to the bar. Counting Electric Sheep's wonderfully campy centerpiece of retro-neon lambs jumped over the bar as he and Inyoni walked in. Outside of the light of the sign, the room was a comfortingly anonymous gloom. In here, people of all stripes and all corporate affiliations minded their own business and held their private conversations in the safely signal-disrupted space. Air filters hummed, blessedly cleaning the smoke out. Finally, Kevin drew a deep breath. Playing his part, Inyoni ushered him into a seat. "Here Dad. 'Scuse me? Can I get cold water with ice? My dad's hot."

"Course!" the bartender called. "One glass or two?"

"Two please," Inyoni replied. A few moments later, two glasses of water beaded with condensation clinked down on the table.

"Getting pretty hot out there, is it?" the bartender asked.

Kevin nodded. "Too hot." He cleared his throat and dropped the pass-phrase as casually as he could. "Looks like there's a storm coming in. Glad we could get in out of the dust."

"Oh yeah?" Studiously, the bartender looked away, calibrating the bar-cleaning bot. "So, you guys want anything else?"

"If you serve scrambled eggs, two plates would be good," Kevin replied, staying in character and as blasé as any other customer. Phil the bartender nodded, setting the cleaning bot to run. "I can do egg sandwiches, that work?"

Sandwiches. That meant he did have GPS scramblers on hand, but he'd have to slip them to Kevin via a dead drop in the bathroom. Not a problem.

“That’ll do,” he agreed easily.

Phil smiled. “Let me get that going for you.”

Turning, he set the food to heat in the induction oven, and slipped out from behind the bar, going about his business.

Kevin had just gotten his sandwich when the tenor of the room changed, sending a shiver up his backbone. Without doing anything so gauche as turning to stare, he took in the room in a bit more detail. What had changed the mood?

And then he heard the voices in the stairwell clearly.

“Four fucking bars. Can’t believe it!” A man was saying over the clomp of boots and the tell-tale creak of body armor. Three Peacekeepers in full patrol gear dropped onto stools, helmets in their hands and complaints in their mouths.

“Hey bartend,” one of them called, “Three fucking beers! Cold!”

Beside him, Inyoni had gone rigid as a block of concrete. Under the bar, Kevin reached over and squeezed his arm. Hopefully that would remind him to do what they’d talked about: keep breathing, stay calm, and don’t look at the opponents.

Kevin followed his own advice as well, but he allowed himself to curse in the adrenaline-buzzing quiet of his own head.

*God damn you to the ninth festering circle of Hell, Fate you bitch. Of all the days for a random patrol to wander in. I can’t run, I’ve got a trainee to watch over, and if we get out of this and Inyoni has so much as a scratch on him,Tweak will shatter, and then she’ll turn me into mincemeat.*

*And if we don’t get out of this…*

Memories of what Cavanaugh Corporation had done to his husband in an interrogation cell skittered through his mind like rats through a sewer. That was what they did to a valuable intelligence source they wanted to keep alive. What they’d do to Inyoni, the trainee they would see as expendable, in order to break a wanted dissident like himself should they be arrested together…

He stomped on that thought. *Damn it all! No, I will not let this happen. Sit still, stay calm, and think. Perhaps they'll simply have their drinks and leave. Perhaps...*

The bartender's words pulled him out of his thoughts with a jolt. "Sorry gentlemen. Your credentials are coming up as restricted."

"Are you fucking shitting me?!" One of the Peacekeepers growled, standing. "Five bars now, and you've all got us down as restricted?! What the fuck for?!"

Slow tendrils of hope unfolded like the first leaves of spring in Kevin's chest. Five bars. That meant...but no, he'd have to be sure. Best to sit tight and wait for confirmation.

Phil studied the readouts. "Says here 'restricted due to multiple examples of obeying unethical orders', sir. Sorry sir. Can't serve you."

"Can't serve us for fuck!" the biggest Peacekeeper snarled. "Listen here, you slap your reader upside the head til it works and get us the fucking beers!"

Laconically, Phil shook his head. "Can't, Officer. The coolers won't open unless I have a registered and approved Citizen to serve. Sorry, sir."

"For fuck's sake," the only woman in the group groaned. "Fine. Water."

"Of course, ma'am. That'll be ten dollars a glass."

Grumbling, the three Peacekeepers downed their glasses of water, paid up and left, cursing all the way.

For a time, the bar was silent.

"Seems like that's been happening to a lot of Peacekeepers," Phil observed, polishing a single glass by hand. "All of them, matter of fact. In every bar."

The hope in Kevin's chest blossomed into elation. He'd heard several Citizen's Assembly meetings talk about the possibility of an action they'd dubbed No Bird Gets Booze. NatBank and EagleCorp citizens had agreed that, with careful work, it was possible to get in and restrict every serving Peacekeeper's credentials to deny them alcohol at bars and stores. So they had put it into action after all. Stupendous! What a way to ruin the Peacekeeper's morale. He kept his face carefully neutral as a matter of course. Inside, he was grinning like a loon. Things were in motion these days, and moving faster than he could believe.

"Must be hard," He observed, sipping his water. Laboriously, he pushed himself off his barstool. "Son, I'm gonna use the pot. Then you'n me should get home."

Shuffling off, he headed down the hall to the gents', the hidden GPS scramblers, and their way out.

## Event File 02
## File Tag: Supply Procurement
## 14:15-06-05-2161/ 09:30-06-08-2161

Kevin flopped onto his rented bed, grinning. "Even EagleCorp's citizens are mobilizing. Everything's happening, Inyoni! Everything's moving."

Inyoni glanced up from his tab. "Guess so," he agreed, smiling a tender sort of smile.

Kevin watched him glance back down at his tab, amused. "I take it Tweak's checking in on us?" he asked, taking in the boy's expression. Neither of the two Gammas would appreciate the appellation of 'adorable' but it was hard to find a better descriptor for their relationship. He wouldn't say it aloud, of course; he didn't want to be skinned alive any time soon.

"Yeah," Inyoni agreed dreamily. "She's checkin' in after that Sleepwalker scare."

"Proactive of her," Kevin murmured, repressing a sigh. "Has she had any luck on her end hunting the Sleepwalker? He's been a thorn in our sides for months now. It's becoming tedious."

The Gamma shrugged. "Nah. No dice. She's pissed."

"I can imagine," Kevin agreed, closing his eyes. "You put the plastic in the fridge? It'll need to stay cool until it's stabilized in printing."

"Yeah, it stayed a good temp," Inyoni agreed.

“Alright,” Kevin agreed, stretching. “So, we make pickups over the next few days, deliver the supplies for the community cooling shelters on day three. And then we head on home.”

“Yeah,” Inyoni sighed, and the happiness in his voice was unmistakable. “Home.”

Thankfully, the rest of the pickups and deliveries went off without a hitch in the next few days. They pulled into the site the Builders’ Union had stipulated at four in the morning on their last Grid day.

“We’re turning an old bus station into a free cooling shelter,” the short-haired woman leading the Builders’ Union project explained as Kevin and Inyoni unloaded the boxes of insulation foam, coolant, hydration salts and the parts to create air filters alongside the volunteers. “It’s out of the way enough that we think it won’t be noticed for a while, and the people who can’t afford the official shelters will have somewhere to go for a change. We’re putting word out on the Common Ground.”

“That’s wonderful,” Kevin exclaimed, thrilled by the work all around him. “Where are you getting the tools?”

The crew lead who’d been introduced as Bobbi gave him a quick, dangerous grin. “Stuff goes missing off building sites all the time. You know how it is.”

Kevin grinned right back, hoping she could see it through the plastic of his respirator. Today he was in a getup that made him look roughly his own age, albeit much stockier. In this guise, he could give this woman the smile one equal gives another. She deserved it; the kind of work the Builders’ Union was doing to provide free community cooling shelters was phenomenal.

“Now that you got us the supplies, we’ve got four more sites in this zip code scoped out for renovation,” his contact enthused. Kevin nodded. “I look forward to seeing it. While we’re here, can we be of use?”

Bobbi grinned. “Sure! Grab a foam gun.”

For the next few hours, Kevin and Inyoni insulated panels, held up equipment while construction folks fixed it in place, and trotted around the area with armfuls of supplies. The air buzzed with the sound of equipment and the steady hum of chill vests. Sweat made Kevin's respirator slip on his face, and he got a lungful or two of smoky air, but thankfully the cough held off for the time being.

By the time the heat of the day came on, the volunteers were standing inside a small shelter that could comfortably seat fifty people, giving each other grins of satisfaction.

Turning to Bobbi, Kevin held his hand out. "It's time we were going. Good luck here."

"Thanks, you too," she agreed, shaking his hand with a smile.

The satisfaction of the day's work stayed with Kevin as they worked their way through public transit and the careful intricacies of exiting the Grid, buoying him like a balloon as they crossed the Dust. That community cooling shelter would save lives this year, when the temperature got into the one-twenties and the prices on seats in the Corporate cooling shelters hiked themselves out of reach for the Poor Standing citizens. It was a community project in the truest sense of the term, and there were projects like it springing up everywhere. The Citizens' Unions had more power every day, and they were using that power to help one another and take their lives back from the seven corporations that owned America. People were pushing back, and the Corps were starting to falter.

It was a good time to be alive. And if what Aidan had whispered to him in the night before he left was true…if their team really was going to be allowed to…just the thought made elation bubble in his chest. *Everything* was happening.

Hope floating his heart like a boat, he grinned at Inyoni as they stepped off their bikes in the cool gloom of their garage. He put a hand on the younger man's back once Inyoni had pulled off his helmet.

"That, my friend, was a very good run."

"Yeah?" Inyoni asked, his mobile ears perking up. "Yeah, I guess it was." He started to say something else, but that was when Tweak cannoned into him, wrapping her arms around his waist.

"Hey, b-Bird."

"Hey Dragon," Inyoni laughed, smoothing her hair. She grinned up at him, triangular face alight as she chirped out a few breathless words. "Inside. Now. C-c'mon."

Inyoni, of course, followed her like a young Great Dane. They really were adorable. Even skittish Cameron smiled a bit as he watched the lovebirds walk away, and Topher had to ask him twice to pass the drill.

Kevin caught Dozer's eyes across the garage, and grinned. The senior transport specialist grinned right back. "You got a fancy word for them bein' stuck like glue?"

"Oh, I've got several," Kevin quipped. "Twitterpaited, moon-calving, enraptured, infatuated. But at the moment, a much shorter and more vulgar word probably covers the situation."

"Yeah?" Topher asked, poking his head up above the bike he had taken mostly apart.

"Horny." Kevin winked. He left the garage with the sound of laughter still ringing off the walls, smiling to himself.

## Event file 03
## File Tag: Mutual Support
## 09:40-06-08-2161

Tweak pushed Inyoni down the hall, into their room, up against a wall, and into a hard kiss, standing on tiptoe and gripping his shoulders for balance.

"You get hurt?" She asked, fingers sliding under his jacket to check his arms for autopads, then his chest. Her head was a nest of live wires. Nerves from the close calls she'd watched Inyoni go through on the Grid, fear, relief that he was safe: all of it was tangling into one giant fizzing ball of *need* to hold onto this guy.

"Nah," Inyoni kissed her back. Turning them, he lifted her and rested her with her back against the wall, her legs on his hips. "Not a scratch."

That was a lot better; now she could really kiss him. "Sure?" She demanded. Inyoni couldn't feel it when he got hurt. If he had gotten hurt and he didn't know...

Her pulse was starting to pound. She'd been so scared when that Sleepwalker warning had come up. So scared when those Peacekeeper signals had shown on the reads and Inyoni's biometrics had shot into the stress zone. It'd made her sick to her stomach. She'd thrown up this morning, that's how scared she'd been. But he'd come back. He'd come back, and she wasn't letting go.

"Definite," Inyoni breathed, kissing her throat.

"Good," Tweak agreed, reaching down and unzipping his pants. "Wanna fuck. Got time?"

Inyoni gave a little snort of a laugh. "Make time." Reaching between them, he unzipped her pants, petting her through her underwear. The thrill of it zinged right up her spine and exploded in her brain. Fuck, she was never going to get over how *good* that was. She ground her hips against him, but the stupid pants were in the way.

"Bird," she gasped out, "Down. My pants. Off."

"You want to get into bed or—" Inoyni started. Tweak shook her head, breathing fast. "Wall. Pants. Off. Now."

"Gotcha," he murmured. Setting her down, he pulled down her pants, then her undies. It took *forever*. Stupid pants!

She grabbed onto his shoulders as he stood and pressed herself against him, wanting to grind her clit on his dick. She wasn't tall enough to get that to work right, and that was a pain, but he gave that little grunt that meant 'I am so horny', and lifted her back up against the wall, and now *everything* lined up right.

She wrapped her legs around his waist, scrambling to get them together. She need need *needed* to ground all this shivering freak-out she'd been keeping down, and she needed to do it fast, and this was The Absolute Best way to do it.

She pressed herself down onto him hard, and the feels blew her brain wide open. Face buried in her hair, Inyoni groaned, thrusting into her hard enough to push her up the wall. The fireworks show started in her muscles, just the little sparklers first, but Inyoni got the big flash-bangs going pretty soon, and then it was one big lightshow, and her legs were quivering and everything, everything, everything in the world was lights and sparkles and GOOD.

Inyoni came, his long ears quivering like grass in the wind. She loved the way they did that when he got off.

"You need more?" He asked quiet, pressing inside her soft and easy now. She kissed him gentle. "Nah. I'm good. You did good."

"Same to you," he chuckled, pulling out carefully. He'd almost dropped her the first time they tried this; he'd been careful since. Leaning in, he snuggled his face down against her throat, holding her. Arms and legs wrapped around him, she held him too.

"Worried about you," she whispered into one ear. It twitched.

"Yeah. Close call," Inyoni breathed, turning his head to kiss her slow. "Wanna hang out and wind down. You got time?"

"Make time," she whispered back.

Inyoni chuckled. "Kay. Let's hang?"

"Kay," Tweak agreed. "Bed. Then w-work. Sound good?"

"Yeah."

Inyoni carried her over to the bed and set her down on it, lying down beside her. A year ago, she never would have believed lying here, touching somebody, could be this *good.* It still threw her for a loop. Sex was *fun,* sure. Plenty of people had told her *that.* But nobody had ever told her that sex shut off all the jitters and all the bad feels for hours.

She rolled her head to look at Inyoni, who was staring at the ceiling with a goofy grin. Sex with him was more than fun. It was *the best.*

Inyoni sighed, closing his eyes. "Any luck with the Sleepwalker thing?"

Tweak snorted. "I wish."

Inyoni nodded. "You'll get the asshole. How's the voting app?"

"Good. Testing. Goes out for approval n-next month." Tweak replied, curling up around her pillow. The stupid stomach ache was still there. Dammit.

"That fast?" Inyoni asked, opening one eye to look at her.

She grinned. "You calling me slow?"

He chuckled, rolling over to wrap himself around her and kiss her a little more. "Nah. Still floors me you can do that much that fast, is all."

"Eh," she shrugged, "had help. All the Code Monkeys are going at this. Got some help from overs-s-seas too. Alpha t-t-testing r-right now."

"Cool," Inyoni murmured, resting his brow against hers. "So, we're gonna be able to do it? Hold votes for stuff? Like, citizen-run and everything?"

"Yep," Tweak agreed.

"On top of all the other protests and stuff?" Inyoni asked.

"Everything's moving fast now," Tweak murmured, head resting on Inyoni's arm.

Tweak couldn't be sure, but the tone in her Bird's voice sounded good. "I get that, but…wow."

"Yeah. Pretty cool, hunh?" Tweak asked quietly.

Inyoni nodded. "Yeah, it's just…it's really fricking fast."

"People're sick of w-waiting," Tweak murmured, stroking his ear. "Time for things to change."

"Guess it is," her guy agreed softly. "Guess it really is…"

Tweak let herself just lay and take in the feels for a bit. Then she bounced up and grabbed her pants. "Kay. Work! My r-rig. C'mon."

Together, they walked down to her office. Inyoni rested his chin on her shoulder when she'd settled into her coding rig, his ear resting on her hair. Tweak brought up the map of Western Quadrant, Sector Fourteen, zooming in on the area where Base 1407 had settled during the latest base relocation. Studying the hologram, she blew out a breath. "Damn. G-Gulch fire. B-bigger."

Leaning in, Inyoni whistled. "Shit. Couple hundred miles it's burned now. How big's it supposed to get?"

Tweak shrugged. "Fuck if I know. G-grass fire. Could do anything." She pointed at her screen. "Fire by the freeway too. Corps will p-put that one out. P-protect the r-r-road. They won't touch the ones in the d-Dust."

Inyoni glanced down at her, his dark ears gone down into their 'I'm getting scared' position. "It gonna get much closer to here?"

Glancing up, she met his eyes and worked up a smile, resting her brow against his for a second. "Aidan has a t-ten mile p-p-proximity r-rule for the b-base. D-dozer and me got an algorithm t-tracking it with the s-sensors we've got up for w-wind and air q-q-quality. We'll know if we n-need to m-move."

She raised her eyes to her screens, thinking their readouts over. "B-Blake said this happens every couple y-years out here. Big f-fire s-s-season."

"You seen it before?" Inyoni asked quietly. Tweak shook her head. "N-not me. But you s-smell it every y-year. Smoke from s-summer fires. S-something's always b-burning." She shrugged. "No big deal. It's always that way."

"Smell it on the Grid all summer too," Inyoni agreed, his skin warm on hers. "Smoke's enough to choke on, some days. But it never felt like the fire was gonna come down the street. It feels different out here, y'know? Closer, I guess."

Tweak nodded. She did know. And it did feel too close.

After a moment, she glanced up. "Hey. We're okay. I'm w-watching. We'll be okay. Y-yeah?"

Inyoni gave her a smile in return. It wasn't a big one, but his ears came up a bit, and that was a start.

"If you're watching it, then I don't gotta worry," he replied, laying an easy kiss on her shoulder. "Thanks, Dragon."

Tweak's heart bounced like a rubber ball. She gave her guy a nod and a smile, bringing up her coding windows. For now, she didn't put on her headphones. Having Inyoni in here gave her what she usually got from tunes.

She started her routine the way she had for a while now: digging down into the corporate chat-boards, seeing what was up, checking what bounties were out and on who. The seven corporations who thought they owned the country were doubling down the only way they knew, now that their workforce was standing up and their backs were against the wall. American AgCo was getting meaner and doling out new punishments. ZonCom was getting frantic with its people-pleasing campaigns, new products full of surveillance chips, and lip service. EagleCorp was cracking down hard on anything out of line, beefing up security on

Citizen Secure and Citizen Excellent Standing property, and putting more drones in the air. ArgusCo was wiring more surveillance into the infrastructure, and more security systems were getting lethal upgrades. TechoCo was paying for tons of subcontractors to do their dirty work out the back door while smiling like maniacs for the cameras, and trying like hell to get control of what went on in cyberspace again. Cavanaugh was buying more hardened bunkers for its top people, working up more formulations for crowd-control drugs, and hiring more and more muscle from Eagle to guard its facilities. NatBank was squirreling away cash anywhere they could and putting new restrictions on how much money lower-Standing people could take out at one time, along with all kinds of financial shenanigans behind closed doors. All seven corporations were hiring every goon, heavy and fixer they could to take apart the growing Workers' Unions, but that wasn't doing them any good. Union action was taking off like a rocket, people demanding decent working conditions and the right to have a say in their lives. It was making the Corps shit their pants.

Beside her, Inyoni sighed. "Tweak…"

"Yeah?"

"The reader's not lettin' me into the base library again."

"Oh. Yeah." Tweak grabbed his tab, typed in the code, and handed it back.

Inyoni gave her a sheepish little smile. "Sorry."

"No big," Tweak replied with a smile. "You're g-gonna r-run outta books soon. Get you on the Common Ground library."

"Be nice," her guy agreed, ears perked. "Never got this much time to just chill and read. Kinda fun." He leaned his head against her shoulder again, getting into his book. Smiling, she turned her head back to her screens.

Tweak listened to her guy breathe as she read through postings on Corporate subcontractor boards that people called 'the Meat Market'. On here, bounty hunters and people hiring themselves out as any kind of goon or fixer got their intel, taking the job contracts they were provided according to rank: Level One contractors got the first pick of the jobs, and what they didn't take went down to Level Two, then Level Three, all the way down to the Level Fifteen debt-collection dickheads who took cash off people too beat down to put up a fight. All the stuff on citizens helping with the movement to bring back some kind of democracy was going to Level One, Two, and Three teams these days, so Tweak took a look at them first. Reading over the job assignments and bounty contracts, she bit her lip.

Information Source: Sleepwalker.

There it was, glowing at the top of the Level One board. The fucking Sleepwalker. That name had been turning up on so many info packets in the last couple months. And the intel in those packets was way too good. Every time she turned around, the Sleepwalker was reporting on something they were doing on the CO-WY Grid. That dickwad had wrecked tons of missions now, and he'd pinpointed Tweak's people more than once. Sometimes even info on National-level stuff that'd been said in meetings Tweak could have sworn they'd locked down tight showed up on the Meat Market because of the fucking Sleepwalker.

This was what she'd been afraid of. A mole, somewhere in the ranks of the Democratic State Force. Leaks were bad enough. She'd known they were going to end up with leaks as soon as they opened up the systems to everyday Joes. A leak she could work around. But this wasn't just a leak; this was a mole, chewing away at the roots of everything they wanted to build.

*Shit.*

"What's up?" Inyoni murmured.

Tweak glanced at him. "Hunh?"

Inyoni shrugged, one ear twitching. "Your breathing picked up. I heard the change."

"Oh." Tweak let out a long breath. "Yeah."

"You okay?" Inyoni looked up at her like a puppy, his chin resting on her shoulder.

“Not great. See this?” She asked, pointing at the screen. “Sleepwwalker?”

“Again?” Inyoni asked, sitting up straight. “That cocksplat.”

“I think he’s a m-mole,' Tweak murmured. “He’s in with us, feeding the Corps intel. Only w-way he could know what got s-said in these t-t-talks.” She glanced through the details. “Could be w-worse. Nothing s-solid. Lots of b-bits and p-p-pieces. Bad s-signal. P-probably bouncing uploads off d-d-drones, using them as h-hotspots for a q-quick and d-dirty upload.” She shrugged. “The r-r-recordings are all c-crap. M-muffled. S-scratchy. Maybe a little bug in the c-clothes. He’s f-f-feeding them l-lots of c-coordinates, though. S-scary.”

“Yeah?” Inyoni asked, glancing at her. “Whatcha gonna do?”

Tweak twitched her shoulders in a shrug. “Dunno yet. We’ll see. Gotta ask K-kevin what he—”

“Speak of the Devil and he does appear!” Kevin leaned through her office door with a smile. “I was just coming to see you when I heard my name. Have you got up-to-date maps on the nearest fire? My consol's lagging again.” He pushed those stupid old glasses he just wouldn’t let go of up his nose, studying the readouts hanging in the air around her. “Is that the Meat Market? My, it’s busy these days.”

“Y-yeah,” Tweak agreed, flicking the images away. “Fire maps? Here.” She pulled up the windows. “Fix your c-consol after l-lunch.”

“Much obliged,” Kevin agreed, studying the readouts. He sighed. “Balls, no wonder we’ve had such poor air quality these last few—”

A coughing fit cut him off, making the skinny guy lean on the door frame as he hacked up a lung. Tweak’s muscles twanged in sympathy. Every time the smoke got heavy outside, Kevin started coughing up his guts. He’d never really gotten back to a hundred percent after the weaponized bug the Corps called MACHA had ripped his lungs up. It hurt, watching him hack up like this.

When Kevin finally got the breath to talk, his voice was rough around the edges.

"Thanks for keeping a sensor on that mess, Tweak. Keep Dozer in the loop if you would; if the conflagration comes down this way we'll need to move with all due haste. Now that we've got the medical-grade plastic, Topher's started printing respirator masks that fit the kids before this gets much worse. Tom, Abigail and little Jenny have outgrown theirs and Don managed to crack his, don't ask me how. I want them properly protected if we do evacuate. On that note, Inyoni, let's talk about getting out into the Dust tomorrow and trading what we picked up with some of our Fringe-camp contacts; we can fetch the supplies that Janice stipulated for her new air-scrubbing system. I'll bring her anything on Earth if it'll get the stink of smoke out of what we're breathing indoors."

"Another run?" Tweak asked, cocking her head. "You guys're g-getting too much stuff."

"You attend to the affairs of your division, madam, and let me attend to mine," Kevin replied with a look over the rims of his glasses, putting on one of his stupid old-world acts again. She rolled her eyes.

"You sure you wanna be out there again so fast?" Inyoni asked as he stood. "I can trade around the Dust on my own. You sound rough, man."

Kevin waved a hand. "I'm fine as long as I wear a respirator outdoors; it makes my glasses fog up dreadfully, but I'll survive."

"Wear contacts, *genius,*" Tweak threw over her shoulder.

"Have manners, guttersnipe," her buddy came back, playing their favorite game.

She rolled her eyes, taking her turn. "Dweeb."

"Cretin," Kevin shot back cheerfully. She flipped him off. That just made him laugh.

"Don't you got a bunch of Sector-level stuff to do?" Inyoni asked, his ears perking up a little as he cocked his head, eyeing Kevin. That meant he was cheering up. He must be trying to tease.

It worked; Kevin sighed. "Damn, I was hoping you wouldn't call that out. I never should have agreed to become a Sector officer; you and Yvonne have all the fun these days."

Tweak snorted at the idea of calling the trading trips across the Dust 'fun'. But that was Kevin for you: batshit crazy.

"I do hope that these summer fires don't cause havoc with transit routes again. That could delay the next inter-Quadrant meeting up in the New Netherlands Quadrant," Kevin went on, giving the maps the fish eye. "I'd hate for that to happen; Aidan says there will be some impressive announcements. How's the security for the big meeting coming, Tweak?"

Tweak see-sawed her hand. "Meh." It wasn't great. It definitely wasn't where she wanted it to be. She and the team of coders spread across the country had focused on picking apart the blanket of drones covering United Corporations territory for almost two years now, and that had paid off; the drones still passed over once in a while, but they were a hell of a lot less lethal these days. Most of them had their bombs deactivated by the Force signals before they got anywhere near a base. So that was getting better, at least. And this next meeting was in the center of a giant city that you could hide anything in, so they should be okay.

"Can you elucidate 'meh'?" Kevin asked with that tone in his voice that meant he was trying to be patient. He was doing the word thing again too. Tweak looked up at him, blinking as she parsed the question. "Can I do what?"

Kevin shook his head. "Never mind. Nobody's going to die, right?"

That she could parse pretty easy. She bobbed her head. "Sure. Nobody's gonna d-die. For now." She pointed at her window on the Meat Market. "We wanna l-live a while, we got s-something to fix."

"Oh? And what's that?" Kevin stepped in. Tweak pointed at the screen, the holographic image distorting around her finger.

Kevin sucked a slow breath between his teeth. "The Sleepwalker. Again?"

"Y-yeah," Tweak agreed. Glancing between her guy and her buddy, she crossed her arms over her chest to keep the nerves in. Her scales scraped little musical notes out of each other as they rubbed together. "I think we got a m-mole."

Kevin nodded, studying the readouts. "Collate a list of times you've seen that name given on bounty contracts as the informational source, will you? I'll add my information on how often the Sleepwalker has scuppered our missions and take it up the chain of command."

"You got it," Tweak agreed. "Gimme an hour."

"Thanks Tweak." Kevin flashed her a grin, giving her a little salute. "Now, Inyoni, I'm afraid I'll have to tear you away from your scintillating inamorata; we've got this supply run to work out, and you need to practice writing your reports."

"Gotcha," her guy agreed. Glancing down, Inyoni ran a hand over Tweak's hair with a smile. The light caught in his brown eyes, making them gleam like pricy wood. "Seeya, Dragon," he murmured. Times like this, it still made her heart do weird, fluttery things to know this guy was into her.

"Seeya, Bird," she agreed, smiling up at him.

"Oh, Tweak," Kevin added, turning like some kind of dance act on one foot in the hall and leaning back into her office, "Aidan told me to check in if I saw you first. Get prepped for leaving the base in a few weeks, they want you up at the big inter-Quadrant meeting."

That sentence totaled all her good feels. Tweak groaned. "Again?" She thwacked a fist into the armrest of her chair. "F-fuck this! I'm w-w-working!"

"Tell Aidan, I don't write the orders," Kevin tossed over his shoulder. "Come on Inyoni, your darling Dragon's started to growl and I'd rather not be flame-broiled."

"Oh. Fuck. You. Kevin," Tweak grumbled at his back, bringing up her search-and-record program to start scraping the Net for mentions of the Sleepwalker.

Once she had her programs running the way she wanted, she pushed herself out of her coding chair and clomped down the hall to her commander's office.

"Aidan. *More* in-person m-meetings? S-seriously?"

In his chair, her commander sighed and turned around. Alpha expressions weren't always easy to read for a Gamma with a brain wired like Tweak's, but this smile she knew. It was the smile Aidan wore when he was thinking 'oh, great. This again.'

"Hey Tweak," Aidan offered. "Yeah, they need you at this meeting. Some new stuff is getting announced, and they want to brief you up front as the coordinator of the Inter-Quadrant Technical Solutions Committee."

"But I wanna w-w-work!" Tweak exclaimed, stamping a foot to get her frustration out. "I got back-end stuff for p-protests to c-coordin-n-nate! I got Unions to help with s-secur-rity! I gotta help c-c-code stuff for Union actions all across the c-country! And I still got work for the S-sector, and the b-base! I c-c-can't keep w-w-wasting t-time at these m-meetings! I gotta get things d-done!"

Aidan ran a hand over his blond hair. She knew this tell too, this was 'I am so tired right now.'

"I hear you," Aidan agreed. "I'm neck-deep in my end of the stuff the Unions are running. They've been organizing and putting on actions like crazy since we gave them their training. Kevin and Liza are even deeper in it than I am, and this is a crap time to get pulled away for a week. But I didn't write the order; it came down to me from Quadrant Councilor Hernandez, and it's co-signed by Regional Commander Hall and Quadrant Commander Ouray. Which makes it as solid an order as it gets." He shrugged, smiling a little. "I might be wrong, and I'm not cleared to tell you details yet, but I can tell you that I think you're going to want to hear what's going down at this meeting. It's big. Trust me on this?"

Tweak gave a long sigh, raised her eyes to the ceiling, and gave up. "Fiiiiine. But I'm taking my tab and I'm w-working while they talk. Deal?"

"Deal," Aidan agreed with a little smile. "Liza, Kevin and I will go out with you."

"When do I gotta be r-ready?" Tweak sighed.

Aidan gave her a crooked little smile. “We leave in three weeks.”

Tweak nodded. She didn’t like it, but she didn’t have to. If Aidan said it was going to be good stuff, then it was going to be good. And three weeks gave her time to get stuff done. “Yeah. Okay.”

“Thanks, Tweak,” Aidan offered, giving her a real smile this time. She did her best to give it back.

“Yeah. Sure.” She cocked her head. “Hey. You okay? No bullshit.”

Aidan gave a little laugh. “Yeah, Tweak. No bull, I’m okay. Things are starting to happen. I can’t talk about a lot of them yet, but trust me: good stuff is coming down the pipe.”

Tweak nodded. She could always trust Aidan. “Kay. Sounds g-good. Seeya.”

Turning away, she headed back to her office. If Aidan thought things were happening, she should get ready for the changes.

## Event file 04
## File Tag: Tactical Planning
## 11:10-06-08-2161

Once he was sure Tweak was out of hearing range, Aidan sat back in his chair, closed his eyes, and sighed.

He hadn't exactly lied to Tweak: most of what was happening was good. Hell, it was amazing. But *man,* it was a lot. Everything was moving so *fast* these days. Everybody wanted to do everything, now that they had the chance. And some days it felt like they were all calling him for something.

He jumped at the knock on his door, and glanced up. His sister smiled down at him.

"Hey. Rough day?"

"Try rough month," he sighed, giving her the best smile he could dredge up.

Naomi grabbed his extra chair, turned it around and dropped into it, resting her elbows on the back. "Schedule getting crazy?"

"I'll say. Take a look." Pulling a couple windows up, he expanded them so that the four holograms hung in the air, detailing actions across the Western Quadrant. "The National map's even busier," he added, flicking it up. "And this is what we're helping the civilians pull off in the next six months," he added, bringing up their own base mission roster.

Leaning in, Naomi whistled low. "You weren't kidding. Shit that's a lot of Grid runs."

"Yeah," Aidan sighed. "And most of it's falling in the middle of peak fire season. I really hate asking people to be out in the smoke."

Naomi studied the list for a beat. "How many of these are Sarah and Yvonne running? I'm seeing their names all over here."

Aidan rolled his eyes. "I know. They begged and pleaded until I gave in and assigned them as Civil Disobedience Action Advisors. They're running a bunch of the actions with the Unions. I'm surprised you didn't hear them dancing around and cheering when I gave the go-ahead." He cracked a grin. "They're calling themselves the Official Head Pranksters."

Naomi cringed a little in her seat. "You gave those two nutcases official orders to go and pull pranks on the Grid. Oh. God. I think that counts as a war crime."

Aidan gave her a crooked smile. "And I'm letting them teach civvies how to pull pranks too."

"You monster," his sister replied, blue eyes bright with laughter.

"I know. I'll probably regret it later. They're gonna love it." He was glad to have something to laugh about for a second. Glancing back at his screens, he waved a hand at the schedule. "All this is on top of the usual stuff we do keeping the base running and getting our people what they need. That makes it a heavier lift for us, as a base. We can't drop normal duties while we're doing all this extra stuff." He sighed, poking at another window. "And we need extra meds right now too. The people who had MACHA really bad are all going to need pulmonary repair nanoids to deal with the scarring in their lungs. It looked like they were going to heal okay, until they started getting smoke inhalation this season. Now the Sector Medical Officer is sending out a recommendation for everybody, and Damian's backing it up with a list of who needs the nanoids the worst. Kevin can't get them through his usual channels, either. They're backordered." He leaned back in his chair.

"That getting to you?" Naomi asked. "Our people needing the really expensive meds? Or is there something you aren't saying?"

Aidan closed his eyes. Naomi could always see right through him.

"Kevin's right at the top of the med list," he admitted. "He keeps coughing himself awake at night, Omi. It's freaking me out."

Naomi blinked. "Wait. I thought a Citizen Excellent guy like him had all kinds of fancy nanoids inside him?"

"Performance-enhancing nanoids," Aidan explained wearily. "Those can't actually fix bigtime tissue damage in his lungs. They were never meant to."

His baby sister nodded, holding his eyes. "Sucks."

Aidan gave her a tired smile. "Yeah. Sucks."

Looking away, Naomi propped her chin on her arms, staring at the screens. The black plastic joints of her off-hand made little tik-tik-tik sounds as she tapped her fingers.

"I still can't believe they used bio-weapons on us," she stated eventually, voice flat as roadkill. Aidan nodded, staring at the screens. "Most people can't. But they sure as hell did; we've got more than enough proof."

Proof like his husband coughing himself awake. Proof like the grave of a little girl their family had lost. So many graves dotted the Dust now. So many people were dead across the nation. All because seven corporations and the men who ran them wanted to hold onto power.

The fuckers.

Looking up from his thoughts, Aidan caught Naomi looking at him. The black thoughts in his head reflected in his sister's eyes.

To flip off the darkness, Aidan quirked his lips. "You know what? All that stuff they did to bring us down? It backfired. Those bio-weapons? That's what's making the rest of the world get off their asses already, and start really backing the Democratic State Force against the Corps."

Naomi studied him for a moment, ice-blue eyes distant. Then she cracked a grin. "Yeah, about that. How's the super-secret international visit going? And how about the Ten Year Plan?"

Aidan had to laugh at that. "I'm not even touching that plan till I'm sure Magnum's serious. And that international visit is super-secret enough that I'm not even telling you it's happening, on the record."

Naomi leaned in, eyes dancing. "Okay, so, off the record, how's it going?"

Glancing over his shoulder, Aidan leaned in. "Word is, the UN observers will be here for the next inter-Quadrant meeting."

"Yeah? For what?"

Standing, Aidan closed the door of his office. Taking his seat again, he gave his sister a smile. "Off the record, yeah? I didn't tell you this, and you don't know it."

"Yeah?" She asked, starting to smile.

He knew he'd closed the door, but Aidan found himself dropping his voice all the same. "Omi? If what we're hearing this far down the chain of command is right, the United Nations are going to formally recognize the Unions as a civilian government, and recognize the Democratic State Force as the legitimate military body of America."

"Seriously?" Naomi breathed, grinning.

Aidan nodded. "Seriously. If we can keep impressing them, they're going to give us international backing."

"And if we get that, we're almost winning," Naomi continued the thought, eyes bright.

"Almost," Aidan agreed. Reaching over, he squeezed his little sister's shoulder. "We're almost there, Omi."

Grinning, she reached out and squeezed his in turn. "We're gonna make it, Big A. We're gonna work our asses off, but we're gonna make it."

"Fingers crossed," Aidan agreed.

He spent the next few hours fielding calls and solidifying this week's plans with civilian unions. It was kind of like working with trainees: they were so excited, so scared, and so ready to run out without prep all at the same time. It was both one of the coolest things he'd ever done in his years of command, and one of the most fucking exhausting. After dealing with them, it was actually a relief to head down the hall and walk into an argument.

"You, woman, are going to *bankrupt* us."

"An' then you an' Tweak will rob another bank, ain't no skin off my nose. If'n you wanna keep drinking those fuckin' awful bloody marys of yours like the snooty showoff you are, I need the funds to keep gettin' water treatment materials an' takin' care of our tomato plants. Period. 'Specially if'n we're gonna have a lot more plants soon."

"*Snooty*?!" Blake's voice shrilled through the pre-fab. "I am not *snooty*!"

"Bullshit. Nose so high in the air it pulls down fuckin' sparrows."

Pulling on a smile, Aidan knocked on the office door. Blake and Janice looked up from their stare-down. Aidan gave them both a quick wave. "Hey guys. Blake? Got a sec?"

Blake turned in his chair and smiled sourly. "Perfect timing, Aidan. Take a seat and help me tell this *crazy woman* that we can't afford *everything* she asks for."

"About that," Aidan sagged into a seat. "I wanted to check on our finances. We need to order pulmonary repair nanoids through approved Cavanaugh routes. Kevin can't get them through his usual channels, so we're going to have to buy legit. Either that or Kevin heads down into the black market and digs around. I'm saying we go the legit route. It's going to cost us, but I'm not real big on our people getting anything black-market in their lungs."

Blake's chair wheels rumbled as his chair was pushed across the floor, and Blake pulled him into a side-armed hug. "Oh *honey*. For *that,* I'll *happily* find the cash. Go ahead and put the order in, you let *me* worry about the money."

"That bad?" Janice asked. Aidan felt her calloused hand on his shoulder. He smiled up at the hydroelectrics specialist. "Well, Damian's saying he's going to ground my husband until he either stops breathing smoke, or gets the nanoid infusion. Kevin's getting threatened with a month's desk duty."

"The *horror,*" Blake observed with that sour humor of his. Aidan smiled, acknowledging the point. He glanced up at Janice, who was staring down at him thoughtfully. Her fingers tapped the back of his chair.

"What's up?" Aidan asked.

Janice looked away, staring into the middle distance. "These fires. Lotta people gonna be in trouble with 'em." She shook her head. "This's fixin' to be a bad summer."

"You can say that again," Aidan agreed. "I hate that we're asking people to be out in the streets in the middle of it."

"Real trick's water," Janice observed, fingers still tapping. "Ain't nobody survives all that long with no fresh water, an' the Corps have been uppin' the water cost again. Been sayin' they'd start shuttin' off water to the houses of folks who unionize, I hear. That's a hell of a thing to hold over people. We gotta figure that out, get some kind of water into these free cooling shelters too. But drillin' water outta the Dust an' truckin' it in just won't do."

Both men nodded with her, contemplating.

"Let's have Kev do some international communication once I get approval on this," Aidan offered. "Other countries are just as hot as ours, but the international news doesn't have so many stories of dehydration and heat deaths as United Corporations land does. Somebody's got to have some solutions out there."

"Hope so," Janice agreed ruefully, "Cause what we got ain't never gonna be enough."

Aidan gave her a lopsided smile. "It never is enough, Janice. But, funny thing is, we keep making it work."

The older woman held his eyes steadily. Then, quietly, she laughed.

"Guess we do," she mused. "Guess we do."

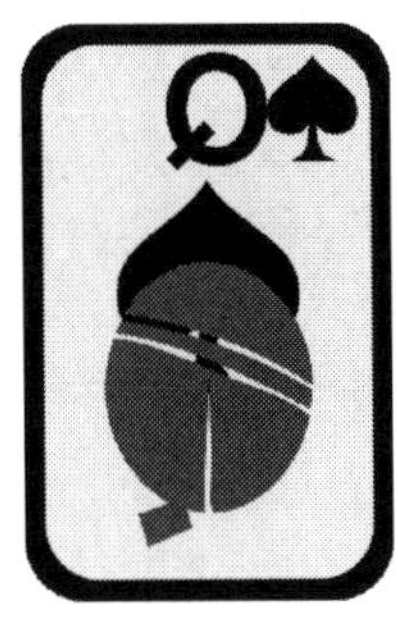

## Event File 05
## File Tag: Deliberations
## Timestamp: 11:30 06-29-2161

"Is everybody here?"

Looking around the long room, Liza gulped.

"Alright, my girl?" Kevin whispered, nudging Liza gently. She nodded, feeling like a block of wood moving on hinges.

"I think that's all thirty-three National Councilors, between the folks at the speaker's table and the line of chairs behind it," she muttered numbly.

"Well spotted," her friend agreed. "And those three bleachers over there are full of observers from the United Nations. See the emblems?"

Liza saw, alright. As if she hadn't been overwhelmed enough.

"I believe everyone's arrived, Commander Ouray," Councilor Williams observed at the central table. Standing, she spread her hands. "Welcome to New York and to this meeting, everyone. Thank you for taking the time out of your schedules to make the trip."

"Like I get a choice," Tweak grumbled on Liza's other side. She shot the girl a 'do not start' look. Tweak rolled her eyes, slouching down in her chair. Satisfied that she'd keep her mouth shut for now, Liza turned to watch Councilor Williams.

"We're gathered today to hear the decision of the American Workers' Unions on our next steps." The Councilor began. She turned to her left, nodding at the seven people seated there. "As the pro-tem representative of the National Council, I'd like to welcome our civilian partners in this work and the ideas they've brought. Presidents? The floor is yours."

Out of the group, Phyllis stood like a queen. "Thank you, Councilor Williams, and thank you to the National Command Council for the welcome." Turning, she addressed the crowd. "I am President Caulfield of the American Writer And Content Creators' Union. The presidents of the American Workers' Unions have been in conference for a week prior to this meeting, and we've come to a decision. I've been asked to present it." She folded her hands behind her back, straightening to her full height. "Going forward, we're asking that our collective work is focused on the following objectives: forcing the seven national corporations to the negotiating table. Compelling each of them to discuss and rework their Corporate Contract with their workers. Each set of unions has their own list of demands, but broadly, this is the thrust." Tapping the tab in front of her, she brought up a list. "Abolition of all corporal punishments and death penalties. Removal of all clauses that link Citizen Standings to the quality of housing and food available to them. Agreed restrictions on hours worked in a day and in a week. Agreed rest and recreation hour requirements for all workers at all Standings. And finally, a signature from each of the Corporate leadership teams that obliges them to abide by the United Nations Declaration of Human Rights of 2115. We'll negotiate hard for the complete abolition of the Citizen Standing System, but realistically we understand that may be a bridge too far. If we can get what we've outlined above, we'll have made a beginning."

Liza glanced around the room in the ringing silence left by Phyllis's words. So many faces. So many expressions. Starry eyes here, grim lines there. A few people looked straight up pissed, and Liza could understand that.

"While that's all well and good, President," one of the councilors for the Appalachia Quadrant threw out in a tone Liza clocked as bad news, "we of the Democratic State Force had our sights set a little higher than that."

"I understand," Phyllis agreed. "But our goals are slightly different, sir. Your goal is to return democracy to this country. A laudable goal, and one we are eager to support." Still polite, her voice took on just the barest edge. "But the Unions have the goal of improving material conditions for everyday people in the here and now. If we can force the Corporations to rewrite our Citizen Contracts in ways that materially improve life, we'll have made a start that you can build on. If we can get concessions today, together we can build democracy tomorrow."

"All the same," one of the Councilors for El Norte began, "That's hardly the bar we've been fighting to set all this time."

"True," Councilor Williams slid into the conversation smooth as oil. "But this is exactly what we've been helping the Unions build their plans around. Nonviolent civil resistance builds on its wins. At each stage, we gain momentum for the next step on the road to the place we all want to be." She turned back to Phyllis. "President Caulfield, could you outline the details of your plan and what you've decided?"

"Of course," Phyllis agreed. "To do this, I'd like to invite a young friend of mine to the stage." Phyllis ran her eyes over the crowd. "Officer Carlan? Would you join me?"

"Break a leg, my girl!" Kevin whispered, standing and offering her a hand up with a formal bow. Of all the times for him to put on an act. Liza was torn between making a face at her buddy and smiling as she stepped down the tiers of the old gymnasium. Whispers rustled like satin wrapped around her as she moved.

"Her!"

"Holy crap, it's the Queen of Clubs!"

"Queen of Clubs!"

"Who?"

"Remember that speech? The one on TV?"

"Oh, *her*!"

Crossing the floor, she joined Phyllis on the dais. Okay. Time to go. Just like they'd talked about in all the vid calls.

"Ladies, gentlemen and colleagues," she began, "working with their Force liaisons, the Unions have worked up and voted on a campaign of action. This work will encompass the next ten months of our joint efforts."

Stepping to one side, she took the tab Phyllis offered her and held it, acting as the projector man for the older woman. The Union president picked her talk up smoothly.

"We now have thirteen unions with several dozen chapters each across the country, and those numbers are growing by the day. During the ongoing Make Good Trouble and Send Them The Bill campaigns, our people have learned coordination, safe communication, and have gained confidence. In the past few years, they've come to a deep understanding of nonviolent resistance. Now is the time for us to put on our biggest campaign to date." She waved a hand at the window Liza was projecting, showing a white circle centered with the silhouette of a black pen spilling ink. Around the emblem, the words 'Pick Up The Pen' blazed.

"We have dubbed this set of actions the Pick Up The Pen campaign," Phyllis continued. "We intend this title as an instruction to the Corporations: we need a new contract. Pick up the pen." She waved her hand at the projection over her head. "Through the voting app we're currently testing for the Force, we Union members took a vote across the nation on the set of concerted actions that will make up this campaign."

Smiling, Phyllis nodded at Liza, who looked out over the crowd. "Working with Civil Disobedience advisors and members of the Force with relevant skills, the Unions will use waves of action to batter the Corporations to their knees. It will begin with acts of political theater, build to several large marches, and culminate in a stay-home event even larger than the Send Them The Bill campaign."

"During each event, we'll build more of a following, more momentum, and more energy," Liza finished. "We'll be forcing the corporate heads to the negotiating table step by step. Kicking and screaming the whole way, of course." She allowed a beat for the laughter of the crowd. "To the earlier point: as union presidents work with the chapter presidents who report to them in every quadrant, they will also be vetting organizers and leaders who would be suited to be the candidates of a National Citizen Council entirely chaired by civilians."

Now it was Phyllis's turn to pick up the ball. Liza turned to her as she began to speak. "We are faced with the task of forcing the Corporations to come to the negotiation table for the first time in centuries, friends. We will bring the new Corporate contracts to the people for a vote. What they approve will be the new Contract they live under." She beamed. "But once we've achieved that, we have in mind the next step. We're not going to let the corporate leaders stay away from that table anymore. Day by day, we're going to work more concessions out of them, until the balance of power is equal in this country between the employed and the employer. The end goal is to create a Citizen Council and positions for Citizen Representatives that Corporate officers must meet with regularly at all levels. We don't just want to make them come to the table once, but *again and again.* From now on, they work with us as equals, taking into account our value, our needs, and our wellbeing. The Corporate heads will do this, or they will not have a single peaceful working day in their lives."

Stunned quiet filled the room, stretching out and out. When it snapped, the applause rang like hail on a pre-fab roof, made even louder when people stood up in their bleacher-seats. Looking up, Liza met her team's eyes where they stood in the crowd, and had to grin at the way they were hamming it up, fist pumping and cheering her name.

It took a while for the cheers to die down. When they did, Councilor Williams stood.

"Alright, everyone. We've heard the wishes of the American Workers' Unions. The American people have spoken, and we serve the American people. We'll now recess for an hour and take lunch in the adjacent room. I'd like to remind everyone not to leave the building until your timed recess window comes up. This is for everyone's safety and security." She clapped her hands. "Lunch, everyone. When we reconvene, we get down to work."

The old cafeteria hall next door smelled of mildew, but it also smelled of good food and bubbled with conversations. Still buzzing with the high of the speech, Liza smiled at her people as they circled up with her.

"Okay," she began shakily, "how did it sound?"

"Couldn't have been better, Liza," Aidan replied with a quick smile. "But man, those details are going to be a bitch."

Liza had to laugh at that as they got in the line for chow. "We're here for five days: two days of work, a day of recess, and another two days of work. We'll get the details settled."

"And in the meantime, we can see how you're doing!" a man's cheerful voice exclaimed behind her. Liza whipped around, but Kevin beat her to it with a happy exclamation. "Brendan! Brandi!"

"Hey you guys!" A man with dark curls replied with a grin, grabbing Kevin in a hug. The woman with him leaned in to give Aidan a hug. "You're looking good, buddy."

"Wow," Aidan exclaimed, caught wrong footed but grinning as he returned the woman's hug, "nobody told me you guys were coming. You're here as Walkers, right?"

"Yep," the man who Kevin had called Brendan agreed, switching places with the woman to give Aidan a hug in turn. "Coomb Olwen wanted representatives here, and that's us."

Finally, things clicked for Liza. Brandi and Brendan. The contacts from the mountain community that maintained the country's unpatented seed reservoir. Holy crap! She grinned, stepping up to shake hands. "Officer Carlan, good to meet you in person. Thanks for everything you did to take care of our people in '57."

"Turned out to be worth it," Brandi chuckled, waving a hand at the room in general. "You guys got an awful lot done. The Diné passed us word from the Mohegan and the Mohawk that you people were hosting this big meeting, and we hear you guys are the reason it happened! Congrats!"

"It wasn't just us," Aidan demurred, ducking the compliment with a one-shouldered shrug. "I mean, there's hundreds of people in here. Everyone did something."

"Yeah, but from what we hear, these two did a hell of a lot." Brandi turned to Liza and, of all things, bowed deeply. She did the same thing for Tweak. When she spoke again, her voice had taken on a note that sent a funny little shiver down Liza's spine.

"Queen of Clubs. Golden Dragon," Brandi spoke quietly, but the words seemed to ring in the air. "The people of Coomb Olwen thank you for your work to create a brighter tomorrow. May the blessing of the rain wash you clean, and may the storms leave you stronger for their passing. May your name be spoken in blessing for seven generations to come."

Tweak blinked, eyes gone wide. Liza watched carefully as Tweak glanced at Aidan, who gave her a small smile and a nod.

"Um…thanks?" The girl managed, and Liza relaxed a little.

She smiled at the two Walkers. "I'm honored."

Brandi straightened out of her bow, shoving her mass of curls away from her freckled face. "Okay, now I did the ceremonial stuff, I can speak for myself: I'm starved!"

The words broke the social ice into crystals of laughter.

Together, the six of them grabbed plates, seats, and snatches of conversation as they settled in.

"How's Topher, did he marry his girl yet?"

"Yeah, last October!"

"And how are you folks anyway? How's Barley? How's the goat herd?"

"It's getting bigger, that DNA reader you got us helped us sort out that glycogen storage disease."

"And Barley and their partner are gonna have a kid!"

"Wow, really? When're they due?"

"Next February, sounds like. Classic Beltane Baby!"

"Are you staying for the whole event?"

"Of course! We gotta see this!!"

"So what's the plan?" Brendan asked between bites of fish. "They said something about details. You got the itinerary on your tabs?"

"It looks like we'll be breaking up into our areas of specialization after this," Liza slid her tab into the center of the table and brought up the window, hanging it in the air where they could all see. "Logistics, Liaison, Command, and Technical Aid will all be doing stuff separately for the next few days. Then we'll have our recess day, and after that two more days of work and two days to get home."

"You guys want to see the sights together on our recess day?" Brandi asked with a smile. "Get out and check out New York? First time Bren and me have been in a place this big."

"Sure!" Tweak agreed. "Only, heads up. Plan to wait hours. In the m-morning. K-Kevin takes *forever* g-getting p-pretty first."

Aidan choked on a laugh and a mouthful of coffee. Kevin pointed his fork at Tweak, who was grinning from ear to ear.

"You, miss, are spouting falsehoods verging on slander. I am not 'getting pretty', I'll have you know, I'm putting on a disguise to keep any and all of us from being tracked or *shot*. And I have to get Aidan, and *you* for that matter Miss Dragon, and Liza as well into your disguises on top of preparing myself! *Pretty* can bugger right off!"

Tweak watched the offended act with amusement in her dark eyes, snorting a little laugh at his antics. She waved a hand. "Okay okay. I t-take it back."

Somewhat satisfied with that, Kevin turned to their friends with a smile. "If we're going out, I've got a list of sites I'd love to see. There's such a treasure trove of history in this city! Some of the really foundational sites are only available if you're on a scuba tour, more's the pity, but there are plenty of things I'd love to see within walking distance. We can see Old Times Square, and there's several sites in Central Park, and…" Catching himself, their poor history geek glanced around the table and ducked his head, his cheeks pinking up. “Er…if it wouldn’t be an imposition, would anyone mind if I drew up a list?”

Liza had to smile. “Sure Kev honey, you can be our tour guide.”

He grinned, grey eyes dancing behind his glasses. “I’ll get the list done this evening, before the workload catches up with me.”

“We’re f-fucked,” Tweak groaned, resting her head on the table.

“Come on Tweak,” Aidan offered, “You can look at other stuff, and Kev can have all kinds of fun.” Leaning over, he gave his husband a quick squeeze. Kevin rested his chin on Aidan’s shoulder with a smile.

“Ugh. R-romance and history. Zonk.” Tweak sighed.

## Event File 06
## File Tag: Historical Intelligence
## Timestamp: 11:30-07-01-2161/ 14:00-07-06-2161

Liza didn't see much of Aidan, Kevin or Tweak for the next two days; everyone was sequestered in meetings for their own spheres of influence almost non-stop. Granted, the food was amazing, and the conversations were incredible, but Liza was starting to feel a bit frazzled by the middle of the week. Her time was split between going over the materials for legitimizing a public voting system, and every second she could spare from that was spent doing back-end work for the actions of the Pick Up The Pen Campaign.

She probably wouldn't have seen anyone from her own team at all if Aidan hadn't put his head into the room where Liza was sitting through another breakfast meeting. He waved at her as a union representative poked the table with two fingers again to emphasize his point.

"And I'm telling you, if we don't train on this, it'll come back and bite us in the ass when—"

"Excuse me, everyone," Liza cut in politely, "My team's scheduled recess is about to begin."

She waited until they were a little ways down the hall before she shot her commander a smile. "Thanks for the rescue."

"I didn't save you from much," Aidan chuckled. "Now you get to sit through one of Kev's costuming binges. Brace yourself."

"Once I've got us sorted out, Brandi and Brendan will fill out our party nicely," Kevin was saying as they walked into his room. He walked around the chair, checking Naomi over. "Yes, that'll do. Aidan, perfect timing! In the chair, thanks."

Crossing the room and grabbing Aidan's hands, the taller man sat Aidan down at the chair in front of a dresser he'd reworked as a makeup table. "Hopefully we'll look like an unremarkable tour party by the time I'm done."

"So what's everybody been—" Aidan started to ask, and got cut off.

"The v-voting app!" Tweak burst out, practically vibrating in her chair. "The alpha g-got approved! Me and the C-code Monkeys! We g-got the w-w-word l-last n-night! We're writing a v-v-voting app the UN just approved!"

Aidan blinked. "Wow!"

Tweak grinned up at him. "They gotta OK the b-beta b-before it's official. Still. Big stuff. We had a p-party last n-night. After this, I'm gonna c-coordin-n-nate it with the UN techs. Let them see ever-rything so they can cert-t-tify l-l-legitimate v-voting," she stammered out, tripping over her words in her excitement.

Slowly, Aidan began to grin. "They couldn't have chosen anybody better, Tweak. Congrats," he offered, wincing as Kevin shoved his hair under a tight skullcap. Tweak beamed at him. After a beat and a little 'ah!' of discomfort, their commander went on. "I've been getting debriefs and technical details of how we schedule discussion sessions and public votes on the new Contracts, without getting everybody arrested."

"Same here, from the logistical angle," Kevin said as he worked. "We're also discussing the creation of covert voting stations for those without access to a tab, and the attendant safety concerns at these locales. We're focusing on restrooms, bus stations and train terminals. With enough of these stations, we'll be able to provide people at all levels the chance to have a say in the community decision-making process going forward. It's going to be quite the undertaking, but it's well within our scope. Hold still love, or this wig is going to be crooked."

"I am holding still," Aidan sighed.

"No love, you're cringing and wriggling," Kevin replied patiently. "At least you won't need contacts; be grateful."

"Our talks have mostly been about trust-building with the population, that's going to be my main assignment for a while," Liza offered before Kevin could pick on his husband any more. "To get everyone we need signed up with the Common Ground app, informed, and engaged is a hell of an ask. But I think we can make it happen, if we keep our heads in the game and we do it efficiently." *And if there were about ten more hours in every single day,* she added silently, but that wasn't something she'd bring the group down with. They needed every bit of morale they could scrape together right now.

"This is on top of the work we're already doing helping the civilians with their campaign and their programs too," Aidan observed wearily as Kevin rubbed on a makeup that acted as a base for the adjustments the holo-mask would make to his appearance. So he'd thought about that too.

Kevin set the tin of makeup down and took his husband's hand, kissing his knuckles. "The man who digs the best holes is given the biggest shovel, love. We'll do just fine."

"Yeah, but will you sleep any time this year?" Aidan asked with a crooked smile.

Kevin shrugged. "Who needs sleep?"

"You do," Liza came back quickly, and found herself saying the words in chorus with Aidan.

"And I'm called out yet again," Kevin observed with a patient little smile. "Oh well. In the meantime, let's go see the sights and take some pics for everyone back home. You're all set, love. Who's next?" He asked brightly, glancing around. "Liza? Your turn in the chair."

They made a pretty interesting tour group by the time Kevin was done with them. He'd taken Liza at her word and done himself up as a geriatric tour guide, complete with vintage uniform. He'd done Tweak and Naomi up as older and younger sister using a mix of wigs, face paints, contacts for Naomi and holo-masks; Aidan and Liza were playing the role of their mom and dad. Liza was still deciding how much that irritated her, but it did work, for the time being.

"I've done us up as CSS folks," Kevin explained as they stood in line to leave the building. "That will get us on the nicer water taxis and through the fence around Central Park. Tweak, don't poke at that wig."

"Itches!" Tweak grumbled, stuffing her hands in her pockets.

"Alea iacta est, my dear Dragon."

"The fuck?"

"The die is cast, it means. In your idiom, it would be, 'shit happens. Deal with it'," Kevin threw over his shoulder.

Tweak sighed like a thirteen-year-old. "We get c-c-caffeine while we're out, yeah?"

"You probably should have gotten more sleep last night," Liza observed quietly. Tweak sighed. "Okay *mom.*" That made Naomi and Kevin both snort. Liza repressed a sigh. What *was* it about reminding people to do something good for themselves that rubbed them the wrong way?

"That's some look," Brendan exclaimed as the Wildcards took their turns to sign out. Kevin gave him a sheepish smile. "You know how it is once you get on the wanted lists."

"You don't have to tell me, pal," the duty officer on the door agreed with a roll of his eyes. "Guess why I'm stuck at the desk. Anyway, remember, all of you gotta check in when you get back, we gotta check for bugs and run the Paulson Procedure. Oh, and watch the first step if you're not used to the Float. Don't look right out; looking at the other buildings can make you seasick. Try to keep your eyes on something that isn't moving."

"Roger," Aidan agreed, signing the team out.

The desk officer hadn't been kidding. Liza braced herself as the front porch outside the door wobbled with the swell beneath it, the incoming tide pushing it towards the part of Manhattan that wasn't underwater. The porch swayed on its cables along with the repurposed high school. Liza glanced up at the subtly shifting bulk of a building on its wide raft of a foundation, and creeping queasiness twisted her gut. *Standing in a city that makes you seasick to look at,* she thought. *What a place. I can't believe people stayed in the Float.*

"Come on, everyone," Kevin offered. "I've got us a route to the nearest water-taxi depot, and from there, we've got quite a tour. We're on the waterwalk from here to Greenwich Street; after that we can grab a water-taxi up as far as twenty-third street and a car will take us the rest of the way. I thought we'd start at Central Park, then the Marcus Z Museum if we have time, and if we're especially lucky we might make it to the Lynch Metropolitan Museum of Art and the—" A water-scooter flumed past, splattering their dock in spray. Tweak and Kevin both jumped backwards; everybody else got soaked.

"Great driving in this city," Naomi muttered, flicking water off her hands.

"Based on what I've read, driving in New York City was fairly catastrophic even when it was land-based," Kevin offered, preoccupied with calling them a ride on his tab. "I don't imagine changing the travel medium altered the attitude much. Anyway, waterwalk! This way!"

Turning, he climbed the spiral staircase built around the former highschool's turret. Liza glanced up, and locked her legs to resist a cringe. Over their heads, walkways spread from building to building like the flexible strands of a net, wandering in every direction. She knew they had to be secure enough, judging by the number of people walking up there. But the idea of walking above the water on what amounted to fancy cobwebs…

Nerving herself, she followed her crew.

The walkways weren't as bad as she'd thought, once she got up on them. They were wide as a sidewalk and surprisingly steady, walled and roofed in a nanomesh weave that helped you forget you were walking on a really sophisticated plank bridge. After a couple feet, Liza was able to relax and look around.

It was hard to take in this much water all in one place. They hoped and prayed for water back home; here they were literally swimming in it. Drowning in it, sometimes.

Liza had heard about the way the sea level rise had changed the big coastal cities, but those had just been stories; reasons that Denver was packed, explanations for why everything had gone screwy. It was a whole new experience really *seeing* New York. When she'd thought about it at all, she'd thought of it and all the other coastal cities as ghost towns. Now she knew better; this place was anything but. Sure it smelled like fish and garbage. Sure some of the buildings looked like they were about to fall over any second. But man, was this place ever *alive.*

Turning her head, Liza stared out over the Hudson. Here and there, the tops of old buildings that ArgusCorp hadn't floated stuck up like the spine of a dead thing under the water. The Hudson threw its watery arms wide ahead, flowing around and through Manhattan. From here, the Venice of the Hudson looked like a bright crystal floating on blue satin. She could almost see the shift and sway of it, moving with its waters.

*What a place,* she found herself thinking again. This time the thought was gentler, freighted with just a little wonder.

"Here's our stop, down this staircase," Kevin threw over his shoulder as he took the steps down. "And that's our ride!" he exclaimed, waving an arm as a long, flat tug wallowed around the side of the building. Roofed in solar panels, the thing looked like a cranky turtle in a shell of blue and black. It sighed up to their dock, mechanical guts grumbling.

"Everyone onboard please," Kevin suggested, falling into his assumed role. None of them had to act like a tourist, but Kevin would have to act like he knew what he was doing. He didn't have much trouble with it; in fact, he went right off into his spiel like a pro the minute the automated ferry started up.

"If you look over here, ladies and gentlemen, you'll see the wall enclosing the Lost Borough of New York. Originally called Staten Island, it has become known as Babylon. When the sea levels first began to rise, the inhabitants crushed their junked petroleum-burning cars into large bricks and used them as an attempt at a sea wall. In spite of this, the area has been badly flooded in the last two decades. As Corporate leadership made their decisions on our strategic adaptation to sea level rise, Staten Island was ruled too costly to maintain and all services were cut off. All workers were relocated. However, some disaffected elements are rumored to maintain a hardscrabble existence there still, and strange rumors abound. It's whispered that unearthly sounds, strange lights, and all manner of oddities are seen in the waters around Babylon. Now, if you'll come to this side of the tug…"

Aidan caught Liza's eye as they followed Kevin, and smirked. "We told him he could play tour guide," he offered in an undertone. "We really asked for it, hunh?"

"Did we ever," she agreed with quiet feeling. "Think he's going to be this big of a ham all day?"

Aidan snorted. "Liza. This's Kevin."

She sighed. "True. I suppose we asked for it…and he is cute when he gets like this."

"Yeah," Aidan agreed, watching his husband with soft eyes.

The tug trundled up the wide canal that had once been a street. Around them, buildings swayed gently on their moorings. Kevin took their group over to the side and pointed down, to where long nano-fiber cables uncoiled into the murky water.

"Each of these cables is driven into the bedrock below us, allowing buildings in the Float to remain resilient whatever the current does. They're counterbalanced by large weights in their upper stories, keeping the building reasonably steady in even the choppiest waters," he explained, nearly grinning. Liza had to smile at him, having such a lot of fun doing his thing.

As the tug eased its way through the water traffic, she took time to watch the city go by. Ad holos filled every storefront and loomed over the water, getting particularly creative with their 3-D elements. Tweak actually ducked when some ad involving a stork swooped past, trailing the banner 'Cavanaugh Corporation! Bringing you the best genetics since 2100!'

"Man," Naomi muttered beside her, "And I thought Denver was bad."

"Welcome to New York," Kevin murmured. "It's always been the place of bright lights and bluster. The Corps have simply put their own spin on the tradition." He squinted a little as a painfully bright ad for a rent-by-the-day boat went whizzing past at head height. "From the reports, there aren't so many ads in the park."

"Good," Tweak snapped. "These're a p-pain in the ass!"

If anything, the sidewalks were worse than the waterways ad-wise: every advertisement got up in your face around here. No wonder so many of them were advertising stress-relief products. This place could stress out a brick.

Finally, they pushed their way over to a kiosk and into the amazing quiet of a Go-car. Liza found that she was rubbing her ears. She glanced around at her friends, who were all various levels of shell-shocked.

Tweak summed it up for them pretty with, "Fucking. New. York. Next time. I'm here. Ear plugs!"

"You and me both, friend," Brandi groaned, rubbing the sides of her head. "Man alive…"

Brendan just groaned, leaning back in his seat and closing his eyes.

Kevin was the only member of their team who didn't seem to be feeling it. He was in love with the city, and he was looking out every window, pointing out things as they passed with the enthusiasm of a kid.

The Go-car dropped them off in a much quieter part of town, shushing away and leaving them to face what seemed to be an understated wrought-iron fence. The appearance was for show and Liza knew it. There would be nanoids in the metal, and probably plas-glass behind the decorative fence. But it did give the place a bit of glamor. Beyond the fence, trees arched for the sky.

"Morning folks," the gate guard offered with surprising deference. "Welcome to Central Park."

And finally, finally, they were through the gate, and there was peace and quiet. And *green*. Green, absolutely *everywhere*. Trees towered overhead. Grass gleamed wetly under their feet. So. Much. *Green.* It was hard to believe this much green existed in the whole world.

"This way, everyone," Kevin offered quietly.

They walked through the green like worshippers in a cathedral. Around them, more casual CSS and CES visitors played lawn games or puffed by, getting their exercise in jogging and biking. The Wildcards and the Walkers barely noticed them.

"Hey boss?" Tweak murmured.

Aidan turned to look down at her. "Yeah Tweak?"

The young woman was staring up into the trees. "In the old d-days…was D-denver like this?"

Aidan glanced at his husband. "Kev?"

"It was never quite this lush," Kevin murmured. "It's always been rather dry in the West. But yes, Tweak. Once, it was more like this." He drew a long breath. "Once upon a time."

"Once, and once again," Brandi added. "In days to come."

"So mote it be," her brother breathed beside her.

She nodded. "So mote it be."

Kevin drew a long breath. Liza watched as he seemed to shake something off, and smiled. "Alright everyone! This way to the historic Wein Walk!"

With Kevin talking a mile a minute, they ambled through the park, breathing in the green. The path wove through gardens and around a lake, showing them vistas of peaceful green at every turn.

*Once, and once again.* Liza considered the words. *Could Denver be like this again someday? Could it be green? Could it be alive like this?*

She was thinking so much that she walked right into her buddy when Kevin stopped in front of her.

"Oh," Kevin breathed. "Oh, look what they've done to you…"

Liza followed her friend's gaze. He was staring at a statue off to one side. It was pretty impressive; on a spur of stone jutting out into the lake to one side, a gigantic arm was holding a humongous cross with flames around its base. Engraved in the rock below were the words:

> *"Central Park, lovingly tended by American AgCo for your enjoyment.*
>
> *'Rule over the fish of the sea and over the birds of the sky and over the cattle and over all the earth, and over every creeping thing that creeps on the earth.' Genesis 1:26"*

Like a man in a dream, Kevin walked down the verdant lawn until he was standing on the stone in front of the statue. Liza glanced at Aidan. He shrugged, and nodded towards the redhead. Liza nodded. They followed their logistics man down to where the statue's plinth rose out of the stone. Kevin was staring at the statue like he'd seen a ghost.

"I've read about this," he murmured. "I'd read where all the pieces ended up, but to see it in person…"

"You okay?" Liza asked, glancing between him and the statue.

"Kev?" Aidan stepped in close to Kevin, whose eyes were riveted on the statue. For a moment Liza thought he'd reach out and touch Kevin, but Aidan was smarter than that.

"Is this something important?" Aidan asked gently.

Kevin swallowed. "It was, once. It's an obscure history. It's been obscured, I should say." Pulling out his tab, he brought up a holo. Liza could tell that he was trying his best to get back into tour-guide mode, but it wasn't working.

"This arm was once part of a larger statue. Out in the bay, there was once an island where she stood. Liberty Island. And this was Lady Liberty."

The image hung between them; a solemn lady holding up her arm, crowned in a starburst of a tiara. What she held in her hand wasn't a cross with fire at the base after all; back then, it had been a torch.

"She stood there from 1886 to 2105. Liberty Island had begun to drown, you see. So they took the Lady apart, intending to raise the island and put her back as quickly as they could." He closed his eyes, swallowing hard. "But then the Dissolution came, and the Incorporation. And instead of putting her back together, the Corps all took a piece of her for displays like this." He waved an arm at the statue on its stone. The acid in his tone should have etched his words into the rock.

"Her head and shoulders stand in the middle of ZonCom's Fifth Avenue Shopping Promenade, with letters spelling 'Luxury' stuck to the tines of her crown. The flagship office of EagleCorp shipped her foot to Denver, and it's—"

"Holy shit, it's in that plaza in front of Union Station crushing a demon," Liza breathed. "I've seen that statue."

"Yes," Kevin agreed tightly. "Her other arm is in Chicago, and the book in her hand has been turned into a banker's ledger on the wall of NatBank's flagship office. You can see what AgCo did with the piece they got ahold of. The rest of her is God knows where. Now Liberty Island is drowned, and there is no Lady Liberty; only a collection of corporate baubles and tawdry stolen trophies." He spat the last words as if they were poison. Maybe they were.

For a moment, they all stood still; Kevin seething, Aidan looking worried. Tweak looking blank. Naomi, as always, wary.

And how did Liza herself look, she wondered. Probably the way she felt. Stunned.

This country had honored Liberty in a statue that, if the arm was anything to go by, had been enormous. A statue that had its own island.

And now it was just scattered bits. Just memories.

She started when Brandi walked forward, laying her hand on the statue's metal.

"We remember who you are," the curly-headed woman said. Though her voice was soft, it carried in the still afternoon air. "You will be whole again one day. By my will, so mote it be."

"By my will, so mote it be," Brendan echoed, joining his sister and laying his hand beside hers.

The morning was still for a heartbeat. Then Kevin stepped up beside the siblings. His hand rested on the metal beside theirs. His voice was soft in the stillness.

"Lady Liberty will be whole again. With God as my witness, this I swear. Amen."

In that moment, Liza swore she heard the future coming.

"Kay. It's a thing," Tweak piped up. "I'm bored. Can we go?"

And the moment was over, and Naomi and Aidan were laughing, and Kevin was grumbling, and they were on the move again. There were days of work ahead, and a couple days of travel too. The world was back to normal.

But the moment stayed with Liza. The words repeated themselves in her head.

*We remember who you are.*

*Liberty will be whole again.*

*One day.*

*So mote it be.*

*Amen.*

It ended up taking three days to get home instead of two, with a train breakdown in the Midlands Quadrant. Liza had never been so glad to see the base when they finally got in, the sun setting behind them. They sat down to plates full of dinner, slaps on the back, and a crew's worth of expectant looks.

*Ten seconds, and someone will ask what the news is,* Liza judged. At his seat, Aidan set a bottle of mead from the mountains out, pouring a glass for himself and one for Kevin. "Pass it around," he offered, handing the bottle along to Milo.

*Eight seconds...* Liza's mental countdown whispered behind her eyes. *Seven seconds...*

"Hey Aidan," Don asked through a mouthful of dinner, "What's the news from New York?"

Liza had to cover a smile with a sip from her mug. *They didn't even make ten seconds before curiosity got the better of them. That's our team alright.*

"Hang on a minute, Don," Aidan suggested with a little smile. "Everybody get a glass of the mead. We're going to want to toast this."

That made the bottle whip around the table in record time. Out of the corner of her eye, Liza made sure that the newest members of the team got into the swing of this little thing. Inyoni had settled in really fast, but Jillian and Cameron were a little slower and more careful about opening up and joining in with the crew. They weren't doing badly, all things considered; just showing caution. Which, given where they'd come from, was no surprise.

"Alright, we all got mead," Janice observed with an easy smile, nodding at Aidan. "Spill, boy."

Now Aidan really grinned. Standing, he held up his glass. "Everybody? The United Nations has approved the Common Ground app and the first step to a certified vote through it. And if we can get the Corps to the negotiating table with the Unions by spring of next year, the United Nations is going to recognize us as a legitimate military force serving a legitimate government. I figure that's something worth drinking to. How about you guys?"

You would have thought a bomb had gone off in the canteen; an explosion of whoops, hollers and cheers made the walls reverberate and the ceiling tiles shake.

Standing, Liza clasped her hands behind her back. "Permission to declare this a celebratory occasion and give the base stand-down orders, Commander?"

Aidan laughed, toasting her as the twins danced around the table and Sarah and Yvonne chanted 'legit-a-mate! Legit-a-mate!' in chorus.

"I think they beat you to it, Liza."

She grinned. "You're not wrong."

Only later, when they were well down all kinds of bottles and the loudest part of the party had passed, did Blake sidle up.

"So exactly *how* much work is all this saddling us with, Liza doll?" the older man asked, lounging into a seat on the couch beside her. "We're already working like *plebes* for the civvies. If we get much more work dumped on us, someone around here's going to *snap*."

She poured him another shot of the good stuff. "From the sound of it, we're in for the workload from hell this year, and probably next year too. Implementing this is going to be a heavy lift. Reinforcing it and defending our wins will be even more work."

"Oh *yay*," Blake groused, "this sounds just *delightful.* As if we weren't *already* working *every second* of the day."

"It's not going to be easy," Liza agreed. She smiled at the man who'd always been right there. People didn't give Blake enough credit. Quietly, in the background and the off hours, he was the one reminding them all to pull their heads out of their asses and be their best. Where her own nagging and Damian's bullying hit a brick wall, it was Blake's sly smiles and elaborately casual comments that got past people's defenses and made them think about doing better. They were going to need him more than ever to get through this.

She took a breath. "It boils down to this: two years of some of the hardest work we've ever done. And after that? After that, we might… Blake, I think we might win."

For a minute, Blake said nothing. Then, setting down his drink, he pulled her into the sideways hug he'd been giving her since she was small.

She smiled up at him. "Think that's worth two year's work?"

Blake sighed, making a big show of it. "I think it'd *better* be."

Liza couldn't help but laugh. "I bet—"

The blare of noise coming out of her tab shot her to her feet. The fire warning. Shit.

"Dozer!" she called, "Fire check!"

Standing, the blocky man spoke to a rec room stunned into silence.

"We've got a mayday call, system authenticated it! Sanctuary Station's on fire!"

## Event File 07
## File Tag: Prioritization Rationale
## 20:45-07-06-2161/24:40-07-06-2161

"This way! Over here!"

The rolling clouds of smoke swallowed Janice's words. She windmilled the arm with the flashlight in it; hopefully the trucks could follow that.

Through the smoke, a scruffy convoy of vehicles moved out, carrying everything that the people of the off-grid community could grab. Frightened people stared out at her through truck and van windows as the convoy rolled. Children sat with their faces pressed against the windows, haunted eyes staring out. Janice did her best to flash thumbs' up as she waved them on. Smiling at them would be pointless, with this respirator mask on.

Fire. They'd had a good run, almost six years without a big fire in their area. Even last year they'd gotten lucky, and Fire had gone off to chew on the Cascadia and El Norte quadrants. But now the beast was back to stalk the West, and Janice could almost hear the crackle of it.

Fire. Not a lot scared her, but fire did. And it would only get worse until the winter rains came down, if experience was anything to go by.

The com in her ear crackled. "Jan, did they make it to you?" Liza asked in her ear.

"Yup," she replied. "They're moving good, no holdups. Got all their coordinates set for a site on the other side of the fire."

"Good. We've got two more sets to load up."

"Fire's moving, folks," Milo added over his crackling mic, "It's slowed up some, but we don't have much more than twenty minutes 'fore it's on top of us."

"Fuck a frag grenade, that ain't enough time!" Janice groaned.

"Gonna have to be," came Dozer's reply. "I got this bus of theirs up and running. Jan, come on back and help them pack."

"Roger," she agreed, turning and dog-trotting back through the smoke. She had to watch her tab for directions; you couldn't see a fucking thing in this mess.

Except the fire, of course. You could always see the fire, blazing all around. The little outlying flare-ups hadn't gotten strong yet, but they were gaining. And if that brushfire caught up before they'd gotten the Fringe community out of here…

Janice shook her head. Fucking disaster, this whole thing. If they had water, they could douse the area surrounding the sad little pre-fab shacks around the old bus terminal that made up Sanctuary Station. If the Corps gave a single flying fuck, they could douse these flames with e-planes.

Fat fucking chance. All these poor folks had was the chance—just the chance—to outrun the fire.

A gust of wind kicked cinders up into her face. For a panicky second, Janice wiped at her eyes, blinded. God*damn* she hated fire.

She danced out of the way of a flaming tumbleweed, and nearly ran into a figure looming out of the smoke. Big Tony was streaked with soot, a bandanna tied over his nose and mouth. He caught her by the shoulder, steadying her.

"You good?"

"I'm good. Where d'you need me?" Janice called, muting her mic so she didn't deafen her team.

"Med store! Last thing we're packing!" the big Fringe camp leader rasped over the crackle of flames.

"Roger!" Janice hollered back. She turned and lit out for the grayish lump in the darkness that was Sanctuary Station's main gathering place and pantry.

The old bus terminal echoed with feet and frantic calls as Wildcards and Sanctuary Station people packed up the medications that would keep the community alive until they rebuilt. The precious barrels of water and the food had already gone out in a covered truck; now it was just the boxes of meds getting packed.

Janice jumped into line, handing boxes along fast as her hands would move.

"Fifteen minutes, people!" Big Tony's gravelly voice called over what must be a loudspeaker. "When I say go, we go!"

"Then let's go faster," a woman's voice called. "Move it people!"

The next minutes scrambled by in snatches. Janice moved robotically, brain turned off, just a bare chatter of "fire fire fire!" in the back of her head keeping time with the sound of her own breathing and the roar of the flames.

"Packed!" someone shouted ahead, and a ragged cheer went up. "Gracias a Dios y los santos buenos." Janice breathed, her hands empty. "Muchas gracias."

"Move it people, we are moving! We are out of here!" Big Tony shouted over his bullhorn.

"Wildcards, here!" Dozer's voice boomed through the smoke. Janice followed the call at a jog. Joining Dozer, Yvonne, Naomi, Alice and Milo, she checked them over. "We all here?"

"All set," Dozer agreed, turning as Big Tony walked up. "Huge props, folks. Give Aidan big love from Sanctuary on this one." The head man pulled Dozer into a hug for a second, slapping his back.

"Thanks brother. We owe you."

"Any time," Dozer replied, slapping the other man's back in turn before pulling away. "Get out of here. Fire's on our ass."

"I hear that," Tony barked a humorless laugh. "See you. We'll send coordinates to pick up your vehicles. Get outta here."

"Already gone," Naomi agreed with two thumbs up.

Nobody needed to tell the Wildcards to pile into their transport and get the flying fuck out of there. Dozer drove steady, but he drove fast.

"Okay, everybody, med check," Alice announced. "Sound off. Who's got what?"

They'd gotten lucky; aside from a couple little scalds, red eyes, and dehydration, the Wildcards were just fine. Alice dabbed on Eze and Janice handed out water from the gigantic backpack cooler she'd brought.

"They're going to make it out, right?" Yvonne asked, her voice rasping. She must have gotten some smoke in her. That wasn't good.

"Course they are," Dozer agreed, eyes on the shrouded wasteland beyond their windows. "Tony's got brains. They'll be fine."

"Tony's good," Janice added. "Been a head man a long time. He'll get his folks out."

*Please, God, don't make me a liar here,* she whispered in her heart. *They've got kids and Gammas and all sorts of people who just wanted a quiet life. Please, just let them get out safe.*

A warm arm wrapped around her shoulders, and Janice looked up at Milo. He smiled, giving her a little squeeze. She smiled back.

In the smoke, it was hard to judge distance if you weren't staring at the GPS. Janice didn't even try. Dozer knew what he was doing. For now, she closed her eyes and leaned against Milo.

They pulled under the base slicktarp and piled out like sticks thrown from a barbecue pit, stinking of smoke and brittle with the heat.

"Alright ladies, I'm gettin' a shower," Janice announced. "You can fight over who's in with me an' who's after us."

"You guys can go first," Naomi offered, waving over her shoulder. "I need to clean out and lubricate my off-hand before I do anything else. That ash stiffened up the finger joints."

"I'll go tell everybody we're home," Yvonne called, jogging past Naomi. "I'll take second round!"

"Thank god, because I want a wash," Alice sighed gratefully. Janice gave her a smile. "I hear that."

"Enjoy, ladies," Milo interjected, stepping over to give Janice a quick squeeze around the waist. She turned in his arms with a tired smile. "Sorry stud. You ain't invited this time."

"I know. Tragedy," Milo chuckled.

"Get a room, you two," Yvonne called over. Janice flipped her off.

"Whew," she remarked, walking down the hall beside Alice.

The darker woman agreed with a drawn out 'mm-hmm'. "I'm never getting that smoke smell out of my braids."

"I hear that," Janice sighed. "Fuckin' smoke holds on like a shitty ex."

Out of the corner of her eye, she glanced at Alice. "Speakin' of suchlike, you an' Damian, hunh?"

"Well we're definitely not exes," Alice laughed. Janice cracked a grin. "You anythin' else yet? One kiss in two years, that's all we seen. Are you two gonna make a move before the Corps come down or not?"

Alice shrugged. And apparently that was all she was going to do.

"Come on girl, give!" Janice exclaimed. "What's goin' on with you two?"

Smile. Shrug.

Janice groaned. "Gettin' anything out of you's like squeezin' blood out of stone, ain't it?"

"Yep," Alice agreed easily as they walked into the women's hygiene room. "And—"

The words shut off like water from a tap. Alice had frozen in the doorway.

"What?" Janice asked, peering around her. "What the…Billie?"

The skinny kid was sitting on the floor with her back against a bathroom stall. She looked up, giving them a weak smile. "Hi guys. Tweak's…" she winced at the sound of someone chucking up in the toilet stall she was leaning against. "Not so great," she finished meekly.

"I'm fine!" Tweak's voice wobbled out of the stall. And that was followed by another round of chucking sounds, which pretty much made saying it pointless.

With a glance for the stall, Billie stood and walked over to them.

"She's been doing that for an hour now," she whispered, eyes full of fear. "She's going to hate me for telling you, but…this is bad."

Alice nodded, face falling into her professional lines. "You did the right thing, Billie. I'll take care of it, okay?"

"Okay," Billie's word was barely audible.

Alice stepped over beside the stall. "Tweak? What set this off?"

"F-fucking s-s-smoke," Tweak groaned through the door. "Made m-me feel sick, and then—" the retching started up again.

"Okay, I'm going to go get you some anti-nausea stuff, and you can take it in there and come out when you feel better. Give me five minutes," Alice called. Tweak grunted something that might have been 'thanks', or not.

*Well, so much for a shower,* Janice thought to herself. Stepping out, she headed for her own room. *A spit bath in peace is better than a shower with someone horking in the next stall.*

Milo was already at the sanitation station when she got in, scrubbing handfuls of wash powder and dribbles of water through his locs. He scrubbed at his head with a towel as she ran a hand over his back.

"Hey stud."

"Hey you," he offered with a smile, turning to pull her into his arms. She pushed back with a laugh. "I'm still dirty, don't go huggin' me yet."

"Thought you were going for a shower?" Milo asked mildly, taking a seat on the bed. Janice shrugged as she pumped up some water and wet down a washcloth. "Hygiene room got occupied."

She stared at the water between her fingers. Water. They needed it so badly. Everyone did. Drought on the Grid and fire in the Dust, and never enough water.

She wished to God they'd been able to save up more of the torrential rains from a couple years back. But that was a pipe dream; there was never enough rain to really meet the Sector's needs. Hell, the whole Quadrant was dry as old bones most of the time.

There had to be something she could do about that.

Milo's arms wrapped her from behind, and his lips rested against her cheek. "You did good today."

"Same to you," she murmured, nuzzling her head against his. "Glad it went off without a hitch."

"Yeah," Milo sighed. "Looked at the fire map, though. Whole Region's on fire right now, seems like."

"Seems like," Janice agreed, breathing in the scent of him. The taint of smoke hung between them.

"Long day," Milo offered.

"Long day," Janice agreed.

"Ready to lay down?"

Janice smiled. "Yeah."

## Event file 08
## File Tag: Hearts and Minds
## 14:10-07-11-2161

"Okay everybody!" Yvonne grinned at the room full of teens. She had officially landed the best assignment of all time. "Today we kick off our action." She clicked the tiny media projector in her fingers. The little player blared the first bars of a song and an ecstatic handful of words: "We built this city!" She tapped it to switch tracks, and the spoken message began. "It's the workers of this country who create real wealth. We have earned the right to access the resources that wealth has created. We demand a new deal. We insist on a new contract between workers and employers. Meet us at the table, and pick up the pen."

She clicked to its last track, and grinned as the anthem of 'We're Not Gonna Take It" came singing out at a volume that was all out of proportion to the tiny device. The kids watched her, eyes dancing. They were some crew: a bunch of NatBank, ZonCom and TechoCo kids everywhere from eleven to eighteen and every rung of the Citizen Standing ladder, all brought together through the kid's clubs some of the Unions were running. The Unions had started the clubs to give kids from lower Standings a chance to get breakfast and dinner, and they offered all the kids somewhere to hang out, relax and get a better education. They had paired kids who asked for help with peers who'd volunteered to do tutoring, so now you had friendships forming all up and down the Citizen

Standing hierarchy, and the kids were pretty happy to forget they had Citizen Standing Scores at all if you gave them the chance. But tutoring and hanging out together hadn't been enough for these teens; they wanted in on the action. They'd pestered the adults in the Unions until they'd caved, and asked their Duster advisors for some safer actions that the kids could take. Once she'd heard, Yvonne had done a little begging and pleading with Aidan, and he'd handed over the assignment. Officially, she was now a Civil Disobedience Action Advisor along with her wife. She was going with 'Official Head Prankster' herself.

One last click turned the little player off as Yvonne held it up. "I'm handing out bags of twenty to everybody. You want to plant these in all the grossest places you can find. What kind of spots are you looking for?"

"Dog shit!" gawky Darnell blurted out, making the other kids whoop and laugh.

"Dead pigeons!" Saoirse suggested with a grin a mile wide, "And rats too!" The other teens obliged her with long, drawn out groans of 'eeeewwwww!'

"Dumpsters!" Cloe called out, standing on her tiptoes to see over her friends' shoulders.

"Awesome! Try the output flows for grease traps around the backs of cheap restaurants too," Sarah suggested with a huge grin. "Don't worry about whether it's too hot to place these things, they're tough little doodads."

"And don't forget spots out of reach," Yvonne encouraged, nodding. "Go for places that lardassed Peacekeepers will have trouble getting to. Where do you guys think that'd be?"

"Up fire escapes?" skinny Jared suggested. Yvonne bobbed her head. "Yep, that's good. Where else?"

"On top of lampposts!" Crash, a kid with a neon red mohawk, threw out.

"And flagpoles too, I can climb a flagpole near my place," Bree added enthusiastically. The teens loved that idea.

"That's great, everybody," Yvonne agreed, grinning. "Just remember to think about the wind when you're up high. It's crazy strong today, and a good gust at the wrong moment—" she mimed a body splatting into the ground, with sound effects. The kids made faces.

"Anywhere you can get that some big guy in body armor can't go, that's where you leave a player." She put up four fingers. "We voted on four rules about placement. What's the deal?"

"Nowhere that it'll mess with mental health, like stopping people from sleeping," Saoirse piped up, copper curls bobbing. Yvonne lowered one finger.

"No violence!" Bree called, followed by Crash with, "Don't put ourselves in danger to drop a player," and Tim right on zir heels with "Nobody goes placing alone, everybody checks in before we go home."

"And if you get caught, you—" Yvonne prompted.

"Tell them we're part of a geo-caching club placing geo-caching clues!" Jared came back with a satisfied nod of the head. "The things don't start to play for an hour after activating, so they'll buy it."

"Nice, guys!" Sarah enthused. "So, that's the plan. We get all the players planted around the inter-corporate shopping areas, and around every main NatBank, TechoCo and ZonCom office we can reach by the end of the day. These things are going to play twenty-four-seven for two weeks. Of course the office staff and the retailers are going to climb the walls, and then they're going to call Peacekeepers in to get rid of the players. And then—" She pointed at Cloe, whose grin bordered on evil. "Then we activate the Mesh-connected cameras we've got stuck around, and we post clips of Peacekeepers going crazy trying to stop a song."

"And getting covered in dog shit," Darnell guffawed. The kids whooped it up for that, laughing like anything. Yvonne could see in their eyes that they were starting to get the buzz of a good prank going.

"Alright!" Yvonne grinned at the kids, and raised a fist. "Let's drive the Corps batshit!"

The kids hollered their agreement, scattering to their pre-assigned exits from the old warehouse four union chapters had retrofitted for a community supply center. Yvonne turned with a laugh and grabbed her wife, kissing her good and hard.

"Ready to get out there, Civil Disobedience Action Advisor Flesher?" Sarah asked, grinning up at her.

Yvonne grinned. "Hell yes, Civil Disobedience Action Advisor Flesher," She stole another kiss, giving her wife a quick squeeze. "Come on."

There was an art to placing the sound broadcasters for maximum impact with minimum threat. Now that they were out in the field together again, Sarah and Yvonne were all over teaching these kids the skills. Step one was acting casual. Step two was using your imagination. Step three was keeping a huge grin off everyone's faces. Everything else came pretty easy after that. Up and down fire-escapes, across roofs, through alleys they went with their kids, Yvonne keeping an eye on the map. Each time the teens placed a player, they activated it. Its playback loop was delayed by an hour, but its locate beacon turned on immediately. Across the map of the area, yellow location dots were flicking to life.

"Here's a good spot!" Yvonne whispered, pointing out a nest that a pigeon had made in a thicket of bird spikes on a parapet to Crash. Ze nodded. "Spot me?"

"You got it," Yvonne agreed. With a nod, the kid handed her zir bag and did one hell of a parkour run, launching zirself off one wall to kick up off a windowsill, landing neatly a ways over Yvonne's head. She flashed zim two thumbs up in admiration. Man, she wished she could move like that anymore. Not that she was losing all that much speed at thirty-five, but every once in a while she got a wakeup call about what her muscles could and couldn't do. And they probably couldn't do parkour.

Crash got the player settled. "On?" Ze called down. She glanced at her tab, where a new reader winked. "Yep!" She called up. "C'mon, let's—"

"Hey!" a voice hollered down the alley, "What the fuck are you doing?!"

"Book it!" Crash yelped. Yvonne didn't need telling twice. She took off.

"Peacekeepers!" the angry male voice bawled behind them, "Peacekeepers, I need Peacekeepers!"

Yvonne grinned. *Yeah, you just stand there and yell. I'm already gone.*

For all the noise that guy put up, it only took running through a handful of alleys to throw the trouble off. Once she was back in the advert-wrapped shopping streets, she pulled her tab out and brought up the Common Ground app. She blinked, wiping her face as a sudden gust of wind blew powdery ash into her face. Clearing her eyes, she typed.

You good?

The response came back from the teen a beat later.

I'm great. Put down another. See you!

Yvonne grinned as she pocketed her tab, sidestepping an obnoxious ad trying to interest her in the ugliest dress she'd ever seen. The ashy yellow of the sky made the holo look even worse. All the advertising holos looked a little drab against the smoky yellow backdrop that wildfire smoke had turned the sky into.

She was riding high by the time she met the kids for their check-in at a different community center. This was the part of the work that always freaked her; holding her breath, crossing her fingers that all the kids she'd encouraged to go out would come back in the door. She knew that one day, someone probably wouldn't.

But today wasn't that day. All sixteen kids came back in, hyped like anything on their prank.

"You guys kicked ass," Yvonne cheered, hugging a couple of the kids who were okay with hugs. "Anybody get hot?"

"I got chased by some guy who works at a shop," Cloe put on her probably-illegal-grin. "He tripped over a trash can."

"We got yelled at by some lardass," Crash shrugged. "He didn't even try to chase us. Loser."

Yvonne glanced over at her wife when a gentle elbow nudged her ribs. "Time, baby," Sarah suggested under her breath. Yvonne nodded.

"Okay, everybody, you did incredible!" She called to the kids. "We need to wrap up now. When the footage comes in, we'll have a watch party on the Common Ground, okay?"

Still babbling, the kids headed for their exits. Yvonne took Sarah's hand and squeezed it. "Yeah, I guess it is time. So what's up next?"

Sarah pulled a face. "Peoples' Assembly. We promised we'd go and represent. But tomorrow's that EagleCorp prank," she added, offering a little sugar to get the pill down.

Yvonne nodded, grimacing. "Alright, let's go get the Assembly over with."

Sitting around with a bunch of civvie organizers as they reminded each other of the obvious was a drag. Obvious Point One: the point of all the actions in the Pick Up The Pen campaign was to push the Corporations to negotiate with their workers. Obvious Point Two: everybody needed to push their people to stop using Corps-controlled net and switch over to the decentralized Mesh. They were going with the snappier name of Cut the Cord for that push, which definitely sounded better than 'pester people to get off TechoCo's Net.' Obvious Point Three: everything this year was building to a big march and a bunch of rallies. On and on they went with organizational details and reminders and lots of talk about how many good things they were doing. *Yawn.* At least there was some energy this time; everyone was thrilled about the news that they'd be voting for new contracts with their corporations soon. Even with these slow and solid citizen types, there was a lot of clapping and cheers when they talked that over. Yvonne did her best to stay involved and offer lots of smiles; seeing Dusters encouraging them gave the civvies confidence. Liza, Kevin and Aidan had been telling her it was this boring stuff that'd make the really big changes long term, and

Yvonne didn't doubt it. These were definitely the kind of people who'd be in charge of local governments when they got democracy up and running again. But it was *so* not her scene. She was more of a run around and do things type.

"I thought I was going to fall asleep in my chair," she groaned when they finally got back to their hotel room and set up their security. "What a *drag*!"

"Yeah, but that's democracy." Sarah said, though she was yawning as she said it. They smiled sleepily at one another.

"Tomorrow's gonna be more our thing," Yvonne offered. "We're all set. I double checked all the prep and details with everybody."

"Great." Sarah leaned in, kissing her. "Sack out?"

"Sounds good," Yvonne agreed. "We gotta move early."

They were out the door before dawn in the morning, sneaking through the stillness of the waking city.

"Stop here," Yvonne murmured in the gloom of an alley. Pulling a blue rag from her pocket, she waved it.

Out of the alleyways and corners all around, people came walking. Everything from masks to scarves to streaks of paint had been used to disguise their faces.

"We ready?" Yvonne asked.

"Yep," a voice whispered back. "Everything's where it's supposed to be."

Yvonne's blood fizzed. "Okay, then everybody knows what to do. The fence is disabled. We've got the cameras looped. Flash mob in twenty minutes. Flash crews in place?"

"Yeah," came the quiet reply.

"Anything comes up, hit the panic button," Sarah reminded. "Install crew, you got the tools?"

All sorts of hand tools were held up. Yvonne flashed them a grin. "Awesome."

Turning, she looked out at the EagleCorp headquarters building squatting across Sixteenth Street from her. She grinned. "Let's do this."

Twenty minutes later, every streetlight flared incredibly bright. From every corner of Sixteenth Street, dancers in brightly colored costumes came flowing. The wind whipped scarves and shawls, spattering gorgeous masks with flecks of ash. A drum corps made up of big bass drums and a couple trumpets came through the center, keeping the whole flash mob on time as they sang.

Surprised Peacekeepers stepped out to see what the noise was, several still holding coffee cups. At every door, they confronted a corridor of full-length mirrors planted in quick-set concrete frames clamped to the sidewalks. Across the top, every mirror carried a motto:

> **Is This Who You Want To Be? Who Are You Protecting? Can You Look Yourself In The Eye?**

"We're not gonna take it!" the crowd bawled, the drums pounding out the rhythm. And then the song was over, and the crowd melted away, and the Peacekeepers were left staring at themselves in the mirror.

"Oh my god, oh my god, oh my god, that was *the best!"* Yvonne enthused, arms tight around her wife as they spun in a giddy circle. "It went just right! The best ever!"

"Did you see their faces?" Sarah laughed giddily. "Oh my god, that guy who dropped his coffee!"

"I know, I know, it was *perfect!"* Yvonne crowed, kissing Sarah. "Oh my god, I can't wait to see the clips go around the Mesh!"

"Some of it's up already, I bet! And we can see how the action went in other parts of the country! That was the best!" Sarah squeed.

They bounced around for a couple seconds more, until they'd worn themselves out and just stood, grinning at each other.

"Time for us to head home, hunh?" Yvonne suggested.

"Yep," Sarah leaned up to sneak a kiss. "Tom will start worrying if we're gone too long."

"Yeah, right, he practically shoved us out the door." Yvonne laughed as they headed out the side door and into the alley. "'I'm seventeen and I can take care of myself, you guys love doing runs together, go on,'" she repeated her son's words with a grinning roll of the eyes. "He's getting so *pushy* these days."

"He probably wanted us out of the way so he could have fun times with Abigail," Sarah teased.

Yvonne snorted. "If that's what he wants, it's not us he has to get out of the way; it's Milo."

"Point." Sarah paused for a moment. "We did get him his sex-health implant already, right? And Abbie's got one, yeah?"

"When they turned sixteen," Yvonne reassured, squeezing her wife's hand. "Damian did Abbie and Tom's birth control implants on the same day he did the new recruits'. You are such a mom these days."

"Yeah, and I make it look good," Sarah parried, her dark eyes full of laughter. Yvonne shrugged, smiling. "Point. Anyway, which out are we taking?"

"The easy one," Sarah replied, "CAS tickets for the train out to the outskirts, through the Sweetwater Station tunnel and thirty miles home on the bikes."

"Awesome," Yvonne agreed. "Might even make it home for dinner. C'mon!"

The sky was the color of a healing bruise by the time they pulled the rabbitbrush and tumbleweeds off the slicktarp that covered their bikes. The wind whipped the crackling weeds out of their fingers, trying to take the tarp away with them. It took Yvonne and Sarah both to fold the thing and stow it in the back-box on Sarah's bike. Yvonne was glad for once to pull on her riding helmet and breathe the recirculated air pumped through its filter; it shut out the smell of smoke, at least.

"Hey Sarah hon, did you check the fire alerts before we got out?"

Sarah glanced up. "Yeah, it looked good on the maps, why?"

"Just checking," Yvonne reassured. She shrugged to herself as she climbed onto her bike. Sure, the sky looked bad, but they'd be okay.

"Ready?" Sarah asked over the comm. "Let's go," Yvonne agreed into her mic, kicking her bike into life.

They tore off across the Dust, the wind slamming them in gusts that came out of nowhere.

"Man, riding sucks today," Sarah's voice grumbled in Yvonne's ear. She made a little sound of agreement into her mic, concentrating on her grip on the handlebars.

Something whipped by her, and Yvonne barely resisted the instinct to duck. A tumbleweed, one of the really big ones. And…she hadn't gotten a good look at it, the wind had whipped it by so fast. Had that flash of red been the sunlight, hitting weird?

"Oh shit!" Sarah gasped ahead of her. Yvonne topped the rise just behind her, and flames speared up to meet them.

"East!" Yvonne yelped into her mic, turning her bike. "We'll go around!"

Another gust sent a plume of smoke racing at them, laying a heavy curtain across the terrain ahead.

"Fuck, fuck, fuck, this is not good!" Yvonne muttered. Sarah's voice laughed nervously in her ear. "You think? The wind's blowing it ahead of us!"

On their flank, the fire roared as it ate up the scrubby prairie, sending plumes of smoke boiling into the air. Rolling balls of kochia raced ahead of the grassfire, spreading it as they tumbled. The wind howled, and the flames raced under its pressure.

"Floor it!" Yvonne yelped, pushing the Go pedal for all it was worth. Sarah matched her pace. Together, they pushed their bikes past eighty, past ninety. Still the fire crackled at their heels. The heat felt like it might bake them in their riding clothes like potatoes in the skin. The only part of her that wasn't overheating was her torso under its chill vest. She could feel sweat running down the tip of her nose, dripping into her helmet. *Hot. Too hot. Have to get out of this heat.*

"Fuck!" Sarah cried as they topped a new hill. "It's ahead of us!"

"Keep going!" Yvonne demanded into her mic. Sweat trickled down her back.

"Baby, I don't know about—" Sarah began, but Yvonne cut her off, her heart in her mouth. "The wheels can take the heat for a little bit. If we drive through the burn, we won't have as much fire coming at us. We just have to move fast!" Matching words with action, she took off.

A stand of Russian Olive trees was belching flame into the sky, crackling as they burned. In another dip in the landscape, an old Black Locust groaned as it fell, smothered in fire. It was like driving into Hell.

"Stay away from the trees!" Yvonne called. She heard her wife snort.

"Ya think?!"

Swerving out of the way of a falling branch, she gunned the bike, eyes scanning the horizon. There, a break in the smoke. "Come on!" Yvonne raced for it, the wind howling like a beast hunting prey.

*Me. I'm the prey.*

A gust of scorching air nearly shoved the bike into a flaming creosote bush, but Yvonne leaned into the turn and pushed the speedometer to ninety-five.

*Almost there,* she whispered in her head. *Almost there. Almost there.*

The wind turned, and now the smoke rolled over them. The crackle and pop of the fire filled her helmet with static. Yvonne could barely see for smoke.

"Sarah, talk to me."

"On your left baby."

"Kay. Don't stop!"

"Don't need to tell me!"

And then they were up and out of the valley, and the air was clear, and they were racing across a gloriously normal section of the Dust with only the yellow sky overhead to tell anyone there was trouble.

They didn't let up until they were within a mile of home.

"Sarah, hon, let's pull up and decompress," Yvonne suggested into her mic. "We don't want to walk into the base freaking out."

They pulled up beside a convenient rock outcrop and killed the bikes. Yvonne pulled her helmet off with fingers that felt numb. Sarah's face, when her helmet revealed it, looked as shook as Yvonne felt. Her gorgeous eyes were huge, and she was white as a sheet.

For a second, all Yvonne could do was stare at her girl and breathe.

Sarah drew a trembling breath. "That was close."

"Too close," Yvonne agreed. Her voice sounded funny in her own ears. She set the bike on its kickstand and slid down, back against the rocks. Sarah joined her.

Yvonne let herself just sit for a second. Eventually, she looked over at Sarah, giving her a shaky smile. "You know what?"

"What?"

"It was kind of awesome, wasn't it?"

Sarah cracked a wobbly grin, a weak chuckle eked out of her. "Yeah. Yeah, it was." She leaned in and kissed Yvonne quick, standing and pulling her to her feet for a hug.

"C'mon baby girl. Let's go home."

## Event File 09
## File Tag: Details Of Procedure
## 09:30-07-12-2161

Kevin came racing up on his bike when they were within half a mile of home, blew right past them, and came back around to fall in line with them in a plume of dust and a squeal of brakes.

"Hey!" Yvonne called into her mic. When her buddy replied, he sounded freaked as hell.

"We saw your trackers pass through one of the new burn areas and stop. I thought…" she heard him take a deep breath over the mic. "I was coming out to check on you two. What was all that about?"

Yvonne winced behind her helmet visor. "Sorry Kev baby, we were just catching our breath. We're good."

They pulled up under the slick tarp, and the second they were parked Kevin yanked off his riding helmet, dropping it as he pulled both women into a hug. "Don't scare me like that girls! I thought—" a spasm of coughing cut his words short, doubling him over.

"Kev?"

"I'm fine, just give me a…" he rasped, but the coughing fit didn't even let him get the sentence out.

Yvonne raised her eyes to Sarah's.

"Damian?" Sarah asked.

"Damian," Yvonne agreed. Grabbing Kevin under the armpits, they marched him, complaining and coughing, down the hall to the medical bay. Damian raised his head, and sighed. "You again. And here I thought it'd be the girls I'd be treating today. Put him here in the diagnostic chair."

"I'm fine," Kevin grated out, giving Yvonne an irritated look.

"Your oxygen saturation says differently," Damian observed dryly, checking the numbers around the diagnostic chair. Turning, he brought up readouts on his tab. "I was hoping those performance-enhancing nanoids you've got would do something given time, but they were never designed to repair serious lung damage. If the smoke is going to keep exacerbating the problem, I'm recommending that you stay indoors until we receive the pulmonary nanoid delivery."

"Damian! I can't stay cooped up indefinitely. I've got work to do!" Poor Kevin was practically whining.

Before Damian got after him, Yvonne stepped in. "No worries, Inyoni and I can take care of getting the requisitions! It shouldn't take more than a month for the nanoids to get here!"

"A month?" Kevin almost whimpered. Damian eyed him patiently for a moment. "Currently that's a recommendation. If you end up in here coughing again, it's becoming an order."

Kevin looked so pathetic that Yvonne leaned down and gave him a hug. "Don't worry baby, we'll get everything all done if you get grounded. You can get all the paperwork and back end stuff done from here."

"Gee. Thanks." Kevin muttered. "You'll be out on public actions, and I'll be doing *paperwork.*"

"Yvonne, the diagnostic chair's trying to read you and Kevin both now," Damian interjected patiently. Yvonne stepped back. "Sorry. We'll get out of your hair." Turning, she took Sarah's hand. "Let's go tell Tom we're home, kay? He'll want to hear about the pranks."

♠

"Are you going to let me out of this chair any time in the next decade?" Kevin sighed once the girls had left.

Damian didn't even look at him. "Are you going to cut the attitude?"

He closed his eyes, taking a moment to calm himself before he spoke again. "Touché. Sorry, Damian. I'm bloody well irritated with this lung issue."

"You'll be worse than irritated if you keep ignoring it," Damian replied, raising his black cybernetic eyes to pin Kevin in his seat. "And if you want to do something for your department, you can sit there and talk to me."

"About what, exactly?" Kevin asked. He only realized that he was rubbing the palm of his hand across his aching chest again when Damian stepped in, took his wrist, and set his hand pointedly back down on the armrest of the diagnostic chair. He gave Damian a sheepish smile, and did his best to relax and sit still. It was a bit of a challenge; the inside of his chest felt as if it had been rubbed with sandpaper. Bloody hell this was vexatious.

"About you training Inyoni," Damian stated flatly.

"This again?" Kevin sighed.

"Yes this, and yes, again." Damian rejoined pointedly. "The kid can't feel pain, Kevin. He's already come in with a couple injuries. Nothing major, but I don't want him missing some wound and coming to me later with blood poisoning when it gets infected. Or worse, bleeding out. If you're going to ignore my recommendation on this the way you do on everything else I recommend, at bare minimum I want to institute some rules when he's going out regularly."

"Sensible," Kevin agreed, relaxing back in the chair as readouts on his condition popped up on either hand. "What would you recommend?"

Damian ticked his points off on his fingers. "I want him in here for a full medical check after every run. I want him wearing a sensor bracelet that will alert him of histamine and kinin release in his system, or dropping blood pressure. That will let him know he's bleeding."

Kevin nodded, thinking through the idea. "That's quite an elegant solution. I'm sure we can engineer the sensor to look like a watch or a fashion statement. Giving him a warning that he's injured will be valuable."

"It'd be better if he isn't injured at all," Damian grumbled, checking his readings. "I don't like sending someone that vulnerable out on the Grid. I told you that before, and I'm telling you now."

"Needs must, Damian," Kevin sighed. "It's not ideal, but he is going to train up into a good logistics man. You know we'll need more supplies than ever, given what Aidan's been passing along from command on high. And if I can't be out there regularly, we need him." Glancing at the readings, he did his best to change the subject. "On that note, how are the readings looking?"

"Your oxygen saturation is still low," Damian grumbled, standing. Staring at the readings, he allowed a grudging nod. "But I suppose you're alright to work. Indoors, for the rest of today, at least. When are we getting those pulmonary nanoids?"

"As soon as we get a lucky break," Kevin replied, pulling on his jacket. "Let me do some digging today, and I'll see."

*I'll see.* That was all he could promise at the moment, and it incensed him to no end. It still galled him to buy anything directly from the bastards at Cavanaugh, especially since it was their God-forsaken disease that had left everyone needing the repair nanoids. But needs must when the Devil was driving.

He was using that phrase so often lately. Too often. Too many situations lately were approps to the proverb.

Stepping into his office, he cued up his music and got to work. Sector paperwork took precedence of course; he worked his way through the Sector logistical assignments, supply calls, and mission coordination. Then he switched gears and started digging into his own base's supply needs. There *had* to be somewhere he could get the nanoids they needed.

A call buzzed on his tab, derailing Kevin's train of thought. Pulling the device from his pocket, he checked the callsign and felt a little thrill of nervous energy sizzle down his spine. Tio Umberto. It was probably nothing, but there was always the chance his godfather was in trouble. He answered quickly, bringing the call window up. "Evening Tio. Anything wrong?"

He blinked as his godfather's grave face transformed itself with an ear-to-ear grin. "Today everything's right, mijo. If I remember right, your crew has a few former AgCo folks on it? Can you go get them?"

"Of course. Give me two minutes," Kevin agreed, pushing himself out of his chair and dog-trotting down the hall.

"Janice!"

"What?" Janice's voice rang hollow from the innards of a machine she seemed to be gutting. When she pulled her head out, Kevin waved his tab. "Call for you."

Tapping the tab, he brought up the window. "Tio? You're still on the line?"

The older man's face resolved out of the holographic fuzz. "I'm here. So, you're the former AgCo personnel?" he asked, looking at Janice.

"One of them," Janice stated carefully, wiping her hands on a rag as she spoke. "Anythin' I can do for you?"

His godfather tipped his head to Janice. "That depends. How much do you remember about animal handling?"

## Event file 10
## File Tag: Creative Disruption
## 11:20-08-16-2161

"I can't fuckin' belive we're doin' this," Janice repeated for what felt like the tenth time. She couldn't have stopped smiling if you paid her.

"If that smell doesn't make you believe it, nothing will," Milo threw out wryly as he smoothed the temporary tattoo showing the name of a corporate board member across the side of the pig, who wasn't too impressed. It had taken a solid month to get all the parts in place for this stunt, but if it worked, the payoff would be more than worth it.

The livestock trailer trundled slow and easy through the traffic, moving along like this was any other day of the week.

Looking up from the last pig that needed labeling, Janice cracked a grin at her partner. "This is gonna be one for the books."

"Isn't it just," Milo agreed, helping her up. "Watch yourself, pigs can and will eat you if you fall down there with them."

"Who's telling who now, plant boy?" she asked, arching a brow. "I got assigned to assist with farrowing in the off seasons, when I wasn't in the fields. I *know* pigs."

"Fair enough," her partner agreed easily, checking his tab. "First stop in fifteen. This is gonna be good."

"Got that right," Janice agreed with a satisfied nod. "These CES folks pay so much to keep farming their premium pork, they can have it.

On the hoof." She gave her partner a quick squeeze of the hand. He squeezed back, smiling down at her.

The truck eased its pace, taking a turn. "Feels like the first stop," Milo observed. Janice nodded. "So that's group one, this first pen." She put a hand down and scratched the head of a porker. "Thanks for the help, you."

Oddly friendly eyes regarded her, before the pig lowered their nose to the pen's trough again.

The truck stilled. Janice grinned at Milo. "Ready?"

Milo held up the rig's door release button. "Ready."

Janice nodded, reaching down for the latch of the first pen. "Alright then!"

The automatic loading dock of the Citizen Excellent Standing restaurant opened in tandem with the livestock rig's door, courtesy of the falsified credentials they'd borrowed from a delivery truck supplying the restaurant.

Janice opened the first pen door right along with it, whistling low and wheedling the way she'd learned to do so many years ago.

"Pig pig pig, hup hup hup let's go let's go!"

Five beefy porkers trotted pretty as you please through the loading bay door, and straight through into the kitchen. Pigs would always follow the smell of food, and nowhere smelled as good as a kitchen. When Janice heard the first yell, she nodded to herself. Pulling out her tab, she brought up the app she'd been provided by the Grapevine, and hit the number one. The metal box on the livestock rig's roof clunked, and a swarm of display drones spread their little rotors and took off over the building. Janice stepped back as the rig's door closed. "Alright. That's one down, couple dozen to go."

One by one, they pulled up to the loading docks and back entrances of the Citizen Excellent Standing bars and restaurants, shopping centers and clubs across the Denver Metro, releasing a set of pigs with names of the people running the seven corporations who thought the people of the nation were livestock. At each stop, another micro-drone swarm released itself to form a banner reading 'Look Who's Feeding At The Trough!' Some of the drones would split off to display prices of what was sold inside the building full of pampered customers getting a wakeup call and pigs squealing fit to raise the dead, side by side with the statistics of life expectancy and causes of death for each Citizen Standing. Those numbers were stark enough to make anyone sit up and pay attention.

They released pigs at a CES cocktail party using the catering vehicle's credentials. Another set got released right onto the main hall of a prestigious hotel via the loading doors intended to bring in the luggage of large groups. Janice had to laugh when they let a set of pigs go into a swanky clothing store, and one pig immediately pulled a dress off the rack and started chewing it up.

Milo and Janice never stayed long enough to watch the fun of course; they could watch the vids later. But what they did see and hear was plenty to leave Janice grinning. She might smell like pigshit, but by the time they pulled in under the slicktarp of their base and shut the garage door, she was more than ready to pull Milo in for a kiss.

"You an' me an' a shower stall, how's that sound?"

"Sounds good," Milo murmured, resting his brow against hers, "Cause I hate to break it to you, Jan: you stink."

"Look who's talking," Janice gently tugged one of her partner's locs. "C'mon stud. Shower."

High on their stunt, they took their time with each other in the shower, and even more time before they got dressed; long enough that they missed dinner. The crew sent up a hell of a cheer when Janice sauntered into the rec room.

"Hey y'all," she acknowledged. "We on the news yet?"

"Are you ever!" Sarah laughed, grabbing the remote. "We've been waiting to watch it with you. Take a look!"

On the screen, clips played one after the other: three Peacekeepers falling over each other trying to catch a pig. A porker eating off a fancy buffet table, and a man in a suit that cost a working family's annual income slipping in pigshit and going over on his ass.

"Down in front Tom," Topher suggested when Tommy's head blocked the bottom of the screen. Grinning from ear to ear, Tom nodded and squeezed in beside Abigail on Janice's left. Dozer pushed a bottle into Janice's hand and gave her arm a squeeze. "Some work."

"Pigs did most of it," she threw out casually, but she couldn't quit grinning all the same. This couldn't have been better. It was an amazing idea from the Grapevine, and the coordination had been something; Janice's pigs weren't alone by a long way. Every big city had an Animal Announcement event. When people saw the news, everyone across the country would see their local swank joints overrun with pigs and turkeys. That'd make it real for people. They'd get a good laugh sure, and they'd get a lift off seeing the upper class get put all out of sorts and covered in pig shit. But mostly, they'd see the people who sat at the top of the Citizen Standing System and the people who held it up, the High Standings and the Peacekeepers, looking like fools. And that, Janice knew, was what people needed to see.

The system depended on people being scared of Peacekeepers and believing the High Standings had the right to be where they were. It was hard to be too scared of a guy who you'd seen chasing a pig around a jewelry store, and it sure was hard for a guy covered in pig shit being chased by a sow to pretend he was some kind of higher life form. People would laugh, and then they'd really look. And maybe, just maybe, they'd see.

"Riiiight, give the credit to the pigs," Blake put in, giving her a broad wink. "Of course *they* did the work."

"The CSS places got turkeys!" Abigail bubbled, grinning up at her. "Wanna see?"

"That a rhetorical question?" Janice asked, grinning as she ran a hand over the kid's soft reddish 'fro.

The CSS vids were just as good, with turkeys bearing placards of CEO's names bumbling in confusion around Citizen Secure Standing pavilions, restaurants and cafes, being chased by Peacekeepers, and in one case chasing some poor sap in Peacekeeper gear. That poor bastard, Janice guessed, was *never* living it down. The CSS-level drone-banners read 'Why Are You Letting These Turkeys Run Things?' The twins were laughing themselves sick watching the birds.

"Man oh man," Naomi chuckled, leaning against her brother, "The CEOs have got to be going apeshit!"

"Pigshit, you mean?" Kevin asked, grinning as a new clip started to play. He blinked at the screen as pigs went through a restaurant like a blowtorch through butter. "Wait, rewind that? Zoom in, left side."

Amiably, Janice did. "Pause it!" Kevin's voice had something she hadn't expected in it. She did as she was asked, glancing down the couch. Everyone was looking at Kevin now, but he was looking at the screen with a grin that had gone feral.

"Go ahead and play."

On screen, a dark-haired man who had been sitting at a big table with a group at the start of the clip was trying to run from a pig. He slipped on another porker's leavings, and went down. The pig ran over the top of him.

Kevin leaned back into Aidan's arms, eyes closed and a grin on his lips.

"Harrington. Face down in pigshit with his croneys on hand to witness the humiliation. That is an image I'll savor till the day I die." He opened his eyes, sighing like a man who'd just had a good meal after a few hungry days. "Oh I needed that."

"Take it you did," Janice agreed quietly. She wasn't sure of the details and she sure wasn't asking now, but she knew enough to know that if Kevin was grinning that way, someone who deserved it was getting comeuppance. She was pretty well satisfied any time that happened.

They were putting on such a party that Dozer had to shout to get a word through.

"Everybody, heads up! Fire!"

A chill skewered Janice. She flipped the screen off. "Where?"

Aidan sat up straight, pushing himself out of the tangle of Kevin and Naomi's arms to step over beside Dozer. "Let's get the details."

"Wind's turned, it's ninety miles an hour and it's pushing a brush fire our way," the big man stated tightly, pulling up maps to hang in the air. "It's fifty miles out. Commander, the algorithm says it'll turn in a bit and leave us alone, but I seen these things go buggy before. I say we prep for a move, and we can chill out if the wind changes."

"Sounds good," Aidan agreed, nodding. "Everyone, you heard Dozer. Prep for a move. Pack and prep everything for transit. We need to be ready to book it in less than an hour if that wind keeps the fire coming our way. I'll send an all clear if we get better news."

Laughter dying on their tongues, everyone got to it. First they packed. Then they waited; either they'd get the all clear, or the order to move.

The waiting stretched time out, leaving them all jangling as the minutes ticked past. The crew played cards, nervous as cats in a dog kennel. Aidan kept circling around, keeping people engaged in games and busy. Janice played because it was something to do, but she didn't really breathe out for the next two hours.

Finally, thank fuck, the all clear went around: the wind had turned, and the brush fire was heading away, staying a good twenty miles off.

"Gracias a Dios," she whispered, setting down the tools she'd been packing.

"Thank God," Milo echoed, giving her shoulders a squeeze. She reached over and gripped his hand, letting herself hang on tight.

That night, she lay in bed with her head on Milo's chest, listened to his heartbeat, and counted her blessings. They'd dodged the fire. This time.

This time.

The thought followed her into her dreams, tainting them with smoke.

## Event File 11
## File Tag: Resource Sovereignty
## 05:45-08-20-2161/ 18:00-08-20-2161

It was early when Janice rolled out of bed and got to work on the idea she'd been thinking through. Pulling up the water-condenser schematics that Kevin had landed, she put a couple hours into studying the designs, comparing them to the list of what she had on hand. She'd tried to do this over the years, tried it again and again. It had never really panned out. But this time, with these plans, it might just work.

She double checked the metal-organic framework she'd started growing in a bin behind her desk a few days ago, based off the notes that had come with the schematics. The stuff stank like fresh blood, but it sure looked better than the gloop it had been when she started. Now that it had crystallized, she could get started.

Studying her parts list, she nodded to herself. "Well, can't hurt."

Standing, she pulled down the first of her extra-parts bags from its net on the ceiling and started digging. Jillian would be on duty soon, and she wanted this done before the girl was here to watch.

Pulling out a beat-to-hell road sign, she pried the solar panel off it and hooked it up to a deep-cycle battery she'd dug out of a portable hand generator that had given up the ghost. She hooked that up to the shell of an old microwave. By rubbing the metal-organic crystals she'd grown and the silica she'd pulled out of a bunch of packing material into the old ace bandages that Tweak had turned over for rags, she'd gotten something that could work for metal-organic framework tapes. She hung the tapes on wires across the inside of the old microwave. Grabbing a drill and some ear protection, she drilled a couple holes in the sides of the box, attached a little fan on the left-hand wall, a heating pad pulled out of old footwarmers on the bottom and a hosepipe on the right side, cementing everything with epoxy. She took the bandages out, sprayed the inside of the gizmo with a food-grade sealant, replaced the bandages, closed the door, put it on the legs from an old wheeled bin and set a bucket under the whole thing. That done, she stood back and studied her prototype. And snorted.

"Well ain't you ugly as sin."

The prototype was an awkward, rickety contraption, without a single point in the looks department. Of course, that didn't matter much. Whether it worked? Now, that would matter.

"C'mon you," she murmured to her new gizmo, picking it up and carrying it out of the building. Getting it up onto the base roof was awkward as hell, but she managed it eventually. The sun was just starting to rise when she set the prototype up on the far end, out of the way. For a moment, Janice stood still and closed her eyes, breathing in the quiet. The cool air fizzed against her skin, making her feel alive. Standing still for a heartbeat more, she smiled. Then she turned, flipped her machine on, attached the outlet hose to the bucket, snapped the bucket lid down tight and walked away. Watched pots didn't boil, and watched experiments didn't do anybody any good.

To kill time, she headed back inside to run phenotype tests on the new seedlings. She had her hand on the door when Blake caught her.

"You're going to want to come see the news," Blake stated. For once, there wasn't a lick of humor in the eyes of the guy she'd trained up with. Not even a hint of sarcasm.

"Who's dead?" Janice asked.

Blake shrugged. "Nobody yet. But it's ugly."

Blake hadn't been kidding. Most of the base had crowded in to watch the news, breakfast in hand. Nobody was eating. In fact, nobody was making a sound.

On the screen, Peacekeepers in full riot gear had surrounded one of the new community cooling shelters. A line of FIDOs stood like leashed dogs from Hell in front of the humans. Janice's gut tightened. Field Integrated Defensive-Offensive units were something she hadn't seen in years, but they were bad news down to the ground.

Behind the Peacekeepers, autonomous earthmovers and black EagleCorp arrest vans idled. The Peacekeepers rattled their nightsticks on their riot shields, the sound echoing around their rec room. Shit, that was scary, even on TV.

Around the shelter, three concentric rings of civilians stood holding hands. They were singing, something old and gospel. It took a second for Janice to catch the words, but yeah, it was 'We Shall Not Be Moved'.

Some asshole from ArgusCorp was yelling over a bullhorn about illegal construction and unapproved cooling shelters. There were a couple beats of quiet. Then the FIDOs moved in. Each autonomous robotic dog moved forward with that terrible mechanical precision that crossed spider and hound. Each unit shot a round of rubber bullets, followed by a spray of what were probably tranq darts. Then they chose a protestor to stand on, holding each person down with a hundred pounds of metal.

The front line didn't stand a chance.

The singing warped into screams as the FIDOS went at the Union folks. And that was when the Peacekeepers moved in. They weren't pulling a single punch this time; they laid into the people with batons, then with boots once they got them on the ground. People did their best to hold, but it was hard to stand when someone had clocked you across the head with a nightstick.

As people went down, they were dragged to the waiting vans by the Peacekeepers. Somebody shouted, and finally, the people still standing broke and ran. *Good*, Janice thought. *No sense all of you going down.*

In ten minutes, it was all over. The FIDOS formed a corridor, and the earthmovers came in. It took the machines less than a minute to knock the little building flat and rip it apart.

"We helped build that shelter," Kevin stated, distant and chilly as the moon. "Inyoni and I were there, not more than two months ago."

"Who turned them in?" Naomi asked.

Tweak's voice was unsteady on the word, brittle as glass. "Sleepw-walker."

"Fuck," Aidan breathed. Janice glanced down, checking on him. Aidan's eyes weren't focused. Janice gave him a beat. He'd pull it together.

After a couple breaths, the man who led them shook it off. "Okay. Liza, reach out to the Union, see what they need. Kevin, start getting a lead on supplies and a logistics plan to drop a med and food delivery off, so they can take care of their wounded. I'm reporting this to Sector. Everybody else, we've got work to do. This sucks, but the best thing we can do for everyone is keep doing our jobs. I'll check in if we're offered opportunities to help. Let's finish breakfast and get back to work."

Nodding, the Wildcards filtered out quietly. Janice gave her daughter's shoulder a squeeze as she passed the girl, giving her a careful check over. Abigail looked freaked, yeah, and broken-hearted. But when she looked up, there was fire in her copper eyes. Good. That anger would get her through. Janice gave her a grim smile, and moved on.

There was nothing she could do for the poor bastards who'd just gotten their asses handed to them. Not her department. So she focused on what she could do: she checked over the watering system for their plants. Checked the power panels feeding solar energy down into the base, cleaning the ash off them as the heat pressed her down. She sweated, and she hydrated, and she took a shower once her outdoor work was done. And she waited.

She did what she could around the base too, of course: a squeeze of the shoulder here, a quick word there. A little telling off when she found Tweak chucking up in the can again.

"You're goin' to see Damian, right?" She called through the door.

"D-don't hassle m-m-me! I'm s-sick!" Tweak's voice moaned in reply.

Janice banged on the door. "Either you go talk to Damian, or I run a wastewater bio-check on what you're chucking up in there an' I send him the report!"

"Fiiiine!" Tweak groaned. "N-now will you p-p-please f-fuck off!"

Well, at least she'd said please. Janice let it drop, and found other things to fix. She had a lot more time to kill.

A little before dinner, she climbed onto the roof one more time and made her check. Methodically, she went through the documentation process. Then she climbed back down, headed into the garage, and sauntered over to Dozer.

"Mind if I borrow Topher for a couple hours 'fore we're off-duty?"

"Sure," her pal agreed, wide brow furrowed. "What's up?"

"Can't be sure yet, till I get some testin' done." Janice shrugged. "Could use Topher's help on that."

"Course," Dozer agreed. "I got him printin' stuff right now, go grab him. Cameron an' me can get the bikes retooled on our own."

"Much obliged," she smiled, turned, and walked inside. Easy, easy, easy. No sense getting excited.

On the way, she stopped in her office and nodded at her trainee. "Jillian? Come'n give me a hand, willya?"

The younger woman looked up, her slotted yellow eyes blinking as they refocused. "Sure. What's going on?"

"Little experiment, lessee what we can do with it," Janice replied, keeping cool. No sense getting excited.

They picked up Topher, and Janice led the two back up onto the roof.

"Got somethin' I need a hand on from you two. I think I got somethin' workable, but I ain't so sure it'll scale."

Leading them to the far end of the roof, she pointed at her jerry-rigged trial run. "Toph, I need your know-how. Let's see how we can work up a printing pattern and an easy-access parts list. Jillian, gimme a hand figuring out where we can improve the water flow."

Under the condenser, the bucket of water glimmered in the last shreds of sunlight.

"This is for what now?" Topher asked, studying the device with interest.

Finally, Janice allowed herself to smile.

"This—" she pointed at the prototype— "is for making that," she finished, pointing at the full bucket. Pulling off the lid, she stepped back to show them the water inside.

Topher and Jillian's mouths dropped open.

Janice grinned, crossing her arms. "Now, you two tell me how we make one of these for as many folks as we can, hunh? That's your job. I done mine."

## Event File 12
## File Tag: Decision Tree
## 06:30-08-22-2161

"Wait, water condensers? You guys actually figured out water condensers?!"

"Yep!" Tweak bobbed her head proudly. "We d-did! I mean, our hydro l-lady did. She kicks ass."

"Holy shit, I guess so!" Fatima agreed, her hologram sitting in its chair with eyes wide. Ethan grinned. "Okay! So, we can get those schematics out there for everyone, they won't have to worry about the Corps shutting off their water. Perfect!"

"Once they got water, and they got the v-vote, they're set!" Tweak agreed, bobbing her head. The other ten Code Monkeys clapped and whooped, holograms fizzing as the projectors Tweak had put on the floor tried to keep up with the movements.

"If they're gonna get the vote, we g-gotta get the app r-right," Tweak announced. "Lessee the front-end chatb-b-bot. Has it got its head out of its ass yet?"

Deniki snorted. "I wish. AI-powered chatbots to guide voters through the registration and vote casting process sounds so good, until we try to do it." The big Haida waved a hand in irritation. "The thing's stiff as a board when it talks. It still isn't picking up anybody who can't speak loud and clear, too."

"Hey," Lulu teased, "could be worse, could be my part of the build that's having problems. The AI may not be doing great talking Grandma through her registration, but the pen-testing is showing a near one hundred percent catch rate for backdoor searches and attacks. We ran a thousand simulated adversarial attacks internally, and the AI's doing great at that."

Tweak's stomach was doing barrel rolls again. Why? She wasn't scared. She wasn't even nervous. She didn't have anything in her stomach either; it was too early for breakfast.

Probably the fucking smoke again. She ignored it.

"The machine learning's run through its final data set," Darnisha added, her hologram wobbling as she demanded more CPU to bring up a full-window display of the data beside her image. "Looks like the biometric verification mechanisms are all trained up and ready to work. People will register using their biometrics, and we backstop that with a password. Once they're validated, their votes go into the blockchain as an anonymized hash with a timestamp. Nobody can get named, but nobody's vote can get changed either."

"C-cool," Tweak agreed with a nod. "D-daniel, you been r-running the ex-ex-external white-hat. What'd it take to fuck the vote?"

Daniel grinned, one of those rare smiles that showed all his crooked teeth.

"I've been running external attacks with all those phones we set up to act as dummy voters. To mess with an election, the black hat would need to have at least fifty-one percent of the vote ledgers on the blockchain. To get them, they'd have to hack multiple, disparate infrastructures, then hack the cryptography on each node infrastructure. And they'd have to do that in a really specific sequence, or the red flags will go up in our blockchain. And all I'm going to say is, buddy, good luck with that!"

"How many tests you r-run?" Tweak asked.

"Three thousand, simultaneous on the quantum servers," Daniel replied with a shrug. "Want more?"

"Nah, three thousand should be g-good." Tweak agreed. "What about the—"

And *that* churn of the gut she couldn't ignore. She covered her mouth, held up a finger, and booked it. She was *not* barfing on her rig.

She made it to the can just in time. There went last night's dinner, and what felt like everything she'd eaten in the last year. Her legs felt like cooked pasta by the time she got to her feet. Her hands shook as she washed up. She could not *wait* for the smoke to fuck off out of the Sector.

"S-sorry," she offered, sliding back into her chair. She gave the Code Monkeys a quick grin. "Fucking s-smoke. M-makes me hurl."

"No shit," Deniki agreed with a little smile. "You okay?"

"Good to talk," Tweak agreed. "And we gotta talk. I'm getting f-freaked. My Sector's got a m-mole."

"The Sleepwalker?" Darnisha asked, her dark face losing its smile. Tweak nodded.

"Yeah, I've been following that," Rhin mused. "Not good. It's not good that we're having so much trouble pinpointing the source. And it's worse that the civvies are getting screwed for it."

"Yeah," Tweak agreed. "Eagle just w-w-wrecked a c-cooling shelter down here because of that fuck."

"We saw," Lulu agreed, her voice edged in anger. "And the Sleepwalker turned in a bunch of intel on that Pueblo march that the Grapevine was doing. It all got passed to Eagle. They opened fire on the crowd, killed a bunch of people. Bastards."

Tweak bit her lip. Sorting through her thoughts, she picked out what needed saying.

"Guys, I'm f-freaked. I track the p-posting ISP for the Sleepwalker, and it v-vanishes. He's like a g-ghost. Can't pin him down."

"Same here," Rhin agreed.

Fatima nodded, straightening her headscarf the way she did when she was nervous. "I gave it a shot too. Someone's covering him really well. I don't like it."

"I'll take a crack at it," Deniki offered. "New eyes might catch something."

Tweak shot her buddy a smile. "Thanks man."

The Alaskan gave her a nod. "I figure you guys have enough going on with those fires. I looked at the map; you okay?"

Tweak shrugged. "For now. Okay, we r-ready to send the final build with the docs for the r-registration and pen tests to the UN for v-vetting?"

"Think so," Darnisha agreed, "here's our bug-test list, it all came out clean. Anybody want to do anything else before we send it off?"

"Yeah," Tweak put in. She swallowed hard. "My name. On there. Gotta c-change it. Put down Lung Tung-Mei"

"Woah," Charlie murmured. "What's up, Tweak?"

Tweak rubbed her throat with one hand, but she grinned at her friends. "The whole w-world gonna see my n-name on here? I want it to be my real name. My family's n-name. Corps took that away, for a while." That wasn't exactly true. She hadn't deserved her name in her own head, for a while. But things were different now. She crossed her arms. "I cleared it with my b-boss. From now on, I take my n-name back."

"Well alright then," Deniki agreed with a grin. "Lung Tung-Mei it is!"

They took a couple of minutes for all ten of them to double check their work and put a digital signature on the app. Tweak brought up the secure quantum-server dropbox, and held up her crossed fingers. "Okay. Here goes."

She dropped their source code and their data files in the box.

**Submission Accepted**, the message came back. **Your submission will be reviewed within seven business days.**

"Fingers crossed," Darnisha sighed.

"Knock on wood," Ethan agreed.

"You guys suck!" Nathan laughed. "I'm gonna celebrate tonight."

"Celebrate after we get approval or you'll jinx it," Deniki replied.

Grinning, Nathan shrugged. "Yeah, yeah. Okay, I'm signing off."

"About time I did too," Deniki agreed, "see you guys."

"Seeya!" Tweak agreed, and shut her end of the call down. The ten holograms blipped out of existence.

Sitting in the empty room, she stared down at her stomach. This nausea was such a pain. It was completely out of control, and she *hated* it when her body was out of control.

"Quit f-fucking around," she grumbled down at her guts. Like that was going to do any good.

She let it go and got back to something she *could* control.

By breakfast she was starving, and that felt weird too. She guessed it made sense though; she had lost all her calories, basically. She wandered down to see what there was to eat.

What there was today was scones and fruit, with a side of potato hash and the plant-based sausages Billie was so good at making. There was even melon, now that they'd figured out what killed the melon vines last year and got it fixed. That was cool.

Tweak was nearly the last person in line for eats, but there was still plenty for her. She waved at Billie. "Hey!"

Her best buddy gave her a small smile. "Hey Tweak. Come back here a second? I could use a hand with the chocolate beans and the grinder."

Tweak bobbed her head. "Sure!" She trotted around the counter and into the kitchen. The chocolate beans were one of the best things they'd ever pulled off; with Abigail's help, she'd gotten a cacao tree gene-tailored to survive in Colorado over the winter, and started harvesting its fruit back in September. Billie had gotten involved at that point, and now they had not just plenty of chocolate on-base and a really neat chocolate-flavored tea made out of the bean husks, but primo chocolate to sell and barter too. That tree was making them bank, and every time Billie came up with a new recipe for the chocolate it sold like that.

"G-grinder fucking around again?" Tweak asked as Billie grabbed a bag of roasted cacao beans.

Her best friend picked at the corner of the sack. “Actually…the grinder’s good. I just needed you to come back here.” Slowly, Billie raised her eyes. “Tweak? We gotta talk.”

“Yeah?” Tweak shoved her hands in her pockets. “Bout what?”

“Tweak…” Billie glanced away. “I think you need to go talk to Damian. You’re throwing up a lot.”

Tweak rolled her eyes. “Billie! I’m. *Fine*. I’m. Good.”

“Tweak,” Billie murmured, “it’s getting to be every day. You’re eating lots at some meals because you’re throwing up other meals. It’s…it’s scaring me, okay?”

That stuck. Tweak nerved herself to look up at Billie, really look at her. Billie was biting her lip, and her eyes were wide. There was that tense set to her shoulders too.

“You’re scared?” Tweak asked.

Bille nodded.

Tweak swallowed. “Billie. S-sorry.”

Billie shrugged “‘S’okay. Just…can you go see Damian? Just to double check?”

The words processed for a second. Tweak was sick of being in and out of the med bay. But if it could help Billie stop being scared…

She bobbed her head. “Sure! I’ll go ton-night.”

“Promise?” Billie asked softly.

Tweak shot her a smile, holding her hands out to the sides.

“Promise.” She could give normal hugs now, but this was the way they’d always done it. This felt right.

Smiling just a little, Billie spread her hands too, touching fingertips with Tweak.

“Okay. Thanks, Tweak.”

Tweak shrugged. “No big. M-maybe give D-damian shit. Him and Alice.”

Billie giggled. “You’re awful.”

“Yep!” Tweak chirped. “And you love it.”

Glancing down, Billie grinned. “Yeah, I do. Love you, Tweak.”

"Yeah, I know," Tweak agreed. "Same. Seeya." With a wave of the hand, she turned and headed back into the canteen.

"Damian!"

The doctor raised his shaved head, looking up from his lunch. "Tweak."

"Put me in the s-schedule. Tonight." She said as she took a seat. "Sick of throwing up b-breakfast. Kay?"

"I'll do that," Damian agreed.

"Scuse the reach," Inyoni offered as he stretched an arm over her shoulder, his riding suit creaking. He snagged the coffee pot, filled a thermos, and stuck it onto the holster at his hip.

Tweak looked up. "*More* trips? Where you going?"

"Out to the Sky House and Dead Horse," Inyoni offered with a smile. "We're trading for the stuff to go in the air filters."

Tweak nodded. Those Fringe communities weren't too bad. Still…

"Got backup?" She asked.

"Me," Yvonne offered, waving a slice of melon. "I told Mister All Ready To Go here that we'd head out after breakfast. Look at you, all ready to move," she teased, grinning at Inyoni.

His long ears drooped. "Was I supposed to wait?"

"Don't take her seriously, Inyoni," Tom offered between bites. "You'll go nuts."

"Listen to this kiddo. Tommy, no teenager ever takes his mom seriously and everybody knows it," Yvonne chuckled, leaning over to give his shoulder a squeeze. Tom gave Inyoni a patient look that was as good as saying 'see what I mean?'

Standing, Tweak gave Inyoni a quick squeeze. "Come home safe. Kay?"

"Gonna try," Inyoni agreed, running a hand over her hair.

She crossed her arms. "Don't try. *Do* it."

He laughed. "Okay, okay. I *will* come home safe."

Tweak nodded. “Good.” Standing on tiptoe, she gave him a kiss. Then she dropped back into her seat. “First, eat. Fuel up. Then go.”

## Event File 13
## File Tag: Citizens' Assembly
## 09:00-08-22-2161

"Come on, Inyoni!" Yvonne called into her helmet mic. "Keep up!"

"Aren't we riding kinda fast?" His voice asked in her ear.

"Yeah, 'cause it's fun!" Yvonne called back. She didn't get an answer to that.

Maybe she should slow down for the new kid. But she loved blazing across open Dust like this. Besides, this wasn't a bad stretch. Sure there were some prairie dog holes here and there, and rocks, and that bush she had to swerve around just now, but that was no big deal.

"Uh…Yvonne?"

"Yeah?" Shit, the kid really did sound freaked. She could hear Inyoni swallow over the mic before he spoke.

"There's a drone."

"What?!" Yvonne almost looked over her shoulder, which was suicide at the speed she was going. "It isn't on our readers!"

"I can hear it. It's up high and to our left," Inyoni's voice said into her mic. "It's keeping pace."

"Shit!" Slowing down, she brought her HUD up. "Inyoni, you sure? I don't see anything on the reads."

"That buzz is right over us," Inyoni stated as she fell back to ride beside him. Her heart kicked up a notch. Tapping her handlebars, she got the HUD to run on all frequencies, not just the usual. A ton of stuff turned up in her vision: delivery blimps way overhead, delivery drones all over the place…and one unaffiliated drone, right over them.

"Shit, you're right," she hissed. "Okay, this is bad. Bringing up specs…okay it's not armed, but we can't go to the Sky House or anywhere else until we shake it. We'd blow their security. Fuckity fuck."

"How do we get rid of it?" Inyoni asked, his voice strained in her ear. Yvonne sighed. "Well, first we try the IR emitters. But some drones are getting around the handheld kind these days, so if they do…okay if they do we'll go with plan B."

She was really glad he didn't ask what Plan B was, because she had no idea.

Twisting the command toggle on her bike's handle, she brought up the IR emitter controls that Topher had added, and hit 'engage.' She imagined she could feel the infrared beam go up.

"IR's going on now. Let's see if that takes it down," she offered.

For a couple beats, they rode in silence. Then Inyoni spoke. "No dice. I can still hear it."

"Fuck me!" Yvonne groaned. "I hate drones!"

"What do we do?" Inyoni asked, voice tight.

"Well right now, you two swerve right and left, and don't look up!" a new voice said in their channel. Yvonne almost fell off her bike.

"Rank! Personnel Number! Passphrase!" she yelped into the line. How the hell had someone who wasn't Duster gotten into the line?!

"Walkers of Coomb Olwen!" A man's voice called over the line. "And right now the passphrase is 'duck!'

There was a high scream overhead, something that rattled Yvonne right down to her bones.

"Swerve, then stop!" a woman's voice ordered in her ear, and Yvonne's muscles did what they were told. She skidded her bike into a swerve, hoping like hell that Inyoni had done the same. She didn't have time to look.

Something crashed to earth right where she'd been, rolling in the dust as she pulled her bike into a skidding stop. She raised her visor, panting.

"Psst! In here!"

A tent flap flickered open in the air, and a hand beckoned.

"Quick now, and bring the bikes!"

If there had been time, Yvonne might have hesitated. But there wasn't, so she didn't. A heartbeat later, she and Inyoni crouched inside the slicktarped dome, breathing hard. The Walkers of Coomb Olwen gave her identical grins, Brandi and Brendan sitting shoulder to shoulder.

"Wait a tick," Brendan suggested. He opened the tent flap and held out an arm covered in heavy blue riding gear, whistling low. And a fucking huge eagle soared through the tent flap to land on his actual fucking arm. He leaned a little with the weight, but he chuckled in Yvonne's direction. Pulling gobbets of bloody meat from a pouch at his waist, he held them out to the bird, who basically inhaled them.

"Is that seriously…" Yvonne breathed for a second, trying to get a thought into line. "Did you seriously just take down a drone with a fucking eagle?" Yvonne managed.

"Yep," Brendan gave her a big grin. Carefully, he stroked the bird's neck feathers. "Yvonne, Inyoni. Meet Gwenafwy."

"She's…uh…pretty," Inyoni offered.

Yvonne swallowed as the dangerous beak swung her way. "She's freaking ginormous."

"Well, not really," the freckled man offered with a chuckle, joggling his arm up and down fondly. "This is her first year. We've got her out to socialize."

The bird changed her razor-taloned grip on his arm, glaring at him. He fed her another piece of meat.

"Sorry about the surprise," the green-clad woman at his side offered, shoving curls just as crazy as his back from her face. "We saw you two getting tracked and thought we'd help out. Looks like someone has something on you."

“How do you know?” Inyoni asked, still breathing hard.

Brandi shrugged. “We had a hunch you guys were going to need a hand.”

“It was a hint, Brandi, don’t get modest now,” the blue-clad rider suggested in the same easy tone. He smiled at the two of them. “We got a couple GPS spoofers for you guys to wear. And a little something extra. We’ll go with you down to the Sky House.”

“Wow…thanks.” Yvonne managed, relieved when Brendan slipped some kind of hood over the bird’s head and set it on a perch off to one side. “But…seriously, how’d you guys know?”

The siblings shrugged, smiling identical little smiles. “We got a tip,” was all Brandi said. Brendan didn’t say a word.

That wasn’t getting Yvonne anywhere at all, so she switched gears. “What are you guys doing out here anyway? Aidan said he saw you at the big inter-Quadrant, but I figured you’d go home after that.”

“Oh, we will,” Brendan replied easily, “but we’ve got work to do first.”

“Work?” Inyoni asked.

Brendan nodded. “Things are changing, folks. Things are headed towards the good. So while you’re gathering the folks on the Grid together, we’re doing our own rallying. Now, you keep this under your hats, y’hear?”

“Sure,” Yvonne agreed, “what, exactly?”

“Our elders have asked us to gather the hidden folk,” Brandi explained, her hands playing with something in the pockets of her riding jacket. “We’re going round to the lost and the forgotten. All those little communities that aren’t on anyone else’s map. You folks are going to make this country a decent place to live again?” Brandi murmured, smiling faintly. “We’re going to bring people you’ve lost back to be a part of it. You’ll need the strangers and the new folks, if a new way of living is to be born from this struggle. You’ll need all the folk to make a new beginning.”

One of those wooden coins Brandi kept in her pocket tonked onto the tent floor. She lifted it, studying the symbol. Yvonne leaned in, getting a good look. The mark was just a vertical line with a horizontal line sticking out of its right side, but Brandi stared at it like it meant everything. All at once, she turned and stared right at Inyoni. "We need a new kind of person for this new world. Remember."

Inyoni's ears went down and back like a scared rabbit's. "Uh…" He swallowed. "I…will?"

"Bran," Brendan murmured, giving his sister's knee a squeeze. "Come on back. You're wandering."

Brandi blinked. Giving a little laugh, she shook her head. "That's what I get for being out in the heat too long," she offered wryly, slipping the little toggle back into her pocket and zipping it up. "Anyway, about those GPS scramblers." Digging in a bag, she pulled out two little grey boxes on strings. "Hang these around your necks and you should be alright. No telling what they're locking onto, but they'll have some fun trying to track anything within thirty feet of these babies. Got them from a community of the Diggers out of Nebraska, real good at disappearing up there."

"They gotta be," Brendan added with a wink. "There's damn all to hide behind in Nebraska. Flat as a pancake all the way to the border."

"True enough," Brandi laughed. "True enough. Fair warning though, they're going to block the signals on your tabs and any other gadgets you got on you, so you might as well turn those off 'til things have blown over."

"Good call," Yvonne agreed, pulling out her tab and turning it off. She made sure Inyoni did the same out of the corner of her eye.

"And here's these," Brendan added, holding out two little bags. Yvonne took one. "What are they?"

"A little bit of luck," Brendan offered with a shrug. "Put them in your pockets. They'll help."

Yvonne liked the siblings, what little she'd gotten to know of them. But she was never really sure what to do about them when they got like this. For now, she just pocketed the thing.

"So, um…can we get moving?"

The Sky House was a relief after the heat outside. Far above, the open roof of the natural rock tower let in a little daylight, but down here in the hollowed-out stone it was dim and cool, the walls breathing out the smell of the adobe they were plastered with.

Yvonne shook hands with the head man, giving him a smile. "Good to see you again."

"Same, girl," the old Fringer agreed with a smile that crinkled the lines around his eyes. "Hear big things these days."

Yvonne laughed. "You're gonna hear a lot more soon!"

"Is that a fact," Pat murmured. Turning, he shook hands with Brandi and Brendan. "Glad you two made it. You're just in time."

"Glad to hear it," Brendan replied, giving a little nod.

"In time for what?" Inyoni asked, almost falling off his bike as he unslung his pack. Man the guy was a klutz.

Pat gave him a grin. "For the big Fringe shindig, kid. Come on, inside."

"I'll be along once I get Gwenafwy settled," Brendan called back, turning to the two-wheeled shed hooked to his bike.

Pat led them through a couple of rooms cut into the cliffside, into the heart of Sky House itself. The central tower of the adobe-and-stone complex built into the concealing rock outcrop was wide enough to serve as a market area, a central square, or anything else the Fringe communities in the area needed. Today, it was a meeting hall, and it was packed.

"Quite the gathering, isn't it, Specialist Flesher?"

Yvonne just about shit a brick. Turning, she saluted her Sector Commander. "Commander Magnum, sir!"

"At ease, Flesher," the big man chuckled. "How's your base doing?"

"Um…good sir," Yvonne gulped. *Magnum*. What the hell was going on, if Magnum was here? What the hell had she gotten in the middle of here?!

"Good to hear it," Magnum offered with a slow nod.

Yvonne turned around, rigid. In a beam of sunlight, Pat stepped onto an upturned box. "Alright, settle y'all." He didn't speak loudly, but the crowd nudged itself into quiet.

"We're going to talk about how this new voting app is going, and how much all us folks want to get involved with what's going on in the cities," Pat explained. "We've got some guests here to say a few words too, but best remember, this is our meeting an' I'm runnin' it. We got a lot to talk about an' some of it's rough, but let's all simmer down and be cordial, alright? No sense gettin' everyone's panties in a bunch."

A little ripple of laughter ran around the room. The rough-edged Fringers shot each other little looks of amusement: a quick grin, a fond roll of the eyes. That was what Yvonne liked about Pat; he made Fringe people show up and behave, but he did it the right way, like Aidan did.

"Now, you may've been hearing, the Dusters is invitin' us to join in on takin' the Corps down," Pat went on.

A rumble of comment ran around the room. Pat panned a steady look around the gathering. "Who's got the floor?"

The crowd quieted.

"They ain't asking us to pick up guns," Pat continued, "jus' to do what we're good at. Growing food. Getting around. Getting supplies. Living out here. An' they're askin' us to start thinkin' about what we'd ask a government to do, if we had one. That's what we're here to discuss today. Now, I'm gonna open the floor, an' all y'all is gonna talk 'bout what you want to see. Keep it civil, and leave some daylight for the next fella. We all got two ears an' one mouth, let's talk an' listen accordingly."

With a grave little smile, he stepped off the box. A woman who shared her looks with an old leather bag took his place.

"Floor's yours, Deanna," Pat observed easily. The woman nodded.

"What I come to say is, my mom got off the grid for a reason," the woman rasped flatly. There was something sour in the twist of her lips when she spoke. "We do our own work out here, and we don't owe a thing to them on-grid. If they don't have the guts to get out of there, that's their problem. Me, I don't want to have anything to do with them. That's all I got to say."

A murmur ran around the cavern of a room as the woman stepped off the box. Yvonne glanced over at Inyoni, who was looking nervous. She flashed him a smile, though she had to work at it.

Someone else, a girl who was barely more than a kid, hopped up on the box. "See, I see it different," she piped. "Way I see it, we couldn't do nothin' afore. Now we can. An' I like the idea of the cities turnin' around an' gettin' straightened out. I like the way cities were in ol' movies. I wanna go on a date in a city someday. If I'm gonna do that, cities gotta get straightened out. I wanna help with that."

"An' what do you know about cities? You're still wet behind the ears!" a man's voice called out of the crowd. Pat stepped forward. "Bill McCormick, who's got the floor?"

The crowd parted, leaving a heavy man all on his own in a circle of cranky looks. He stammered. "I…uh…" He swallowed. "Cindy's got the floor," he admitted.

"That's right," Pat agreed, nodding slowly. "She does. Say your piece, Cindy."

"Did," the girl squeaked, hopping off the box.

A boy who couldn't be more than twenty stepped up onto the box next. "See, a government should be like Grandpa Pat," he threw out, getting a laugh from the congregation. "But in all seriousness, it should, folks. We had enough of the Corps; they don't listen to nothin' or nobody. We want somebody around here who'll look us in the eye an' listen to us. Sure, they might not be perfect. But they gotta be a damnsight better than the Corps. I say we get in, help, and vote."

There were a few ‘yeah’s’ around the room, and a couple whistles as the boy stepped down.

“Quite the event, isn’t it, Specialist?” Commander Magnum offered quietly. Yvonne bobbed her head. “Yes sir. Did we organize this?”

“Why would you think that?” Commander Magnum asked quietly.

Yvonne didn’t have a good answer, so she shrugged. “Shot in the dark, sir.”

“Hold your fire until there’s some light on the situation,” the big man suggested. “It usually gets better results.”

“Yessir,” Yvonne agreed meekly.

Up and down on the box, people stepped to speak their piece. Some spoke in bitterness, resentment against the whole world pouring out. Some were timid, and some were cynical. But just enough people spoke with hope on their tongues that Yvonne started to wonder if they might win over the others.

After what felt like hours, Pat stepped up. “Now we all thought about it together, I’d like to offer the floor to a guest: Bran Ap Llyr has come from Witch Mountain to say a few words.” He nodded over in Yvonne’s direction.

“That’s your cue,” Brendan whispered to his sister. They shared a quick grin. Brandi shoved her long mane of curls back over her shoulder and strode into the circle.

“Witch Mountain?” Yvonne whispered. Brendan shrugged, smiling easily. “Fringe name. People give us names, and we use them. You think we tell everybody we’re from Coomb Olwen?” He winked. “Now let’s see Brandi do her thing.”

In the center of the circle, Brandi held her arms out, encompassing the room.

“A blessing be upon this roof, and all those beneath it.” She took the box with a soft smile. “Thanks for inviting me, folks. The Curanderos of Witch Mountain have been here when you needed us for generations.

We've made sure you had your medicines and sent folks to teach your midwives and doctors across the West. Now you know us; we've always kept ourselves to ourselves."

A ripple of agreement ran around the room. Brandi smiled impishly. "In fact, there's some who say we don't even exist."

Laughter.

"What I'm here to say today," Brandi went on, "is that we who keep the Vow, the Curanderos of Witch Mountain, are stepping up to join in this movement. We were the first to test the voting app and make sure it could be trusted. We're standing at the left hands of the Dusters. We have always midwifed and healed. We have always brought balance to the Wheel of Life. In the name of my elders and my people, I tell you this: we are come now to midwife a new time, and see to the healing of the cities." She spread her arms. "We shall do the work of healers in this time. We shall stand at the left hand of the warriors and in the care of the folk. There is a place for you to stand beside us. Will you stand up? Will you join us?"

A cheer filled the cavern like the sweetest rainwater. Brandi stood and smiled until it died down. "Good. But if we're to come together, we need a gathering place where we can all stand on equal ground: Dusters and Fringers, grid folk and hidden folk alike."

"I'd like to offer that space," Commander Magnum's voice rolled like a mighty river through the room. He walked forward. "Curandera of Witch Mountain, may I have the floor?"

"That you may, Sector Commander Magnum," Brandi agreed with a weirdly graceful bow.

The upturned crate creaked as Commander Magnum stepped onto it. He surveyed the room thoughtfully.

"Friends. I am Sector Commander Benjamin Magnum, the Democratic State Force Commander of the area known as the Front Range. And I am completely in agreement with the suggestion of the Curandera.

"In the past seven years, a base of mine has been working towards the creation of a sedentary farming community. I propose that the communities represented in this room work hand in hand with Unit 1407 to found Four Aces Farm, a multi-stakeholder community that will serve as an equal standing space and a place of exchange between Dusters, Fringers, Grid organizers, and those who call themselves the Hidden Folk."

Yvonne's brain stalled out. She turned to Inyoni. "Is…is he saying what I think he's saying?!" she whispered.

Inyoni blinked at her. "Lady, you're asking the wrong guy."

"Do you think Aidan already knew?" Yvonne hissed. "If he knew and he didn't tell us…that guy!"

"He had good reason, motor-mouth," Brendan teased, elbowing her gently. "Shush, that's your boss an' my sis talkin'."

Yvonne did as she was told, brain spinning. A farm. Their base was getting *turned into a farm.* Commander Taylor's Ten Year Plan was coming true. Holy. Shit.

"We're not asking you to pick up weapons," Commander Magnum continued, "But we are asking anyone who is interested to come and help us build Four Aces Farm. It will be supplied and protected by Unit 1407, governed by democratic vote, and designed to feed and provide for the communities of the Fringe in this Sector. It will provide safety to those who live in its environs, seeds to all the other farms that want to get started, as well as medical care and agricultural expertise. We have the plants and the tools already. What we need are the hands and the minds. Will you come and help us make this real?"

For a beat, the room was dead silent. Slowly, a murmur built like a wave. Little whispers floated like foam on the crest.

"A farm…a real farm…"

"Impossible. Corps will take it down ..."

"But what if they don't?"

"Pat will be collecting the names of those who would like to sign up to join Four Aces Farm this week," Commander Magnum continued.

"All of us have lived out here in the Dust for generations. We know what it's like to live with barely enough. Some of us may have stolen from each other to survive another day. But today, we can do this differently. Together, side by side, we can build places where we can all live in abundance. I want to build these places with you. My people want to build these places with you. That's our offer. All you have to do is step up and say 'yes'."

With a gracious nod, he stepped off the crate.

"Holy…shit…" Yvonne breathed. Her Commander gave her a nod as he passed, smiling gravely. "Make those trades for your base and head home, Specialist," he suggested over his shoulder. "They're going to need all hands on deck."

Yvonne was too thrown to do anything but salute.

"That fink!" Yvonne laughed as she strapped down their trades. "That little…and I bet Kev knew too! I just bet he did! I can't believe those two! And I just bet they're going to tell me that I can't say anything until the official announcement!"

"You'd almost think it was supposed to be a secret, yeah?" Inyoni asked, head cocked. Yvonne heard the tease, but she had more steam to blow off.

"The boys have known all this for months and they haven't said word one!" she exclaimed. "We're going to get to go through on something we've been begging to do for years, *years*, and it's going to be *amazing,* and they didn't say anything at all! And now they're probably going to tell me to keep quiet about it until it's time, and that's going to drive me nuts! That pair of sneaky little weasels! Ooh when Sarah and I get ahold of them!"

"Okay then," Inyoni chuckled. "We'll get home, and you can go at them."

"Hell yes I will!" Yvonne agreed, not sure whether she was going to hug Aidan and Kevin or knock their heads together. "Come on Inyoni, we're riding."

She raced home like a bat out of hell. She circled twice to make sure Inyoni could keep up, but she couldn't help flooring it. She wanted to be home and calling Aidan out, wanted to be home and telling Sarah and Tom the news, wanted to be home where she could cut loose about every incredible word she'd heard and everything she'd seen.

She was riding so fast that, at first, the change in the landscape didn't register.

The burnt shrubs. The charcoal-stick branches of the trees.

Slowly, it got through. *Fire.* Fire had burned through this area.

Fire had burned through her neighborhood.

Yvonne's gut clutched like the fingers of a hand, tightening into a fist under her ribcage.

"Um, Yvonne?" Inyoni asked in her ear.

She sucked in a breath. "Hang on Inyoni. We're not on our coordinates yet."

Two miles. In two miles they'd be home, and everything would be fine. Everything would be great.

Pulling up on their coordinates, Yvonne hopped off her bike and reached out to pull aside the slick tarp that hid the garage.

And hit empty air.

It was stupid, and she knew it. She did it anyway. Both arms out, she walked forward, feeling for the base. Her base. It had to be here. *Had to.*

"Yvonne?" Inyoni asked weakly.

Yvonne did her best to steady her voice. "Inyoni, I…I think the crew had to bug out."

"Where'd they go?"

Yvonne swallowed hard. "I don't know. I…I don't know."

## Event File 14
## File Tag: Return To Base
## 16:20-08-22-2161

For a moment, Yvonne couldn't move. Couldn't think. Couldn't breathe.

Then she smacked herself in the head. "Augh! Idiot!" Feverishly, she switched the spoofer around her neck off, pulled her tab out, and turned it on.

A flood of messages poured down her screen. It started with a warning from Aidan, and went on with a couple from Tom and Sarah, followed by a string of messages from Liza that started with,

> 'are you okay? Write back'

and ended with,

> 'I swear to god Yvonne if you've turned your tab off and there isn't an incredibly good reason, I'm putting you on latrine cleaning for the next two months! WRITE US! TELL US WHERE YOU ARE!!!'

"Woah," Inyoni murmured. Yvonne glanced up at him. He held up his tab. "Tweak blew up my tab with texts."

"Same with Liza on mine," Yvonne agreed, glancing back down. Out of the mess of text, she dug up a set of coordinates with a wash of relief so strong that her knees wobbled. She raised her head, laughing over at Inyoni. "They're okay! They moved when we were at Sky House, that's why it didn't come through." Leaping for her bike, she kicked it into life. "Come on, let's go!"

If anything, she rode faster now. She needed to see her family. Needed to see home. Needed to *be home.*

The new site was on a little rise, well away from the fire and the smoke. The base was still half-put-together, and Yvonne skidded up to a bunch of whoops and cheers. Running over, Tom hugged her before she'd even got off the bike. Sarah was right on his heels, and she tugged Yvonne off the bike for a long, tight embrace. Then she tapped her shoulder crankily. "What the hell Yve?! Why didn't you pick up?!"

"We were starting to think…" Tom swallowed hard, and yanked her in for another tight hug. "Don't do that," he whispered, voice cracking against her shoulder.

Yvonne put her arms around the boy, giving Abigail a reassuring smile as she came trotting over on her boyfriend's heels. "Sorry Tommy, I didn't mean to. I kinda got into the middle of something and had to keep my tab off; security reasons."

"They better be damn good security reasons," Liza snapped, tromping over to grab Yvonne by the shoulders and shake her a little. "You scared everyone, Yve! You know better, damn it! You're not a teenager anymore! Where the hell—"

"Liza," Sarah interrupted, stepping in to push Liza's hands off Yvonne's shoulders. "My wife, my job to bitch her out. She's going to tell me what happened, and then she's going to report to Kevin, and if she was a dipshit then she'll end up in your office, okay?"

Liza stood stock still for a moment, biting her lip. Yvonne realized that her friend's hands were shaking. Stepping over, she gave Liza a quick squeeze of the arm. "I followed procedure, Liza. I was safe the entire time. I was with Commander Magnum, and we were wearing spoofers to make sure we stayed safe. I'm sorry you got freaked."

"What were you…where was Magnum?" Liza asked, finally yanked back into using her brain again.

Yvonne gave her a smile. "Tell you later. Right now, we got a base to set up."

Liza looked around as if those dots had just gotten connected for her. Then she nodded once, decisive. "Right. Right. Okay, Yvonne, Inyoni, put the bikes away and jump in." Then she was turning on her heel and trotting away. Leaving Yvonne with the solemn eyes of her wife and son on her.

Sarah managed a sorry little smile. "We got a pretty good scare."

"Me too," Yvonne laughed weakly, "thought my heart stopped when I reached out for the tarp and got a handful of air."

Tom nodded. "That would be bad."

"It was," Yvonne agreed, returning the nod.

"You're okay, right?" Abigail asked, eyes wide.

Yvonne chuckled. "Yeah Abbie, I'm good."

"Good," Abbie offered. She took Tom's hands. "We got work. C'mon."

"Same goes for us," Sarah suggested. Yvonne nodded. "Yeah, let me get my bike put away and I'm on it. Inyo…wait."

"Cameron and Inyoni took the bikes to the garage while we were talking." Sarah cracked a grin. "Guess I can still keep your attention?"

"Guess Liza can still scare the crap out of me when I piss her off!" Yvonne laughed. Stepping in, she pulled her wife in for one long kiss.

"Sorry I scared you, honey."

"Sorry you got so scared, baby doll," Sarah murmured against her, hanging on tight. Then she stepped back with a grin. "That's for later, we got work, c'mon!"

"I'm gonna remind you about that later," Yvonne agreed with a laugh, falling into step with her wife.

The base setup went pretty smoothly, or as smoothly as it ever went in the baking heat of August. Yvonne was one of the last to start work, so she was one of the last to head inside for a shower, base officially secured and set for normal operation. The hygiene room was empty by the time she got in. She shucked her stuff, shoved it all into the wash-dry unit inside the stall, and turned on the water. It felt incredibly good to be clean again. She took a bit of a long shower, hoping Janice wouldn't notice. She needed it. Eventually, she turned off the water, pulled her clean gear out of the wash-dry unit that had used her washing water to clean her clothes and taken the heat energy from the hot shower to dry them before the water went back into the base recycling system. She headed down to her room to get back into base clothes and out of the Dust gear.

"Hey you," Sarah's voice murmured when she'd closed the door. She turned, and her wife gave her a little smile from her seat on the bed.

"Hey," Yvonne murmured softly, crossing the room to sit down beside her. She slung an arm around her girl's shoulders, resting her head on Sarah's collarbone. "Some day?"

"Some day," Sarah agreed. Her soft little fingers tipped Yvonne's head up, and Sarah kissed her.

"I was really scared for a minute there."

"Me too," Yvonne agreed, drawing soothing circles over Sarah's back with the flat of her hand. "Me too."

Sarah's fingers played with her ponytail. "You're still in your Dust gear."

"Mm," Yvonne agreed, "I came in here to get it off."

"Oh yeah?" Finally, Sarah's sweet voice had a laugh in it again. "Think I can do something about that?"

"Oh I don't know, can you?" Yvonne teased, running a hand up and down Sarah's flank. With a grin, Sarah took Yvonne's wide khaki hat off her head and spun it like a frisbee. It donked into the wall, but Sarah was already busy with the buttons of Yvonne's jacket. Yvonne wriggled loose and yanked at the hem of Sarah's shirt. Her wife slithered out of it like a snake, dark eyes gleaming. Yvonne grinned.

"Lock the door?"

"Everybody's at dinner, don't need to," Sarah breathed, kissing down Yvonne's throat while her quick fingers undid Yvonne's bra and pulled her hair tie loose.

"You sure about—oh," Yvonne trailed off as Sarah's tongue flicked one of her nipples. The sudden sensation on skin that had just been exposed to air made her gasp. Sarah always did know how to get the last word.

"I was scared to death," she whispered in the quiet of their room, "When the base wasn't there, I thought…"

"Me too," Sarah agreed, fingers playing with Yvonne's other nipple and sending hot squiggles of electricity zipping down her body. "For a minute there, I thought…" She surged up, kissing Yvonne so hard that they both fell back onto the bed. "Don't do that to me, baby girl," Sarah whispered in her ear, running a line of kisses down her throat.

"Yeah. Sorry," Yvonne agreed. "Really glad to be home."

"I'm going to make sure you remember why you come home," Sarah chuckled. Sparrow-flicker fingers traced across Yvonne's breasts, teasing her. Tingling heat tensed her belly.

"Yeah?" Yvonne asked, a little breathless. "How are you going to do that, hunh?"

"Oh, I got some ideas," Sarah laughed. Sitting up, she peeled off her own bra, revealing that gorgeous body that was still as toned now as she'd been when she was eighteen. Grinning, Yvonne sat up fast and got one of Sarah's strawberry nipples between her lips, licking and teasing.

Sarah squeaked. "Ooh…two can play that game, baby girl." A hand snaked up to make Yvonne's nipples burn and tingle with touch, and the other slipped down to undo the fly of her pants and slide inside. Yvonne sucked in air. Sarah chuckled in her ear, and slid off her to shimmy out of her pants. "Lay back, baby."

Grinning, she did. Standing at the bottom of the bed, Sarah got ahold of the cuffs of her pants and pulled them off. Then she climbed onto the bed, prowling up Yvonne's body like a sleek little black cat. Yvonne wrapped her arms around her wife and rolled her so that they lay side by side, snaking a hand down between them to pet her wife. "Want to play?"

"What's the game?" Sarah breathed. Yvonne grinned as she laid kisses along her shoulder. "We see if we can come at the exact…same…time." She drew little circles on Sarah's undies with one finger.

"Mm," Sarah murmured. "I like that game. You want to stay like this?"

"Yeah," Yvonne agreed, "I want to see you come."

"Oh yeah," Sarah purred. Reaching down, she stripped her underwear off, kicked it off the bed, and yanked Yvonne's down her legs. When Sarah ran out of reach, Yvonne wriggled and kicked hers off the rest of the way.

Sarah's breasts pressed against hers, their nipples brushing like their lips as Yvonne slid two fingers around and around Sarah's clit. Sarah's delicate fingers slid inside her, curling until they made Yvonne's entire body twitch and tighten. Sarah ducked her head and sucked at Yvonne's breasts, and Yvonne arched. She sped her fingers against her wife, keeping up and keeping time with what Sarah was doing to her. Sarah groaned and wiggled, grinding against Yvonne's hand. She grinned and put a little more pressure in. Sarah whimpered, and started playing on Yvonne's clit with her thumb while her fingers worked to drive her crazy. Yvonne tightened up with the heat and the tingle of it, her muscles locking. That was fine, all she needed to move were her hands and her mouth, but now here came the shivers, and…

"Sarah," she gulped, "Sarah, honey, I'm this close, I…"

"Same here," Sarah gasped. "Harder, baby girl. Hard."

Yvonne didn't need telling twice. She opened her eyes and stared as Sarah arched back, eyes closed, lips parted, and felt her heart ache with the joy and the beauty and the…and the…

And oh man, the orgasm hit like a train. Her body shook with the first wave, hot flares running up and down her insides as the first wave of spasms came on.

"Yve!" Sarah whimpered, bucking and grinding against her, and that set Yvonne off all over again, and she got back to work making sure Sarah came a second time too. Sarah gripped her hair with her free hand, pulled her into a hard kiss, and fingered her so hard that Yvonnne felt the hot wet spread between her thighs. Sarah rolled them so she was on top and kept at it, and Yvonne lost all control of what was going on as wave after wave of orgasm took over every nerve in her body and she spiraled into the stratosphere. She yelped and whimpered and shook under her girl's hands and lips, caught like a fish in a net of sensations that had no end, no end at all, and now Sarah was rubbing her clit hard against Yvonne's, and…and…and…

And her whole body breathed out in satisfaction. That last orgasm had some serious kick. Sarah squeaked one last time and lay her head against Yvonne's collarbone, kissing it. "So, see why you should come home?" She whispered.

Yvonne giggled. "Yep. Good reason." She stroked Sarah's feathery hair soft and slow, drawing the strands between her fingers. "So, about dinner. Think we should…"

The door of their room banged open. "Sarah! Yve!" Tom yelped. "Tweak's screaming!"

Sarah yelped. Yvonne blinked. "Wait, what? Say that again?"

Tom had already clapped both his hands over his eyes. "Tweak's screaming at Damian, guys! Don came and got me, he needs help! Put on a shirt and come help, please!"

"Shit," Yvonne sighed, grabbing for her shirt. "Two secs, Tommy. We're coming!"

## Event File 15
## File Tag: Behavioral Health Situation
## 19:00-08-22-2161/ 22:30-08-22-2161

"Tweak, what the hell?!" Aidan demanded, skidding into the medical bay. For a breath, he took in the entire shitshow. It looked like a storm had hit the med bay. An exam tray had been thrown against the wall, from the looks of it. Something green was leaking out of a broken bottle. Damian was standing over the eye of the storm, who was currently curled up in a ball on the floor.

Shit, and Tweak had been doing so good lately. Aidan had thought she was past this. He shot Damian a 'what the?!' look, but the doctor was preoccupied with his patient.

Kneeling, Aidan did his best to get on eye-level with his technical officer.

"Tweak? Can you talk to me about what's going on?"

Tweak turned eyes like two lit coals on Aidan. She was breathing so fast that the words came out as gasps. Every word ended in a ragged little sob. "B-b-bastard! L-lied to me! *Lied. To. Me!* Lab rat! God-d-d-damn l-l-lab rat! Fucker!" Tears sparkled on her skin.

"I didn't—" Damian began, but Tweak twisted around, snarled at the doctor like a wounded animal and pushed herself to her feet. Damian did the stupidest thing he could have done at that moment, which was put his arm out to try and stop her. Shoving him out of her way, Tweak darted through the door and bolted. Damian's back thumped against the wall. The sound of Tweak's combat boots rang down the hall, fading into silence.

His own breath and the sound of something dripping from a broken bottle filled the room for a moment. Brain on standby, Aidan turned to his medical officer.

"Okay…What just happened?"

Damian shook his head. "Give her some time. She just got some bad news."

"What kind of bad news?" Aidan asked, blinking.

Damian sighed, shaking his head. "Not my place to tell you. When she's ready to talk, she will."

Aidan glanced between the open door of the med bay and the defeated man in front of him. "Um…Damian, I'm going to need to insist on more details this time. I need to know if Tweak's going to be a danger to—"

The sound of running feet whipped Aidan around, but it was just Yvonne and Sarah this time, Tom and Donovan jogging in front of the girls with panic in their eyes. Yvonne's hair was down, she wasn't wearing a bra, and Sarah's shirt was on backwards. *So that's why they disappeared the minute the base was set*, Aidan thought distantly. *That figures.*

"Tommy said Tweak was…" Yvonne trailed off with a bewildered shrug.

"Stand down, you guys," Aidan stated, working for a level tone. "I've got this handled. Go find Liza, tell her there's a situation, and—"

"What's the situation?" Liza demanded, striding up behind the girls. "Sarah, your shirt's backwards," she added distractedly. Sarah glanced down at herself, and shrugged.

"Deliquisha told me Tweak was screaming at her brother," Liza continued, walking into the medical bay.

"We have a behavioral-health situation with Tweak," Aidan explained. "I don't want her chased around; go get Billie, get Inyoni, and tell them to find her and—"

"Not Inyoni," Damian sighed. "Not him, not now."

"Hunh?" Aidan turned, blinking. "Why?"

Damian straightened from the lean Tweak had shoved him into. From the way he moved, she must have really packed a punch.

"If you're not in the Command division," the doctor stated flatly, "then you're not in here. Close the door behind you."

Yvonne and Sarah gave each other looks, but they each put a hand on the boys' shoulders, steering their younger basemate and their son out and closing the door behind them. Damian waved Aidan and Liza to his office, moving like a scarecrow with some of the stuffing pulled out.

Watching him, Aidan took a seat. "Okay, so..."

Damian sighed. He ran a hand over his face.

"Tweak's…" He lowered his black plastic eyes. Aidan couldn't be sure, but he guessed Damian was staring at his hands.

"This is confidential," the doctor stated quietly.

"Of course," Aidan agreed. "What?"

Damian raised his head, and the face around his blank eye implants was drawn.

"It looks like the interactions between medication and Gamma biology are a little more complex than I realized." Standing wearily, he brought up his flickering desk screen. "Male contraceptive blocks the luteinizing hormone needed to produce sperm, and the female contraceptive blocks ovulation. In ninety-nine percent of patients. Unless your system has such a high turnover rate that the doses are burned through."

A lead sheet folded down over Aidan's chest. He wet his lips.

"Are you saying…what I think you are?"

Damian ran a hand over his smooth head, letting out a long sigh. "I didn't do as well as I thought at calibrating the dosages for Tweak's birth control implant. Or Inyoni's. She's… Six weeks along."

“As in…” Aidan had to clear his throat to get the word out. “As in pregnant?”

Damian nodded. “As in pregnant.”

“Oh…shit…” Liza breathed, her voice tiny. “Oh shit.”

*Oh shit is right,* Aidan thought numbly. Slowly, he nodded. “Okay. Liza, I need you to go out, get Billie, and send her to find Tweak. And then tell everyone else to leave them alone. This isn’t anybody else’s business until she’s ready to talk about it.”

“Should we tell Inyoni?” Liza asked.

Damian shook his head. “Breach of confidentiality. If and when she wants to, she can ask us to tell him. Or she can do it herself. In the meantime…” He sighed. “In the meantime, we do our jobs. And we let her work it out.”

Tweak sat under her coffee tree, knees drawn up to her chest, and rocked herself in the spangled shade. Her head felt too tight to hold all the feels packed inside it. Fear choked her throat as her muscles tried to find a way out that wasn't there. Her gut hurt.

"Tweak? Are you okay?"

Abigail. That was Abbie's voice.

Shit. A kid. She couldn't lose it on a kid. But she *couldn't* take people and talking, not now.

"Get l-l-lost kid." Tweak muttered at her feet.

"You need someone to talk to?" Abigail's voice asked gently.

Tweak’s gut clenched like a steel trap. "You know Eng-l-lish. G-g-get lost means g-get lost." Her muscles ached with the tension of holding still.

Abigail's feet stayed there in her line of sight for way too long.

“Be right back," her little voice murmured. Then she was gone. Thank fuck.

Turning, Tweak wrapped herself around the coffee tree and hugged it tight, letting the tears go. At least the water could make something grow.

Something growing. A baby.

*A baby.*

She *couldn't* have a baby. She was a *fucking disaster*. Genetics, brains, feels: all of it was fucked up. She'd destroy a kid. She'd be lucky if she didn't kill it in week one.

She couldn't do this.

She *couldn't.*

A cup of coffee sent up a little puff of dust as it was set on the earth beside her boot. A plate of brownies settled down beside it a beat later.

Tweak glanced at the treats, then up. Abigail and Billie smiled down at her.

Part of her wanted to scream at them to get away, because she could explode at any second and she didn't want the shrapnel to hit them when she broke. But this was Abbie. This was Billie.

She drew a breath. "T-t-t-thanks." she croaked. Bille's fingers shoved a cloth into her hand. "Blow your nose, sis."

Tweak gave her a smile, wiping away snot. Grabbing a brownie, she bit down.

"Wasn't crying. Just thinking," she muttered between bites.

"Thinking about what?" Abigail asked, taking a brownie for herself.

Tweak glared at her. "C-c-cut the shit. Base g-gossips like c-c-crazy."

Abigail blinked. "Huh?"

Tweak dropped her head back against the bole of her tree. Might as well admit it and get it over with.

"I'm hacked, k-k-kay?"

"Did someone get around your codes or something?" Billie chewed on her brownie, eyes soft and sad and worried.

Tweaked rolled her eyes. "Hacked, B! T-trojaned?" She sighed at the blank look on her buddy's face. "I g-g-got p-pregnant. You know that w-word?"

Abigail swallowed her bite of brownie. "You, uh…you and Bird, huh? Um. Congrats?"

Tweak gave a choked groan and dropped her head back into arms, fingers burrowing into her hair.

"Want to talk about it?" Billie's voice was just a murmur, soft as the wind through the scrub. "I'm here to listen, if you want?"

Tweak made a small animal sound in the back of her throat. "C-c-can't..." she coughed, drew a breath. "C-can't k-keep it. Have to tell D-damian. C-c-can't have a b-b…c-c-c-can't…."

"Why?" Abigail asked quietly. "I mean…why can't you keep it? I understand if you don't *want to*, but that's different than 'can't.'"

The question doubled Tweak up in a knot of emotions. Why couldn't she keep a baby? Because she was a freak. She was a disaster. She couldn't bring a kid into this life just to watch them get broken. And die. She'd tried to protect a kid before, and he'd died. Her brother had *died* because she wasn't good enough to take care of him.

"Tweak?" Abigail murmured, the word grating like a no-connection signal across her nerves.

Billie's voice was only a little better. "Let's just sit, Abbie. She needs to get it out before she can talk, okay?

The storm raged all through her. It battered her, raking her insides with heaving sobs. She was going to die from this storm. She knew it. This time, she wouldn't make it. She squeezed the tree's trunk tight, fingernails and scales scrabbling against bark. She couldn't make it. She couldn't hack it. She couldn't save Bao Li, and she couldn't save this baby. She was too messed up. Too weird. Too dangerous. She was a freak, and because of her the baby would be a freak too, and then it'd die, and it'd be her fault. Again.

*Again.*

*It's all going to happen again.*

“Ssh, Tweak,” Billie soothed, sitting close enough that Tweak could feel her body heat. “Ssh. It’s okay. It’s gonna be okay. It’s all gonna be okay. Ssh. Just gotta let the storm go through. Sssh. Storm’ll be over soon. It’ll be okay.”

It was all bullshit, what Billie was saying. Total bullshit. But her voice was something to hide under as the lightning went through Tweak’s insides and the tears pounded down.

Slowly, the storm inside Tweak blew away. It got a little easier to breathe. She wiped snot and tears away.

“You okay?” Abbie’s voice was quiet, but it still pissed Tweak off to no end. She glared at the dumbass kid, her gut seething. "Abbie. Two Gammas. M-making. A b-b-baby?! That. Sound. *Okay.* To. You?!"

Abigail shrugged uncomfortably. "I mean…it could be okay?”

Tweak’s hands balled into fists. “C-could be okay? Are you c-c-crazy?”

“Tweak,” Billie offered softly. “She’s trying to help.”

Tweak shook her head. “Bullshit.” She curled into a ball. “Just l-leave me al-l-lone.”

“I mean, we will if you want,” Abigail said quietly, “But I think you should hear this first. I've been looking at Jenny's blood with Damian when he’s doing therapeutic DNA work for her, and her DNA's actually in good shape. Maybe…maybe two sets of gamma DNA kind of…negate each other. I mean, she’s got the eyes, and there’s something with her lipid cells that Damian hasn’t figured yet, but that’s pretty much all we see. That’s no big deal. Maybe your baby will be the same way."

Tweak shook her head. "Doesn't work that way. G-g-genetics. Screw up is screw up." Her fingernails scraped on her scales. “I’mma s-screwup. I’ll s-screw the k-k-kid up. Be a shit mom." she whispered. "I’m n-no good. I h-hurt people. I b-b-break things. I l-l-lose it. I’m d-dangerous."

"You were in danger most of your life," Billie said gently. “And you didn’t break me, Tweak. You made me better.”

Surprised, Tweak looked up. Billie smiled, nodding.

Tweak had to think about that. Billie *was* better these days. She was quiet still, sure. But she was so *brave* now. She was married. And she was so sure of herself in the kitchen, as sure as Tweak was in the code room.

Tweak had protected Billie in detention, sure. And she'd backed Billie in lots of stuff. But had she really helped Billie get better?

Abigail smiled. "You've gotten loads better since I first met you. And Dad says most parents are shit at first; you get used to it, he says. And you've got Inyoni and all of us to help if you want a baby, right?"

Tweak gave her a long, level look while she waited out the lightning-flash of panic. Inyoni. When Inyoni found out…

"Who says he wants to be a dad?" She asked, flat.

"Well, did you ask him?" Abigail suggested.

Tweak shrugged, nerves sizzling with tension. "No. No point. C-c-can't k-k-keep it."

"Maybe you should talk to him? I mean…if you want to." Billie reached over to pick up the rest of her brownie. Tweak watched her sister eat. She leaned back, staring up into the branches of her tree.

"S-s-scared." she whispered.

"Dad said he was terrified when he found out Mom was pregnant with me," Abigail offered. "I think…I think it's a pretty normal thing. Freaking out. Being scared. Doesn't make it easier, I know, but…well, you got the base behind you."

"Whatever you want to do, we'll be there," Billie added. "You tell us what you need, and we'll help. You got people here who'll back you on whatever you want."

Her sister looked so worried and so sweet that Tweak reached over and gave Billie a little hug. "Yeah. Yeah, I do."

Drawing away, she drew in a deep breath, nose stuffy from crying. "Guess I'll check with B-bird," she managed eventually.

"You should probably wait a bit, till you're not all snotty and gross," Billie suggested.

Tweak snorted. “Well y-yeah. Duh.” She looked towards the door that led inside. “Everybody knows n-now, y-yeah?” And man was that going to suck to face up to.

“Nobody knows,” Billie murmured. “Liza just told me to come talk to you. She didn’t tell me why; just told me you got bad news.”

“I just knew you were crying,” Abigail offered.

“For real?” Tweak asked, glancing between the girl and the woman. “B-base talks all the t-time.”

“Not about this,” Billie stated quietly. “Till you make the call, it’s nobody’s business.”

Abigail mimed the pull of a zipper across her lips. “I’m saying nothing. Swear.”

“Same,” Billie agreed, reaching out to put her hand beside Tweak’s. “You okay?”

Slowly, Tweak nodded. “Y-yeah. Think so. Yeah. Thanks, B.”

“Course, sis,” Billie murmured, giving her a quick squeeze.

Pulling away, Tweak patted Abigail's shoulder. “Thanks, k-k-kid."

Abigail grinned her big sunflower grin. "Any time.”

The next couple hours, Tweak stayed in the garden: getting her brain straightened out, double checking the slick tarp, and finding stuff to do with the plants. Anything was better than going inside and facing…all of it.

There was so much *all of it.*

The moon was riding high by the time she could get herself to walk to the door, open it, and head inside.

She found Inyoni in their quarters. "Hey," she murmured, leaning against the wall.

Inyoni looked up from his tab with his easy smile. "Hey. Sounds like you had a wild day.”

“What?” Tweak asked, freezing.

"Heard there was a mess in the med-bay that you had to help fix," Inyoni continued, flipping a page on his tab. "Liza told me it was no big deal, but I heard you yell. Liza said something was broke in there and fixing it was really shitty. You guys get it figured out?"

She swallowed hard. "Yeah. Fine. It's…yeah."

God, that smile. When she said what she had to, he was never going to smile at her the same way again.

Everything was going to change.

*Everything.*

She crossed her arms. "You got t-time? D-Damian says he w-w-wants to talk to us t-together. N-next couple d-d-days."

There. She'd said something, and she'd bought herself a couple days. A few more days of normal and good.

Besides, this way Damian would be the one who had to say the words to Inyoni. It wasn't the payback Tweak wanted to give him—she wanted to break the dickhead's nose—but it was the best she was getting while she kept her promise not to hit people on her team. At least the doctor would have to see what he'd done, close up and in his face.

"Sure," Inyoni agreed carefully. Sitting up, he set his tab aside and walked over to put his hands on her shoulders, his long ears gone all cockeyed. "You okay, Dragon?"

Tweak shrugged. "S-s-stressed. Lots g-going on."

"You wanna talk about it?" Inyoni asked, bending his head to brush his lips over her brow.

Dammit, why did he have to be so awesome? Why did this have to change?

She shrugged. "Nah. Okay. Not s-s-sick. D-d-Damian says. But yeah. Find time. For us. Go have a t-talk."

"I got time," Inyoni agreed. "How's Thursday?"

Thursday. On Thursday, everything would fall apart.

But she had till Thursday.

She nodded. "Kay. Thursd-day."

Raising her eyes, she looked Inyoni in the face. He smiled down at her, all love and easy comfort.

Losing this was going to fucking *suck.*

Stepping close, she hugged him tight while she could.

## Event File 16
## File Tag: Identity Correction
## 11:00-08-26-2161

"Quit giggling, they'll hear you!"

"I can't help it!"

The can slopped between them. Sarah hefted her end with a grin a mile wide. "This is going to be the best!"

"I know," Yvonne laughed back, her black gloves slipping a little on the canister's handle. Pressing a hand against the door to the roof, she checked it for give. "Yep, the coders got it, it's unlocked."

"Awesome!" Sarah whispered back. "Wish they could have got the shopping center itself, but yeah, this'll work. Got the line and the cradle?"

"Yep." Yvonne checked her tab. "Cameras loop and drones go offline in three…two…okay let's go!"

Stepping out of the doorway's shade, they pulled on their sunglasses and crunched across the heat-reflecting cinders glowing white across the expanse of the roof. Standing at the parapet, Yvonne set down her end of the canister and shrugged off her backpack. Pulling the long nanofabric line out, she tapped the activation dongle on its end. Activated, the nanites making up the rope flowed out, formed themselves into a clamp, and dug themselves into the concrete of the parapet.

Yvonne eyed the distance between the roof and the next one over, calibrated the line, activated the dongle on the other side and tossed it out into the air. Uncoiling like a dancer's ribbon in the air, the zip line spiraled across the space between the office building and the inter-corporate CSS shopping zone, sinking its clamp into the metal railing across the way.

"See you," Sarah murmured, pecking Yvonne's cheek. Pulling the grip bar out of the bag, she set it on the rope and slid across the zipline, catching herself easily on the roof across the gulf. She waved, and Yvonne waved back. She heaved the canister up, set it in the gear cradle that fit the line, and slid it across. Sarah caught it neatly.

Looking up, Yvonne grinned at the black figures ziplining in on the other side of the roof. The rest of the pranking crew was here. Right on time.

Throwing her pack on again, she caught the handle Sarah shoved back to her across the gap and zipped down the line, both feet thudding into the roof of the luxury shopping center. Stepping over the railing and onto the roof, she waved at the other crew. "Heya. You got it?"

"All set," the man carrying one end of a long bundle agreed, grinning. Yvonne matched his grin. "Okay then. You do the sign, we got the paint. Our tech girl's watching our backs over the Mesh. Let's go."

Together, Yvonne and Sarah pulled gauntlet gloves out of their packs, slid them on, and got to work opening the canister. The nano-enhanced paint gleamed an obscene red inside its can.

Looking up at her wife, Yvonne grinned. "Ready honey?"

"Hell yeah," Sarah agreed with relish. Pulling the paint cup they'd brought out and handing it to Yvonne, she grabbed the spray can of restrictor paint out for herself, spraying the edge of the roof with it to make sure the smart paint didn't do something dumb and spread in the wrong direction. Yvonne mirrored her in the other direction, careful not to drip any smartpaint on herself. They'd gotten the best-quality stuff they could land, the good smartpaint for fancy houses with programmable nanoids in the mix. The little machines were usually programmed to make nice straight lines and stop drips in the paint, but with a little reprogramming it worked great for their project.

As she dripped the red from her paint cup, the dribbles of paint expanded, the nanoids taking in the dust and grit of the rooftop and manufacturing it into more paint. The spreading pools flowed down the sides of the building in patterns that, honestly, made her a little queasy. But that was the point.

Yvonne kept spreading the red. At the front of the building, the banner team secured the top of their bundle to the railing. Yvonne heard them count off 'one, two, three!' With a heave, they shoved the twenty-foot-long bundle over the railing.

With a clap like thunder, the massive banner unfurled, spreading itself like wings. Yvonne joined in the cheering as she dropped her last cup of paint. Tucking the cup into its sterile baggie, she jogged over to join the rest of the team. Laughing, she high-fived and slapped shoulders, hugged and whooped with the others, all of them chattering.

"This is going to be so good!"

"Wait till we see this on the news!"

"Wait till the building owners see it!"

"The coordination worked, this same prank is happening all over the country!"

"Awesome!"

"Fuck yes! Can't wait to see it on the news!"

"Time, guys," their designated keeper stated, tapping his tab. "Let's book it."

"Right," Sarah agreed, "See you around!"

With waves over their shoulders, Sarah and Yvonne headed back to their exit spot. Jumping on the zipline, Yvonne pushed off and skated across thin air to the unlocked building and her way out.

Hitting the ledge, she turned and shoved the handle bar back to Sarah. Near-empty paint canister on her hip, Sarah hopped onto the edge and grabbed the handlebars light as any bird. She flew across the zipline, and Yvonne caught her on the near side with open arms and a quick kiss.

"Take a look at this, hon."

Side by side, they took a moment to look at the building across from them. It looked as if the building had begun to bleed, organic vein patterns exploding at their ends in spatters of gore. The paint was still oozing down the sides, and it would keep on oozing for a few hours yet, until the nanoids ran out of charge.

Across the roof, a banner blazed the statement in letters twenty feet tall and shimmering red.

It's Your Blood. It's Their Profit Margin.
Demand A New Worker's Contract Now

"Man," Sarah breathed. "That looks good."

"Yeah," Yvonne agreed, leaning her head against her wife's. "It does, doesn't it?"

BANG!

Yvonne whipped around, and felt her heart seize up. FIDOs, three of them, stood in the doorway, taking aim. Rubber bullets thunked into the ground, sending up sprays of cinders. Pain exploded in Yvonne's thigh as she hit the ground, aching as if someone had hit her with a brick. She gritted her teeth against the scream. Beside her, Sarah grunted.

Yvonne's brain kicked into high gear. First round, rubber bullets. Second round, either gas, mace or darts. Probably darts. Maybe mace. Shit, how were they going to get out of this?

"Hearts!" Sarah hissed, switching from names to call signs. Just like training. "Can. Now."

The spraycan pressed cool into Yvonne's hand.

"Got one too. Dodge and weave. Three mice."

*Right,* Yvonne whispered to herself. *Field code. Three mice means go for the eyes. Okay, we can do this.*

"Three mice. Dodge and weave," Yvonne agreed.

Sarah nodded. "On three."

"On three," Yvonne whispered back.

She could hear the motors of the FIDOs' legs revving as they walked forward.

One…

Two…

"Three!" Sarah exclaimed, exploding out of a runner's crouch. Yvonne shoved herself off the ground. Her thigh screamed, but she ignored it. This wasn't the time. Taking off to the left, she ran a sidewinder circle out and around the FIDOs. Get behind them, that was the thing. Get behind them, confuse their gyros. And then…

*Shit shit shit shit,* she whispered inside her head, breaking her zigzag and running straight up behind the nearest FIDO. Reaching to the side and around, she sprayed her paint can full in its camera sensor 'face' as its mechanical 'head' was turning towards her. For good measure, she painted a stripe down its flanks where other cameras could be.

One down. Sarah would have got hers. That meant one to go

She jumped as another round of rubber bullets hit the cinders beside her and the FIDO in front of her. The metal dented on the side of the thing, the impact wobbling it.

Yvonne danced back. "Shit!"

The FIDO that just shot its buddy was triangulated on her now. It rotated, aiming. Sarah stared at her over it, terror in her eyes. She was within touching distance, if it turned and shot her point blank…

"Hey, hey asshole!" Yvonne yelled, jumping around. Shit, bad idea. Both blinded FIDOs triangulated on her, focusing on the noise. Yvonne picked up handfuls of the white roof cinders and threw them out to right and left, scattering noise and keeping in motion. The blinded ones got distracted, but the sighted one was still fixed on her, and it was taking a step forward, and—

And Sarah reached around and covered its face in spraypaint. It wobbled, freezing as it tried to calibrate based on the senses left to it.

Yvonne held up both hands, miming rain. Sarah jerked her head in a nod. Reaching in her bag, she got out the extra thing they'd picked up on their way in: a couple containers of corn syrup out of the cooking aisle in the nearest grocery store. She yanked the top off and poured it over the place where the FIDO's mechanical neck joined its head, right where its sensory apparatus and gyroscope was kept.

The FIDO froze solid. Sarah casually walked over to its friends, still bumbling after the sound of the little rocks that Yvonne was throwing, and did the same thing to them. They wobbled into immobility as the sticky syrup killed their balance and their sound sensors.

Yvonne gave a whooping laugh of victory, running over to give her wife a squeeze. "Nice!"

"Thanks," Sarah murmured. "But if they sent FIDOs here, Eagle's people aren't far behind. Let's get into the stairwell and get changed."

"Got it," Yvonne agreed. Stepping back into the stairwell, they stripped out of their gear and pulled on the janitor's jumpsuits they'd kept in the bottoms of their bags. Down one turn in the stairs, they got onto a floor of offices and headed for the maintenance closet that Tweak and Kevin had made them key cards for.

Grabbing a maintenance cart, they wheeled it down the hall to the break room, emptied a can, and wheeled it along. All the time, Yvonne was thinking about the timing. They needed just about ten minutes of cover. Ten minutes would be enough time for the Peacekeepers to get worried about their doggies and come check on them, which would leave the exits clear. But it wouldn't be enough time for Eagle to lock down the office building.

Ten minutes. About five had already passed.

Their maintenance cart full, they got in the freight lift and rode it down to the dumpsters on the bottom level.

*Bing!*

The door slid open. Eight EagleCorp officers stood there on the other side in full battle rattle.

Yvonne froze solid.

"Move it!" the head man growled through his helmet mic. "We need this lift."

Yvonne gulped. "Yessir," she squeaked, shoving the maintenance cart out through the grudging corridor the peacekeepers made for them.

"Hey," one of them grabbed Yvonne's arm in a gloved fist.

*Breathe,* she told herself. *Don't fight yet. Wait.*

"You see anybody who doesn't work here on your way down?" The Peacekeeper demanded.

"No sir," she replied, submissive as she could.

With a grunt of dissatisfaction, the Peacekeeper shoved her away and got in the freight elevator with the rest of them.

*Bing!*

The door shushed closed. Yvonne's heart started to beat again.

Swallowing hard, she turned to Sarah.

"Holy shit."

Stepping over, Sarah squeezed her tight.

"Let's get out of here, baby. C'mon."

## Event File 17
## File Tag: Forward Planning
## 16:00-08-27-2161

"Alright," Quadrant Commander Ouray stated, his holographic representation setting aside the tab and resting his darkly wrinkled hands over the walking canes in his lap. When he glanced up, the light where he was sitting caught in his long black braids. "That concludes our preparations for the next large-scale Force-civilian joint venture during the Pick Up the Pen march. I expect all personnel to be in position on or before the twenty-fourth. Any other business?"

Nobody brought anything up. Maybe this meeting was almost over. That'd be a relief. It was an honor to be included in a Quadrant meeting, Aidan thought privately, but here he'd thought Magnum was intense. A Quadrant Commander and a Ute tribal chieftain both, Quadrant Commander Ouray radiated power even through a hologram. Aidan wasn't sure if he ever wanted to find out how intense the man was in person.

The Quadrant Commander's black eyes fell on Aidan. He resisted the urge to hide under his chair.

"Headly-McIllian. How's the site determination for your new farm coming along?"

*I'm actually doing this,* Aidan thought, caught between wanting to grin and run. *Me. A little Base Commander from the middle of the Dust with a handful of years under my belt. I'm actually sitting in on a Quadrant-level meeting and talking about starting a farm. How the hell did this ever even happen?*

"We have a site we like, Commander," he offered, clearing his throat. "It's set over a natural aquifer, and the tests my agricultural officer and my senior hydroelectrics specialist have run all came back looking good."

"Have you prepared your information packet?" The Quadrant Commander asked, voice as calm as the high desert.

"Yes Commander," Aidan replied. "It was sent to Sector yesterday."

Commander Ouray nodded, a grave smile gracing his lined face. "Then I look forward to reading the details. Given the nature of this project, it will be arriving on my desk after Magnum and Hall have looked it over."

"I'll have it for you on Tuesday, Commander Ouray," Commander Hall agreed from her holographic seat on Aidan's left. Aidan glanced her way, and he could have sworn she shot him a smile.

"Very good," Commander Ouray agreed. "If no issues arise, I'll pass official approval by the end of next week."

"Thank you, Commander," Aidan agreed. "Am I cleared to inform my unit? I know you said you wanted this to be a day of implementation announcement in light of the security situation, but…"

The Quadrant Commander smiled. "Let's compromise. You can inform your senior staff—officially—and begin making arrangements with them." The look on his face told Aidan that he knew damn good and well Aidan had spilled the beans to somebody. He resisted the urge to squirm as the Quadrant Commander went on. "But your junior staff will be informed at implementation. They can wait for a few more days. You have the bulk of the supplies you need, and you have a more pressing event to prepare for prior to that."

"Yes, Commander. Thank you, Commander," Aidan agreed calmly. His crew was going to give him no end of shit for keeping all this to himself for so long, but that was just them being them. In the meantime, he could continue prepping for the big day. Kevin could help him out with that. He could help plan the mother of all parties, too. When the gang heard that they were actually making Commander Taylor's Ten Year Plan happen, they were definitely going to go into high-gear party mode.

"Then I believe this meeting can be adjourned," Sector Commander Ouray stated. "Good luck with your work, everyone. Keep your heads down in the storm."

With a chorus of 'thank you, Commander', the holograms of Regional Commanders and invitees winked out one by one. Once the room was empty, Aidan leaned back in his chair and closed his eyes.

*Breathe....*

*In for seven...*

*Out for seven...*

*In for seven...*

*Out for seven...*

*Wow. Okay. So that was something...*

He'd almost gotten back to baseline when somebody knocked on the closed door, and the adrenaline spiked right back up into the red again. He sat up. *What now?*

"Come in?"

His door opened, and Damian stepped in.

"You free right now?"

"Sure," Aidan agreed, standing. "Something wrong?"

Damian shrugged, a move like two construction cranes rising and falling in tandem.

"Nothing yet. Tweak's asked for your presence while we go over her options and discuss her situation."

Aidan blinked. "Um…okay. But I don't know if I'm going to be any help. I'm not a doctor."

Damian sighed. Glancing down, he crossed his arms, "You're a trusted authority figure. And right now, I'm not. That's my guess. So if you have time, I could use the help."

Aidan studied his medical officer for a second. Damian was taking this hard, wasn't he? He looked almost as frustrated as he'd been when the gene-tailored bacteria that caused the MACHA disease had been shrugging off everything he threw at it.

Crossing his office, Aidan put a hand on Damian's shoulder. "No problem. Are they down there already?"

Damian raised his head, and gave him a ghost of a smile. "They will be, when we get there."

"Then let's go," Aidan offered, returning the smile in kind.

Tweak and Inyoni stood stiffly by the door of the medical bay. They looked small in the expanse of white all around them.

"Tweak says we gotta talk?" Inoyni asked, his long ears twitched down and back like an unhappy dog's.

"Let's go into my office," Damian offered, gesturing to the door.

Aidan grabbed a seat, stealing a glance at Tweak as she thumped down into her chair. Her face had that unreadable china-doll look it wore when she didn't trust the situation.

Behind his desk, Damian steepled his fingers. "There's an issue I'd like to talk to you about."

Inyoni stiffened, his ears flattening at Damian's tone. "Wassit?"

Damian managed a small smile. "Don't worry, nothing's wrong per se. But Tweak....well, maybe I should be congratulating you, Inyoni. If you and Tweak agree to bring it to term, you're going to have a baby in a few months."

Inyoni's eyes went wide. His ears twitched. He glanced between Damian and Tweak. "Wh-what? You're…you're kiddin', right?"

"I'm afraid not." Damian stated solemnly. Aidan shot him a look. That brick wall act he was using to keep his own chill really wasn't helping right now. He really wished the doctor would thaw out and give him some help here on the emotional end of things.

He watched with a sinking heart as Inyoni froze solid. Shit, he wasn't taking this well at all.

"Fuck," the younger man breathed, staring at Tweak. "You're seriously…"

"S-s-seriously," Tweak agreed, nodding. She smiled a tiny, broken smile.

"This could be a good thing, you know," Damian suggested. "A blessing in disguise. The fetal DNA is in good shape, barring a few easily edited areas."

Aidan just about winced at those words. A sentiment like that at a time like this was *so* not going to fly.

Inyoni stared at Damian as if he had just realized the guy was nuts. "A good thing?" he managed, his voice hitching. "A double-Gamma baby on a Duster base. That ain't a good thing, Damian. That ain't a good thing at all. Fuck."

Damian nodded. "If that's how you both feel, it's simple to terminate the pregnancy safely. If that's what you want, Tweak, I can perform the procedure. Or we can contact a specialist."

"All your options are on the table," Aidan added. "You two tell us what you want to do, and we'll make it happen."

"We will need to make our decisions within the next month," Damian added, "but within that time frame, I have a lot of options for you. We can help you bring the pregnancy to term with healthcare and gene therapies to make sure the fetus develops within healthy parameters. With a few regular tests, we can be sure your pregnancy remains viable and comes to term successfully. Or we can terminate the pregnancy. You tell us what you want to do, and we'll do it."

Tweak stared at Damian with murder in her eyes. Inyoni looked over at her, ears flat against the sides of head. When he spoke, he sounded like a lost child. "What're we gonna do?"

His words cracked Tweak's armor. Aidan watched as she dropped her eyes, shaking her head helplessly. "We c-c-c-c-can't do it."

*Man*, Aidan hated seeing the two of them in this spot.

Inyoni took a deep breath, closed his eyes and nodded. Then he shook his head. "I…if…he said it was early enough, if you wanna…." Groaning, he reached up and tugged at his ear with one hand. "I don't know Tweak, what do you want?"

Tweak shook her head, eyes fixed on her boots. "Don't g-g-g-got a choice."

And that was his cue, Aidan decided.

"Tweak," he murmured. "I know you feel that way right now. But you *do* get a choice. You get *all* the choices. You two are the only ones who get to say what happens next, okay? *You* get to decide." Getting out of his chair, he knelt in front of her, putting his hand on the armrest of her chair. "Whatever you want, you tell me, and we'll make it work. Promise."

Tweak glared at him, tears rimming her eyes. "Make it work?! Make it work?! Are you batshit?! Nuts! Total fucking n-n-n-nuts!"

"Yeah, sometimes I am," Aidan agreed. "But right now, I'm steady. Right now, your fear's talking for you. And I want to hear from *you.* Not your fear. You get to make this decision, either way. Your fear doesn't."

Tweak surged out of her chair, her scales standing up in ridges along her arms like the fur on a scared cat. "What d-decision?! A b-b-baby, from *us*? You want me to play the odds? Odds are million to one! Odds always w-win!"

Aidan stayed where he was, holding her eyes. "Yeah. I hear what you're saying. And I don't *want* you to do anything. You're the only one who has the right to make this decision." He drew a breath. "But we're Wildcards, right? The house might win most of the time. But the wild card can beat the house. If that's what you want."

Tweak snorted, pushed herself to her feet and stalked the room, arms crossed over her chest as she paced.

Aidan watched her, feeling useless. Slowly, he stood.

"Why don't you and Inyoni take some time and talk this out?" He could offer that, at least. "Take the afternoon off. Take some time together. I have to leave the base tomorrow to get ready for the next big Pick Up The Pen march. I'll be home in a couple days. Have Damian run some tests if you want, think stuff through, and we'll sit down and talk about all this when I get home. Okay?"

Inyoni swallowed, his ears plastered down to the sides of his head. "Yeah. Yeah."

Carefully, he stood, and gently touched Tweak's shoulder. "Dragon? C'mon."

Tweak's fingers danced over her scales as the door of their bedroom closed at her back. Her head was so full of static that it was going to explode. Fear choked her throat as her feet tried to find a way out that wasn't there. Her gut hurt.

Finally, she leaned against the corner of the room, slid down, and clasped her knees with her arms, closing her eyes.

Now he'd leave. Now he'd walk away. Now everything would end, and…

Inyoni slid down the wall beside her. His warm hand rested on the scales of her arm.

"Tweak..."

Tweak rocked herself, shaking her head. "Sorry. Sorry. D-d-didn't mean…d-didn't w-want to f-f-fuck up like this…"

"Hey, hey Tweak," Inyoni murmured, his arms wrapping her up. "Hey, no. You didn't fuck up. That was Damian, not you. No saying sorry, you didn't do nothin'. C'mere."

Gently, he rocked her as her shakes eased up. "'Sokay," Inyoni whispered. "'Sokay. You done good. Hey, hey. 'Sokay."

She gulped. "Thanks."

"Yeah," Inyoni whispered into her hair.

For a time, the room was quiet.

"So," Inyoni murmured, "Um…what're we gonna do?"

Tweak shook her head. “Don't know. I d-dd-d-don't k-k-know. D-d-don't know..."

"'S'okay," Inyoni muttered, pulling him into her arms. His hands were shaking. So was his voice. "'S'okay. We don't…we got time, yeah? Let's…I dunno, get coffee or somethin'. Talk 'bout it.”

Tweak shook her head, shivering in his arms. It was so fucked up. But he was still here. He was holding her. He wasn’t gone.

She buried her face in his chest, and tried to smother a sob.

"'S'okay," Inyoni repeated over and over, until the words became a nonsense sound. It was something to hold onto. Something to tell her she wasn’t alone. She held onto it, held onto his hand, and let the sobs come.

Finally, Tweak's crying jag let up. Sitting up, she wiped her eyes. "S-s-sorry."

"Nah," Inyoni muttered, smiling weakly. "I'm sorry. I mean, weren't for me, you wouldn't be…weren't for me, you'd still be fine."

Tweak shook her head. "Don't talk stupid. D-Damian's fault. M-messed up the m-meds. Asshat."

Inyoni gave a tiny snort of a laugh. "Yeah. Guess so."

"Know so." Leaning up, Tweak wrapped her arms around her man.

Inyoni sighed. His soft fingers trailed up and down her scales.

“It’s gonna be okay, Tweak. I’m…we’ll get through this, you and me.”

The wave of emotion came down again, right when she thought she’d got on top of it. She rolled over, curling in a ball with her head pillowed in Inyoni's lap. She lay like that for a long time, fighting to get her cool back.

"They think we can have the kid. If we want,” she whispered. “They got t-tricks. If we want."

Inyoni was quiet, fingers running over her hair. She could hear it when he swallowed. "I, uh…um. Good? I mean…I…you wanna have it?"

Tweak couldn’t answer that. She wiped her tears on his pants. "What d-do you w-w-want?" she whispered.

"I dunno," Inyoni admitted in a whisper. "I never…didn't really think 'bout it till…I mean I don’t know if I can even be a decent…I just…I dunno."

Tweak wrapped her arms around her stomach, curling in on herself like a snail trying to defend itself from the bigness of the world outside. She didn't know either. She had no fucking idea whether she would be a decent mom, even if this kid wasn't a total freak. She *wished* somebody knew what she should do, because she *did not.*

Inyoni’s hand stroked her shoulder. "We could get the tests done, then choose? Or somethin'…"

Tweak sighed, and forced herself to sit up. Tests. That meant more time. More time to figure everything out.

Wiping her face with the back of her hand, she got a smile together. "Yeah. Tests. Sure."

Aidan was incredibly glad to shut the door of his room at the end of the day. Crossing to the bed, he flopped onto it.

“Hey,” he muttered at his husband, voice muffled by the pillow.

Kevin’s long fingers brushed through his hair. “Hey. Bit of a day?”

“I’ll say,” Aidan agreed. Rolling over, he rested his head on Kevin’s belly. The other man stroked his hair with soft fingers.

“Anything in particular?” Kevin asked.

Aidan sighed. “Yeah.”

“Want to talk about it?”

Aidan debated it. Tweak hadn’t gone public, so he really couldn’t…but he could trust Kevin with a secret. And he *needed* to talk.

“Yeah,” he admitted. “Something big’s going on here at home.”

"Oh?" Kevin asked, setting aside what he'd been reading. "What's that, then?"

Aidan closed his eyes. "It's Tweak. She's…pregnant."

He felt the jolt go through Kevin's muscles.

"She's…really?" Kevin asked.

Aidan nodded. "She wanted me to sit in on a consultation with her, Inyoni and Damian. She's working on deciding if she wants to have it or not. She's not ready to tell the rest of the base, heads up."

"How did this happen?" Kevin asked, fingers absently running circles over the back of Aidan's hand. "Do I need to change suppliers for our sexual health implants?"

Aidan shook his head. "It's not the implants. It's Tweak and Inyoni being Gamma. Their systems burned through their doses, basically. Damian explained it better than that, but yeah."

"Oh," Kevin murmured distantly. "Oh…Oh dear…"

"I'll say," Aidan agreed. Rolling over, he curled up against Kevin, resting his head on the taller man's shoulder. "I got her through the consultation, but…I have no idea what to say to her about this, Kev. I don't know what to *do* for her."

His husband was quiet for a moment, stroking his hair gently.

Kevin sighed quietly. "Right now love, I think all we can do is be there for her as she deliberates." Turning his head, he kissed Aidan's brow. "But not for the next few days. We'd better get some sleep; it's a big day tomorrow. The general march down Sixteenth Street is going to be something. We need to be on-site by noon. Everything starts at five in the evening."

"Yeah, I know," Aidan agreed wearily. He knew he had things to get ready for. Things to do. Things to take care of. But it felt so good to just lie here, for now.

Soft hands gently tugged at his shoulders.

"Come on love. Let's get you out of your boots and into bed."

Gratefully, Aidan let his husband take care of him. A little bit of softness before the insanity. A little comfort. A little rest.

Maybe it would be enough.

## Event File 18
## File Tag: Mass Civic Action
## 16:55-08-28-2161

"Sign crew?"

"Here," the voice came back in Naomi's ear. She checked the box.

"Okay, Guardians?"

"Here!"

Check.

"Great. Lookouts?"

"In position."

Check.

"Medics?"

"All set."

Naomi raised the window showing her list for her brother to see, flashing him a thumbs' up in the hotel room's low light. He gave her two thumbs' up and a nod in return, leaning back-to-back with his husband at the head of the hotel bed. He gently elbowed Kevin, who started out of his work zone, looked up, got a clue and nodded. She returned the nod.

"Okay, we're all set," Naomi relayed into the mic, checking her screens. "The Force has shut down all surveillance in the area. Drones are out of operation. Remember your route: down Sixteenth to Wynkoop, back up Seventeenth, onto the lawn in front of the Inter-Corporate Cooperation Center, and then disperse."

"Our people are prepared to guard you against the Peacekeepers when they arrive. We have your routes into and out of the area secured," Aidan added into his mic. "Remember, Eagle and Argus aren't going to be caught off their guard this time. We've seen a lot of equipment being moved around. Guardians, eyes up."

"You got it, Ace of Spades," the head of the team acting as civilian protection agreed.

"Okay," Naomi stated, checking her reads from the other Munitions officers in all their assigned positions, "We're as ready as we're going to be on the Force end. You can give the signal when your people are set."

"Got it," the head of their Union liaison team agreed with excitement in her voice. "Hang onto your hats everybody!"

"Good luck out there," Naomi offered, signing off. She sat back. "Okay. Now we wait and see."

Below them, Sixteenth Street blazed in all its attention-grabbing glare. Naomi really hoped the trick that the ZonCom folks had come up with was going to work.

"Two minutes to five," Kevin observed tightly, eyes on the Cavanaugh flagship office shining in its blue-steel glory at the top of the street.

The room filled up with quiet. Naomi double-checked her contacts' positions. Aidan studied his own screens.

One minute to five.

Kevin pushed himself off the bed and walked to stand by the window, staring down into the mess of competing lights scrabbling to grab an eyeball and sell a product.

At five on the dot, the lights went out.

Naomi grinned. The ZonCom folks had said they could shut off all the ads. Turned out they weren't kidding.

Out in the streets, streams of people came flowing, gathering in strength. Micro-drone swarms formed into a gigantic banner at the head of the crowd: a fist made of many hands, holding a pen. Around it, words blazed in light.

We Demand A Seat At The Table. We Demand A New Contract. Pick Up The Pen!

Below, people held signs and controlled personal drones displaying messages. The Unions had agreed that this would be a masked march done in silence, and Naomi approved of the tactic: it meant that any troublemakers would immediately stand out by the noise they made and could be isolated. As a bonus, the silent swell of people was more impactful than any chant could have been. The river of mute humanity was downright eerie.

A few faces looked up as the speechless crowd flowed below, and Naomi got flashes of their masks: a white oval with night-black circles for eyes, the black silhouette of a pen spilling ink from the tip standing in for a mouth.

The crowd flowed on, silent and powerful as a river. The sound of sirens rose off to the east, far down Sixteenth. Naomi checked her screens. Yep, right on time. Eagle had figured out that their drones weren't operating. Now they were scrambling.

"Eagle's moving," she offered to the room.

Aidan nodded, eyes on the text communications between organizers scrolling in front of him. "Can we pin down what they're deploying yet?"

She checked the cameras around Eagle headquarters, zooming in as much as she could, and studied the grainy mess of moving bodies and vehicles through her feed. Bringing up her image recognition software, she set it to start matching the silhouettes her eyes might miss against the shapes of known munitions and equipment.

"Based on the reads we're getting, three trucks of FIDOs, and four Screamers."

"Four? Crap," Aidan sighed. "Okay, have we got the gear ready to go?"

"Yeah," Naomi agreed. "We just need to get in eye-line so we can control it real-time."

"Okay, let's move then," her big brother agreed. Shutting down his tab's external window, he stood. "Kev?"

Kevin was still standing at the window, watching. Quietly, Aidan stepped across and laid a hand on his husband's shoulder. Kevin started a little at the touch.

"Let's move," Aidan murmured. Kevin nodded once, sharply. "Right."

Stepping out of the hotel room, they headed for the back exit. Naomi ran a visual check of the space, double-checked her tab for any anomalous reads, and waved her basemates on.

"We stick to the alleys."

"Roger," Kevin agreed just behind her. "As soon as we're set up, I've got the swarm ready to deploy. You're sure we've got what we need for the opposition involved, Naomi?"

"If I wasn't, I wouldn't be walking in there," Naomi replied patiently. "Let's go, boys."

The silence of the evening was eerie. Usually the sidewalks were packed with shoppers, holo-ads filling the air with their noise and movement, cars driving themselves down the street. But this evening the Go system had been rerouted to avoid downtown. The ads were disabled. The only sound was the shuffle of their own feet, and the sirens wailing in the distance. Far away, for now. Getting closer.

Naomi clocked Aidan and Kevin both as they threaded their way through the streets, checking where they were in terms of headspace. Her big brother was tense, but his head was in the game. Good.

Kevin, though…

Naomi liked the guy, and he did good work. But times like this, she got a little leery about having him on a mission. He had a streak of crazy in him. Ninety percent of the time he kept it buried deep, but Naomi had seen it come out when his face looked as blank as it did now. She didn't trust it an inch. He'd shot unarmed people when he let that vicious streak get the better of him, and he'd acted like an idiot more than once. In a good headspace, Kevin was a big tactical and logistic asset. In a bad one, he was an unpredictable liability. She had to hope he'd stay in the driver's seat tonight and stay on the asset side of the line. They really didn't need trouble.

Naomi checked her reads again. If she was right, Eagle would confront the crowd when they reached the Union Station Hub. If they were smarter and less reactionary, they'd wait until the crowd gathered itself on the sweeping lawn of the building that had been the state capitol in the pre-incorporation days, but they weren't. Seeing a big crowd coming at them, the Peacekeepers would put on a show of force.That was what the Dusters were here to handle.

Naomi knew they were getting close when she heard the rumbling. It was the sound of machines, yeah. And it was the sound of a lot of people on edge. Not the protesters, she was pretty sure of that. This was the sound of shouted orders and threats; Peacekeepers growling as they waited to slip their leashes.

"Stop," Kevin whispered. Naomi glanced at him. He pointed upwards. "Here. Unit four-sixteen."

Together, the three of them pulled down a fire escape ladder and climbed up onto the deck of the vacant unit in the luxury apartment complex that Kevin had scoped for them. He'd done good. From here, they could practically see the whites of the Peacekeeper's eyes. The bastards were going through all the steps Naomi had expected; flanking out in squadrons like black ants protecting their nest, rallied around the statue of a foot crushing a skinny demon in the center of the old Union Station plaza, massed in numbers intended to scare the crap out of the citizens.

Across the gulf of retro cobblestones, those citizens stood still and silent.

A Peacekeeper spoke into the mic, and mounted speakers around the courtyard amplified his voice.

"Pursuant to your Corporate Contracts, you are required to remain in good order at all times. This gathering is a breach of your Corporate Citizen Contracts. Unless this crowd disperses immediately, we are authorized to use all necessary force to remove you."

The crowd didn't say a word. Didn't move. Across the gulf, blank white masks and heavy black helmets stared one another down. Ten minutes crawled past like eons.

"Begin!" the Peacekeeper barked.

The rattle of batons on shields hammered the evening. It was the kind of sound that seemed to work its way out through your bones, not in through your ears. It rattled your guts, making the little monkey in every human brain beg to run and hide somewhere.

Eyes narrowed, Naomi studied the protestors. They'd been trained for this. They knew the drill. Now she just had to trust them to keep their nerve.

Eyes panning, she studied the Peacekeepers.

"Movement," she offered. "Bringing up the gear."

"I see it," Aidan agreed. "Kev?"

"Drones are ready," Kevin agreed quietly.

"Great. Omi?"

"Mine too," Naomi agreed, checking her readings and setting her gauntlets ready by her side. "Say when, Big A."

"Roger."

Under the incessant hammering of the batons, the FIDOS came strutting through the ranks to take their places, a wave of metal and plastic pain waiting to wash over the people. A few protestors shifted, but they held their ground.

With a hiss of tires, four trucks came barreling out of alleyways. Aidan stiffened. "Kev, Omi. Now!"

Naomi was way ahead of him. Cueing up her four prepared windows, she brought her drone swarm to life. The terrestrial drones rose from their hidden places in alleys and basements, swarming together like a million spiders, abdomens full of white fluid.

Naomi's eyes flicked from her drones to the trucks. The gigantic speaker-like apparatus on top of each vehicle had begun to warm up. She checked her readings.

"Screamers are set at a hundred and sixty decibels, sound in one minute."

"That enough time?" Aidan murmured.

"It's going to have to be," Naomi replied tightly, staring down at the Screamer devices. In a minute, they'd be releasing waves of sound in tones that could burst eardrums and rupture blood vessels at thirty feet, deafen at fifty, and make people run for hundreds of feet around.

*But not today, they won't,* Naomi thought with a grim little smile. She pulled on the gauntlets and began to draw movement paths in the air. Her terrestrial drone swarm had been designed to insulate buildings in construction work. They had repurposed for this better than she could have hoped, once she'd played with their control programs a while.

At her gestures, her swarm broke itself into eight, and two swarms created pincers around each sound cannon. She gave the command gesture, and the drones began their work. Long plastic legs clamped themselves to the sides of each vehicle. White bodies and black appendages obscured the windshield as the wave of terrestrial drones clambered up each vehicle. It was incredible how fast the drones moved. One second they were on the ground around a truck. In the next second, there was no truck; just a ball of moving drones.

Out of the corner of her eye, Naomi stole a look at Kevin's work. The skinny guy was grinning as the micro-drone swarms he was using swept down to smother each FIDO, blocking its vision and balance sensors with paint. As it was blinded, every machine followed the programming Naomi had heard about: playing it safe when EagleCorp personnel were in proximity, the blinded FIDOS hunched down and went into hibernation mode. Eagle had meant them to be the shock troops bringing the terror, but now that table was turned. A line of FIDOS had become a six-foot wide, waist-high wall of scrap metal hemming the Peacekeepers in. Perfect.

Satisfied, Naomi turned her attention back to her own drones. They were hard at work. Thick white liquid insulation poured out of them, muffling the sound weapons in coat after coat of foam.

Naomi checked her timer. Fifty-nine seconds. And…time.

The screamers went off. The foam around them shuddered, but it held. The sound squeezed itself out as a strangled whimper of reverb.

Standing shoulder to shoulder, the crowd cheered. Naomi wasn't sure it was time for cheering yet, but you couldn't blame the civvies.

As one, the cheering crowd swept past the trap that had been set for them, laughing at the enemies who'd fallen into it. Peacekeepers hollered and swore as they tried to get their legs over the dead FIDOs. A few drew guns, but Kevin was on that with swarms of micro-drones instructed to watch for the shape of a gun and programmed to clog the barrels.

Naomi glanced at her brother, and caught him laughing. She grinned.

"Pretty good, hunh?"

"Hell yes," Aidan agreed. "Kev? Where's the head of the protest crowd now?"

"Headed up seventeenth!" Kevin crowed, watching through his screen. "Eagle put all its force into stopping them here, there's absolutely nothing to impede the rest of the march!"

"Then I guess we just sit back and watch the show for a while," Naomi offered, grinning. "All we have to do is—"

BANG.

A cloud of greenish gas billowed out of the curled white seashell of station exits. Men bulleted out of the doors, running headfirst into the Peacekeepers.

"Zoom in on that," Aidan asked. "I want to know what's going on there."

"On it," Kevin agreed. "Turning the sound on for a few of the micro-drones in the vicinity. Mind your ears."

The blatting of angry voices, the thump of feet, and a hell of a lot of curse words came over the tab speakers.

"You fucking morons, what the fucking hell?!"

"You fucks weren't doing jack to subdue the rioters!"

"You didn't hit the fucking rioters, cocksucker, you hit us!"

"Fuck you up sideways, you and your assclowns! I was hired to protect Mr. Harrington, and that's what I'm going to fucking do! Your job is to protect property, *my* fucking job is to protect a citizen!"

Out of the corner of her eye, Naomi watched Kevin go tense. When he spoke, the word came out like a breath of ice.

"*Harrington.*"

Naomi tensed. *Uh-oh.*

Down below, the pale man in the tailored suit strode out. "Who's denied my vehicle access? I have a meeting to attend."

"Sir," the Peacekeeper who'd done the yelling offered in his best 'I want to keep my job' voice, "We've been trying to clear rioters from the area, and—"

Harrington cut him off with a wave of the hand. "I don't care about that, I have an appointment to get to, and I expect you people to do your job and keep the streets passable!"

Naomi missed the rest of the conversation when Kevin drew his gun.

## Event File 19

## File Tag: Planned Maneuvers

## 17:30-08-28-2161

"You hear anything from the action team?" Inyoni asked over Tweak's shoulder. "Topher and Dozer want to know if they should stay on duty or catch some sack."

Tweak waved a hand over the back of her coding chair in a 'who knows' gesture. "N-news looks good s-so far, that's all I see. D-drone feeds are out, cameras are out down there, so I'm b-blind." She winced as her rig buzzed. "Fuck…"

"What's wrong?" Inyoni asked. Tweak sighed. Pushing back from her rig, she curled into the big coding chair, wrapping her arms around herself to keep the shakes in. She'd been holding it together, focusing on work. And now…

She so *did not* want to think about this right now.

But she didn't get a choice. She had to.

"What is it, Tweak?" Inyoni asked, voice gone all soft as he knelt beside the chair. "What's the buzz?"

Tweak swallowed. "T-tests. Our appointment. For the t-tests."

Inyoni's ears drooped. "Oh."

For a moment, the room was dead still.

Slowly, she forced herself to raise her eyes. "Bird? Go with m-m-me?"

Inyoni managed a smile. "Course."

It felt like it took a month to walk down to the medical bay.

Damian raised a brow when she opened the door. "I was starting to wonder if I'd see you today."

"Working," Tweak muttered, slumping down into the diagnostic chair. "Tests. Get it over with."

"Yes your majesty," Damian replied, throwing shade dry as the dust outside. She thought about calling him out, but she didn't have the juice to go at it.

Damian studied his tab, calibrating the chair's readings. "I'll have to take a blood draw."

Tweak rolled her eyes and stuck out her arm. She'd had so many blood draws by this point that she didn't give a crap anymore.

"So?" she asked, as her blood filled the tube.

"So, we'll let the test run," Damian stated.

Tweak sighed, slumping back in the diagnostic chair. She heard Inyoni swallow, and glanced up at him. Fuck he looked scared.

Reaching up, Tweak squeezed his arm with her free hand. He gave her a wobbly smile as Damian studied the readouts.

*Bing!*

"Okay, now?" Tweak asked, looking over at the doctor. Damian let out a slow breath. "Let's go to my office."

Tweak pushed down a snap of anger at the words. Damian wasn't really doing anything bad. Yet.

"Spill," she stated when they'd taken seats.

Damian steepled his fingertips together over his nose. Tweak clamped her fingers on the chair to keep herself in her seat.

*Think about something besides this. Anything besides this. Think about something else before the nerves get a foothold.*

You could never tell what he was looking at with those eye implants of his. She should talk to him about programming visible pupils and irises sometime.

How would that code work? If she started from the haptics…

"You're nine weeks along, and we can get direct DNA from the fetus now," Damian began, bringing her back to this place she so *did not* want to be. He cued up his desk's image projector, showing a set of DNA strands and a laundry list of results. Tweak stared at the scrolling words.

"So?"

"The short story is, the system isn't picking up any known congenital diseases. But we're starting to see irregularities."

Damian held up a hand as static buzzed through Tweak's muscles. "Not major irregularities, don't worry. But the child's showing odd DNA patterns. Non-human in some areas, which isn't unexpected."

Tweak's gut turned over. "Point?"

Damian rounded the desk and sat beside her, pointing out the DNA strands. "These areas are for GI tract formation. They're the areas of abnormality I'm concerned with, and I'd like to get this fixed as soon as I can source the right DNA. These are for ear formation. I think the child might have Inyoni's ears. This can also be changed, though it is an area that involves more gene pairings and is more complicated because of it."

"Fuck. Can you tell yet?" Inyoni asked, staring at the readouts. His ears had gone down like popped tires.

Damian glanced over at him, gave him a smile. "At worst, the baby will take after you. Don't worry too much."

Inyoni stared at him as if he'd said cannibalism was a great hobby.

"Which brings me to my point." Damian flicked his fingers, bringing up a new set of images to twist beside the ones Tweak had been looking at. "We can do a fetal injection with healthy DNA sequences, once I source a compatible DNA template. We can tailor out the abnormalities, if that's what you and Inyoni want."

Tweak blinked. "S-serious?"

Damian met her eyes levelly. "Am I ever anything else?" He glanced back at his work. "The main question is what direction you'd like me to go at this point. If we're planning on bringing the pregnancy to term, we need to begin genetic treatment. If we're planning on termination, it's better to do that sooner than later."

Tweak bit her lip. She glanced at Inyoni, away again.

*No more time. Sooner rather than later. Fuck.*

She swallowed hard a few times, rubbing a hand over her throat. Hopefully the words would come out. "Heart? L-l-lungs? B-brain? S-s-skin?"

"I'm monitoring all the vital body systems," Damian repeated. "I'm currently sourcing clean genetic code for the fetal injection on the GI tract; as a backup I'll use the template the system has stored, though that isn't ideal. So far, most of the life-sustaining organs are within normal genetic parameters."

"How long we got before we gotta make a decision?" Inyoni asked before Tweak could get it together to talk.

"I wouldn't leave it longer than a week." Damian suggested quietly. "This isn't a decision you can make at the last minute."

Tweak nodded. "Okay. Okay." She drew a long, slow breath. "We'll talk ton-night. Tomorrow n-night, we'll t-t-tell you. What we want. Day after. Tops. That w-work?"

"That'll work," Damian agreed with a nod. "But make sure it *is* by the day after tomorrow. I know this is a lot to decide, but for your health, I need you to remember that the clock's ticking."

*As if I can forget,* Tweak snarled in her head. She almost said it out loud, but there was no point. Damian couldn't change the timeline on this train wreck. Neither could she.

All she could do was decide.

Their bedroom door made almost no sound as it slid closed. Tweak leaned against it, arms crossed.

"So?"

Inyoni stared at her like a scared rabbit, his ears flat against his throat. He shook his head. "Ain't givin' a kid my ears. We can fix it, right? Damian said we could fix it."

Tweak closed her eyes. "Said m-m-maybe. Said we have to m-m-mess with lotsa d-DNA to do it. We do that? N-n-no w-way."

"Ain't givin' a kid my ears," Inyoni repeated, his voice caught somewhere between ordering and pleading. He yanked one quivering ear out from his head. "These ears are so…fuckin' hell, Tweak, I ain't makin' a kid put up with this if I can stop it!"

Tweak shook her head. "Your ears are f-fine. I like 'em."

"You're the only one," Inyoni grumbled, folding his arms over his chest. "I hate 'em. You know that. Kid'll prob'ly hate 'em, too. No use givin' 'em to them if we can help it."

"And so we just change the kid? Like we know what's b-b-best?" Tweak paced down their room. "You get d-DNA w-wrong, you k-kill somebody. Sides, we do that? We're b-b-bad as people who f-fucked us up. Bad as C-cavanaugh!"

Inyoni shook his head. "No, we ain't. We ain't fuckin' 'round with animal DNA and shit. We're making sure the kid's *human*, not somethin' else." Groaning, he yanked on both his ears. "I…fuck, we don't even know if we're gonna have it or not! I don't think I'd make a good dad, I…oh goddamn, Tweak, I dunno! And if we do have it? You want our kid to be a freak like us if it don't have to?" He waved a hand her way. "What would you do if it was your arms 'stead of my ears? Those pretty li'l scales you hate so much? What if the kid had *that?* Bet you'd wanna do something then, huh? Bet you wouldn't want him dealin' with *that* all his life. It ain't fair to the kid, Tweak! It just ain't."

Tweak threw her arms wide in frustration "So what, we d-decide what's g-good and what's n-n-not? We g-gonna d-d-decide the eye and h-h-hair and s-s-s-skin c-c-color too?" She glared up at Inyoni. "This is people, not code. You don't just hack *people*."

Inyoni stared at her for a long moment, his ears and hands trembling. "You'd hack it in a heartbeat, meant it fixed some problem with the brain. You'd hack the DNA no problem if—"

"They hacked my b-b-brother and he d-d-DIED!"

It scared Tweak, how loud her voice came out. It froze her in place.

Inyoni stood hunched, hands clapped over his flattened ears.

Slowly, he straightened, watching her with fear in his eyes. He swallowed.

“It…I ain't doing this, Tweak. I just…ain't."

She opened her mouth, but he hunched up his shoulders and shoved the door open. The door rattled shut behind him. His footsteps echoed down the hall.

Tweak turned and kicked the wall until her leg ached, cursing until she stuttered. "G-g-goddamned IDIOT!" she yelled at the walls. Who the idiot was, she didn’t know.

She dropped onto their bed and wrapped her arms around her knees, rocking herself as the tears came down.

## Event File 20
## File Tag: Unforeseen Event
## 18:45-08-28-2161/08:00-08-29-2161

"What the fuck Kev?!" Aidan hissed, but Naomi didn't waste her breath. She landed on Kevin, tackling him to the floor of the deck. He writhed under her, grasping for the gun she'd shoved out of his reach. Great. Just great. Right when they didn't need it, the streak of crazy was going to show up and fuck them all over.

Kevin bucked and scrabbled under her, his words coming out like birds startled into flight. "I can take the shot! I can take him out from here! We'll never get another chance like this! Please Naomi, please, you have to let me up, you have to let me take the shot!"

Her brother's hands clamped down beside hers on the struggling man. Together, they turned and pinned Kevin spread-eagled, Naomi sitting on his legs. Aidan glared down at his husband. "You are going to fucking *stop*, Kevin. And you're going to do it *now*."

Naomi's skin prickled at the tone in her brother's voice, but she wasn't actually sure Kevin took it in. He looked up at Aidan with wild eyes, still trying to wriggle and buck as he gasped out his words. "Aidan, Aidan please! Everything he's done, everything he's taken, he has to pay! He has to pay for it! Henrietta! MACHA! Everyone he's killed! I've got to make him pay for it! Please!" The words were ragged as sobs, fury and desperation tangled in them like bugs in a spiderweb.

Aidan stared down into Kevin's face for a second. Then he pulled the other man up, clasping him in a grip like steel.

"He will pay, Kev. Remember the plan. We're going to arrest that bastard. The international court is going to hold human rights hearings. That's how he'll pay. He'll pay for all of it in front of the whole world. He needs to live so the whole world can see him pay his debts."

When Kevin spoke, the words were sharp and grating as broken glass. "He deserves to die, Aidan. He *deserves* it."

Her brother nodded, holding his husband's eyes. "I know. But you deserve to keep thinking of yourself as a good guy. Good guys don't shoot people in cold blood, Kev. He's going to pay, okay? Just not like this."

Kevin's body heaved, once with the last of his struggles, then with a couple quiet sobs. Finally, he was still in Aidan's arms. "Not like this," the logistics officer murmured, repeating it in a strange sort of resignation. "Not like this."

For a moment, silence crystallized in the air between them.

Finally, Kevin let out a long breath. "You can let me go now. I'm under control."

Warily, Aidan drew back, letting his grip on his husband loosen. Kevin sat up calmly, breathing deep and staring at Aidan. Naomi was pretty sure that a bug flying into the beam of that stare would have fried.

"He will pay," Kevin stated quietly, and the tone made a little shiver run up Naomi's backbone. "I'll hold you to that."

Leaning in, Aidan squeezed his shoulder. "I know you will, Kev. I'll keep my promise."

"You'd bloody well better," Kevin stated flatly. Carefully, he stood.

"They'll be distracted for some time. We should move."

Shooting looks at one another, brother and sister followed his lead.

♠

By the time they made it in that night, the base was wrapped in stillness. They came in as quietly as they could, hanging their riding gear up in silence.

Reaching over, Naomi pulled Aidan into a side-arm hug. He gave her a quick squeeze. Raising her eyebrows, she nodded at Kevin; a 'you got this?' sort of move. Aidan nodded in return, though his insides felt as if they had been weighed down with lead shot.

Naomi gently fistbumped his chest. Then she was gone into the base, leaving him alone with his husband. Kevin was meticulously going over his bike.

For a moment, Aidan wasn't sure he wanted to speak. The silence between them felt like it might explode.

"Come on, Kev," he murmured. "We need sleep."

Head hung low, Kevin followed him without a word. He moved like a machine programmed to crack eggs as he got out of his Grid gear, put it away neatly, and fell into bed. Aidan followed his lead. After a couple seconds of lying still in the dark, he scraped his courage together, and rolled over to cup Kevin's cheek.

"Kev? Talk to me. Please."

For a minute, he thought Kevin was going to play statue. Then the other man turned his face away from the touch, sitting up.

"I'm sorry. What I tried to do was inexcusable. Insane. I could have gotten us all killed. If you need to write me up, do your duty. I'll understand."

Aidan sat up, rubbing his hand over Kevin's back. The other man flinched at the touch, but Aidan knew better than to stop now.

"You almost did it. But you *didn't* do it. And it's going to be okay."

Kevin shook his head. "It's…not until he pays. He *has* to pay. Until he pays…" Kevin covered his face with both hands.

Aidan shifted in closer, cradling his husband as he fought his demons.

"He will pay, Kev. And things are changing. Remember tomorrow? Remember what we're doing? We're starting the farm. We're changing things."

"He killed Henrietta," Kevin choked out. "He took Jim away from us. He killed our friends. He killed Mom and Dad. And I had him in my sights, and I let him get away!" It hurt to hear the broken way those words came out.

"You held your fire," Aidan amended gently. "Because you're a decent guy. And you know that shooting somebody doesn't make it right. Changing the system, that makes it right. And that's what we're doing, Kev. I promised, remember? One day Harrington will stand in a courtroom and be made to pay for every one of the things he's done. On that day, we'll prove that we have real laws. A real system that works. A real country, one worth living in. I promised." He squeezed his guy tight. "I promise."

Kevin shook his head against Aidan's shoulder, his tears tracking down Aidan's skin. "I didn't hold my fire. You and Naomi…" He swallowed hard. "I had to be stopped."

"You needed to think for a minute. I gave you a chance to think about it before you did something you'd regret," Aidan offered gently. He pulled the sheet up, wiping Kevin's face.

"Things are changing. Remember what we're doing tomorrow. It might not fix everything. But it fixes something. And something… sometimes something *is* everything."

Kevin was quiet for a beat. Then he gave a watery little laugh. "Maybe so." Turning his head, he nuzzled into Aidan's neck.

"Thanks."

Aidan kissed his brow. "Sure."

They sat like that for who knew how long. Slowly, Kevin's breathing evened out. Moving carefully, Aidan lay down with his husband in his arms, holding him as he closed his eyes.

Tomorrow. Tomorrow would be better.

It had to be.

Waking up in the morning wasn't easy, and heading outside was harder. The sunlight hit like a hammer, searing Aidan's eyeballs even behind the sunglasses and Duster-issue sun hat. Damn, he needed more sleep.

But he could catch up later. Right now, he had a ton of people standing in front of him. He had to get them to work together.

Aidan stared out at the mixed crowd of almost a hundred Fringers, Grid refugees, and his own crew. The Wildcards were giving him puzzled looks, shifting their footing and glancing at each other. They'd been told to expect a bunch of strangers, but not why, and a lot of them were looking nervy. Well, everyone except Yvonne and Sarah, who were grinning like a pair of maniacs. Yvonne was literally bouncing in place. At least she hadn't spilled the beans ahead of time. The rest of his crew hadn't found out a thing beyond the fact that they were getting a lot of company, and now they were looking at him with 'what the hell?' written all over them.

He was starting a farm today. A farm. A haven. A place for all these waiting people to be.

*Holy shit.*

A rustle fluttered through the people assembled in front of him, and Aidan snapped himself out of it.

"Um…" He swallowed. Kevin's hand squeezed his. He drew a breath.

"Okay. Everyone, it's good to see you here. It doesn't look like much yet, but I want to welcome you to Four Aces Farm."

Among his crew, jaws dropped open.

Aidan cleared his throat. "Our chain of command has approved the creation of a sedentary supply and coordination hub at this site. Basically, it's going to be a farm. Our main goal is to feed and provide for the communities of the Fringe in this Sector, as well as providing a place where Fringers, Dusters, and Grid citizens can freely interact and exchange ideas. I will act as the custodian and military advisor. The

Wildcards—Unit 1407— will provide defense and supplies. We'll be governed by consensus democracy, facilitated through weekly meetings and the Common Ground app." He scuffed a boot through the dirt. "Below us, there's an aquifer that can support a farm for the next hundred years. But that's our backup, not our main source of water. Specialist Danvers?"

Janice stepped out of the crowd, Jillian and Topher carrying their newest take on the water condenser behind her. It was a lot nicer than the first try Janice had walked him through; a clean white column on stilts with wing-like projections on either side, making the whole thing look like a weird butterfly.

"'Lo," Janice offered easily, patting her contraption on the lid. "This's a personal water condenser. Stick it in the sun, it'll make about fifteen gallons of water a day. We're gonna be makin' big ones that'll produce a hundred'n fifty gallons each. An' these dew-catchers on the sides add another ten gallons or so overnight, if'n you keep 'em outdoors where they can get some early morning condensation."

Amazed murmurs ran through the crowd. Janice spread her hands in something halfway between a shrug and a showman's razzle-dazzle.

"You'll need some specifics, but if you got a decent printer, you can make these yourselves outta chitin an' agar-plastic real easy. I'm gonna be passin' the schematics along. You can test 'em yourselves. Shoot me a note if you find anything you ain't likin', or if'n you find any way to make 'em work better. With these, we got enough water to irrigate 'round here."

"What about the drones?" somebody called.

"We've got a number of IR emitters that will incapacitate any drone within a mile," Kevin offered smoothly. "Our Technical officer and myself—Logistics officer, at your service—will see to the drones"

Aidan shot his husband a grin. Kevin mirrored it, eyes dancing.

"So, everyone here today has a job to do," Aidan continued. "Today, we're going to be receiving a couple of building printers that we'll use to put together buildings for this sedentary base. I'd like you to work with our senior engineers—that's Specialist Short here, and Specialist Danvers—to stake out sites for the water condensers, new storage tanks, and new buildings. Specialist Danvers has a map. If anything comes up, Officer Carlan here will give you a hand with all personnel issues. If you need anything—toothbrush, clothes, anything—come talk to Officer McIllian-Headly here. Officer DuCoss would really appreciate help on the orientation and siting of the new garden plots, and clearing brush. Any of the Wildcards can and will help you find supplies or tools if you need them. There's a water station set up over there, and hats and chill vests on the rack by the side door."

For a moment, the crowd stood frozen. Aidan swallowed. *Shit, where do I go from a bombshell like that?*

"First thing first, I need at least thirty people helping us set up slick tarps!" Kevin called out. "We don't need satellites ruining our day!" He pointed into the crowd with a smile. "You folks there, and you over here, anyone who isn't sure they've got specific skills, you can help Officer Lung, Specialist Amanzi and myself to set posts and string slick-tarps around this property"

"I need fifteen people over here with me!" Janice called into the crowd.

"I need thirty over here," Milo added a beat later, bass drawl pouring out into the hot air. "Grab shovels and let's make gardens."

"If you wanna learn plumbing and building, I need about twenty folks over here," Dozer added in his gravelly rumble.

"And I'll need a crew of at least twenty people to help bring water to workers and hand out supplies," Liza interjected, voice sharp on the air. "Anyone who's ever worked in a kitchen, Specialist Jeffries, Specialist Coson and I can use your help." At her side, Deliquisha beamed from ear to ear. Billie managed a little wave.

With a quick grin for his team, Aidan clapped his hands. "After we finish, big meal tonight. Heat index is okay today, so let's get some work done."

And holy shit, did they get work done. It got loud and a little crazy while people divvied themselves into groups to do work they wanted to do, but they made it happen. For the next eight hours, everyone was doing something: setting and monitoring building printers, lifting walls, hacking down kochia and clearing cholla from the places that would be planting beds. Everywhere people were doing something, making something. Tweak's team set beams and strung gigantic slick tarps, as much for sun protection as anything else. Printers churned away on all sides, and people talked everywhere.

It felt like everybody in the crew stopped him to exchange a hug, to babble their excitement, or to smack his arm and gripe about being left out of the loop. Yvonne's groan of, "Dude, so not cool! That was just un*fair*!" summed up the reactions pretty well.

As the day wound down, Billie and a bunch of people who'd been helping out with the refreshments set the canteen tables outside and piled them with so much food that their legs wobbled. Once that was ready, Aidan walked to the center of the space.

"Okay, everybody," Aidan called, cupping his hands around his mouth to get his voice across the area. "Pack up the tools, we're calling it for the day!"

"Party time!" Yvonne whooped, and that set all of them off cheering. Aidan had to laugh.

Dozer, Topher and Cameron started a bonfire at the center of the half-built compound as the workers put their tools away. Liza broke the newcomers into groups and gave them numbers to schedule hygiene room time. Everyone filled plates, spread out bedrolls, and plunked down. Bottles came out from who knew where, and somebody pulled a media set out and started some music going.

In the flickering light and the last shreds of sun, Aidan glanced around for his husband. Kevin would be over the moon, seeing this whole thing come together. Aidan wanted to share that with him.

He spotted Kevin joshing with Yvonne and Sarah as they shared a bottle. Sarah punched him in the arm as he came up.

“You!”

“Ow,” he grumbled, rubbing the spot. “You already hit me there once.”

“And I’ll do it again, you fink!” Sarah laughed, fitting words to actions. “You made us keep quiet fooooorever! *So* not cool!”

“Worth it though?” Aidan asked, smiling as he took the bottle and Kevin’s free hand.

“Very much worth it, my love,” Kevin agreed, bending his head to kiss Aidan with the taste of whiskey on his lips. He was so different now, out here under the sky. It could make you forget how broken he’d been a few hours before.

“Not bad, hunh?” Aidan asked as he looked over the crowd of Dusters, Fringers, and Grid refugees starting conversations.

Kevin smiled fondly. Dipping his head, he brushed his lips over Aidan’s again. “Not bad.” He took the bottle back from Aidan, sipping. “Let’s find some dinner and a seat, love.”

The heat had let up, and the night wind cooled the air into a sweetness on the skin. Over by the media center, people had started to dance. Everywhere he looked, Aidan saw people laughing. People smiling. Shaking hands.

Leaning back against his husband, he sat and stared. “Wow…”

“Indeed,” Kevin agreed, leaning his chin on the top of Aidan’s head. He chuckled. “Seven years. I can hardly believe it. We’ve been talking about this for ages, and now it’s real.” Leaning down, he kissed Aidan’s cheek. “All because of you, my love.”

Aidan had to laugh at that. “My ass. This is all of us. Not just me.”

Kevin chuckled, stroking his hair. “Ah, you. Only a life lived for others is a life worth living, hmm?”

“Who said that?” Aidan asked, curling into the sinewy warmth of his arms. He rested his head against Kevin’s chest, listening to his heartbeat.

“Einstein, if I’m right,” Kevin replied.

Aidan nodded. "Right. The guy who figured out quantum computers? The guy with the hair?"

Kevin's quiet chuckle wrapped around him. "Close enough for tonight, love. Here, help me finish this bottle and I'll go get us another. Tweak helped me out and we landed a crate of them."

"Nice," Aidan agreed. He glanced around. "Where is Tweak anyway?"

"I'm not really sure," Kevin murmured. "Inyoni asked me to keep an eye out for her in passing; she seems to have wandered off." He took a thoughtful swig. "This might be too many people for her. Our dear Dragon's still a tiny bit reticent, you know."

Aidan's brow furrowed. "Hunh…maybe I should go check on her?" He started to stand, but his husband gently pulled him down.

"Ah. *I'll* go check on her. *You* stay here and enjoy the celebration for once. You've earned it, Commander." With a quick peck on Aidan's temple, he was sauntering off.

Aidan started to stand again, but that was when the kids found him. Delquisha and Don landed on him in a tandem hug, chanting 'we're gonna have a farm, we're gonna have a farm!' and Abigail was right behind them, talking a mile a minute and pulling Tom along by the hand. Aidan had to laugh.

## Chapter 21
## File Tag: Advisory Capacity
## 21:20-08-29-2161

Stepping out of the circle of firelight, Kevin glanced over his shoulder. He had to smile at the sight of the kids overwhelming his poor man.

He headed around the side of the building, watching the shadows for Tweak's silhouette. The girl often chose a quiet corner to watch from. Once he'd spotted her and taken stock of her state of mind, he'd know where to go from there. If he was in luck, she'd simply be in a mood to wallflower, and he could tip his hat to her and pass on by.

But then his luck hadn't been the best of late, had it?

In the shreds of firelight, he did spot a silhouette, but it certainly wasn't Tweak's. Only one person had limbs and ears that long.

"Evening," he offered, leaning against the wall Inyoni had slouched down.

Inyoni took a sip from the bottle in his hand. "Lo." The syllable had the fuzz of inebriation to it.

Drinking in the dark, sporting a pair of ears like a kicked dog. Yes, that was relationship trouble if Kevin had ever seen it. Those ears were like sign posts. If only everyone had such tells.

"Having fun?" Kevin asked quietly. That got him a snort. He looked back at the party rather than discomforting Inyoni with staring eyes.

"How's Tweak?" He asked quietly. "And as an addendum, have you got a drop of that to spare?"

"Have it," Inyoni grumbled blearily, passing him the bottle. "Thought it'd help. Didn't."

"I know the feeling," Kevin agreed. "Alcohol usually helps a bad mood get worse, if anything." He took a nip from the bottle. "Is Tweak the reason you're in the mood to drink?"

"And sleep on a cot," Inyoni sighed. Kevin raised a brow at that. "Was that her choice or yours?"

"Mine, I guess," Inyoni shrugged. "Figured she doesn't want to see me."

"Want to talk about it?"

Inyoni stared at the dust between his feet.

"I don't know, man. She…shit, I don't know if I can be a dad."

"It's quite a prospect," Kevin observed quietly. "Have you decided to have it, then?"

Inyoni flinched like a kicked dog. "Dunno if I get to say shit about it."

"Is that what you argued about?" Kevin probed gently. Inyoni wrapped his arms around himself, tattoos gleaming in the dusty night. It took time for him to speak again.

"Damian says the kid's gonna have my ears. I said we gotta fix that. Tweak said if we touched the DNA, the kid could die. And then…" He groaned, tugging on his ears with both hands. "And then it all went to shit and there was her yelling and me yelling, and I fucking *hate* yelling, and…and then I needed out."

"Some days are like that," Kevin commiserated gently. "I remember a few times Aidan slammed a door on me. And vice versa."

Inyoni shook his head. "I don't know, man. I just… I don't know."

"You don't have to decide tonight," Kevin reminded. "Especially not with this much of a bottle in you. Maybe you should go to bed?"

Inyoni looked up at him dully, He nodded, ears flopped askew. “Guess so. Yeah.” He straightened—or tried to—and almost toppled over.

“Steady,” Kevin chuckled, grabbing the boy’s arm. “Here, lean on me.”

Getting the younger man into the rec room and onto his cot took some work, but Kevin knew about leverage and getting drunk men into beds. Once he was sure the boy was settled in for the night, Kevin left him to sleep it off. He had a dragon to beard. If he was right, she’d be in her den.

He found Tweak where he’d expected; curled in her rig chair, going over raw command code.

“Anything interesting?” He asked, taking a nip from the bottle he’d brought along. When she looked his way, he held it up. “Celebratory drink?”

That would tell him a bit about where she was mentally.

For a moment, she stared at him. Then she shook her head. “C-can’t. B-baby.”

Ah. So she was thinking in terms of a baby, not a situation. Well, that was a definite clue. Now he knew how to calibrate his approach.

"You and your bird got into it, I hear?" Kevin asked quietly, pulling up Tweak's spare office chair and folding into it. "Funnily enough, ‘bird’ used to be a term for a lovely lady."

"Since when?" Tweak snorted.

"Oh, the mid twentieth century," Kevin rejoined easily, sipping at the bottle. "So, are you two alright?" Between their two opinions, he’d get something approximating the truth.

Tweak didn't reply for a long moment. "None of your b-business," she snapped eventually, eyes riveted on her phosphorescent windows.

"As your fellow officer and your beau's training officer, I can't agree with you there." Kevin replied as he watched her. "Personally, I'd like to be advised in case a lover's spat is leaving my subordinate prone to distraction. Best way to avoid another bullet wound, in either one of us."

"B-Bird won't get you s-shot. You j-jackass," Tweak grumbled half-heartedly, tapping a few keys.

"Watch who you call jackass," Kevin replied with good humor he didn't feel. "From where I'm sitting, your boyfriend looks like a fairly big jackass too."

That got him only a snort.

"Let me guess," he offered. "Inyoni told you he didn't want his child to suffer as he has."

Tweak shrugged, saying nothing.

"I'll interpret that as a yes, then. And you're afraid of doing more damage by tampering with the DNA. You don't want the child going through the hell you have, either." He sighed, studying the bottle in his hand. "And you and your man talked right past one another, given that you both have the emotional intelligence of a brick. Does that sum up the situation?"

This time, Tweak shifted uncomfortably and gave him an actual answer. "I l-listened…just…don't think he's r-right."

"No, I imagine you didn't listen," Kevin murmured. "And neither did he. You both said what you thought."

"Fuck you."

"You don't have the equipment," Kevin replied easily.

Tweak snorted. "Gross."

Then she was silent.

Kevin said nothing for a moment. If he misstepped even slightly, this situation would go off like a landmine in his face. But if he was careful, if he chose the right angle…

Putting on just a bit of a wince for show, he stretched.

"Let's go get some coffee and continue this chat in the canteen, shall we? This Lilliputian chair is going to distort my spine out of all hope of salvation if I sit in it any longer."

Tweak rolled her eyes. "Wimp."

"I have a keen sense of the finer things in life," he retorted with a smile. "Including that coffee and chocolate you and Billie have been making. Come on; midnight snacks and a chat."

Tweak clucked her tongue, but she did shut her rig down.

He kept an eye on her as they walked down the hall. Usually Tweak moved with all the focused precision of a guided missile. Tonight she had her arms crossed, every element of her body language turned inward.

He let the silence rest easy between them, balancing it like a man building a castle of cards.

"Dark or light roast?" he asked as he switched the canteen lights on.

"My b-blend," Tweak answered as he headed into the serving area. "Has a d-dragon on it."

"Of course it does," Kevin laughed. Finding the bag on the coffee shelf, he opened it, measured out the beans and ground them as the water heated, savoring the aroma. One of the finer things of life indeed.

And then there was coffee between them, and the silence, and nothing to do but sit.

"We need music on a night like this," Kevin suggested, putting his tab between them and switching on his player. "Not rock and roll, cross my heart," he added, hearing Tweak draw in a breath to speak.

"B-better not be," his companion grumbled. He let the comment pass.

The music twined softly into the room. "This alright?" He asked. Tweak shrugged. "Eh."

"The folks from Coomb Olwen gave me this. Quite a rare vintage track. Appalachia Rising, the band was called. Nice, isn't it?"

Tweak shrugged. "Guess so."

She said nothing else, staring into her brew.

*Well, fingers crossed,* he told himself. *No time like the present.*

"Ever heard of population adaptability dynamic?" He threw out as lightly as he could.

"What?" Tweak asked, glancing his way irritably.

"It's one of the dynamic laws of evolution," Kevin offered as he sipped his brew. "Read about that?"

Tweak shrugged. "Nope."

"In a nutshell," he continued carefully, "It means that a species without a sufficient breadth of variability is dead in the water. That variability is the key to preventing any one thing from wiping the organism out. You following me on this?"

Tweak actually glanced at him this time, which was a step in the right direction. Slowly, she nodded.

"Our world isn't what it was." Kevin rolled his coffee mug between his palms as he spoke. "It's hotter, drier, less productive and less salubrious. That's already killed a lot of people, and it's going to kill more." He watched his fingers move as he chose his words. "But some people can thrive in these conditions. People like you and Inyoni. Your more obvious traits are called 'phenotypic offsets' in medicine. It's a way of saying side-effects. Also a way of saying they don't matter. What matters is that we get the traits we need into the gene pool." He glanced back up, and smiled self-deprecatingly. "What I'm trying to say and rather mangling is this: perhaps the traits you hate so much aren't actually the problem. Maybe they're something our species *needs*."

Now Tweak actually raised her head. She stared at him for an impressively long time as folk guitar played. Finally, she gave an irritable little snort.

"What good're b-big ears? What good're s-s-scales and s-s-stutters and three fingers? M-makes it harder to s-survive."

"Given the state of our society, that's true today," Kevin acknowledged. "But tomorrow may be different. A current society's reactions to differences are beside the point. What I'm talking about is the gene pool." He waved his free hand, trying to capture what he believed in words she could understand. "Look at it like this. What good is sickle cell anemia? It seems a genetic dead end at first glance. But look a little deeper, and you see it for what it is." He leaned forward, resting his elbows on the table as he spoke. “Those who have a single copy of the gene are immune to the depredations of malaria. And that trait saved the population in places riddled with the disease.”

Tweak tapped her fingers on the table. “L-like c-c-code s-snippets.”

“In what way?” Kevin asked, glad to see her engaging in the discussion.

Tweak shrugged. “Code doesn’t do a lot one p-p-place, you save it. Might do s-something better s-somewhere else. Later.”

“Exactly,” Kevin agreed, nodding. “In the same vein, consider what your DNA did for us during the MACHA attack." He shrugged, smiling half-heartedly. "In another time and place, that trait you dislike may be the reason your descendents thrive."

"Makes us freaks," Tweak sighed, staring at her fingers as they ran up and down her scaled arm.

Kevin's jaw set. "Sorry to tell you this, my friend, but your child’s already going to be a ‘freak’ if you have it here. It's going to be a Duster.”

"D-dusters aren’t f-f-freaks," Tweak grumbled. "Not like g-g-Gammas."

The comment was as good as a slap. Kevin felt the irritation ricochet through his system. "Really. Really? Have you actually looked around this base?" He asked, tasting ice on his tongue. "You think you're the only one here who’s been labeled a ‘freak’? You know better than that, Tweak."

"Fair. C-c-corps hate everyone," Tweak agreed quietly.

Kevin took a deep breath, steadying himself. Tweak didn’t deserve such a reaction for an off-color crack made in the midst of her own pain. Given how he’d acted the last time he’d lost his temper, he owed it to her—and everyone else—to keep his anger on a tight leash. Breathing slow, he watched her. She lifted her coffee cup with exaggerated care, sipping at it like a bird at a stream.

"P-p-people are more choosy about it. Who they h-hate." The words were little more than a whisper, but Kevin heard the pain in them.

Reaching over, Kevin rested his hand beside hers on the table. "Is that what you're afraid of, Tweak? Of people hating your child?"

Tweak closed her eyes. One small hand rose to massage her throat. The muscles tightened in a few convulsive gulps.

"Here," Kevin offered, holding out his tab. "I was just using it, it's unlocked. Note-taking app's in the upper right-hand corner."

Tweak took his tab with a weak smile, brought up the window and typed.

> "I don't know what this kid's genes are going to be like. My little brother. He was born with two stomachs. His guts were all twisted up. I tried, and Mom tried, and nothing we did could help him. Mom found this gene splicer who said he'd fix Bao Li. But when the work was done, he"

Her fingers froze on the tab. She stared at her hands, shaking her head.

Kevin wished he knew the words that could comfort her. But he knew better than to interrupt her train of thought. Quietly, he sat back and listened to one of Gordon Lightfoot's tunes segue into one of S.J. Tucker's pieces of down-to-earth poignancy.

Finally, Tweak's fingers moved again.

> "After they messed with his DNA, Bao got even more sick. The guy said if we could pay for better, he could live. I sold stuff to get the money together. You know about that. That's what got me thrown in jail."

Her little hands shook as she typed.

> "My little brother died because I couldn't do good enough. If we do nothing the baby could die, and if we do anything we could make it worse, and..."

The cursor blipped as Tweak froze. Slowly, she typed.

> "It's all going to happen again, and I'm so scared I can't do good enough this time either and this baby will die too. It'll die because

I'm not good enough. I don't think I'm good enough to keep it from getting killed. If I can't keep it from dying, I shouldn't have it at all."

Carefully, Kevin nodded.

"That's a substantial weight to carry on your conscience." He knew better than to tell her what had happened to her family wasn't her fault. He'd tried that once, years ago. She'd scoffed at him. Having known her and Aidan both for some years now, Kevin had learned his lesson; he wasn't here to reason those he cared about out of their emotions. He was here to listen while they talked it out.

Tweak coughed out a laugh like a shard of glass. "No shit."

Kevin stared down into the dark mirror of his drink. Which path through this minefield wouldn't explode in his face…

*Too much silence is as dangerous as the wrong word here…*

*God and all your Hosts, help me get this right…*

"You're incredibly strong, you know. To have carried on with all that weight inside you," he offered softly.

Tweak rolled her eyes as she set his tab on the table. "Like I got a c-choice."

"But you did, Tweak," he corrected gently. He nodded at the tab between them. "Just like the song says."

"Your music, not mine." Tweak grumped. Kevin cocked a brow.

Tweak sighed. "Tell me what it s-says. You're gonna anyway."

Kevin paused the track, skipped back thirty seconds, and sang along with S.J. Tucker's sweet words.

*"But is this not the life we choose?*

*To be in so deep, so broken hearted,*

*and so bravely sing these blues?"*

"You are such a dweeb," Tweak muttered at her cup, but at least his performance had made her smile a bit.

"Guilty as charged," he agreed, "But that doesn't negate my point. You were brave to carry on when you could have given up. You chose that in spite of everything. And you can choose now. If you don't want to bear a child, I can more than understand that. It's exhausting and gut-churning just to think of caring for a child out here." He sipped at his smooth brew, enjoying the taste and pacing himself. "I'll never know how Andrea and Jim pulled it off with such equanimity," he continued conversationally.

"Jillian and Cameron too, for that matter. If you don't want that stress on your shoulders, we can certainly get you out of the predicament. No trouble at all. Just say the word." He drew a steadying breath. "But if you're saying you *do* want a child, and you don't think you *can* have it? If you're hesitating because you fear what could go wrong genetically…well. We can fix that too." Kevin caught Tweak's eye, smiling carefully. "If I can help, I'd like to."

Tweak looked up at him, blinking for a few beats. "How?" she asked.

Kevin laid one hand on the table, palm up. "Use my blood, if you like. My genetic code has only the tiniest set of deviations from the medical standard, and Damian knows exactly where each aberration is. It's nearly the best DNA that Cavanaugh provides. And since we've got the same copyright on our DNA, the codes will be compatible. Damian can use my code as a clean template for editing your child's genome."

Tweak looked away. "C-cavanaugh code," she spat the words like a curse.

Kevin gave a humorless laugh. "Don't remind me. Cavanaugh put its fingerprints on both of us. It gave me unfair advantages and expectations, and it gave you unfair handicaps. It was wrong, and it was cruel." He glanced down into his drink. "But if we can use what they've done to me to heal what they've done to you…maybe we can make some of it right, here and now."

Tweak closed her eyes, her shoulders hunching. For a few moments, she breathed hard. Then she put out a hand and typed.

> "If we do that to a kid who doesn't get a choice, hack a person with no say, how are we any better than them?"

"Because what you choose to do is in love and in protection, Tweak," Kevin stated quietly. "It's not done in pursuit of profit or control. We aren't going to make this child fit anyone else's standards when we edit their genome. Not yours, or mine, or even Inyoni's. What we're going to do is make sure that the child is healthy and able to enjoy life; that's all, my word on the Good Book. Damian wouldn't countenance anything else anyway. We're using Cavanaugh's tools, yes. They're the only tools we have, for now. But when we use the tools they made in greed and systemic callousness to subvert the systems they've created, when we use those tools in compassion, equality and solidarity to make just one life better? Perhaps we cleanse the tools just a little of the sin that stains them when we do that. We take something made in evil, and use it to do good."

He toasted her. "What happened to you and your family. To your brother. It was terrible. But please don't forget: you're not working with a cut-rate splicer and whatever you can scrape together now. You'll be working with Damian, and me, and the Wildcards. Competent people who care about you, and Inyoni, and this baby. And if I can be excused saying something selfish at a time like this, I'll mention that you'd be doing me a favor too if you chose to use my DNA."

Tweak's head canted to one side. "How?"

Kevin shrugged. "Aidan and I won't have children. If my blood were to be carried into the next generation by your child? That would be the best thing I could imagine imparting to the future. From a genetic standpoint, passing your genes to the next generation is how you win the game."

Tweak snorted. "What, your perfect CES genes in a half-black Gamma freak?" She snapped, hiding behind her battered shield of vitriol.

He kept his smile, looking through the words to the scared woman. He knew all about lashing out when emotions got the better of you. Didn't he just.

"My genes, carried in the beautiful child of my friends," he offered as gently as he could. "Nothing in my life could equal that."

Tweak stared at him for entirely too long, her chest moving in hummingbird gasps.

If the landmine was going to go off, it would be now.

He sat still, and he smiled, and he waited.

Slowly, her breathing eased. She closed her eyes. Took a swig of her brew.

"Kev?"

"Yes?"

"Thanks."

Kevin's gut unknotted. Standing, he drained his mug.

"Anything for a friend. Think about it and let me know. Night."

For just a moment, he smiled down at her. Then he took his leave. He'd done what he could. The rest was up to her.

## Event File 22
## File Tag: Advisory Signal
## 22:00-08-29-2161

In the empty canteen, Tweak stared into her coffee, and listened to her own breathing.

She could hear her heartbeat in her ears.

Heartbeat.

The baby had a heartbeat now.

Bao Li's heartbeat had been so fast. They'd shared a bed as kids. She'd fallen asleep listening to his heartbeat. She'd missed that so much, later.

She fell asleep to Inyoni's heartbeat now. And that was good.

Would it still be good if there were two heartbeats in the dark? Could it be good, with three of them?

Could they do this parent thing, and not completely fuck it up?

"Hey, Tweak…you okay?"

Tweak's muscles twanged. She whipped around, and there was Billie watching her. The taller woman stepped into the canteen.

"You okay?" Billie asked softly.

Arms across her chest, Tweak leaned against a table with a shrug. "Fractal. Every time."

Billie gave her a patient look, waiting for more explanation.

Tweak sighed. "Inside every question, more questions. Get it?"

Billie nodded thoughtfully. "So…take it that means 'not okay.' What can I do?"

Tweak glanced up, then managed a smile for the person who knew her best. "You're doing it. Thanks, Billie. Lots. I'm just....freaked."

“About the baby thing?” Billie asked, taking a seat beside her.

“Yeah,” Tweak sighed. “Whole thing. A mess.”

"I know," Billie agreed with a weak smile. "Wish I could do more. I mean…something more…solid, you know?"

Tweak shrugged, hands wide spread. "What to do? Allyar Yaktar Est. Just is."

"Did you just speak another language?" Billie asked with an incredulous laugh. "Damn, girl, you gotta get out more. You been around Kevin too much."

Tweak grinned. "Fancy. Means shit happens, deal. In Latin. Cool, hunh?"

Billie laughed again and shook her head. "Yep. 'Round Kevin waaaay too much."

"Somebody's gotta tell him where to g-go and w-watch his ass when him and b-Bird run stuff." Tweak replied, trying for a smile. But she couldn't work up to eye contact. “What you doing up?”

“Party's still going, I came down to get more snacks,” Billie explained, tipping her head towards the pantry.

Tweak nodded. Party. The new farm was worth partying about, no question. But she had absolutely zero chill right now. No way was she going up to hang with strangers.

Besides, Inyoni would be there. He'd still be mad at her. What was she even going to say to him?

“You look bummed,” Billie observed gently.

Tweak glanced up at her, trying for a smile. "I am. B? Talk?"

Billie nodded. "Gotcha. What's it?"

Tweak stared at her boots, massaging her throat. "This baby thing? Don't know. Can't d-decide. Help?"

Billie nodded slowly, biting her lip. Finally, she glanced up, and gave Tweak a tiny smile. "I think I got an idea. I'm gonna run the snacks up and be back, kay?"

Swallowing hard, Tweak nodded.

For a few minutes, Billie messed around in the pantry and cupboards behind the big serving table. Then there was just the sound of her footsteps fading away, and Tweak's heartbeat again, and her thoughts.

*What can I say to Inyoni to make this right?*

*What can I say to a kid who hates their life later, if I fuck up now?*

*What am I going to do?*

It was a relief when she heard Billie's footsteps again. But that sound was doubled, and more.

Not just Billie. Fuck.

She jumped to her feet, facing the door. And in came Billie, and Alice, and Jillian with little Jenny in her arms.

"Let's get more coffee and sit down," Billie suggested.

"What the—" Tweak started, but Billie raised her hands. "I know, I know. Let me brew, Tweak. Chill."

Billie headed into her kitchen. Tweak took her seat again, and her basemates joined her at the table. Jillian shifted Jenny in her arms, smiling awkwardly when Tweak glanced her way. "She's having a fussy night. Won't sleep unless I'm holding her."

Tweak glanced back down at her hands, nodding. "Noise?"

"Maybe it's the party noise keeping her up," Jillian agreed ruefully, "or maybe it's just her. She does this on and off, sticks to me like glue."

"Bet you'll be glad to wean her next month," Alice observed with a gentle elbow bump. Jillian let out the biggest sigh on the planet.

"Will I ever, she's getting *so heavy*!"

The coffee frothed into the cups as Bille poured. "I mixed this with a little of the cacao husk and some other things," Billie murmured in her softly competent voice. "Give it a taste-test for me." She set a plate of her signature chocolates down beside it.

"So," Alice began, taking a chocolate, "You're working on making a decision? Want to talk about it?"

"With you? Why?" Tweak demanded. She spared a glare for Billie. Her friend dropped her eyes.

"I can't talk to this, Tweak," Billie explained to her coffee cup. "I can't tell you anything. But Alice and Jillian can. They can help you make decisions here."

"We can tell you what we decided, anyway," Jillian corrected. "We made two different decisions. We figured you can see how it went for us both, and that'll help you make your decisions."

Tweak groaned, laying her head in her arms "Wish this shit was just d-d-done! Too many d-d-decisions. Every d-decision, fractals!"

"Sounds familiar," Alice murmured. "I was there when I was deciding about my abortion."

Tweak blinked at her hands. Carefully, she looked up. "You?"

Alice nodded. "Me."

"Can I ask things?" Tweak murmured.

Alice smiled. "Sure honey."

"How come?" Tweak asked, staring at this fucking amazeballs medical specialist. What would make somebody as on it as her think she couldn't be a mom?

Alice shrugged. "How come I got an abortion? I was nineteen and raising four brothers and sisters. My boyfriend's birth control was cut-rate, and it didn't take. I was too broke to be on anything, so…" She shrugged. "Yeah. I was just lucky I was NatBank-contracted back then; they allow the procedure in their Corporate Contract. Otherwise…" She sucked air between her teeth.

"Was it b-bad?" Tweak asked, nearly choking on the words.

Alice shrugged. "Going to the doctor and getting talked to like I was something defective, yeah, that was hard. The procedure? It was two pills, and that was that."

"You feel b-bad?" Tweak asked. "S-sad?"

"Not wrong. And not bad," Alice replied. "It was sad, a little bit. Sometimes when I see our kids at the table here on base, I think my little kid could be there too." She shook her head. "And the guy dumping me the moment he found out, that was…that was hard. That was really hard." She blinked, raising her head to smile at Tweak. "But no. It wasn't bad getting it done. And it wasn't a bad choice. If I'd had the kid, I probably wouldn't be here talking to you today." She held Tweak's eyes. "It can be the right thing and still be sad."

Tweak nodded. "S-sorry."

"Nothing to be sorry for," Alice reassured. "I told you that you could ask questions; that's what I'm here for. I did what was right for me. It was sad. And it was hard. And I'm glad I did it."

Tweak nodded, thinking it over. It made sense.

She looked over at Jillian, who was nursing Jenny. "You?"

"You mean, why'd I have Jen?" Jillian asked. Tweak nodded.

Jillian stared down at her daughter, her yellow eyes soft.

"A lot of things, I guess," she began quietly. "For one thing, I knew the hoops to get medwork officially would suck jumping through. They'd ask who the dad was, and Cameron wasn't contracted. They'd want to screen me, and that'd be bad too. So… there was that."

She smoothed baby Jen's soft white fuzz back. "And…well, they keep telling us we're not supposed to exist. Keep saying they don't want us Gammas. When I found out…something sat up in me and screamed 'I want you to exist, I do!' Sort of, screw the rest of the world, *I want you to exist*. I guess that was it." She shifted her arms under her baby gently. "And there was this other thing. Cam and me talked about it. Having Jen meant having a tomorrow. Meant believing there was gonna be a tomorrow worth getting to. We didn't always believe that, some days. A baby meant that. Meant we were telling the whole world, like, 'we're here, and we're not going away, and we've got a future. So there.'

"Future?" Tweak asked, watching Jen nurse contentedly.

"Yeah," Jillian agreed. "A future. This kid is here, and she's going to have a future. And that means…I guess that means I am too."

"On the worst days," Alice added quietly, "When I was so damn tired that I thought I'd fall over at my keyboard and die from it, that's what kept me going. Knowing my little sibs were there, and they needed to make it into better days. Whether I did or not, I wanted them to make it." She sipped her coffee. "That's what kids are, basically. They're the future in a little package. Tomorrow on two legs."

"What if t-t-tomorrow's m-messed up?" Tweak barely got the words out.

Alice glanced at Jillian.

Jillian shrugged. "What if it isn't?"

That hit Tweak. She stared at her coffee. "That's the p-problem. Don't know."

"None of us do," Jillian murmured. "All we got is us. All we got is what we think. And I guess…I guess I thought 'maybe it can work'. And 'maybe we get tomorrow'...maybe that's enough for today."

Tweak studied Jillian's bowed head, watching her smile down at her child.

Mom and Bao Li used to look at each other like that.

Kevin's words ran through her head again, mixing into Jillian's and Alice's like milk in tea.

*From a genetic standpoint, passing your genes to the next generation is how you win the game.*

*Tomorrow on two legs.*

*We were telling the whole world, 'we're here, and we're not going away, and we've got a future.'*

In all of it, she could almost remember the sound of her dad, whispering… something in Chinese.

What had it been?

Something about Tweak having kids, and not being alone.

What was it?

Tweak stirred her coffee with a finger as the words spun round in her head. Finally, she glanced up. "Billie? If it was you. What'd you do?"

Billie hesitated, mulling the question over. Finally, she let out a long breath. "Honestly, Tweak? 'Less there's something wrong with the vitals, I say let it come. You and Inyoni turned out okay, and the baby's gonna be here on the base, with folk who don't care what you guys look like. But…your choice."

"Turned. Out. Okay?" Tweak snorted. "Billie, Imma freak. You. Know. That."

Billie gave her a dry look. "Tweak, you're here. You got a man who loves you and friends and the most wicked-fast brain I've ever seen. You got issues, sure, but everyone does. You're not one of them Gammas that's got real wiring problems—the ones that hit the newsfeeds now and then 'cause they decided to shoot up the city for no reason."

Tweak stared at her mug. "We're not. But the kid...."

"Damian got a test for that kind of crazy?" Billie asked gently. "'Cause from where I'm standing, he was just talkin' about the looks."

Tweak shrugged. "Says he's got it handled."

"We do," Alice agreed. "Once you give the okay and we find a clean genetic template we can use, we can handle anything."

Tweak glanced at her. "But if he's wrong..."

"If he's wrong, you ain't gonna know till the kid goes crazy, anyway," Billie cut in. She reached out and placed her hand beside Tweak's.

Tweak winced at the words. "What I'm s-scared of." she muttered.

Billie bit her lip, glancing between Alice and Jillian.

After a moment, Jillian leaned in. "You gotta take a risk one way or another, Tweak."

Tweak swallowed. "Don't know. D-don't know."

"Try this," Billie suggested. "Say you don't think about the rest of it. Say you just want to ask yourself, 'is being a mom something I want'? Jillian, you said there was a little voice saying 'I want you to exist'." She leaned in. "Tweak? Lot of folks have that voice in them. Lot of folks don't. Either way, it's cool. Either way, we make it work. But you gotta say if you *want* a kid." Her lips quirked up in a tiny, sad smile. "So…so yeah. Is that voice saying 'I want this', or not?"

Tweak swallowed. She closed her eyes. Ignored everything else. Tried to hear herself thinking.

Slowly, she nodded.

"Is. It is."

"Okay," Billie murmured. "That's your answer. The rest is…I guess it's just checklists and fixes. Yeah?"

Tweak opened her eyes and studied her basemates' faces for a moment, and her best friend's. Then she drew herself up. Reaching over, she touched Billie's hand, just for a moment. "You're smart. Know that?"

Billie gave her a little smile. "Says the smartest girl around."

Tweak shook her head, black hair swinging. "Quick isn't smart."

"It is when you're you," Billie replied.

Tweak's smile eased into something less bleak. She nudged her shoulder into Billie's. "So...kid's gonna get called Donkey. Or Rabbit. Or some shit. Gonna have to teach her to kick some ass, hunh?"

Billie laughed. "Oh yeah."

"We'll help," Alice added.

"Jen will back them up," Jillian added with a little smile. "They'll never be alone."

"Thanks," Tweak murmured. Standing, she picked up her mug. "Wanna go. Gotta think. But yeah. Thanks. Lots."

"You got this," Billie replied quietly.

"You tell us tomorrow, kay?" Alice added. Tweak nodded. "Yeah. Will."

Turning, she headed back to her office, and closed the door. Plugging in her 'buds, she sat back, stared at her sleeping console, and let herself think.

The words ran around in her head, bouncing off the inside of her skull. With nobody to bug her and all night to herself, she just let them do their thing. Her shrink app had taught her how to let the brain run all its routines without getting pulled into any one thought. She watched the thoughts run by like lines of code, sipping at her coffee now and again.

*Children. They're tomorrow on two legs.*

*What if I screw it all up?*

*I say let it come.*

*If I get it wrong, the baby will die.*

*Maybe we can make it right, here and now.*

*I'm a mess. If I mess up, lose my temper...*

*If I hurt the kid...*

*Do I want to be a mom?*

*Yes.*

*Risk either way.*

*Either I risk this baby being born... everything that could go wrong...*

*or I risk how much it hurts to never even try. Knowing I could have been a mom and chickened out...*

*From a genetic standpoint, passing your genes to the next generation is how you win the game.*

*Can I make a kid carry this disaster that's my gene code?*

*Use my code. We're going to make sure that the baby's healthy and able to enjoy life.*

*Damian can use my code as a clean template for editing your child's genome.*

*They'll never be alone.*

In the dark, another voice rose up in her thoughts. Her mother's voice.

*Don't worry, my little Dragon Girl. See the incense sticks burning? These are for your ancestors. Even when you're very, very scared, you will never be alone. Your ancestors will always be with you, making things better. They want to see you do well, because you are how they continue. While you breathe, your ancestors are alive.*

Her father's voice was there too.

*One day, you and your children will burn joss paper and incense for us, just like we're doing for your grandparents. And you will know that we are here with you, and we are smiling for you, when you do.*

Tweak found herself on her feet. When she'd decided to stand, she didn't know. Heading down the hall, she grabbed a lighter from her room, and headed outside.

The party was winding down, just a lot of folks around the fire talking now and a whole bunch in sleeping bags laid out. Tweak picked her way between them to the raised garden beds. Gently as she could, she cracked a couple dry stems off the agastache plants they used to attract pollinators. Three stems were what she needed. On her way, she stopped at the booze table and poured three shot glasses of something that looked good. Nobody talked to her. That was something to be grateful for.

Stepping out until she could see stars, she found a spot and scuffed the dirt clean of anything flammable. Carefully, she knelt.

There were things she was supposed to say, she knew. Things she was supposed to do. She remembered her dad bowing three times and clapping. She remembered that there were important words, special things to say and do. It had been so long, though. The words were all gone. All she could remember was the flame and the rising smoke.

She did what she could. She lit the sticks of agastache, and she ducked her head three times. Clapped her hands.

"L-lung Li Mei, I'm burning this for y-you. Lung Jia Hao, I'm burning this for y-you. Lung…Lung Bao Li, I'm b-b-b-burning this for y-you." She swallowed a couple times, setting the lighter to each glass of booze. They flamed blue, contrasting with the red flicker at the tip of each agastache branch.

"Hey, Mom. Hey Dad," She whispered. "Hey Bao. I…you t-t-t-told m-me you'd always b-b-be there. If you're not…then I'm a d-d-dumbass. But if you are…" She swallowed hard. "I'm gonna b-burn this for you guys more. I'll get the j-j-j-j…the p-paper, okay?" She massaged her throat, watching the flames dance.

"And g-guess what?" She choked out a tiny laugh. "There's a b-b-baby coming. And…" She rubbed a hand over her belly. "And I'm gonna show it how to b-burn the incense too. Okay?"

The flame at the end of Bao Li's stick rose high, dancing bright orange for a beat.

Overhead, the stars wheeled on.

It was early when Tweak came around in her borrowed sleeping bag between the planting beds. She basically woke up and chucked up, glad that all she had to do was roll to get out of the path.

"Dragon? You okay?"

Tweak groaned, raising her head. Up on a stepladder beside her coffee tree, Inyoni stood with his ears stuck out all different ways.

"You fall and break branches, I kick your ass," she managed.

Inyoni's ears lifted a little. Smiling, he tossed one of the beans down at her. "I ain't gonna fall, Dragon Girl. Check me, these are ripe, yeah?"

Tweak caught it without looking, staring up at him. Then she was up and climbing the ladder steps, until she was standing face to face with her guy.

"Hi." One of her hands, gently, touched his.

"Hi," Inyoni murmured. Carefully, he turned his hand to run his thumb over her fingertips. His other hand held out a bottle. "Here. Rinse your mouth out."

"Thanks," Tweak agreed, taking it. She swished a few mouthfuls of water around, spitting it down onto her tree's roots where it would go to good use. When her mouth didn't feel like the bottom of a trash bin, she glanced up at Inyoni. He was staring at her with something she couldn't name on his face.

Tweak held up a hand. "We talk, we fight. Don't want to."

"Me, either," Inyoni muttered. He took a deep breath and let it out slow. "Come on. Everybody's still passed out. Let's go to our room."

Tweak nodded.

It felt good to have Inyoni back in bed with her. For who knew how long, she lay with her head on his chest, and just let the world float.

The words bubbled up in the silence.

"Bird?"

"Yeah?" He murmured into her hair.

"We're doing it."

Inyoni's head jerked up, "Wh-what? We are?"

Tweak met his eyes, and nodded, once. "I am. You want in, or not?"

Inyoni's ears went down. He swallowed hard. "Tweak…I…I don't think I'd make a good…I…" He drew in a breath so deep it seemed to pump his ears back up. "Okay. I'm scared, okay? But I said I'd be with you. An' I ain't goin' back on that."

Tweak nodded. "Okay. Good." Reaching out, she laid her hand over his. "Want to tell you why."

Inyoni flopped down on their bed and watched her, his ears finally perking forward. "That'd be nice."

Tweak rubbed a hand over her flat belly. "This? This means…." she trailed off, unsure of how to say what she felt. It felt as if this child was growing roots as well as a body; roots into the past and the future, connecting her and Inyoni and whatever came next. This child was a promise that there *was* a future, and a safe place in the world. How could she put all that into words that she could get past her stutter?

She circled her belly with her hands. "Means.....means we're here. And we're n-not going away. And it m-means we'll b-be here tomorrow. And it m-means we're… we're home."

Inyoni took a deep breath, and let it out slowly. "Tweak, I…I ain't ever really had a home. Or a dad. Not that I remember. I'm scared I'll fuck it up."

"Me too." Tweak agreed in a whisper. "But I think…I think it's w-worth it."

"You really wanna take the risk?" Inyoni whispered. "I mean, with the DNA? If we leave it alone?"

She snuggled against him. "Gonna use Kevin's DNA for her c-core s-systems. She'll be okay. Leave all the other stuff up to her. Tell D-Damian today. Deal?"

Inyoni sighed. "Why d'you keep calling it a 'her'? Could be a boy."

"Feels like a girl." Tweak murmured, resting her head on his shoulder. "Feels right."

"What're we gonna name her, if it is?" Inyoni asked quietly. "Somethin' Chinese? Somethin' Zulu? Wait till we know it's gonna be a girl for sure, maybe?"

Tweak nodded. "Maybe." She closed her eyes, smiling slightly. "Wanna hear something stupid?"

"What kinda stupid?" Inyoni asked.

"Name. In my head. Baby, in my head...." With a little laugh, Tweak shook her head. "Nah, skip it."

Inyoni tilted his head. "Nah. Tell me."

"Bao Li. Treasure." Tweak shrugged. "Told you. Lame."

Inyoni turned that over for a moment, then smiled. "Ain't lame. I kinda like it. Bao Li Amanzi sounds good."

"Yeah?" Tweak asked quietly. Her hands closed over his. In the quiet between them, Inyoni smiled.

"Yeah."

## Event File 23
## File Tag: Project Completion
## 11:00-11-1-2161

Time was funny stuff, Aidan thought as he straightened and heard his spine pop. Sometimes you went through nights that seemed endless. And then you started a farm, and two months ran through your fingers like sand.

And now there was a cow.

"They brought a cow?" He repeated, handing off his bag of potatoes to the folks doing harvest and joining his officers.

"They brought a cow," Milo agreed, locs swaying in the breeze.

Aidan couldn't fit it into his brain, no matter which way he turned it.

"What's it take to feed a cow?" He asked, completely out of his depth.

Milo shrugged. "Not so much that we can't make it work. I can draw up a resource sheet for you. Its manure would be good for our soil, and a little animal fat from the milk wouldn't be terrible in our diet. If nothing else, we can have burgers later."

"So do we let them in?" Dozer asked. He'd ended up as unofficial gate guard in the last couple months, given that he was always on the lookout for vehicles in transit around their base. It was more of a ceremonial job than anything, but Aidan was happy to see the guy doing something that was more about accepting respectful nods and smiles than breaking his back. Dozer had earned a spot like that.

Aidan ran a hand over his hair, sighing. "For now, sure. Can you find a place for the cow, Milo?"

"No problem, Commander," the taller man agreed.

For a beat, Dozer caught Aidan's eye, and cracked a grin. "A goddamn cow. Seriously, a goddamn cow."

"A goddamn cow," Aidan laughed, acknowledging the complete ridiculousness of it. But then again, this whole thing was ridiculous. It was crazy. And it was happening. Standing by himself for a second as his officers headed off to do their things, he took in the view. An acre and a half had been covered with raised beds, irrigation lines gridded between them. Around their space, Janice's new irrigation pylons were rising one by one as the 3D printers worked. Milo and Janice had worked together on the siting, and what they'd come up with amounted to a stockade wall of water-production units. At the moment it blocked the worst of the wind, but by the time they were done the wall of water-producing units would enclose their little compound. On the very edge of vision, the guard outposts that Naomi had set up with the more militant-minded Fringers winked in the sun, a little more than a mile away from the compound wall. It was those perimeter posts, deals and treaties the Fringers joining them had made with communities all around the area, security and fire patrols that the new folks had agreed to run with a few new Force members who'd joined the Wildcards, and of course Tweak and her people writing bots that scrubbed every mention of the Four Aces Farm from the corporate Net that made Dozer's gate guarding more of an honorary position than anything. If it weren't for those layers of people cooperating to protect what was growing here, they'd be dead already.

It had all grown incredibly fast, but it looked like they were hitting a sustainable stride finally; most of the people who were staying here had already shown up, topping out right at a hundred and some. This group with the cow was the last one to sign up for official residence. The Wildcards had set aside a barracks for refugees who were being moved on or people visiting, and that usually had a handful of people in it, but nothing they couldn't handle.

It made Aidan nervous to even think the words, but if he didn't know better, he'd say things were going okay.

Of course, he wasn't the one who got final say on that. Command had passed down the word: there'd be an inspection in a month, and they'd decide whether his crazy little community out here was viable or not.

A month. It wasn't a lot of time. And they wouldn't be looking their best either; all the autumn crops would be pulled out of the ground already and it'd just be cover crops in half the beds. The other half of the beds would be covered over and used to produce fruit and veg in the winter; those would get switched to cover crops during next year's heat peak in July. Cover crops were great for the soil, but they just looked so damn scrubby. Aidan had seen the pictures, and there was no nicer word for it: cover crops looked like weeds. That wouldn't be a good look during inspection.

All the same. All the same, when he looked out at people working between the rows of peppers and zucchini, tomatoes and quinoa, he couldn't help but smile to himself.

Maybe they were doing okay. Maybe they really were.

He didn't get many moments like this to himself these days. Billie's little voice reminded him of that.

"Hey Aidan?"

Pushing down the thought of 'oh no, what now' that wanted to rise to the top of his brain, Aidan turned to give his base services officer a smile. He'd had to argue long and hard to get Billie an officer position; cooks usually got shoved into Logistics and Requisitions as specialists and told to cook up whatever the rest of their division could bring them. But Billie had taken on a whole new set of duties, and the way she worked with Janice, Damian and Milo to plan the crops they needed to cover their nutrition baseline and the meals she could make from them deserved the recognition. Not to mention the way she coordinated the child care for everyone. She had five people under her these days full time, and who knew how many volunteers day in and day out. She more than deserved to be called an officer for managing all that.

The woman smiled a little, and he snapped himself out of his train of thought.

"Hey Billie. What's up?"

"Here's the readings on our food supplies you asked for."

Aidan took the tab she held out to him, looking it over. "So…am I reading this right? We're…running a surplus?"

"Yeah," Billie agreed, grinning now. "That freezer-shed Topher and Dozer put together for me is doing a great job keeping everything in deep freeze. I wanted to check in and see when our final harvest is, so I'll make sure to leave lots of room."

Aidan nodded, still processing the information. Based on Billie's numbers, they'd have plenty of food through the winter, more than enough to get them to the first harvest of cool-season crops in May.

"This is great, Billie," He offered with a smile, passing the tab back to her. "Really great. You're good on coolant and everything, yeah?"

"Sure," Billie agreed as she pocketed her tab. "Kevin and I drew up a supply plan. We should be good."

*And that's what a good officer does, draws up supply plans without me even asking,* Aidan thought in wonder. *I'm so glad I fought for her on this.*

"That's great news, thanks Billie. What's for lunch?"

"Quinoa salad, eggplant burgers, sweet potato fries, raspberries and brownies," Billie scrunched her nose, making a face. "If Tweak doesn't eat all the brownie batter first. Used to be I couldn't get her to eat, now she won't stop!"

Aidan had to laugh at that. "Yeah well, at least she's not throwing up all the time anymore. Anyway, thanks and—"

And because things never got boring around here, that was when his tab went off. Grabbing it out of his pocket, he checked the call, saw his husband's name, and pulled it up.

"Hey Kev, what's up?"

Kevin's face was neutral in a way that made Aidan's heart sink. "Aidan, could you join me in my office?"

"Sure," Aidan agreed. "Be there in five." Switching off the call, he gave Billie a quick nod and a smile, and headed inside.

Aidan had to open Kevin's office door when he got to it, and that was never a good sign. In his office, Kevin was already on the line with his godfather, three windows spread out around the call.

"Shut the door behind you if you would," the redhead asked distractedly. "Right Tio, Aidan just got in; now we can make some decisions."

Turning in his chair, Kevin split a glance between the screen and Aidan, fingers tapping on his arm rests the way they did when he was making logistical plans. "We've currently got thirty beds, plenty of water, and a food surplus, Aidan. And we've got refugees on our hands. They're going to need medical care."

"From what?" Aidan asked, stepping in. "Is everyone on your end okay, Mr. Ojeda?"

"Umberto, son. And no, they're not," the older man sighed. Everything about him seemed to droop today. His mustache hung like washing on the line. "You remember the Who Feeds Who demonstration?"

Aidan nodded. "That was supposed to kick off today, right?"

"It was," Umberto agreed. "We did what we planned, brought the trucks full of produce into town and opened them up for a free farmer's market in the CPS AgCo neighborhoods. Everyone who'd been told was waiting. But AgCo and Eagle had been told too."

"What?" Aidan leaned in. "Who leaked the intel?"

"I'm tracing the leak now," Kevin offered tightly. "We'll know where the information came from by this evening."

"They moved in to arrest everyone setting out the food," Umberto stated dully. "And when the crowd tried to de-arrest them, the pajeros opened fire. Point blank opened fire. Rubber bullets, thanks be to God, but they shot for the heads." He closed his eyes, sighing into his mustache. "We have a lot of wounded."

"Fuck," Aidan whispered. "Okay. Umberto, we can offer thirty beds if you can set up a way to get them out here safely. Damian and Alice can call in some favors and get some docs in from the nearest bases. We can handle this."

"We're hiding them in a rig right now," Umberto stated. "We've been using that as a mobile hospital. What's the best way to get a rig to you folks?"

Aidan blinked. A semi rig. Driving in here. It would be like a giant flashing arrow pointing at their compound. The surveillance net thrown over the continent might be unraveling, but an entire semi was bound to get noticed. And if it was noticed, they were sitting ducks.

He could feel the adrenaline dump into his system. He took a second to count his breaths and ground himself before he spoke.

"Okay…I'm thinking. If we strapped a slicktarp over the rig, would that do it?"

"For the satellites, of course," Kevin agreed. "But on the ground, even a dead Peacekeeper would sit up and wonder why there was a colossal gap in city traffic."

"Yeah," Aidan agreed. "Shit. Okay, if we got it out on the highway and then…no that'd be just as bad, if the thing parks on the side of the road and disappears."

Kevin pulled off his glasses, fiddling with the legs. Pulling out his cleaning cloth, he went to work on the lenses. "I wonder…" he murmured, fingers working. "I wonder if…" His hands froze. "Hah! Perfect. Gentlemen, hold that thought. I'm going to run and get Tweak, we need her for this."

He wasn't kidding either; shoving his glasses back on, he just about vaulted out of his chair and shoved the door open. The sound of running feet trailed away down the corridor.

Aidan closed the door, and faced the man on the other side of the screen. "What kind of injuries are we looking at? What's the survival rate likely to be?"

Umberto sucked a slow breath between his teeth. "Higher if we can get them to you sooner. The ones who were sure to die have died already. The rest…we've got autopads on them. I'm no doctor. That's all I can say."

"Okay, thanks," Aidan agreed. "That's something. I'll alert my medical people. Kevin's cooking something up. We'll take care of this."

For the first time in the conversation, Umburto managed a smile. "Thanks, Commander. We're grateful."

Aidan shrugged. "Solidarity. Let's just hope Tweak and Kevin can pull something off. And it's Aidan, Umberto."

They shared a weary smile.

A heartbeat later Kevin was back, Tweak right behind him. It was still weird seeing such a round belly on her stick-skinny body, but she was moving as fast as ever.

"Idea," she began without preamble. "Gimme a t-tarp. I'll r-reprogram it. We'll p-program it to p-play images of a c-couple cars on it. Motion. Keep it m-moving so it looks r-real. T-terrain change will t-trigger it back to d-default p-programming. Hide it across the d-dust. That work?"

"Excuse me?" Umberto asked, but Aidan nodded along.

"Yeah, if you can pull that off it'll work. Kev, do we have an extra tarp big enough?"

"Three," Kevin agreed. "Tweak, do you have canned code you can start from? We've got bleeding people out there."

Tweak bobbed her head. "Gimme t-twenty m-minutes, you got a t-tarp."

"Okay, half an hour for the tarp, half an hour for somebody to take it down there, and an hour for the rig to make it up here at safe speeds," Aidan explained for his contact on the other side of the screen. "Two hours. Tell your people to hang on for two hours, and they'll be somewhere safe getting fixed up."

"Appreciate it," Umberto agreed. He glanced at Kevin, and managed a smile. "Gracias, mijo. Vaya con dios."

"Vaya con dios los todos, Tio Berto," Kevin agreed. With a quick thumbs up, he ended the call and was on his feet. "I'll get ready for the trip. Tweak—"

But Tweak was already out the door.

Two and a half hours later, Aidan stood with Damian in the overflow dormitory, watching medical staff check over the wounded. They were a mess. Umberto hadn't said the half of it when he said 'bullets'. There were rubber bullet wounds all over. But there were folks doused with fear gas trying to come down off the chemical overload, and there were plenty of people who'd been straight up beat to crap.

"What do you think?" He asked quietly. Damian lowered his head.

"We've stabilized everyone. I've handed out some games that help people keep the trauma from evolving into PTSD, along with the meds. I don't want them on calls with UN representatives yet, but if you want to do some soft intake interviews that'd be alright. I'm stressing the soft in that sentence."

"You don't have to tell me," Aidan agreed. The people in here looked like they'd been dragged through hell.

Damian gave a grunt of acknowledgement. "Liza helping you on the intake interviews?"

Aidan shook his head. "I've got this." He meant, *this is my job,* and they both knew it.

Crossing his arms, Damian turned away. "Call me if anyone gets agitated. I can help."

"Roger," Aidan agreed. Stepping over to the first bed in line, he knelt beside a young woman with a toddler.

His stomach dropped when the kid turned their head. Their eye was covered in a medical patch. Shit, the kid had lost an eye in this mess. *Shit.*

He reached for his best smile. "Hi. I'm Aidan. I run things around here. I wanted to check in and see how you're doing."

The young woman gave a tiny laugh. "How I'm doing. They opened fire on us." Tears sprung up in her eyes. "They opened fire on us."

"If you want to tell me about it, I'm listening," Aidan offered quietly. Later, he could record these stories. Later, he could document the situation. Right now he just needed to listen.

The woman in the bed talked until she was exhausted, tears tracking her face as the words came out. At one point, Aidan took her nervously fidgeting hand. She gripped his fingers like a lifeline.

"Thanks for telling me," he offered when she was worn out. "Get some rest. You're safe here."

Standing, he passed on to the next bed. The next awful story. The next person who needed to be told they were safe.

The stories collected inside of him, all thirty of them. He felt weighed down with them by the time he'd listened to the last words.

Damian caught him as he passed. "You alright?"

Aidan shrugged. "Are they alright?" He asked, gesturing at the room full of the wounded and the shattered. Damian nodded, acknowledging the point.

Aidan slipped away, carrying the weight of knowing with him.

Slowly, he walked down to his husband's office. Stepping inside, he closed the door.

"I need to know who ratted them out. I need to know ASAP." His own voice scared him, the way it came out.

Kevin turned in his chair, looking at him for a moment. Slowly, he stood, closing the scrap of space between them. He leaned on the wall beside Aidan.

"The Sleepwalker. It was him. Again." Kevin stated quietly. His eyes fixed on nothing, empty and cool. When he spoke, the words had a bite of ice to them.

"We have some calls to make. We've got to plan. This mole needs to be dug out of his hole and nailed to the wall."

"Yeah," Aidan agreed. "Yeah, he does."

## Event File 24
## File Tag: Project Report
## 10:30-12-1-2161

They went hunting. Tweak dove down into every dark pool in the Net. As a team, they drew up an Internals List of everyone on the ops that had been compromised, and started there. Kevin called in favors with all his contacts, including some he wouldn't tell Aidan about. Aidan wasn't sure he wanted to know, if he was honest with himself. When Kevin closed the door for those calls, he left it closed.

Liza went talking to all the civilians, asking about any whispers they'd heard before they left the Grid. Blake got in on the game too, calling a bunch of contacts he'd kept in touch with. Aidan focused on reaching up the chain of command and out to other reconnaissance bases; somebody somewhere had to have *something.*

But nobody did. Weeks went by, and there was nothing. And now weeks were turning into a month. Still, there was *nothing.* Nothing but hints and tips that went nowhere. Nothing but wounded people and wrecked plans where the Sleepwalker had been. Nothing but empty nets and curse words and time wasted chasing leads that went cold. And now it was inspection time for the farm. Aidan stared into his own frightened eyes in the mirror. How had three months gone by so *fast*?

"You sure I look okay, Kev?"

Behind him, there was a chuckle, and then there were long fingers massaging his shoulders. Kevin smiled at him in the mirror.

"You look dashing, my love. And very dignified." Kevin kissed his brow. "You also look more nervous now than you did when we started all this."

"Of course I'm nervous," he grumbled at his husband. "When we got started we didn't have all this on the table. Now we've put three months of work in and started something, and we still didn't nail the Sleepwalker, and if the brass don't like what we have to say, then—"

"Milo and Janice will explain all the details of why our new water production and winter crops are doing well," Kevin cut in smoothly as he straightened Aidan's tie, "and I'll help with the details of how close to self-sufficient we are. And you'll reassure everyone, the way you always do." Dipping his head, Kevin kissed his throat. "You *are* good at this, love. Trust me."

"Yeah, but am I good enough for *this*?" Aidan asked, feeling just the hint of tightness begin in his throat. "I'm not just talking to Dusters here, Kev. This is a citizen's assembly, and I'm just a—"

"Ah." Kevin rested a finger over his lips. "Enough of that. You're not *just* anything, and everyone knows it." Leaning in, he brushed his lips over Aidan's. "You're going to do incredibly well out there."

"Says you," Aidan muttered.

Kevin tapped his nose with one finger. "Stop that."

Aidan couldn't help but smile. "Okay, okay, fine. Love you."

"And I you, my dear pessimist," Kevin replied, eyes twinkling like the sky at twilight. "Now, kiss me and let's go out there."

Aidan did as he was told, staying in the safe quiet of his husband's arms for a second. Then he straightened his shoulders, checked his tie one more time and opened the door.

The canteen had gotten huge in the last few months. They'd had to rebuild it twice. It was four times the size it had been, and the Quadrant reps for every Union, every Regional and Sector Commander for the

Western Quadrant, a handful of UN people and the ten visiting National Councilors all fit comfortably alongside his own people.

His people. Shit, they were practically a town now. He ran his eyes over so many faces he'd come to know: his crew, of course, but all these awesome new recruits and civilian folks too. Mika, who was amazing with the slicktarps. Evelyn the research whiz and her partner Blackbird and the kids smiling over here, Taz over there with his boyfriend Ryan, and Opal and Beryl sitting together practicing the knitting Alice had taught them with their gnarled fingers. So many great people were here these days.

So many people he had to protect.

Quietly, Aidan took his seat at the right hand of the Regional and Quadrant Commanders on the staging area they'd set up across from Billie's kitchen. Given how many layers of cooperation and protection he'd needed to work out just to take care of this one compound, he was a little in awe of these people higher up the command chain. He didn't even want to think about the million tangled threads his superiors had yanked and woven together in the last year. So many people, doing so many things, making so many plans and deals. It made Aidan a little giddy, picturing all the threads of command and cooperation and interaction, weaving all these people together into…into what?

Into something good, he hoped. Something powerful.

He ran his eyes over the crowd one more time, picking out Yvonne and Sarah. He'd have to grab the two of them as soon as this was over. Then he ran his eyes down the line of crew sharing the stage with him. Milo gave him a nod, and he returned it.

Janice leaned over towards Aidan. "Ready for this?" She asked in an undertone.

"Guess I better be," Aidan murmured back.

Down the stage, Quadrant Commander Ouray stood.

"Everyone. Let me welcome you to the second Citizen's Assembly. I'm pleased to welcome you to Four Aces Farm, which has come about through the hard work of Unit 1407, the Metro Chapter of the

Builders' Union, the Grapevine Union, and the many Unincorporated communities in this area."

Aidan was still getting used to that term, Unincorporated. It sounded *weird.* But it was a lot more respectful than Fringer, he had to give it that.

In his seat, Quadrant Commander Ouray turned to look down the row. "Commander Headly-McIllian, would you take the stage?"

*Here goes nothing,* Aidan sighed to himself. Standing, he walked to stand at the center of the stage, falling into parade rest.

*Okay, you know how this goes. Don't lock your knees, don't say 'um'. Just talk.*

*Just.*

*Talk.*

"Thank you, Quadrant Commander Ouray. Good afternoon, everyone," he began, with a quick nod for his superior officer.

"Today, I'll present details on the setup and running of Four Aces Farm. Hopefully, this setup can be duplicated in other places in the West, El Norte, and Cascadia where the environment has similar requirements.

"With the advisement of myself and my unit, our civilian population has created a stockade of water-producing units enclosing the area we farm. This serves four purposes: the creation of water for agricultural and human use, the production of shade, a windbreak, and a stable substrate we use to hang shade cloth and slicktarps."

Over his head, an image of the water-production pylon hung; three times as tall as a person, it looked like a surrealist's representation of a tree. The wings on the sides of the personal water condenser had become a spreading ring of horizontal hoops on the top, with the finest moisture-catching nets strung between them. The whole thing funneled down into the white plastic trunks. The image didn't show it, but on the inside of the compound, the pylon walls had been painted with murals. AIdan loved seeing them when he walked outside.

"Within the protection of the stockade, the base now grows forty varieties of open-source crops and medical plants that are used in the production of foods for us and our satellite communities, as well as medicines for many units in the West," he continued. "My Agricultural officer and my Hydroelectrics specialist will present details."

Nodding to Milo and Janice, he took a step to the side. As casually—but not as rudely—as she ever did, Janice talked the gigantic assembly through everything she and Milo had done and how they'd pulled it off.

"Here's the list of winter crops we've got in the ground now," Milo picked up where she left off. "We'll harvest in January and replant with our spring and summer plantings in rotation. Our list of warm season crops is shown here—"

A new window flipped up into the air, displaying the plants.

"With these rotations and our expanded staff processing food in the kitchens, we are nearly self-sufficient in food, insulin, penicillin, heart medications and mood-modification drugs, as well as sexual health implants and a variety of nanoids produced from the biowaste we now use as our plastic substrate," Kevin continued, stepping in smoothly beside Aidan. "Friends, dignitaries and officers; in the past three months, we have been able to provide sixty percent of our material needs and eighty percent of our food needs on this compound. At our current pace, we will be fully self-sufficient by the end of next year."

A wave of clapping washed the room. People whistled, stamped their feet and cheered at the top of their lungs.

When it had faded, Commander Ouray nodded. "Now, present the leadership structure please."

"Of course sir," Aidan agreed. "I sit as one of four permanent members of a ten-person steering committee, with my agricultural officer, my logistics and requisitions officer, and my hydroelectrics off—specialist." Damn, one of these days he was going to have to get Janice to accept the rank of officer or get the brass to let her have the rank without the paperwork load that usually came with it. Convincing the brass would probably be easier; Janice had told him time and time again what she thought of 'pantywaist paper shuffling with the bean counters', also known as the administrative duties that officers took on for their divisions. He'd have to try, because he was always calling her an officer accidentally; in his brain she *was* an officer. And then he realized that his brain was wandering off. While he was on stage. Shit.

He cleared his throat. "Every three months, six civilian members are chosen from a pool of possible candidates by sortition; that is, a random selection out of the candidate group. These randomly selected individuals give us civilian insight and feedback on the needs of our community. We present our options to the community at weekly Meets, and the community takes votes on decisions as they're presented through the Common Ground app. Between us, we've been able to come to consensus on all issues that have come up."

For a moment that seemed to take a century, Councilor Ouray stared at him. Aidan felt his chest begin to cinch in on itself.

Then the older man nodded and, holy shit, *smiled.*

"And it seems that you've handled everything that's come your way, Commander. Our congratulations and commendations." With a quick nod, Commander Ouray took his seat, his black braids swinging. Now Councilor Hernandez stood, taking the Commander's spot.

"Thank you for sitting through the formalities, everyone. As anyone who has walked through the gates of this compound knows perfectly well, there is no question that Four Aces Farm is a resounding success. Now, we'd like to hear the plans and concerns of the Unions."

*Formalities?!* Aidan sputtered inside his head. *I thought we were getting reviewed for mission success today?! This was a formality?!* He stole a glance at his crew. He could read Janice's lips as she mouthed 'formality?!' at Milo. The big man gave just a hint of a shrug, a tiny smile. Aidan looked to his other side. Kevin was lounging in his chair like a cat who just drank the world's supply of cream. Aidan didn't have to hear him talk to know he was thinking 'see, I told you it would be fine. There was never any question.'

Aidan shot the other man a smile, dizzy with relief.

"Presidents, I'd like to invite you to take the floor," Councilor Hernandez offered.

Thirteen people trooped to the front of the room.

"Thank you for the welcome, Councilor Hernandez," Phyllis acknowledged graciously. "Today, we'd like to discuss and vote on the next large-scale action the Union would like to take. Bobbi?"

A woman with a dark pixie cut stepped forward. "Good afternoon, ladies gentlemen and friends. I am Roberta Lyons of the Architects', Builders' and Construction Workers' Union. Today, I'd like to present the action we'd like to take next for a vote. If approved here, it will be taken to the participating Unions for community voting and approval."

She gestured, and three windows rose. Each showed the Halcyon Hotel from a different angle.

"As you know, only two of the seven corporations are based out of the Western Quadrant, and both have their flagship offices in Denver. Cavanaugh and EagleCorp are here, but they're not likely to fold before they see someone else give in. That said, we do think we have a target who will cave to worker demands." Glancing at the crowd, Bobbi smiled. "We've been informed that several members of the TechoCo Board are in town for important meetings, and will be staying at the Halcyon Hotel.

"With this in mind, here is what we propose: We want to stage an event on New Year's Day we're calling Come To The Table. Beginning on New Year's Eve, the entire Unionized workforce of ZonCom and TechoCo will begin a stay-home strike. On New Year's, several thousand members who have signed up for what we call Loud actions will gather in Denver. We'll set up a large table on the lawn in front of the Halcyon and host an outdoor carnival and camping event, making the lives of the Board impossible until they agree to come sit with us and speak about a new contract for the TechoCo-contracted people in the new year." Displays of street fairs played behind her as she spoke. "Once we've got one set of CEOs at the table, literally, we prove it's possible. And once we prove it, we can do it again and again."

A ripple of murmurs ran through the room. Aidan felt his heart rate kick up as Bobbi paced the stage.

"We bring this idea to the meeting, ladies, gentlemen and friends, because there are a number of details we need help working out," she continued. "How will we protect the crowd? How will we make it difficult for guests to simply leave, without using violence? How will we organize? We need to plan these details with everyone. But first, we want a vote on the general concept."

A wave of rustling filled the room as people pulled out their tabs, and windows showing the Common Ground app winked into existence. People were really getting used to using the app for their voting these days. All you had to say was 'vote', and they grabbed their tabs. That was seriously cool to see.

On the main holographic window, a bar chart appeared showing four possibilities: Approve, Provisionally Approve, Provisionally Disapprove and Disapprove.

"Voting begins now," Councilor Hernandez announced. "Three minute window. We will have a listening period later when those who disapprove can suggest changes."

Aidan watched the bars of the chart as they rose. The Disapprove bars went up a little, but the Provisionally Approve bar shot through the roof. The Approve bar was a ways behind it, but way higher than the Disapprove bar.

"Time," Councilor Hernandez stated. "There it is, everyone. Our next major local action. Now that we've agreed, our international contacts would like to sweeten the deal. Special Envoy? Please take the floor."

From the United Nations group, a big man that looked like what you'd get if you shaved a bear and put a blonde wig on it walked to the front of the room.

"Good afternoon, everyone. I am Brynjar Pettersen, special envoy for the United Nations Security Council. I'd like to come before you with the proposal of the United Nations Council." Carefully, he read from his tab.

"The Working Group on International Affairs In The Western Hemisphere has resolved that all countries signed to the International Abundance Accords will present the United Corporations of America with this ultimatum: any more attacks on the civilian population will result in the cancellation of all international purchases for a period not less than five years." Looking up, he gave the room a huge grin. "If they think shooting at you will get them out of this problem, they will want to think again very quickly."

The clapping was thunderous.

"Thank you for the support, Special Envoy," Councilor Hernendez acknowledged with a smile, before turning to the crowd. "We'll take a thirty-minute recess, and after that we'll begin planning our approaches and methods."

With a bit of clapping, the gathering relaxed into movement and chatter.

"That's our cue, love," Kevin murmured at his side.

Aidan nodded. "Yeah. Help me spot the girls?"

"Right over there, they're allied with Mally in teasing Mouse. Let's go rescue the poor bastard, shall we?"

"Sure," Aidan chuckled.

Sarah and Yvonne were taking turns with their friend Mally, making faces at the small turbanned logistics man who was waving his hands around.

"Through a fire?! You two are fricking nuts!"

"Aw you're no fun anymore, Mouse!"

"Fun? Yve, it was a *wildfire*! You coulda *died*! And let me tell you—" He trailed off, catching sight of Aidan, and straightened. "Good morning sir."

"Morning, Singh," Aidan agreed, nodding his way. "Sarah, Yvonne? With me please."

"Roger," Sarah agreed, giving her pal a quick punch in the arm. "Seeya, Mouse."

The girls in tow, Aidan headed down the hall to his office. "Inside."

Yvonne halted a couple steps back. "Is this 'I'm gonna yell at you for stuff in private?' Whatever it was, we didn't do it."

Aidan had to smile at that. "Come on Yvonne, it's not trouble. Inside. Once Liza shows up, we're set."

"Liza?" Sarah asked.

Kevin glanced down the hall over her shoulder, and waved. "Speak of the devil. You get away alright, my girl?"

"No problem," Liza agreed, marching up to them. Aidan waved at the door. "Alright, let's head in."

Inside, Quadrant Commander Ouray, Phyllis and Bobbi, Sector Commander Magnum, a couple other base commanders and logistics folks, and Quadrant Councilor Hernandez had already taken seats in the chairs Liza had put in there prior to the meeting.

Stepping in, Sarah and Yvonne glanced at each other with wide eyes. Yvonne shot Kevin a look, and Aidan just heard her whisper 'you never tell us anything anymore!' as everyone took their seats. Aidan gave a quick salute.

"Councilor. Commanders. Presidents."

"At ease, Headly," Magnum offered. "We don't have a lot of time, so let's set formalities aside." Turning, the big man nodded to Phyllis. "Madam President?"

"We wanted to clear this with everyone in person, based on the conversations we've been having," Phyllis explained with a smile for Yvonne and Sarah, the last ones getting clued in. "You see ladies, the plans being discussed out there are a decoy. We won't be heading to the Halcyon."

She waved her tab, and a set of images popped up. "Bobbi?"

"Thanks Phyllis," Bobbi acknowledged. "Everyone, these are the vacation homes of Chief Human Resources Officer Melanie Carnegie, Chief Operations Officer Arthur Marshall, and CEO Braxley Bezo-Mars of ZonCom. The Democratic State Force has informed us that these three have recently been in town on business, and are currently all staying at their vacation homes: Mr. Bezo-Mars in Cherry Hills Village, Mrs. Carnegie in Greenwood Village, and Mr. Marshall in Columbine Valley. All three homes are within easy travel distance of the city center, all have security systems that the Union of Guardians has infiltrated, and ZonCom is the most sensitive to public opinion of the Corporations."

Bobbi was almost vibrating as she spoke. "With this in mind, here is what we propose: we let everyone think we're headed to Halcyon…until the last second. And we do the Come To The Table event we just voted on. But we do it at these three houses, all at once. We'll set up a large table on the lawns of each of these three homes, and camp in their yards until they agree to come sit with us at these tables and speak about the Corporate Contracts of ZonCom folks." Her grin was gigantic. "In the meantime, EagleCorp will start off on the wrong foot, and we'll have time to set up protections."

"Bait and switch," Yvonne mused, nodding her head slowly. "I love it!"

"But why are we talking about the bait and switch in here?" Sarah asked. "What's with the closed door?"

Aidan wet his lips. He glanced from Commander Ouray, to Councilor Hernandez, to Commander Magnum. His superiors gave him the nod.

"Because this is how we're going to catch the Sleepwalker," he offered quietly.

Both women stared at him.

"Say what?" Yvonne asked.

"The Sleepwalker," Aidan explained. "At this point, we know he's listening in our meetings somehow." He shrugged. "So this is how we know. If the Sleepwalker passes along intel that we're going to be at the Halcyon on New Year's Day, then we know it was someone out in the canteen or someone they're close to. But if Eagle's waiting for us at the execs' houses…"

The air hung heavy on the words Aidan didn't want to say.

"Then we know it's someone in this room," Kevin finished. The words were very precise, and so very flat. They hung in the air like smoke.

## Event File 25
## File Tag: Implementation
## 22:58-12-31-2161

Tension filled the air like static before a storm, sizzling between people in glances and gestures. All the time, more people were streaming into the warehouse.

"How soon?" Sarah asked, eyes glimmering in the deep sockets of her skull mask.

Yvonne checked her tab.

"Two minutes. We said we'd head out right at twenty-three hundred." She shifted her weight, her blood singing with anticipation. Turning her head, she gave her wife a grin. So much prep work. So much drilling. So much planning. And it all came down to this night.

"Ready?"

Sarah's grin mirrored hers.

"Hell yes."

Yvonne checked her tab. One more minute, and it'd be time.

Thirty seconds.

Fifteen.

"Go time," she murmured. Giving Sarah a quick peck on the cheek, she jumped up on a stack of old packing crates, grabbing the bullhorn Sarah handed up.

"Okay everybody! Circle up!"

The packed crowd turned her way. She gave them a grin.

"Hey all! This is the New Year, New Contract action we've been talking about since November!" She let the crowd whoop and holler for a second, jigging on the spot in time to their cheers. "Here's the plan! Your written material said you'd get directions and coordinates when you got here; well here it is. Our group is marching down Belleview and into Cherry Hills Village. Our back-end folks are blocking all the Go systems, stopping traffic coming our way. They're running dictionary and DDOS attacks on every security system in Cherry Hills Village to make sure the people opening Bezo-Mars' doors for us aren't implicated. They're in EagleCorp's systems jamming their intel and shutting down their gear. We're marching onto the property of Braxley Bezo-Mars. We're putting a big table on his lawn, and we're staying there having a New Year's party until he comes out, sits down, and agrees to pick up the pen and start writing you guys a new contract!"

Cheering rocked the building.

"You guys all brought your party gear, your costumes, and all the camping stuff and spare clothes you need, just like we agreed!" She went on. "Our Caretakers have got enough extra food, hygiene stuff, camping gear, and party supplies to keep us on the guy's property for two months if we need to stay that long! Find them if you need them, help them if you can when we get there, they're the ones in blue." Yvonne continued through the horn. "Our Guardians are carrying the stuff we need to shine a light on the CEOs and their goons, and they'll keep any trouble off of us," she went on to whoops and hollers. "Talk to them if you see trouble, they're the ones in orange with the hard-hats. And remember what we're going in there for! We're not there to fight. If there's violence, it won't be us making it. We're not going for blood, people! Remember, blood washes away. What we're going for is *change!* Change is what we want, change that's written in stone, and change is what we're going to stay and demand! And change is what we're going to get!"

The room was a cacophony of cheers.

"Alright!" Yvonne waved an arm. "Let's go!"

And the big warehouse door opened. A sea of people deluged the street. The band that had been checking their instruments in the back started to play.

Stepping down off the crates, Yvonne grabbed Sarah's hand and got to the head of the crowd.

The brass band filled the air with wild noise as the night air hit them. It was a little nippy, sure, but Yvonne couldn't have cared less. She'd dressed up as the heroine from *Death In Tulsa*, and the big poncho from her favorite film was plenty warm. Sarah had done herself up as the Grim Reaper with a sash that said 2161 on her chest, and her skull mask bobbed like a star under her cowl. Around them, dragons and clowns, movie characters and cows and astronauts danced down the street.

They went out of the old supply warehouse and down Belleview Avenue like a king tide up a beach, filling the winter night with music and color. The streetlights flowed with them, glowing up ahead and flicking out behind.

A quarter of a mile down the road, Yvonne started spotting the bright lights above. News drones. Perfect. Right on time. And the plan was working too, it looked like; they'd fed the information that they were headed to the Halcyon to the general network months ago. Every EagleCorp body the security giant could spare was dug in down there. It'd take them time to scramble and get up here, especially with Tweak's people fragging their Go systems. By the time they made it, the marchers would be settled in and ready for them.

Over the sound of the brass band, the voices of the crowd raised in song. The United People's Band had sent out the lyrics to a freaking ancient tune, and everyone had got the words down. It was nothing much when you sang it by yourself, but with everyone here singing it rolled up like thunder, the brass band backing it up.

*" Is there much we have in common with the greedy parasite*
*Who has chained us into service and has crushed us with his might?*
*Is there anything left to us but to organize and fight?*

*For the union makes us strong!"*

It gave Yvonne chills, the words swelling up into the cold air and filling her lungs as she carried them with everyone else.

She turned her head, watching the gigantic table with the ridiculous fluffy quill pen and inkwell stuck on carried by so many hands. The words 'Come Sit At The Table. We Need A New Contract. Pick Up The Pen!' gleamed in the streetlights, painted bright white across the tabletop. Chairs bobbed along around it like pieces of wreckage in a storm surge.

Up ahead, a blue-clad set of Caretakers held up arrow signs pointing them off Belleview and down onto Holly. Gorgeous houses sat in sprawling lawns that drank more water in a year than five families, rolling out on either side of the road.

Down off Holly, they took El Camino, and marched right up on what looked almost like a fenced park, singing all the way. The place might look pretty, but Yvonne knew for a fact it had been built like a fortress. It had tons of hidden protection, everything from hands-off arcs in the pylons of the gates to anti-theft drones and self-repairing fences. There was no way you could get through that. At least, there was no way if the folks who maintained and repaired the entire security system weren't on your side. Lucky for the marchers, the folks in the EagleCorp Guardians' Union had handed the Dusters everything they needed to take over the security on the Bezo-Mars system and control it remotely.

Sarah waved her scythe, helping to direct the crowd as she hollered out the lyrics.

*"We can break their goddamn power*
*gain our freedom when we learn*
*That the Union makes us strong!"*

And just like they'd planned, the tech folks had made sure the heavy gates that enclosed Bezo-Mars's property swung open ahead of them. The electrical arcs didn't fizz as they entered. The sound of their feet gave percussion to the song, the words flying like a banner as they walked through the gates.

> *"We can bring to birth a new world from the ashes of the old*
> *For the Union makes us strong!"*

Along the crescent of driveway that fronted the gigantic Pueblo-Revival house, people started showing up: staff poking their heads out of upstairs windows like gophers, a couple guests for the CEO's New Years party looking out the door with fear in their eyes.

Striding in, Yvonne stepped off concrete and onto sweet green grass, pointing. The table and its chairs were bobbed forward through the singing crowd, set down and spread with analog paperwork detailing the demands of the ZonCom Unions. Standing on a chair, Yvonne lifted her bullhorn. Just like they'd talked about and drilled on, the band and the marchers fell quiet on cue. Yvonne's ears rang with the silence.

"Mr Bezo-Mars!" She called through her bullhorn, "Mr. Bezo-Mars, your workers are here to talk to you! It'll be a new year in an hour. For a new year, your workers want a new contract with you and your Corporation. And we're not leaving until ZonCom workers have got it!"

Right on cue, the fireworks they'd planned went off behind her, lighting up the night sky in blazes of display-drone color. They shimmered in soundless explosions, drifting down into the words 'New Year, New Contract!'

The people began a chant.

"Come to the table, pick up the pen!

We want dignity again!"

At her side, Randy of the Guardians put up three fingers, orange sleeve catching the light. Yvonne nodded. Three fingers, that was personal bodyguards on the move towards the front of the house. A couple people on the serving staff inside the house were feeding Randy details, and they'd drilled for this.

"Union, circle up!" she called through her bullhorn.

Just like every Union had drilled on for months now, everyone formed up behind Yvonne and the table, making her and it the spearhead of the crowd.

The front door burst open, and Mr. Bezo-Mars's personal bodyguards came pouring out, a couple in tactical gear but most of them wearing riot-helmets over fancy suits. They looked like fascist penguins, as nasty as they were ridiculous. And yep, there were the snipers on the roof.

"Hey everybody over there!" Yvonne waved. Over and around her, news- recording drones and display drones winked their little lights. "Just want to let everybody know: we're not here to hurt you. We represent workers contracted to ZonCom across America. If anybody but Mr. Bezo-Mars wants to go, that's fine; we won't get in your way. Now, let me talk to you folks doing bodyguard duty on the front steps! I just want to tell you, the people out here aren't your enemies. We've got more in common with you than you've got with the people in that big fancy house. You've got Citizen Credit scores in the five hundreds and six hundreds, right? Seven hundreds, maybe? You've got just enough to keep you living a decent life, but you're never really safe, right?"

She shook her head. "Hard times for all of us, guys. We're in the same boat. You want a decent life for your kids, right? You want to live a life where a number on your cards doesn't decide if you get a good place to live or medicine for somebody in your life? That's what we're here to talk about! That's what we're here to fix! I figure that's worth standing up for. Is what you're standing over there for worth protecting?"

The bodyguards stood like statues.

Yvonne made a big show of a shrug. "Okay, you stand there tonight. We're going to celebrate the New Year until Mr. Bezo-Mars comes out and talks to us about rewriting the ZonCom contract with his workers, 'kay?"

Sarah passed up a bottle. Yvonne pointedly turned around. Sure, one of the bodyguards could shoot her in the back right now. But in front of all these cameras? In front of a whole watching world, after she'd just said she wasn't violent? When that shot could cancel every international purchase on the books?

The Force had run psychological algorithms and simulations on this all last month. Everyone had told them that if they did things like this, just like this, they'd be okay. Between ZonCom's big focus on the way they looked on camera, the shock and the weirdness of the situation, and the international sword hanging over the company profits, any bodyguard would shrink from pulling the trigger.

All the algorithms and all the simulations had said so.

Yeah.

Yvonne's back prickled as she lifted the bottle and toasted the crowd.

"Let's start this party!"

The band struck up a new tune, something more danceable and fun but still making the point.

*"We're the first ones to starve, we're the first ones to die*
*The first ones in line for that pie-in-the-sky*
*And we're always the last when the gravy's shared out*
*For the worker is working when the fat cat's about!"*

And on the sweet softness of grass that drank more precious water than they did in a day, the people danced.

Stepping off the table, Yvonne glanced at her tab. Half an hour to midnight. She read up on the word from other Dusters: everything was going great at the other two houses. Eagle was losing its mind. Their Go vehicles were grounded, everything from cars to planes, so they'd been scrambling for two hours to find every manual vehicle they could and get it up and running. Then there was the problem of putting somebody who could drive a manual in the things. But they were coming. They wouldn't have drones and they wouldn't have planes, but they were coming.

*Okay, fine,* Yvonne told herself. *You knew they'd come. Better dance while you can.*

Turning, she took Sarah's hands and danced along to the song.

*For the worker is working when the fat cat's about!*

They had another twenty minutes of fun, with Bezo-Mars's guests slinking out through the back doors. The Guardians kept an eye on who was leaving; they didn't stop anyone who wasn't the CEO, but they made sure he wasn't sneaking out.

Some of the guests seemed to think they were in a spy movie, and got pretty elaborate about sneaking away. One guest tried to go over the wall onto Belleview and got stuck, hanging by his tailcoat until laughing protestors found him, took a couple pics and helped him down, setting him on the empty street. The brass band took a break and gave a turn to a bunch of folks who'd brought drums and guitars. Caretakers set up pop-up showers, a canteen full of good things to snack on and latrines with compacting toilets. People got into their really fancy costumes. One group did gymnastics on the driveway, and they were incredible. Overhead, the drone fireworks lit the sky.

Yvonne was really starting to have fun when Randy caught up with her and held up four fingers. Icewater dumped itself into Yvonne's system.

*Well okay, here we go!*

"Bad eggs!" she called, and heard the call picked up all through the crowd by the Guardians. All around, people started getting ready.

The first vehicle to come lumbering up the road was a repurposed ambulance, a bunch of Eagle's goons hanging off the sides. Two fire trucks came next, and another four ambulances. Out of them poured EagleCorp personnel in all their gear, ready for a fight. Thank god that they'd turned the Hands Off feature on the gates back on behind them. Eagle couldn't fire bullets through the electric arc without making the rounds explode, and they probably wouldn't risk that in front of these cameras, not on ZonCom's precious property.

At least, she hoped.

Randy came jogging over. "Fuck, Bezo-Mars cleared them to ram his gate!"

"Fuck," Yvonne hissed. "Get everybody back!"

And an ambulance hurled itself into one of the gates, backed up, and did it four more times. The gate fell in a shuddering heap.

The wrecked vehicle backed out of the way. Eagle goons started marching through the fallen gate.

Yvonne slipped on her costume's sunglasses.

*Please please please let this go the way we planned,* she whispered in her head. On the stairs, the guards fanned out, weapons trained.

"They think they can bring us down in the dark," she called through the horn. "They think they can shoot us here in the night. But night's almost over! Dawn's coming! So let's shine a light!"

And every one of the Guardians turned on the flashing diodes on top of their hardhats. They turned as a drilled team, orienting the incredibly strong beams that were built into each little optical-interference device on their helmets. Every beam was something on its own. When all two hundred beams were shining together, they created a wall of shuddering, vision-scrambling light; a Duster answer to the Screamers that Eagle loved so much. Difference was, the Spear of Light messed with the people it was targeted at, and not everybody for a half mile around. The Dusters actually gave a damn about not fucking over the civvies. But if you were the one that the Spear was defending against, it had the same debilitating effects as Screamers.

Eagle goons dropped what they were holding and covered their eyes with reflexive little screams. Some of them threw up, some of them covered their heads with their arms. All of them reacted to the optical suppression tools that were temporarily ruining their ability to see, orient, and navigate, not to mention making them feel like their eyes had gotten chili pepper rubbed into them.

"Yes!" Yvonne whispered. She'd watched as Sarah drilled the teams with the Spear, but seeing the whole thing in action was a serious thrill.

In no time at all, the goons were scrambling back behind their vehicles. A few of the idiots opened up with live rounds, but all they did was shoot either bullet-proof plas fence or an opening covered by a hands-off arc. When the slugs interrupted the arc's field, two lightning bolts met around them, which set off a whole new kind of fireworks as little slugs popped into dust in midair.

The crowd went wild.

Over their heads, the fireworks spelled out a countdown. The ZonCom Workers' Union shouted it out in time.

"Three!

Two!

One!"

Then everyone was cheering, and laughing, and kissing. They had EagleCorp stuck helpless outside, and a CEO cowering like a weasel in his house, and it was a whole new year.

It was just one giant outdoor party from there, that was what Yvonne remembered later. All across the ZonCom CEO's sprawling two acres of lawn and garden, tents were pitched. People were dancing, singing, and cooking food. People were teaching classes and giving talks. Performance artists went at it with dance and spray paint and chalk on the sidewalk, with music and acrobatics and all kinds of things.

Outside, the EagleCorp forces waxed and waned. They tried all kinds of things, but Bezo-Mars's property had been built to protect its owner, and he'd had the money to do that right. Tear gas and fear gas canisters got fried in the air, ditto bullets. Eagle tried firehoses a couple times, but that was easy to handle; the Guardians just got everybody out of range the minute the hoses unrolled. The techies had Eagle's attempts to get in and control the security system via the back door handled. The only things flying overhead belonged to ZonCom and those drones were run by the Unions right now, so they were good on food and supply drops. A couple folks faked controlling some of the drones with dud remotes, just to fuck with Eagle's heads and send them chasing signals that didn't exist.

The workers made sure to leave food at the front door and the gate for Bezo-Mars's people and the Eagle guys both. They kept education holos aimed over the wall and at the house, telling everyone what they were there for in all kinds of ways: from personal stories of ZonCom kids and EagleCorp kids to explanations of what other countries looked like without a wage gap of four hundred percent between the boss and the worker. There was something to watch all day if you were stuck on guard outside the wall.

The gathering made a point of letting anybody leave if they wanted to, as long as they weren't the CEO. That meant that Bezo-Mars was pretty much on his own by the end of the week. Outside, there were a lot more EagleCorp goons, but they looked even more bewildered and bored. All their usual tools were out of commission, from tanks to assault vehicles. If they came near the gate they got blinded. So they mostly asked a lot of questions, sat around, drank coffee and watched the vids the Union was playing for them.

All over the compound, people relaxed and had fun. They talked all night, woke up and watched the sunrise. They climbed trees, hung out, swam in the heated pool with the koi fish, played ball on the lawn. And they waited.

Yvonne didn't mind the waiting. It was weirdly relaxing, being here with nothing to do but hang out. She'd probably never been this relaxed in her life. It sounded funny, with Eagle a couple hundred feet away, but it was true.

She was lying in her tent on another lazy morning, their fourteenth on the property already, and thinking it all over with her fingers stroking Sarah's silky hair. Outside, a gigantic cheer went up.

"Wanna see what that is?" Sarah murmured.

"Probably," Yvonne agreed, stretching. "C'mon."

Dressed, they stepped out of their tent. Yvonne grabbed the first person she spotted.

"Charley, what's up?"

The boy with the beautiful eyes stopped his jog to grin at Yvonne. "It's the CEO, ma'am! He's on his front steps! He's talking!"

"Holy shit!" Yvonne laughed. "What're we waiting for, come on!"

And Charley was right. On the stairs, a man stood flanked by two bodyguards, practically shaking as he clutched his tab. His family line was another one that had gone for gene modding; Yvonne could see a couple things that reminded her of her buddy Kevin. But where the tall and super-pale thing worked on Kevin, it just made Bezo-Mars look underdone. He'd tried to imitate the bald and bold look of his famous ancestor, but he was too—what was that word Kev used…oh yeah!—he was too insipid to pull it off. Standing on the steps of his mansion, Bezo-Mars looked like something that lived under a rock, and he didn't like it that they'd just taken the rock away.

He cleared his throat. "First of all, welcome, everyone. I hope this is the first of many of these meetings with my workforce. And I commit to you to be more accessible than I have been historically."

"You weaselly fink," Sarah snorted.

Yvonne gave her hand a squeeze. "You said it."

Bezo-Mars shifted from foot to foot like a guy who needed to take a piss. He tapped his tab, and a hologram window floated up to hang in front of him. Licking his lips, he read from it.

"This company has a tremendous legacy of supply chain and marketing achievement, thanks to your efforts and the contributions of generations before you."

A ripple like the growl of a wolf pack ran through the crowd. Yvonne glanced around, the tiniest seed of fear pricking her insides. If this twit said the wrong thing now, in front of all these people his company had *abused* for generations…

"I honor that legacy, and I appreciate your tireless commitment," Bezo-Mars tried, and that got him a wave of derisive laughter. He swallowed. "I also recognize the lessons – many of them painful – from the experiences of the last eighteen months that you are bringing to the way we do our business and take care of you, our valued employees."

More howls of derisive laughter. This guy was trying to shovel shit, and the crowd was *so* not having it. Yvonne glanced around, glad to see the Guardians reminding people to keep their cool.

"This is a crucial time for ZonCom," the twerp went on. "We have a lot of work to do to uphold our values and to build on our strengths. I…I have a lot of work to do. And part of my work includes engaging my stakeholders with greater transparency, holding myself accountable to the highest standards of our legacy, and incorporating bottom-up perspective on what we do and how we do it. On that note, I will be listening closely to you, my committed workers. And we'll rework your corporate contract together. In doing so, we'll become stronger as a corporation."

Crossing the lawn, he took a seat at the table and picked up the pen.

## Event File 26
## File Tag: Negotiation
## 02/11-2162/ 03-28-2162

"You headed out?" Tweak asked.

Naomi checked her fighting stick, tightening its harness as Billie put away the last of the dishes. "Yep. Can I raid the pantry, Billie?"

"Sure," the girl agreed with her soft little smile. "Snacks are on the left-hand side, top shelf, now that I did the reorganizing."

"Out of the reach of the kids, hunh?" Naomi observed.

Billie nodded. "After the whole too many snacks and puking kids thing, yeah. Out of bounds from now on."

"No kidding," Naomi agreed ruefully.

"N-next big m-meeting?" Tweak piped behind her.

"Yep," Naomi agreed. "Whole set of them. They requested Kevin, Liza and me for liaison on this one."

"Why you guys?" Billie asked. "I thought the Commanders and the Councilors were taking over?"

"I think Liza's a good luck charm for our people these days," Naomi offered as she studied what the pantry had to offer. "And Kev's being asked to sit in as an observer; makes sense, he's used to exec culture and he talks their lingo. He'll see things our people might miss, and he can advise. And I'm there in case any Corps get any bright ideas, and we need an out. You got the paperwork, yeah Billie? Don't bother planning us as part of the meal plans for a while. We're going to be in and out a lot until the last week of March."

"Yeah, I told her," Tweak put in.

Naomi glanced over at the little coder as she packed food into her bag for the trip. The smaller woman had tucked herself into the corner of the kitchen she hung out in when she was spending time with Billie, curled up like a little animal in a den. Naomi smirked.

"You know you look like someone put a balloon down your shirt when you sit that way?"

"Yeah," Tweak sighed, rubbing a hand over her belly. "C-can't get c-c-comfortable. Sucks." She stood, but sat down almost as quickly, head in her hands. "Ack..."

"You okay?" Billie asked, stepping over.

"Here," Naomi offered, dropping her bag and pulling one of Tweak's arms around her waist to help her stand again.

"'M'okay. Dizzy. Hate it," Tweak grumbled.

"Only two months to go, Gurgi," Naomi reassured. "You got this."

"Yeah. Still sucks." Tweak grumbled. "Okay. Time. Billie, I got work. Omi. Get me to my r-r-rig?"

"Can you fit in your rig?" Naomi asked as she helped the smaller woman down the hall.

"F-fuck off," Tweak retorted as Naomi walked her to her office. "Smartass."

Naomi chuckled as she settled the girl into her chair. "So what're you working on? The voting app, still?"

"Nah," Tweak replied. "Hunting."

"Hunting, hunh? Well that'll be fun, you seven months pregnant and walking funny. Heads up, I'm not giving you a gun."

"Ha. Ha. Ha," Tweak retorted, deadpan to the hilt. "I'm after the S-s-Sleepwalker," she explained as she pulled up her windows. "The New Year. Proved it. He was in the b-big m-meeting. Not the l-l-little one. So I'm doing a d-d-deep dive on everyone who was in the c-c-canteen."

Naomi nodded. “Good plan. I’m getting really sick of that asshole putting a wrench in things.”

“Same,” Tweak agreed. “Sides, I’m n-not going anywhere.” A yawn cut her off, and she finished it with a curse. "Fuck.” She smacked the armrest of her rig. “Always tired! Don’t wanna sleep! Wanna work!"

"You're growing a human, kiddo," Naomi replied mildly. "You’re gonna get tired."

Tweak rolled her eyes. "Better be human," she grumbled under her breath, scrubbing at her eyes. "Better stop knocking me out too."

"Talk to Damian, if it's bugging you,” Naomi suggested offhandedly.

Tweak snorted. "Damian's a jackass."

"He's a doc,” Naomi observed. "All docs are jackasses when they have to be. Or think they have to be."

Tweak nodded. "You guys are going out to another meeting with the execs. How m-many now?”

Naomi ticked them off on her fingers. “We’ve got the joint one with two execs, another three with ZonCom this month, and four with TechoCo’s execs, two with Argus. The other four haven’t cracked yet. Next month it’s a ton of Union meetings and international meetings. And we’re leaving time in case we can schedule meets with the execs who are holding out right now.”

“Figures,” Tweak sighed. “M-m-meetings g-going okay?”

Naomi shrugged. “Ask Liza and Kevin. I’m just there to pull triggers.”

“Lame, Omi.” Tweak grumbled.

Naomi shrugged. “True.”

Tweak didn’t say anything to that for a second.

“Hey? Omi?” Her voice was a lot smaller now.

“Yeah?” Naomi asked.

Tweak glanced down at her hands. Then she raised her head, and two eyes like dark pools pinned Naomi to the wall. Man, Tweak could get you with those big eyes. She looked so vulnerable for a second. So breakable.

“C-careful. ‘Kay?" She asked in a little voice.

Naomi couldn’t help but smile. She gave a salute. "Roger that.”

She was still thinking about Tweak’s worried eyes as she stationed herself with two other Dusters on security detail across the room from the exec’s bodyguards. She eyed her opposite number warily, noting her people taking their seats out of the corner of her eye. At the other end of the room, a couple UN representatives sat quietly taking notes.

At the center of their side of the table, Marcus Z the Fifth and Braxley Bezo-Mars sat with their aides murmuring in their ears. The Union Presidents sat quietly, waiting. Among the Union aides, Kevin sat unobtrusively, made up today in a mousy look that faded him into the background.

Z5 cleared his throat. People talked about whether the family line had overdone the genome shaping; based on the history docs Kevin was always showing them, Naomi was pretty sure the family had always had a little weird in them. He sounded a little like the family founder too when he talked.

“Good morning. Thank you for agreeing to meet with us again at this site. We have some new people here. So I think we should go around and quickly introduce ourselves, just say our names.”

“Reasonable,” a man on Naomi’s side agreed. “I am Mr. Steve Ragomo, president, Shippers and Loaders’ Union.”

Down the table, people gave their names.

“Mrs. Jamie Lebron, president, Multimedia Entertainment And Event Union.”

“Ms. Phyllis Caulfield, president, Writer And Content Creators’ Union.”

“Ms. Tamika Strasser, president, Retail Service Peoples’ Union.”

“Mr. Paulo Madiara, president, IT Workers’ And Coders’ Union.”

"Ms. Lam Ti, president, Warehouse Workers' Union."

"Mx. Noct Fredriksen, president, Fabricator and Hardware Installers' Union."

"Mr. Brynjar Pettersen, special envoy for the United Nations Security Council."

"Ms. Ravitri Kumar, special envoy for the United Nations Economic and Social Council."

"Ms. Punthea Chea, special envoy for the United Nations International Court of Justice."

Naomi could have sworn she heard Marcus Z the Fifth gulp.

"I think that is everyone," Bezo-Mars stated. His voice was almost steady. Almost.

"Then let's begin," Phyllis offered crisply. "On the first page of the proposal, some of this might seem familiar to the Company, because this is language that has passed back and forth between the Union and the Company multiple times. To begin, and I quote, "'in addition to all previous tentative agreements, the Federated Unions counter with the following offer:

"Discontinue the ZonCom Citizen Acceptable Standing Day Off Practice in conjunction with an agreement." She looked up from her tab, pinning Bezo-Mars to his seat like a teacher with a naughty pupil.

"The ZonCom Day Off Practice is something that was afforded to us as part of the package when we agreed to bargain this agreement through arbitration. We did bargain to this, but currently this tentative agreement is contingent on the rest of the agreement. However, given that the Company has declared impasse and attempted to implement a different proposal…"

Naomi relaxed into the proceedings and zoned after that. These things were becoming mostly routine; it was a lot of nitty gritty details and arguing over the everyday things that changed life in small ways: just as important as cleaning her guns regularly, but about as interesting. Once in a while, she'd surface for a moment in the talks, especially when emotions heated up or one of the CEOs started to raise the temperature.

"I'd like it in the record that I continue to state my objection in regards to the structure of these talks," Z5 tried at one point. "We can't effectively discuss rights, privileges and terms across so many types of workers at once. I repeat my request to split these meetings into discussion groups for high-skill and low-skill work sets, and create working meetings focusing on the specific needs of each Citizen Standing in order to better assist our workers."

"With all due respect," Phyllis stated in a voice that clearly said the amount of respect due was nil, "we know our history, sir. We will not be wedged apart along class or work-type lines. That has been the tactic of management throughout history. It has been the original sin of many movements of the past. We will not commit the sin of dividing and ranking ourselves in a way you can exploit. You're right, sir. There are many people of many work types and walks of life represented here. We are a union of unions. We are all people of value, we are all paying the price under the current conditions, and we are *all* standing together today. And no, we will not be divided. That is *final*. I *hope* that is clear."

At the end of the table, one of the UN reps whispered a little 'yes!' Naomi had to smile.

"Now," Phyllis went on, "Mx. Fredriksen, you've brought up several important points about mental health support. Please continue."

"Thanks, Ms. Caulfield," Noct agreed. "I'd like to point out that the Company has offered the terms of twenty percent payment for all mental health care, and no days off. the Federated Unions counter the offer and propose the following counter offer…"

And Naomi zoned out again.

"I'm giving Aidan a call," Naomi called into the bathroom where Kevin was peeling himself out of the onion-skin layers of his disguise that night. "Want me to wait till you're done?"

"No need, get him updated and give him my love. I'll be some time in here," Kevin replied as he worked to remove pasted-on eyebrows.

"'Kay," Naomi agreed. Taking a seat on the bed, she put her brother's call sign into her Mesh app.

"Hey big brother," she offered when he picked up.

He gave her a wave on the other end of the call. "Hey Omi. How's it going over there?"

"Pretty good. Kev says to tell you a bunch of mushy stuff like he loves you," Naomi offered, poker-faced.

"I heard that!" Kevin's cranky voice called out of the bathroom. Liza snorted. Naomi cracked a grin. Aidan rolled his eyes, chuckling.

"Yeah well. How're the meetings?"

"Pretty good; Kev and Liza got all their notes sent up the chain of command. We're in good shape."

Aidan nodded. "What's the vibe?"

"Execs are pissing themselves," Naomi stated. "They're scared shitless of actually having to talk to their people on equal terms, and oh man, it shows. Any luck getting anybody else to the table?"

"Looks like Lynch is starting to wobble over at NatBank," Aidan offered with a smile. "Our sources say he's this close to coming to the table. But we're having trouble getting solid intel on that."

"Working on it!" Kevin's voice called.

Naomi sighed. "I told him to tell me if he wanted to be in on this call."

"Yeah well," Aidan shrugged, smiling a little. "The threat from the IMF to shut NatBank out of international banking has Lynch softened up, and that last piece of political theater, the Pieces of Silver one? Yeah, that got through."

"Awesome," Naomi agreed. "How about Cavanaugh?"

"Harrington's keeping his nose in the air, from what we hear," Aidan offered. "Keeps saying 'ignore the plebes and they'll give up.'"

In the bathroom, Kevin barked a laugh. "Only in his dreams!"

"Is Kevin saying something?" Aidan asked. "I can barely hear him."

"That's because he's catcalling from the other room, getting out of his gear," Liza observed dryly. "Kevin, quit trying to shout from in there, just come in when you're done."

"Yes nanny," Kevin threw out. Liza sighed.

On the other end of the call, Aidan chuckled. "Okay people, enough hassling my guy. We've got more good news: the people from Eagle are saying the Corporation's basically cracking up along Quadrant lines: in Cascadia, the New Netherlands, Freshwater, the Midlands and the First Nation, they're quitting like rats jumping ship or turning around and unionizing. Whole departments are defecting. Out in Cascadia a whole platoon put down their weapons and joined a free food bank event as protestors. In New Netherlands, every one of the departments disbanded and rebranded themselves as a chapter of the Guardians' Union."

"Holy crap, that's great!" Liza leaned in. "And what's the word on the management, are they going to cave?"

"From what we hear, they're doubling down," Aidan admitted. "Problem is, their troops in El Norte, Tidewater, here in the West, and over in Appalachia are just getting that much meaner now that they're up against the wall. They're being called up and deployed outside their own Quadrants in what amounts to occupation troops in the areas where the local people have come over to our side. That's where things might really get messy."

"Shit," Naomi sighed. "I mean, no big surprise, but yeah. Shit."

"Yeah," Aidan agreed. "That may be where we need to step in and do some mop-up operations. Command is talking about us doing a military action to oust Hamilton from his seat as CEO if he tries to hunker down on Sixteenth Street and barricade himself in. There's a good chance he will, with his psych profile. Fingers crossed it won't come to that, but we'll be ready if it does. There's a Union vote scheduled for next month on what to do now that we're getting the upper hand."

"You really think we're that far?" Naomi asked. Aidan gave her a cockeyed look. "Who was sitting in a room with a couple CEOs pissing themselves?"

Naomi nodded. "Point. Still weirded out by that." Drawing a breath, she shook it off. "So, what's next, boss?"

Aidan sighed, running a hand over his hair. "Well…we've got the ball rolling. Now I guess we just keep pushing until it rolls us right into a real democracy."

"And rolls over every bastard trying to keep his grip on power along the way," Kevin quipped, poking his head out of the bathroom.

Aidan laughed. "That I heard. Yeah. What Kev said."

It wasn't as easy as they talked about in that conversation between friends. It never was. In the next weeks, Naomi barely saw her home. She was always out on security detail somewhere: security detail for UN reps, security detail for Union heads. A couple times she got called in to clear bombs planted in Union headquarters or the homes of prominent folks in the movement. She heard about folks who weren't so lucky in other Sectors and other parts of the country. Planting bombs was a new EagleCorp tactic; bombs in cars, bombs in houses, tampered solar panels or wiring that overheated and caught houses on fire. Damn they were playing dirty these days.

Naomi and a couple other munitions folks got together on the Mesh, talked things out and wrote up a primer on civilian personal security. They vetted and posted it on the Mesh in record time; it had a million reads in the first day. That was good, Naomi thought. It would save some lives.

Seeing the ball roll was good. All the same, she grinned when she finally read the orders she'd been waiting to see on her tab.

Message Handle: Sector40COM
Message Authenticated

Message: The 1407 unit is given three weeks out of Grid rotation. Good work, people. Go home.

## Event File 27
## File Tag: Reassessment Of Priorities
## 08:30-03-30-2162

"You've gotta be kidding, you're gearing up? You just got home last night!"

"Yes, well, we're low on nanoids we need, Yvonne," Kevin replied distractedly as he pulled on his riding gear. "You've let that supply become perilously low, and I've got to rectify that."

"Perilously nothing, we've got three weeks for the base, the whole base!"

"Yes, and three weeks is nothing if the Fabrication Union implements the sit-down strike they've been discussing. We need at least two months' worth if we don't want our teeth rotting out of our heads, thanks very much. I thought we talked about this."

Yvonne gave a drawn out sigh. "You are such a workaholic, Kev."

"And you, my girl, are ungrateful," Kevin retorted, easing himself down to lace up his riding boots. Naomi watched the girls give her brother-in-law shit with an easy smile. After the last weeks of craziness, it was nice to fall back into everyday goofing and bickering.

"You sure you want to be sitting on a bike seat after last night?" Sarah cooed in mock concern. "I mean, you are kind of walking funny today Kev baby."

"And no wonder, after what we heard last night," Yvonne added, shooting a grin Aidan's way. He ducked his head, pretending to be really interested in breakfast. A flurry of snorts and giggles ran up and down the crew table.

"Kindly fish your mind out of the gutter, dear girl," Kevin threw out lightly. Naomi caught her big brother's eye, and cocked her head. He grinned, shrugging. Naomi gave him a quick smile and a wink. It was good to know he was still finding time to have some fun.

"Ready, Inyoni?" Kevin asked. "You've got your GPS spoofer? And your new bracelets?"

Inyoni tried to say something through the half a bread roll he'd just shoved in his mouth. He held up an arm, showing off the silver bracelet with a stylized blue bird swooping across it as he swallowed hard. "Got 'em. Ready." Leaning over, he pecked Tweak's cheek and tucked the rest of the roll into her hand.

"Seeya Dragon."

"Bye Bird," she chirped, biting into the roll.

"You'll eat anything these days, hunh?" Naomi observed as Tweak made the food disappear. She shrugged.

"Growing a human.You said." She loaded a plate. "Need food. For that."

"What's all that for?" Billie asked.

Tweak shrugged. "Snacks. When I'm w-working. Gonna go. B-bye."

Plate held in front of her, she trotted away.

Naomi glanced at Billie, who was biting her lip. "She been doing that a lot?"

"Yeah," Billie agreed. "She's got a lot on her plate."

"We saw," Janice observed dryly. Out of the corner of her eye, Naomi spotted Aidan catching the older woman's eye and giving her a 'not now' look.

Beside her, Topher scooted in and gave Billie a quick squeeze. "She's doing good, habibti."

Billie gave him a little smile. "Yeah," she sighed. "Only I wish…" She glanced up, cutting her eyes from Aidan, to Liza, to Naomi herself. That was new, Billie actually looking her in the eye. "I'm just worried."

"Relax, Billie," Naomi offered. "We're all here. We're all going to watch the Dragon with you."

Billie smiled shyly, bowing her head and leaning against Topher. "Yeah, I know. Thanks."

"It isn't hard to watch her either," Topher reassured. "She barely ever leaves the code room these days."

"If she's not careful she'll end up giving birth in that coding rig," Alice added with a chuckle. "Her and that Sleepwalker, I'm telling you. She never talks about anything else anymore."

"No kidding," Jillian sighed. "She came out to do a movie night, and she talked through the whole thing."

Beside her, Cameron gave an irritated little grunt. "Didn't hear the vid. She wouldn't shut up." Baby Jen snagged a few blueberries and squished them between her fingers with a delighted coo. Jillian leaned over to wipe her off.

"That bad?" Naomi asked, looking her brother's way.

He rolled his eyes. "That bad. She's kind of obsessing right now."

"*Kind* of?" Blake demanded tartly. "Try *completely,* honey. I can't *tell you* how long I have to talk at her before she'll come help me with a little funding work."

Naomi nodded. "I'll go sit with her later on, I guess. Hear what she's got so far, since I've been out of the loop."

"*Please* do, she's bored the rest of us *to death* with the details already," Blake groused.

The crew wasn't kidding either: Tweak barely looked up when Naomi walked into her space three hours later.

"Hey," Naomi offered.

Tweak jumped a little, but she didn't look away from her screens. "Hey."

"How's hunting?"

"Slow," Tweak sighed. "Doing a d-d-deep dive on almost t-two hundred p-people. Slow."

"Damn," Naomi murmured. "Any hints?"

"N-no," Tweak grumbled. "And I keep on t-t-trying and I get n-nowhere."

Absently, she flicked up another set of windows. Naomi watched Kevin and Inyoni's Force tracking dots run down the highway. Good thing the kid had figured out a work-around that let them track their people even when they were using GPS spoofers.

Settling in, Naomi pulled up her hand-to-hand and marksmanship recertification signoff papers for the crew, and started doing the gruntwork of her department. It needed doing, and it was a good way to kill time. Sarah hadn't done any of it in the month Naomi had been gone. It gave her a good excuse to hang out and keep an eye on the little coder.

They'd been working for twenty minutes when Tweak winced, shifting in her seat. "Ow..."

"You good?" Naomi asked, glancing up.

"Yeah. Fine." Tweak muttered. "I just…" She squeaked, doubling over. "Shit!"

Naomi stood. "Tweak, you're…" Then she saw the spreading wetness soaking Tweak's pants. "Stay put. I'll get Damian."

Tweak nodded, though her smile was more of a grimace. "R-r-right."

Naomi jogged down the hall, dodging people. "Clear the hall! Gangway!" she called, heading for the med bay. Sticking her head inside, she waved a hand. "Damian! We need you in the code room! Now!"

Miles away, Kevin calibrated the binoculars and tried to ignore the look Inyoni was giving him.

"Man, I don't like this," Inyoni muttered. "You said we were comin' out to pick up dental nanoids, not do all this spy shit."

"I know, I know, Inyoni," Kevin soothed. "But there are times when Logistics and Requisitions is given clandestine orders from on high in addition to our routine responsibilities. With the Sleepwalker nosing around, certain orders really are on a need-to-know basis."

Inyoni gave a little grunt. "What're we here for, exactly?"

"A meeting," Kevin explained, checking that both his slick poncho and the younger man's were doing their work. Lying on his belly in the dust, he calibrated… calibrated…

There. Fire. Perfect.

"Inyoni, stay here with the bikes, alright?" He murmured.

Inyoni gave a nod, though he sighed. "Yeah. I'm spotting for you?"

"You are indeed. And it's very much appreciated," Kevin agreed. Standing, he waved a blue bandanna he'd brought for the purpose, and began to walk.

He stopped just shy of the campfire's warmth, nodding deferentially at the two poncho-cloaked people. "Commander. Councilor, sir. Good morning. I apologize for the security measures on such short notice."

Reaching up, Councilor Hernandez pushed back his hood. Weak winter sun played off the silver in his dark hair. "McIllian-Headly. Bit melodramatic, having a meeting out here."

"I thought it was best, given our recent mole-related issues," Kevin agreed. "As we discussed in the call."

"And as I agreed," Sector Commander Hall agreed, pushing back her hood. "At ease, McIllian. Take a seat."

"Thank you, ma'am," he acknowledged, dropping down onto the piece of aged wood that had been set to one side. "As we've discussed in our calls, I've been in touch with a contact in EagleCorp who regularly acts as bodyguard for his CEO, and a meeting has been scheduled this afternoon between the four hold-outs among the oligarchs. I would like to propose an adjustment to the scheduled action, for your approval. Rather than a union-led recording of the event, I'd like to make this a one-man infiltration mission. This mission would be three-fold: a chance to gather intelligence, an opportunity to catch the Corporate heads on tape…" he gave it a beat, building up their interest, and smiled. "And a chance for us to take a leaf out of their book. If the Corps can have a sleepwalker in our midst, why can't we have one in theirs? Or four, perhaps?"

Councilor Hernandez studied him. "Interesting."

"No more showmanship, McIllian-Headly," Commander Hall stated flatly. "Spit it out."

*Fair point, I am showing off. Enough of that,* Kevin told himself. He cleared his throat. "My proposal is to smuggle in a set of bio-based surveillance nanoids and see that they're drunk at this meeting. A dose for the wine bottle is prepped and ready to go, as well as a dose for the water that will be delivered to the table. Once the nanoids have integrated into the systems of the CEOs, we will be able to track them, use their ears to listen to their meetings, and follow their every move. Turn about is fair play, after all." He waved in the direction of Denver. "With your approval, I'd like to enact this mission myself. It's a risk, but I think it's both more efficient and more reliable than asking our contact to carry these actions out while we sit back. I have the necessary skill-set to perform the mission, and the knowledge base to note details of the Corporate heads' behavior that recordings or other operatives might miss."

Hernandez sat back. "Now that...is something."

Proposal made, Kevin sat quiet and let his superiors process.

Hernandez nodded slowly. "That is certainly something…" Turning, he nodded at Commander Hall. "Your thoughts?"

"It's an opportunity," Hall agreed. "Might turn out to be the edge we need. And McIllian-Headly's right: he is the only operative I'd put in there. In most circumstances." Turning, the raptor of a woman pinned him with a look. "I've got questions, Officer."

"Yes ma'am," Kevin acknowledged.

"What's your infiltration plan?"

"Disguise myself as the double of a volunteer. We've worked out a dead drop for me to switch clothes with him. I have everything I need to disguise my physical appearance."

"Everything's in place?"

"Yes ma'am. What I need is on my bike. All plans are in place. I only need to give the go-ahead."

"You will inform me directly. Not your Base Commander, and not anyone else. Are we clear?"

"Yes ma'am," Kevin agreed. And of course that meant he was lying to Aidan again. But that was for later. Focus on now. "Currently I've written this foray down as a routine nanite pickup in my base's records. Only one person on my base knows otherwise: Specialist Amanzi. And he's been informed that it's not to be discussed. He'll be acting as my spotter."

"And can he be trusted?" Hall came back. Kevin nodded. "Yes ma'am. He's young and undertrained, but he's capable. And to be very frank, he's having a child with our Technical Officer and she does an intensive background check on you before she shakes your hand, never mind lets you into her bedroom. We've had such a lot of new people on my base that it is rather difficult to implicate or exonerate anyone with any certainty, but I trust Tweak's checks on someone that close to her."

Those sharp eyes didn't waver. "And where's your head? Is it in the game?"

There it was, the question Kevin was hoping he wouldn't be asked. "Ma'am?"

The lines of the Regional Commander's scarred face didn't so much as twitch. "Your history, McIllian-Headly. With the targets. One target in particular. It hasn't been ideal. I need you to tell me honestly: can you do this?"

Well. That, of course, was the question. For a beat, Kevin's mind flashed back to that night of protest. That night when he'd drawn his sidearm. Fire and ice streaking through his body and twanging every nerve on the way. The desperate need to inflict pain on someone who had hurt *so many.* The corrosive hate. The unchained need to do violence.

He'd nearly done something unforgivable that night.

What would happen if the opportunity was in front of him again?

"I believe my record displays my ability to put the plan into action, ma'am," Kevin stated.

"Not what I'm asking, McIllian," Commander Hall rapped out, seeing his bluff and calling it. Damn. "I'm asking, can you stand in a room where Harrington's drinking wine and keep your head on straight? If you have any doubts, any at all, then we're not doing this."

Kevin swallowed. He had a national year's supply of doubts. And worse, he had memories. What he'd done the last time he'd seen his enemy…

For a moment, he wondered if Aidan or Naomi had written a report on what he'd done. But no. Aidan would have told him if he'd sent in a reprimand; he would have been right to do so, and they both knew it. Aidan wouldn't leave him in the dark about a thing like that. And Hall wouldn't have countenanced this mission for a moment if she knew just how close he'd come to the unforgivable.

Putting himself on this mission wasn't wise. He knew it. But he needed to know if he *could* do it. If he couldn't face Harrington as a man rather than a raging beast, he could never look himself in the eye again. Until he did this, he could not trust himself with his family's lives. He *had* to do this.

He nodded. "Ma'am. I understand your caution. But this action would be the first step to the ultimate punishment of a man who has… of a man who richly deserves it. I admit freely, *I need* Harrington to be punished. Badly. But I've had time to think about this. And I can say, without a shred of doubt, that a mission to make that first step towards his very public comeuppance is worth more to me than any short-term satisfaction I could get from blowing his brains out." He gave a bleak, tight smile. "I want him to *pay,* Commander. A bullet out of the blue isn't a payment. One day, I *will* see him up in front of the Hague being tried for crimes against humanity."

Hall studied him for a heartbeat. Two. Three. Then she checked her tab.

"If you leave now, you'll be in more than enough time for the meeting. Councilor?"

"The Council has voted and approved similar actions in the past against specific high-threat targets. There's precedent. And the World Court has approved these measures in the cases of proven human-rights and war criminals," Councilor Hernandez considered for a moment. Then he nodded. "If you approve, I do,"

Regional Commander Hall took one more moment to study Kevin, one more moment of waiting stillness before she spoke. "Approved, McIllian-Headly. Come back in one piece. That's an order."

"Orders received, ma'am," Kevin agreed. Standing, he saluted.

## Event File 28
## File Tag: Covert Infiltration
## 13:30-03-30-2162

Inyoni sighed and pulled out his tab. "Tell me when you're done."

"Roger," Kevin agreed, checking his disguise one more time against the pic of the man he was impersonating and the mirror.

"So let's run through the code. I won't be able to talk into my mic. I'll tap my tab and use the haptics to ask you for a report. You'll be here watching through the binoculars. One beep means…"

"One beep means all good," Inyoni recited reluctantly. "Two beeps means I see trouble. Three beeps means get out now."

"Very good," Kevin agreed, quietly grateful that the boy was such a quick study.

"Walk me through what you do if I can't get back to you," he asked, and nodded along with Inyoni's answers. Good. Whatever happened to him, the boy would be safe. If someone was going to die because he couldn't control himself, it would be him and him alone.

He met his contact in the basement. The Peacekeeper looked him up and down. "Nice."

"Thanks. Where's my double?" Kevin asked in the voice he'd practiced.

"Joe's waiting for our word in the sub-basement. He needs to step back into his spot, he's here," the man offered. For a moment, he looked

Kevin up and down. "Never thought I'd be working with you guys, you know?"

"Same," Kevin agreed. "What's your story?"

The man made a face. "I don't shoot kids. Period. You order me to shoot kids, I'm done with you. Hamilton did that to our unit, so yeah. Fuck 'em."

Kevin clapped him on the shoulder. "You done good."

"Hope so," the Peacekeeper murmured, eyes turned away. Then he drew himself up. "Here's Joe's creds and gear." He shoved a suit, gun, and set of credentials into Kevin's hands. "Get kitted, we gotta get upstairs and on duty."

"Yeah," Kevin agreed.

He fell into line with the nicely dressed Peacekeepers sweeping the intimate little club made from a retrofitted clocktower, going over every inch of it. Twice Kevin tapped his tab. Each time, a reassuring single beep sounded in his ear.

Kevin took his time giving the kitchen its sweep. Using the sensor wand he'd switched with the original, he dispensed the surveillance nanoids into the water carafe. The nanoids would die without a heat source to draw energy from in a few hours, so there was no fear of an innocent ending up inadvertently bugged.

Checking each of the wines for poison with a needle-thin sensor through the cork, he used his modified version to add the nanoids. Then it was time to check the pots and pans, and finally the undersides of tables in the dining room itself. A routine sweep. Steady. Easy.

He just had to keep reminding himself of that. *Easy. Slow, steady breathing. Smooth movements. Easy.*

Eventually, the leader of the squad snapped out an order.

"Superiors in the building. Attention!"

Kevin straightened up, fell into his at attention pose with his hands behind his back, blinking four times to set the recording chips in his contacts to work.

One by one, the CEOs entered the room. There was Augustus Lynch of NatBank, skinny as a rake and about as attractive. The powerfully muscled Jack Hamilton of EagleCorp was behind him, giving the Peacekeepers of his corporation proprietary nods. Steven Evers of AgCo was resplendent in green with his ostentatious gold cross on a chain around his neck. *Sacrilegious show-pony,* Kevin whispered inside his head, though he kept his face neutral. *And to think I nearly ended up as a member of this noxious boys' club.*

Then the fourth man stepped into the room, and a cold fire lit in the pit of Kevin's gut.

Harrington didn't look well. Though his stride was assured, there was a stretched appearance to his finely gene-sculpted features. The bracketing lines about his mouth had deepend in the years since Kevin had been in the same room with him. The furrows of his brow were deeper, the bags under his eyes far more visible under the exquisite makeup work that had been applied to polish his veneer of effortless wellbeing. Under the polish, the man looked stretched. Exhausted. Strained.

*So you are feeling the pressure, are you, Mister H.?* Kevin asked silently. *Good. I'll make sure the vice around you tightens a little more every day from now on. I'll see to it that you feel a great deal more before this is done.*

His fingers clamped into fists behind his back.

They'd equipped him with a sidearm. How long would it take him to reach for it? How long to fire?

A stupid idea. A suicidal idea.

And yet.

And yet. To watch the bullet open a wet red hole in Harrington's chest. To watch the shock as he realized that he, too, could die at any moment. That he too could have life stolen from him.

Kevin could be that thief. It would be so *satisfying* to be that thief.

But who would the act benefit? What good would it do? It would feel incredible, true. For about a minute. It would certainly cost his life.

And his reputation as the Wildcard who could pull these clandestine missions off, for that matter. And it would cost the Force years…no, decades of work.

A minute of satisfaction wasn't worth that price. He wouldn't pay it. He wouldn't make his people pay it.

And yet…

His fingers ached. A slow drum beat was pounding in his ears. He fixed his eyes on Harrington as the man took his seat. The waiters offered menus obsequiously. Food was chosen. Drinks were poured. Drinks were sampled. And the Trojan Horse was through the gates. *Yes. Yes, yes, yes.*

Finally, the CEOs cut to the chase.

"Gentlemen," Lynch began. "I've called this meeting to let you know that, once this month comes to a close, I will be meeting with my employees. I advise that you do the same."

Two of the men erupted, spitting insults and curses at Lynch. Harrington sat completely still. Some part of Kevin's mind noted distantly that the tape of this meeting was going to be informational gold. Noted all the words said, the physical tells of the men shouting at one another. But it was Harrington that he couldn't look away from.

*You saw this coming, didn't you, you cold-blooded reptile?* Kevin asked in the drumbeat silence of his head.

"Gentlemen, please!" Lynch was trying to shout over Evers and Hamilton. "We have two choices now: either we negotiate with unions, or we deal with mobs! We're sitting on a country like a powder keg, playing with matches. Every time we retaliate against a union the following backlash burns up millions of dollars in assets, and it'll get worse if we put a foot wrong! It doesn't make any sense! See reason!"

"Fuck your reason!" Hamilton snarled, "you think I'm giving in to these anarchist shitsuckers because they're bitching and moaning and smashing windows?! If they want smashing, I'll smash their heads! The only thing I'm giving them is bullets!"

"Gentlemen!"

*And what will you do, Harrington?* Kevin whispered silently. *Will you stand and hiss, or will you lie down and try to crawl away?*

*I could crush you now, you venomous wyrm. Remove your poison from the world. It would be well and truly justified.*

But it wouldn't be justified, would it? An extrajudicial killing wasn't justified. It was just another vicious circle in the downward spiral they were all trapped in.

And yet.

The man was a serpent in human skin. Compassionless. Amoral. Death was the only answer for such a clear and present danger.

And yet.

A cramp spasmed through Kevin's wrist.

And yet.

And Lynch was standing and storming out, the remaining men calling slurs after him. Harrington was still as a sand dune. Would he sit that still when the whole world called him to account in a court of law? Kevin had said it to Commander Hall: *A bullet out of the blue isn't a payment. One day, I will see him up in front of the Hague being tried for crimes against humanity.* And he did believe that.

But would Harrington sit that still in a box at the Hague one day? Or would he escape to keep spreading his poison in the world?

That *could not happen.*

Harrington was right there. Soaked in the blood of all those he'd put in the grave. All the innocents. All the citizens. All the people Kevin had cared about. All the people he'd loved.

And yet.

Aidan's words.

*He needs to live so the whole world can see him pay his debts.*

*You deserve to keep thinking of yourself as a good man.*

Was he good? That, of course, was the question. Was he good enough to withstand this temptation?

His forearm began to ache.

And there were three beeps in his ear. They repeated a moment later.

"Gentlemen," Harrington stated, "Take a moment. My sources are informing me that we may have an infiltrator in the building."

"What?!" Evers demanded.

That was Kevin's cue. He didn't step away immediately; that would be a giveaway. He stood for fifteen minutes with the executives screaming at one another, guards who weren't on personal detail rushing around, and Inyoni's warning beating a tattoo inside his ear. Minute by minute, he added the body language of a man who really needs the bathroom. On his double's work watch, he sent the code for taking a bathroom break and stepped away. In the toilet, he set the scrambler that would short out the surveillance cameras, stripped down to the cleaning jumpsuit he wore underneath the Peacekeeper uniform, and peeled off the mask he wore. He donned the tight skullcap he'd tucked in his pocket, added a gimme cap, and streaked reflective cream over his face. He hid Joe's gear behind the ceiling tile over the toilet.

On his own tab, he sent Joe the code to come back and reclaim his place. Then he was out the door, his heart still pounding in his ears.

*That was close.*

*Too close.*

*But I did it. I got the information. I inserted the nanoids. And I can face Harrington,* he repeated, dizzy with the elation of it. *I can face Harrington without becoming a beast. I can face him as a man! I can!*

He was practically dancing as he entered the attic where Inyoni hid. "Well done Inyoni, thanks for the heads up, what's—"

"We gotta go!" Inyoni cut in, ears flat against his head.

Kevin blinked. "What?"

"I called you man!" Inyoni cried, his voice cracking. "I called you, come on!"

"I thought you called because Harrington was onto us?" Kevin asked, brows knit.

Inyoni stared at him with bewildered eyes, panicking. “Hunh? No! We gotta go, it’s Tweak! She’s in labor! Fuckin' hell!" He grabbed his ears with both hands, yanking in his agitation.

"Get it together." Kevin ordered, words clipped. "I'll get you back to the base.”

Inyoni looked at him like a trapped rabbit, but at least he let go of his poor ears. He smiled in relief. "Thanks."

"Don't thank me yet." Kevin replied dryly as he shoved the door open. "We haven't gotten there. But we will directly."

Luckily, the strictures across the Grid had been loosening ever more in these past months. Exiting was almost easy. They crossed the Dust in record time, arriving in a plume of grit that powdered the plants just inside the pylon wall.

Inyoni was off his bike before it stopped moving, panic on his face. Kevin did his best to keep up with the panicking boy; no telling what he’d do if he didn’t have a guiding hand on his shoulder.

“Take care of the bikes please?” He threw over his shoulder as he blazed past the motor pool crew. Ahead of him, Inyoni was skidding through hallways, almost running people over. Chest on fire, Kevin caught up with him just as he blazed into the med bay.

"Where's she?" Inyoni demanded.

Damian poked his masked head out of a curtained corner. "She's in here, but I want you masked and washed up before you—" a high scream cut him off, and he pulled sharply back into his hidden alcove.

Inyoni made to move again, but Kevin caught him by the shoulders. “No, no, you want to listen to Damian here, Inyoni. Here. Let me get you scrubbed up and sterile. It’s for Tweak’s health, and the baby’s health,” he reassured when Inyoni opened his mouth in protest. Fighting down the urge to cough, he led his subordinate to the sinks. “Here, come over here, don’t waste time arguing.”

He grabbed masks from the wall and slathered hand sanitizer on Inyoni’s hands and arms along with his own. Inyoni squirmed like one of the kids.

“Man, my dragon’s screaming, I ain’t got time for—”

“Screaming is a normal part of childbirth, Inyoni,” Kevin soothed. “Here, put your arms under the hot water. Alright. Now the antiviral UV beam. Good. Now, gloves, and a gown, and a cap…damn, your ears, I didn’t think…alright forget the cap. Come on.”

Stepping past the curtain, Inyoni gasped. "Holy fuck…"

It wasn’t a pleasant sight, even for those who’d seen it before. Tweak's body was bowed up against the bed, her face a mask. Her hands were balled so tightly into the sheets that her knuckles were white.

"It's nothing to worry too much about. Stay calm," Damian said, but he sounded nervous himself. "Her system is having a heightened reaction to labor. I've got her on something to help."

“Where are we?” Kevin asked.

“Second stage of labor, eight centimeters,” Alice replied quickly. “Water broke a few hours after you left, she’s going through a transitional phase now.”

“Then everything’s right on schedule,” Kevin clarified cheerfully. “Tweak, I brought your bird home! Here you are, Inyoni.”

Inyoni nodded mutely, swallowed hard, and moved to the bedside. "Hey…Tweak, you hear me?” He murmured, voice a little wobbly. “I'm here. You're gonna be okay."

"Asshat!" Tweak spat. "You were s'posed to be gone. Don't want you to see—" that was all she got out before she screamed.

"Forget that," Inyoni muttered when the scream faded. He was ashen under his dark skin, ears fluttering like sickly moths against his neck. "I should be with you."

"Don't want you to see!" Tweak gritted between her teeth.

“Everyone’s been in to check on her,” Alice added patiently. “She keeps saying she doesn’t want anyone to see.”

“Cause I don’t!” Tweak ground out.

Inyoni frowned and put his hand around hers, squeezing gently. "Too bad. I wanna…I wanna see. Said I'd be here for you, didn't I?"

Tweak gulped down a breath. "Fine. You guys. And Aidan. Nobody else. D-don’t want the whole c-crew in here."

“You got it,” Alice agreed.

"I'm just going to check a few things. We'll be right back." Damian added, taking Kevin by the shoulder. Outside, he met Kevin’s eyes. "I don't want to scare you exactly," he stated in an undertone, "but I've got some misgivings about this delivery. If we ask you to get Inyoni out of here and keep him occupied, help me out?"

Kevin nodded. Holding the doctor’s eyes, he tipped his head toward the curtained alcove. "And you'll make sure she gets through this." It wasn't a question.

"I'm going to do my absolute best," the doctor agreed solemnly. Then he returned to his patient. Carefully, Kevin stepped in behind him.

Another contraction had set in. Inyoni had taken a knee beside the bed, holding Tweak's hand. "Hey. I'm here,” he was murmuring softly. “You're gonna be fine." Tweak's grip probably would have made a normal man scream in pain. Finally, the contraction released. Tweak lay back, panting.

Kevin put a hand on Inyoni’s shoulder. “Right. Inyoni, come on. Let’s go get dinner, this is going to take a few hours yet.”

“But I—” Inyoni began.

Blowing out an exasperated breath, Tweak pointed at the door. “Bird! Go. Come back. Later.”

“You heard the all powerful Dragon,” Kevin offered with a chuckle. “Come on.”

“What if she has it while I’m in the canteen?” Inyoni asked weakly. Kevin shook his head. “Alice said she was at eight centimeters. The dilation process is, roughly, about a centimeter an hour if everything is perfectly smooth. Often, it takes longer. Birth really begins at ten centimeters. So we have at least two hours to kill.” He reached over and squeezed Inyoni’s shoulder. “All that said, you’re frazzled, you haven’t had anything to eat for some hours, and everyone will want to spend this time together while we wait for the new member of the family. Come on.”

Everyone in the canteen greeted Inyoni with the appropriate level of cheering and boxes of diapers. The parents in the group circled up, giving him all the reassurance and tips a man could want. Kevin let them take charge, stepping back.

"Hey," Aidan's quiet voice offered behind him.

Turning, Kevin smiled at his husband. "Afternoon, love."

Stepping in, Aidan put an arm around his waist. "How's Bird doing?"

"Oh, panicking as much as any expectant father," Kevin offered, kissing the top of his husband's head. "Don't worry, love. The crew's got this."

"Yeah, I see that," Aidan agreed, leaning against him. "You hear the news? Lynch is going to sit down with the NatBank unions."

"Is that a fact?" Kevin asked. For a moment his mind flashed the images of men hurling abuse in their luxurious room. So, all their vitriol had backfired. Lynch had gone ahead early. He smiled. Served them right. And they'd be able to listen to the details with Lynch's own ears, to boot.

"Gonna be some party tonight," Aidan murmured, "between Lynch giving in and the new kid getting here."

"Some party indeed," Kevin agreed with satisfaction.

Time passed. Inyoni paced the med bay until Kevin thought he'd put a hole in the floor. Now and again, Aidan would deliver coffee for Alice and Damian, ice cubes for the expectant mother, and a word of comfort for the father to be. Mostly, Kevin's work became keeping Inyoni out of everyone's hair and off everyone's nerves.

"It's been hours and she's still screamin' here and there," Inyoni fretted, finally coaxed out into the hall for a bit to sit with his support crew and eat something.

"And that's normal," Kevin reassured, looking up from his book. "I've seen several women go through this. It's not like shelling peas; it'll be hours yet, and that's perfectly natural. Sit."

"But the meds ain't helpin'," Inyoni muttered anxiously, though he did as he was told, flopping gracelessly into a chair.

“If anything was wrong, Damian would know,” Aidan soothed in that soft voice he had such a talent with at times like these.

“It’s actually going really well,” Alice reassured, Aidan handed her the sandwich he’d brought for her, and she gave him a smile before biting into it.

Inyoni glanced up at her like a puppy afraid of being kicked. “You sure?”

“I’m sure,” Alice agreed between bites. “This labor’s going nice and fast, and yeah her cortisol and heart rate are elevated, but she’s doing alright.” She patted Inyoni’s shoulder. “Everything will be alright.”

Inyoni hunched his shoulders. “Yeah. I guess…”

Time passed. Alice finished her meal and headed back in. Kevin did his best to keep his subordinate distracted.

In the medical bay, Tweak screamed again and again. In the hall, Inyoni covered his ears and rocked to and fro in his chair. Aidan looked between him and the door with furrowed brows.

All at once, Inyoni was out of his chair and running into the medical bay. The man moved in such a burst of speed that Kevin, to his chagrin, barely caught on for a beat.

“Inyoni!” He hissed. “Oh damn it.” He followed as quickly as he could.

"Blood pressure's through the roof," Alice called over the noise of Tweak's screams. "Fetal's fine but Tweak's—" she winced as Tweak's body bowed into an arch of agony.

Inyoni was back down beside her again, mumbling things that couldn’t be heard over her screaming. Then the scream cut off.

“Shit!” Damian growled. "I knew that dose was too high! Alice, paddles!"

"Tweak," Inyoni yelped, his voice cracking. "Come on, no. Don't do this. Come on, come on, you can do it."

For the next little eternity, the room was very quiet. Tweak's body was small enough to bounce off the table every time it was hit with a charge. Kevin whispered his Pater Noster under his breath and held Aidan's hand tight.

The line of the monitor ran on and on in that ghastly, supine finality.

"Again," Damian stated. The charge bounced Tweak's body into the air.

"Again."

Kevin traded Our Father for Hail Mary. The Virgin knew more about this sort of situation anyway.

"Again."

"Holy Mary, Mother of God, pray for us sinners now," Kevin whispered.

The room smelled of ozone.

And the monitor blipped. And blipped again. Tweak sucked in a breath. So did everyone else in the room.

Damian grinned. "That a girl."

It was not a fun half an hour for anyone. But at the end of it, Damian was wrapping a squalling little girl in a blanket. "They're both in good shape," he reassured the new father. "Tweak's system is bouncing back. She'll be pretty woozy for the next day or so, but she's fine." He smiled down at Inyoni, the squalling infant in his arms. "Want to hold her?"

Inyoni's hands trembled as he reached for the baby. He sank down into the chair beside the bed. The expression on his face made Kevin's heart ache. Putting an arm around Aidan's waist, he smiled as he watched a father fall in love with his daughter.

Inyoni stared at the child in wonder for a few beats. Then he raised his head, and looked at Kevin.

"Hey man…you wanna come hold her? You're her daddy gene-wise too, yeah?"

A hard lump rose in Kevin's throat. He swallowed. "I…I'd be honored. Thank you, Inyoni." Stepping to the bedside, he knelt and held out his arms. With infinite care, Inyoni passed the little bundle over.

The child was absolutely miniscule, wrinkled as a prune. Two tiny brown rabbit ears flopped aimlessly, moving out of sync with the child's elfin hands.

Kevin felt his heart crack wide open. So many emotions ran through his chest that it was a wonder his frame could contain the flood of them.

He glanced back at Aidan, feeling tears prickle behind his eyes.

He was a father. In this wonderfully off-kilter, jerry-rigged fashion that was so very Wildcards, he was a father.

Carefully, he leaned over the side of the bed. "Tweak, wake up. Look. It's your baby. We have a daughter. You and Inyoni and me. We have a daughter."

"Bao Li's here, Tweak. You done good," Inyoni murmured, massaging her hand. "She's here. You're here. You done good. You done so damn good, babe."

Tweak opened bleary eyes and smiled weakly. "Yeah. I did. Kickass." Then she closed her eyes, and fell fast asleep.

## Event File 29
## File Tag: Personnel Induction
## 04:20-03-31-2162

It was dark when Tweak woke up, and she *fucking hurt.* Everything hurt. Her muscles twanged. Her head throbbed. Her guts felt like they'd been scraped out with a blunt spoon.

"Hey," Alice murmured. "The readings say you're coming around and doing good. How're you feeling?"

Tweak gave a long groan. Alice chuckled.

"Yeah, I bet. We're getting some fluids and stuff into you, and now that you're coming around we can get you some nerve blockers for the pain."

"You had to wait till I w-w-woke up feeling like this?" Tweak grumbled. Sitting on her bed, Alice nodded. "Yeah, we did, because you had a cardiac event. But it turned out okay."

"Y-yeah?" Tweak turned her head. "Bao Li. Where?"

"Right here," Alice offered, patting a little wheeled cart. Tweak swallowed. The fear made it through everything else, cutting like a knife. "You checked? She's good?"

Alice smiled gently. "She's great, Tweak. She's got everything she should have, and nothing she shouldn't. She's got her mom's eyes and her dad's ears. Her genome is in great shape; only a couple irregularities that were tricky to iron out, and none that'll hurt her."

Tweak nodded. She was so tired, but her baby was here. Safe. Alive. In good shape.

She drew a breath. “Bird? Where?”

Alice nodded. “In the chair across from you, dead asleep. He’s been planning this big party with the rest of the crew for a couple hours. When you’re feeling better, they’re going to throw a huge welcome party for Bao Li. Hope you’re ready for that.”

Tweak snorted. “With D-Damian, it’ll be n-next y-year before I get out.”

Alice tipped her head, acknowledging the point. “You do look pretty rough.”

“Feel it,” Tweak agreed. “But I wanna see Bao. And Bird. Can I g-get up?”

“Not for a bit,” Alice chuckled. “If I sit your bed up, you can see them both. Want me to?”

Tweak nodded. Alice tapped the screen beside the bed, and Tweak felt it shift under her.

“Patient Control activated,” Alice said to the bed’s controls. “Okay, now just say ‘bed up’ or ‘bed down’, and you can lay down and sit up when you want.”

“Thanks,” Tweak agreed. Now she was sitting up, she could see Inyoni splayed out across a chair, ears twitching as he dreamed. Turning her head, she looked into a repurposed storage bin on wheels. Now it was a wheeled crib lined in soft white blankets. A tiny baby lay curled in them, only her ears and one brown fist peeking out of the whiteness.

“You want to hold her?” Alice asked quietly.

Tweak couldn’t take her eyes off the baby. She couldn’t say a word. Swallowing, she nodded.

Gently, Alice reached into the crib and lifted Bao Li. She was settled in Tweak’s arms like a fluffy little bird, all blankets and lightness. Barely there at all.

Reaching in, Tweak stroked her face with two fingers, following the line of her little jaw all the way up to the tip of one ear. Bao Li turned her head at the touch, waving a little fist like she didn't know it was attached.

Gently, Tweak touched the tiny fingers with one of her own. The little hand grabbed ahold.

Tweak thought her heart was going to split.

"I'll be over here if you need me," Alice offered softly. And then it was just Tweak and this tiny little person wrapped in blankets. She still felt like somebody had scraped her out with an ice cream scoop. She still ached all over. But right now, that didn't matter so much.

Bao Li turned her tiny face Tweak's way, and opened her eyes. Dark eyes, set at the same angle as Tweak's. Her baby had her eyes. Her baby was looking at her.

"Hi Bao Li," she whispered, stroking the little girl's cheek. "Hi. You're Bao Li, okay? I'm m-Mom."

The tiny girl took her in for a second, staring at her like she was thinking it all over. Then she closed her eyes.

Tweak swallowed. There was so much inside her, and she wanted to put all these feels somewhere. Maybe she could talk. What could she say to this little girl on her first day in the world? What should she say?

What had her own mom said?

Tweak closed her eyes, remembering. Trying, anyway. There weren't very many conversations in her memory.

What was there?

Her mom giving them sponge baths when they were tiny. Bedtime, and her mom singing. There was that song. Mama had always sung that same song. The tune was still there in Tweak's head, that tune from way back. She dug down to it, pulled it up. A lot of the words were gone, but she could remember the tune. Slowly, the first words came. She let them out into the air carefully, afraid they'd fall apart any second.

*"Zhe lü dao xiang yi zhi chuan..."*

Quietly, she sang to her daughter. She stuttered, got words wrong, stumbled and messed up. But she kept singing. She sang about green islands in the moonlight. She sang about a river of love pouring out for a child to float on like a boat. In the dark, the song wrapped them up and made them safe, and everything was good.

They had to delay the party a few days when all was said and done; Tweak was in the med bay for a week before she was feeling well enough to start complaining and get out of medical supervision. Kevin couldn't help but note that she was a bit wobbly even then, leaning on Inyoni as she walked. He wasn't alone in the observation either.

"Can't wait to be normal," she grumbled, cradling Bao Li with one arm and holding onto Inyoni with the other.

"You grew a baby," Inyoni replied with a chuckle. "Gonna take a while to get back to normal."

"Yeah." Tweak agreed softly. "Good job, though." In her arms, the baby gurgled.

"Yeah." Inyoni grinned teasingly. "Three of us did damn good. 'Cept her ears, 'course."

"Shut it," Tweak replied as they entered the rec room. The whole place had been done over in Alice's softly crocheted blankets, and a huge banner reading 'Welcome To The World Bao Li Amanzi!' graced the back wall.

The cheers were muted in order not to frighten the baby, but no less fervent for that. Tweak was ensconced like a queen in the center of the couch, and everyone circled round. Gifts piled up at her feet: snacks for Tweak, soft toys for the child. Alice had outdone herself with a blanket showing a phoenix and a dragon circling one another on a golden background; Kevin had never seen her knit something so intricate. The baby was wrapped in it immediately, and the colors made her lovely dark skin shine. The little hair she had puffed dark reddish-brown between her vaguely waving ears.

"She's so little!" Donovan murmured in wonder.

"She looks like a tiny adorable bunny rabbit!" Yvonne enthused, making happy little wiggles of the fingers at the child.

Tweak gave Yvonne a look. “Bunny. R-rabbit. *Seriously.*”

“She really does though,” Billie chuckled, sitting on Tweak’s other side. “Like a little bunny in a nest.”

“There are worse nicknames than Bunny,” Kevin offered with a smile. Tweak raised her head, and he prepared himself to parry her newest barrage of insults.

Of all things, Tweak smiled at him. “C’mere CES. C-come sit.”

Since it was Tweak and Bao Li’s day, he did as he was told. Giving his husband a kiss, he crossed to the couch and took a seat at Tweak and Inyoni’s feet. Tweak looked around the room. “S-somebody g-get a pic?”

“I’ll grab someone from the hall to take it,” Topher offered. “Two seconds.”

“You wanna hold her?” Tweak asked, smiling at him. Kevin had to clear his throat to get the words out. “Yes please, if you don’t mind.”

Tweak snorted. “You. Arms. Open.”

Gently as a sigh, he accepted the little girl in his arms. Their daughter. His friends’ daughter. *His* daughter.

For a moment, he was swamped again with that tidal wave of love and gratitude, nearly breathless with the joy of it.

“Watch out, or Kev will dump holy water all over her,” Yvonne teased. He rolled his eyes, the intensity of his emotions relieved with the teasing of daily life.

“For your information, a baptism done on a newborn without the consent of the caretakers isn’t canonically legitimate, and I can’t sanctify water under the aegis of the Catholic faith; I’m not ordained. Therefore your argument is invalid and you can stuff it.”

Soft laughter ran through the room. Kevin felt hands on his shoulders, and looked up into his husband’s bright eyes with his daughter in his arms.

For a breath of time, life was immaculate in its endless marvels, redeemed of all its sins.

And then reality crashed back down over them all.

"Guys!" Topher's boots clattered against the floor as he raced into the room. "Guys! Argus shut off the water and power to the Denver Metro! They shut it all off!"

"What?!" Aidan almost ran over to Topher. "What neighborhoods? How many people are cut off?"

Topher's eyes were huge. "All of them. Every neighborhood. Everyone."

Fingers fumbling, he brought up the reports. Everyone stared.

Janice let out a long sigh. "Well fuck a fire hose. Here we go again."

## A Note From The Logistics Specialist: if you need resources to help you improve your community and your world, there's help. Reach out.

Heya. Name's Inyoni, I'm new(ish) around here. Anyway, I just wanted to say…look, sometimes things suck. But you're not on your own, okay? In your own world there are resources for the stuff you're working on. Here's a bunch.

Hang in there.

-Inyoni

## National Suicide Prevention Lifeline-1-800-273-TALK (8255) Code 988

The National Suicide Prevention Lifeline is a national network of local crisis centers that provides free and confidential emotional support to people in suicidal crisis or emotional distress 24 hours a day, 7 days a week. They're committed to improving crisis services and advancing suicide prevention by empowering individuals, advancing professional best practices, and building awareness.

## Crisis Text Line-Text HELLO to 741741

A live, trained Crisis Counselor receives the text and responds, all from their secure online platform. The volunteer Crisis Counselor will help you move from a hot moment to a cool moment.

## Substance Abuse and Mental Health Services Administration-1-877-726-4727

SAMHSA's National Helpline is a free, confidential, 24/7, 365-day-a-year treatment referral and information service (in English and Spanish) for individuals and families facing mental and/or substance use disorders.

## National Alliance of Mental Illness

What started as a small group of families gathered around a kitchen table in 1979 has blossomed into the nation's leading voice on mental health. Today, they are an alliance of more than 600 local affiliates who work in your community to raise awareness and provide support and education that was not previously available to those in need. www.nami.org/Support-Education

## Channel Zero Network

Channel Zero is an english-based anarchist radio/podcast network run by radical media makers. They present anarchist analysis & context to deepen people's understanding of the situation and broaden the struggle. They share stories from the front lines, lessons from history, and battle-tested ideas to spread revolutionary practices. Check them out at https://channelzeronetwork.com/

## Beautiful Trouble Network

The Beautiful Trouble Network is a global network of organizers, artists, trainers, and writers who form the community of praxis called Beautiful Trouble. They equip social movements with an ever-growing suite of strategic tools and training to help grassroots movements be more creative, effective, and irresistible.

Check them out and get involved at https://beautifultrouble.org/

## The Ruckus Society

Ruckus has trained and assisted thousands of activists in the use of nonviolent direct action. They either bring activists to them (at Training Camps or Skillshares) or they go to the people (community-requested tailored trainings). Through these trainings, they help people learn the skills they need to practice nonviolent direct action safely and effectively. These trainings contain cerebral elements as well as physical, classroom-style instruction for action planning, communicating with the media, building leadership and political analysis, and nonviolent philosophy and practice.

Ruckus promotes and teaches:

- Implementation of strategic nonviolent direct action against unjust institutions and policies;
- Organized strategic development and coherent planning to advance campaign goals;
- The establishment of broad coalitions with common objectives;
- Effective methods of media outreach and Internet/Technology activism to inform the general public;
- Respect for all living things and a commitment to the power of diversity.
- In addition to hosting Trainings, Ruckus also provides Action Support at a wide variety of levels (from helping you brainstorm action ideas to pulling off an action for you) for groups who desire assistance with their action campaign.

Their Action Support program goes hand in hand with their Training program, and they love nothing better than helping folks who have trained with them take action in order to build their skills and experience, and most importantly – create positive changes! Check them out and get involved at https://ruckus.org/

## International Center on Nonviolent Conflict (ICNC)

ICNC is the leading global organization advancing the study and practice of nonviolent civil resistance to achieve rights, freedom and justice around the world. Their programs, achievements and impact reflect their ongoing dedication to using social science insights and lessons from practitioners to improve outcomes for civil resistance movements worldwide. Learn more about their impact and theory of change at https://www.nonviolent-conflict.org/

## CANVAS-Center For Applied Nonviolent Actions and Strategies

From CANVAS' headquarters in Belgrade, Serbia, CANVAS operates a network of international trainers and consultants with expertise in building and running successful non-violent movements. They work to build more just, democratic, and responsible societies. CANVAS' offices in Washington DC, Kuala Lumpur, Male, Tbilisi, Johannesburg and Belgrade aim to provide maximum support to the activists on the ground, and they serve as a hub for local and regional initiatives that rely on principles of nonviolent struggle and creative activism. Their organization disseminates knowledge through a variety of media, including workshops, books, videos, and specialized courses.

CANVAS has produced several publications on nonviolent resistance over the years, based on intensive research and our members' decades of experience in the field. These revolutionary manuals are available for free download on their website. Their trainers regularly teach courses on nonviolent strategy at a variety of educational institutions worldwide. Get in touch with them at https://canvasopedia.org/

## United for a Fair Economy

(http://www.faireconomy.org/resource-library)

The resources on UFE's website feature online data and analysis revolving around CEO Pay, Taxes, Union demographics, wealth gap rates and other elements of corporate power. Most sections are accompanied by UFE's analysis on corporate wealth and the economy, often presented in viewer-friendly formats such as charts and diagrams. Homepage:

http://www.faireconomy.org

## The American Federation of Labor and Congress of Industrial Organizations (AFL-CIO)

The AFL-CIO is the democratic, voluntary federation of 58 national and international labor unions that represent 12.5 million working people. They strive to ensure that all working people are treated fairly, with decent paychecks and benefits, safe jobs, dignity, and equal opportunities. They help people acquire skills and job-readiness for the 21st century economy, operating the largest training network outside the U.S. military. With millions of workers taking collective action, the AFL-CIO is showing that together we can win better pay, better benefits and safer working conditions. Get involved at https://aflcio.org/about-us

## Responsible Shopper

This database is designed to help you discover the good, the bad and the ugly behind the products you buy everyday — from clothing to shoes to toothpaste. It's searchable by company, brand or category, and provides an overview for each company with specific problems, praise, ratings and industry comparisons. A program of Green America, at http://www.greenamerica.org. Check out the accessibly-formatted Co-op America's Guide to Researching Corporations, with its useful appendix full of gems like the Resource Sources, searchable by type of information. Though some listings are dated, it's still a very useful reference tool. http://www.responsibleshopper.org

## SumOfUs

SumOfUs is a community of people from around the world committed to curbing the growing power of corporations. We want to buy from, work for and invest in companies that respect the environment, treat their workers well and respect democracy. SumOfUs is not afraid to hold them to account when they don't. Check them out and help out at https://www.sumofus.org/

## Top 100 Corporate Criminals

The Top 100 Corporate Criminals is a compilation of corporations that were criminally fined for a variety of crimes, including environmental, antitrust, fraud, and campaign finance. The ranking is done by the amount of criminal fine. The list is all on one html page, so you can do a search, enter your corporate target's name and see if it's made it to this list. The longer version of the same list that includes criminal offense summaries follows on the lower part of the page. http://corporatecrimereporter.com/top100.html

## Empower Oversight Whistleblowers & Research (EMPOWR)

Empower Oversight Whistleblowers & Research (EMPOWR) is a nonprofit, nonpartisan educational organization dedicated to enhancing independent oversight of government and corporate wrongdoing. EMPOWR works to help insiders document and report corruption to the proper authorities while also seeking to hold authorities accountable to act on those reports. Check them out at https://empowr.us/

## Queen City Cooperative

QCC provides inclusive, democratic, affordable, member-owned housing. They offer ongoing education to members regarding cooperative ownership, creating an inclusive culture, effective democratic participation, and stewardship of the property. QCC strives to educate the public about cooperatives.

Check out their work at https://www.queencitycooperative.org/

## Colorado Community STD Testing Centers

Community-based STD testing organizations generate awareness and foster social change while providing access to testing and treatment.

If you're concerned about visiting your regular doctor or can't afford the cost of private testing, a community testing center may be able to help. You can find free or low-cost testing from the resources on this page:
https://www.testing.com/std-testing/colorado/#_colorado_std_testing_directory

## Civics Unplugged

Civics Unplugged (CU) is a nonpartisan 501(c)(3) social enterprise whose mission is to empower the leaders of Generation Z to build a brighter future for humanity. While Generation Z is deeply motivated to contribute to addressing the challenges we collectively face, traditional empowerment structures were simply not designed to equip young people with what they need to understand and address impediments to human flourishing. This is where Civics Unplugged comes in.

At CU, they are creating a new way to empower thousands of civic-minded youth around the world each year to devote themselves to radically increasing the health and resilience of humanity's collective future.

CU is powered by a digital-first team and community of thousands of Gen Z leaders committed to fostering human flourishing around the globe. CU's core team is based in NYC and represents decades of experience across politics, law, education, social impact, tech, venture, pop culture, media, and community building. It's at this intersection of these many domains that the magic of CU emerges.

Read more and show it to the young people in your life at https://www.civicsunplugged.org/

## Government Accountability Project (GAP)

The Government Accountability Project (GAP) is a nonpartisan, public interest group that promotes government and corporate accountability by providing legal representation to whistleblowers. It offers pro bono legal and strategic advice and support to employees considering reporting, or who have already reported, misconduct. GAP also leads campaigns to enact whistleblower protection laws both domestically and internationally.

Get in touch at https://www.whistleblower.org

## Public Employees for Environmental Responsibility (PEER)

Public Employees for Environmental Responsibility (PEER) is a national alliance of local, state, and federal government scientists, land managers, environmental law enforcement agents, field specialists, and other resource professionals committed to responsible management of America's public resources. PEER provides advocacy and legal support to employees who speak up for environmental ethics and scientific integrity within their agency. Touch base with them at https://peer.org

## Project Vote

Project Vote is a national, nonpartisan, nonprofit organization founded on the belief that an organized, diverse electorate is the key to a better America. Project Vote's mission is to build an electorate that accurately represents the diversity of this nation's citizenry, and to ensure that every eligible citizen can register, vote, and cast a ballot that counts. Check out their work and get involved at http://www.projectvote.org/

## Alliance for Emerging Power

The Alliance for Emerging Power provides trainings on organizing, base building, and get out the vote (GOTV) to develop the next generation of civic leaders. Their trainings have prepared students to run campaigns for Student Government, city council, and issue areas they are passionate about like student loan debt and the treatment of unhoused community members. Their alumni network holds campus, community, and non-profit leadership positions.

Learn more at https://www.commoncause.org/emerging-power

## Native American Rights Fund

Since 1970, the Native American Rights Fund (NARF) has provided legal assistance to Indian tribes, organizations, and individuals nationwide who might otherwise have gone without adequate representation. NARF has successfully asserted and defended the most important rights of Indians and tribes in hundreds of major cases, and has achieved significant results in such critical areas as tribal sovereignty, treaty rights, natural resource protection, and Indian education. NARF is a non-profit 501c(3) organization that focuses on applying existing laws and treaties to guarantee that national and state governments live up to their legal obligations.

## Gapminder

Gapminder is an independent Swedish foundation with no political, religious, or economic affiliations.Their work identifies systematic misconceptions about important global trends and proportions, and uses reliable data to develop easy to understand teaching materials to rid people of their misconceptions.

If you want to fight false information, join them at https://www.gapminder.org/

## City Repair Project

City Repair Project collaborates with communities to cultivate and facilitate community-led artistic, equitable and ecologically-oriented placemaking. Their immediate service area is the Portland Metro Area, and they have worked with communities in Portland, Gresham, Beaverton, Hillsboro, Oregon City, Tigard and Vancouver. They consult with and support communities and organizations across North America and internationally.

Check them out and get involved at https://cityrepair.org/mission

## Food Revolution Network

This network is committed to healthy, ethical, and sustainable food for all. Guided by John and Ocean Robbins, with more than 700,000 members and with the collaboration of many of the top food revolutionary leaders of our times, Food Revolution Network aims to empower individuals, build community, and transform food systems to support healthy people and a healthy planet. Check out their extensive resources at https://foodrevolution.org

## Honor The Earth

Honor the Earth develops these resources by using music, the arts, the media, and Indigenous wisdom to ask people to recognize our joint dependency on the Earth and be a voice for those not heard.

As a unique national Native initiative, Honor the Earth works to a) raise public awareness and b) raise and direct funds to grassroots Native environmental groups. They are the only Native organization that provides both financial support and organizing support to Native environmental initiatives. This model is based on strategic analysis of what is needed to forge change in Indian country, and it is based deep in our communities, histories, and long-term struggles to protect the earth.

Check them out and lend a hand at https://honorearth.org/

## Urban Symbiosis

Urban Symbiosis took roots in Aurora, Colorado with a purpose to build long-standing symbiotic relationships between locally owned and community-driven businesses. To bring their vision to life, they pursued one of the community's greatest needs: healthy food. By growing and sharing their own food throughout local communities, they have witnessed tangible results that people benefit from, both in and out of their gardens. Check them out and lend a hand at https://www.urbansymbiosis.org/

## The American Community Gardening Association (ACGA)

The ACGA is a grassroots non-profit advocacy organization focused on community gardening. Their mission is to build community by increasing and enhancing community gardening and greening across the United States and Canada.

With over 1,000 individual and 252 organizational members, they link 2100 gardens across Canada and the US, ranging from family allotments to tiny pollinator pocket parks, and from school gardens to urban farms. Our proudly diverse membership includes active community gardeners, supportive volunteers, garden organizing and sponsoring organizations, governmental agencies, and horticultural professionals including teachers, horticultural therapists, Cooperative Extension agents, landscape architects, and academic researchers. Get your hand in at https://www.communitygarden.org

## The Speed And Scale Plan

Speed & Scale is a global initiative to move leaders to act on the climate crisis. Our work focuses on education, advocacy, and solution-scaling.

With 10 objectives and 55 key results, the Speed & Scale plan shows how we can get to net-zero emissions by 2050—and halfway there by 2030.

A well-formed objective is significant, action-oriented, durable, and inspirational. Each objective is supported by carefully chosen and crafted key results. Strong key results are specific, timebound, aggressive (yet realistic) and most of all, measurable and verifiable. OKRs stand for Objectives and Key Results. They address the critical facets of any goal worth achieving: the "what" and the "how." Objectives are what you aim to accomplish. Key Results (KRs) tell us how we'll get the objectives done.

OKRs aren't the sum of all tasks. They focus on what's most important, the handful of essential action steps for a given pursuit. They enable us to track our progress as we go.

To learn more, visit https://speedandscale.com.

## Bioneers

For 30 years, BIONEERS has acted as a seed head for the game-changing social and scientific vision, knowledge and practices for environmental and social restoration. They do so through their annual national conference, award-winning media, local Bioneers conferences and initiatives, dynamic programs, and special projects.Check out their work and get involved at https://bioneers.org/

## Project Drawdown

Drawdown is the future point in time when levels of greenhouse gasses in the atmosphere stop climbing and start to steadily decline. This is the point when we begin the process of stopping further climate change and averting potentially catastrophic warming. It is a critical turning point for life on Earth. To reach Drawdown, we must work on all aspects of the climate equation—stopping sources and supporting sinks, as well as helping society achieve broader transformations. Read more about the work and get involved in making the drawdown happen at https://www.drawdown.org/drawdown-framework

### Transition Network

Transition is a movement that has been growing since 2005. Community-led Transition groups are working for a low-carbon, socially just future with resilient communities, more active participation in society, and caring culture focused on supporting each other. They are using participatory methods to imagine the changes we need: setting up renewable energy projects, re-localising food systems, and creating community and green spaces. They are sparking entrepreneurship, working with municipalities, building community connection and care, repairing and re-skilling. Find out more about the characteristics of Transition at https://transitionnetwork.org/

## EarthJustice

Earthjustice is the premier nonprofit public interest environmental law organization. They wield the power of law and the strength of partnership to protect people's health, to preserve magnificent places and wildlife, to advance clean energy, and to combat climate change. Give them a hand at https://earthjustice.org

## A Wildcards Playlist, Part 7

- Walela, 'Is Everybody Here', Walela, 2002 Triloka Records
- J.Folk, Sleep Walker, Chillhop Beat Tapes: J.Folk, 2022 Chillhop Publishing
- Jon Bon Jovi, 'Walls', This House Is Not For Sale Deluxe, Island Records 2018
- Vienna Teng, 'In The 99', Aims, Soltruna Records 2013
- Atomic Drum Assembly, 'We Out Here', Atomic Drum Assembly, Island Life Recordings 2016
- The Score, 'Revolution', Atlas, Republic Records 2017
- L.A Salami, 'Desperate Times and Mediocre Measures', Ottoline, Sunday Best 2022
- The Pretty Reckless, 'Fucked Up World', Death By Rock And Roll, Fearless Records 2021
- Konowoulen, 'Toukan Toukän', Le Merveilleux Voyage 2020
- Republica, 'Ready To Go', Republica, Deconstruction Records 1996
- The Interrupters, 'Divide Us', Say It Out Loud,

Hellcat Records 2016

- Sham 69, 'If The Kids Are United', The Best of Sham 69 [Essential], Anagram Records 2012
- Cut And Move, 'Run', Day Of Fire, Essential Records 2006
- Jon Bon Jovi, 'The Devil's In The Temple', This House Is Not For Sale Deluxe, Island Records 2018
- Deap Valley, 'End Of The World', Sistrionix, Island Records 2013
- Train, 'The Bridge', Bulletproof Picasso, Columbia Records 2014
- The Avengers, 'The American In Me', We Are The One, Dangerhouse Records 1977
- Dropkick Murphys, 'Worker's Song', Blackout, Hellcat Records 2005
- The Interrupters, 'Broken World', Fight The Good Fight, Hellcat Records 2018
- The Interrupters, 'Control', Say It Out Loud, Hellcat Records 2016
- Against Me!, 'Transgender Dysphoria Blues', Transgender Dysphoria Blues, Xtra Mile Records 2014
- No Doubt, 'Just A Girl', Tragic Kingdom, Interscope Records 1995
- Twisted Sister, 'We're Not Gonna Take It', Stay Hungry, Atlantic Records 1984

***Quoted Chapter 08***

- The Interrupters, 'Babylon', Say It Out Loud, Hellcat Records 2016
- Dropkick Murphys, 'Smash Shit Up', Turn Up That Dial, Born & Bred 2021
- Tom Petty And The Heartbreakers, 'Makin' Some

Noise', Into The Great Wide Open,1991 Geffen Records

- Jon Bon Jovi, 'Livin' On A Prayer', Slippery When Wet, Mercury Records 1985
- Minuit Machine, 'Don't Run From The Fire', Don't Run From The Fire, Synth Religion 2020
- Rebel Diaz, 'American Spring', 2012
- Grandson, 'Dirty', Death Of An Optimist, Fueled By Ramen 2020
- Playing For Change, 'Get Up Stand Up', PFC 3: Songs Around The World, Playing For Change 2016
- Mike Shinoda,'World's On Fire', Post Traumatic, Machine Shop 2018
- Starship, 'We Built This City', Greatest Hits (Ten Years And Change 1979-1991), RCA Records 1991
- TobyMac, 'Help Is On The Way', Help Is On The Way (Maybe Midnight), ForeFront 2021
- Alabama Shakes, 'Hold On', Boys and Girls, Rough Trade Records 2011
- The Score, 'Born For This,' Born For This, Republic Records 2019
- Royal Deluxe, 'No Limits', Savages, 2019
- Lawrence, 'Casualty', Hotel TV, Beautiful Mind Records 2021
- U2, Where The Streets Have No Name (Remastered), The Joshua Tree, Island Records 2007
- Florence + The Machine, 'Dog Days Are Over (2010 Version)', A Lot of Love….A Lot of Blood, Iamsound Records 2009
- Lindsey Stirling, 'Til The Light Goes Out', Artemis, BMG Rights Management 2019
- Grandson, 'Thoughts and Prayers', Death Of An Optimist, Fueled By Ramen 2020

- Passion Pit, 'American Blood', Gossamer, Columbia Records 2012
- SuperKnova, 'Goals', Goals, 2021
- Tracy Chapman, 'Talkin' Bout a Revolution', Tracy Chapman, Elektra/Asylum Records 1988
- Taboo and Hip Hop Caucus, 'Stand Up / Stand N Rock #NoDAPL', Printz Board 2019
- Billy Bragg, 'King Tide and the Sunny Day Flood', Bridges Not Walls, Solar Music 2016
- Nahko and Medicine for the People, 'Wash It Away', Take Your Power Back, Medicine Tribe 2022
- Vienna Teng, 'Shine', Warm Strangers, Virt Records 2004
- Aurora, 'The Seed' The Gods We Can Touch, Decca Records 2022
- Millie Turner, 'Underwater', Bathing In Blue, 7k! 2022
- MF Tomlinson, 'Sum of Nothing', Sum of Nothing, Awal Digital 2016
- Heather Mae, 'Stand Up', I Am Enough, 2016
- Satsang feat Wookiefoot, 'Speak Up', Pyramid(s), 2017
- Playing For Change, 'Higher Ground', PFC 3: Songs Around The World, Playing For Change 2016
- Jon Bon Jovi, 'Miracle', Miracle, Island Records 1990
- The Who, 'Street Song', WHO, Polydor 2019
- Tom Petty, 'You Wreck Me', Pretty Wildflowers, Warner Records 1994
- Train, 'Bulletproof Picasso', Bulletproof Picasso, Columbia Records 2014

- Imagine Dragons, ‘Believer’, Evolve, Interscope Records 2017
- Sam Tinnesz, ‘Even If It Hurts’, 2017
- Joan Jett, ‘World Of Denial’, Pure and Simple, Blackheart 1994
- Imagine Dragons, ‘Whatever It Takes’, Evolve, Interscope Records 2017
- The Score, ‘Unstoppable,’ Born For This, Republic Records 2019
- Marlon Craft, ‘State Of The Union’, How We Intended 2021
- U2,’Fire’, October, Island Records 1981
- Bon Jovi, ‘These Days’, These Days, Mercury Records 1995
- Svrcina, ‘Meet Me On The Battlefield’, Meet Me On The Battlefield 2016
- Crys Matthews, ‘Armor’, Come What May 2014
- Marcus Miller, ‘Let America Be America Again’, Marshall (Original Motion Picture Soundtrack), Warner Records 2017
- MILCK, ‘Quiet’, Quiet, Atlantic Records 2016
- Katy Perry, ‘Rise’, Single EP, Capitol Records 2016
- P!NK, ‘What About Us’, Beautiful Trauma, RCA Records 2021
- Pete Seeger, ‘Which Side Are You On?’ Almanac Singers Labor Songs, Columbia 1931
- Mandy Harvey, ‘This Time’, Single EP, SoNo Recording Group 2019
- Rhys Lewis, ‘Better Than Today’, Things I Chose to Remember, Decca Records 2022
- S.J. Tucker, ‘Rain Falls Hard’, Tangles, 2005

*Quoted Chapter 20*

- Rivers Monroe, 'Against The Odds', Smart Girls, Ingroove 2015
- Pat Benatar, 'Brave', Go, Bel Chiasso Records 2003
- OK Go - All Together Now (Official Video)- Internet Release 2020 https://www.youtube.com/watch?v=a5j50F4rlzA&list=PL8HyB52xsG8WPKL-VwkNpOfH4CtacWJtW&index=77&ab_channel=OKGo
- Low Lily, 'Hope Lingers On', 10,000 Days Like These, 2018
- Vienna Teng, 'Level Up', Aims, Virt Records 2020
- Phil Collins, 'Take Me Home', No Jacket Required, Atlantic Records 1985
- S.J. Tucker, 'Chalk On The Sidewalk', EP Single 2020
- Crys Matthews, 'Call Them In', Changemakers 2021
- Des'ree, 'Gotta Be', I Ain't Movin', Epic 1994
- Bishop Briggs, 'Champion', Champion, Island Records 2019
- Against The Current, 'Wildfire', Wildfire, Atlantic Records 2022
- J.Folk, Sleep Walker, chillhop beat tapes: J.Folk, Chillhop Publishing 2022
- Steeleye Span, 'The Dark Morris Tune', Wintersmith, Park Records 2013
- Charles Onyeabor, 'They Can't Pull Us Down (feat. Miriam Taylor)', Single EP 2020
- Benjamin Booker, 'Witness', Witness, Rough Trade 2017
- Pat Bentar, 'Invincible', Seven The Hard Way, Chrysalis Records 1985

- Gavin DeGraw, 'Fire', Finest Hour, RCA Records 2014
- Florence+the Machine, 'Shake It Out', Ceremonials, Island Records 2011
- Crys Matthews, 'Hope Revolution', Changemakers 2021
- Roxette, 'Dressed For Success', Look Sharp, EMI 1988
- Aaron Taylor, 'Get Through This', The Long Way Home, Believe Music 2020
- American Authors, 'I'm Born To Run', Island Records 2017
- Erik Larsen, 'Solidarity Forever Pete Seeger Trap Remix', EP Single 2020
- Rozzi Crane, 'Psycho', Space, Interscope Records 2015
- Barenaked Ladies, 'Odds Are', Grinning Streak, Vanguard 2013
- Pat Benetar, 'Shine', EP Single, Ingrooves 2020
- Christopher, 'Against the Odds, EP Single, EMI Music 2011
- Lindsey Stirling, 'Something Wild', Disney's Pete's Dragon Original Soundtrack, Walt Disney Records 2016
- Creed, 'With Arms Wide Open', Human Clay, Wind Up 1999
- Alanis Morissette, 'Guardian', Havoc and Bright Lights, Collective Sounds 2012
- Me First and the Gimme Gimmes, 'Danny's Song', Have A Ball, Fat Wreck Chords 1997
- Alanis Morissette, 'Ablaze', Such Pretty Forks In The Road, Epiphany 2020

- Vienna Teng, ‘Lullaby For A Stormy Night’, Waking Hour, Virt 2020
- Vienna Teng, ‘Green Island Serenade’, Warm Strangers, Virt Records 2004

***Quoted Chapter 27***

# Other Books By The Author

**The Aces High, Jokers Wild Series**

Aces High, Jokers Wild Book 1: The Hands We're Given

Aces High, Jokers Wild Book 1.5: The Boys of Summer Have Gone

Aces High, Jokers Wild Book 2: Call the Bluff

Aces High, Jokers Wild Book 2.5: After Hours Game (A Wildcards Christmas)

Aces High, Jokers Wild Book 3: Raise the Stakes

Aces High, Jokers Wild Book 3.5: Bad Hand (A Wildcards Halloween)

Aces High, Jokers Wild Book 4: Aces and Eights

Aces High, Jokers Wild Book 4.5: Follow The Lady

Aces High, Jokers Wild Book 5: Draw Dead

Aces High, Jokers Wild Book 5.5: Draw Out

Aces High, Jokers Wild Book 6: Deuces Are Wild

Aces High, Jokers Wild Book 6.5: Fill The Pot

**Anthologies**

Neon Dreams and Nightmares: Mixed Punk Works of Dystopian Futures

Dark Horizons: A Collection of Near-Future, Dystopian, and Cyberpunk Sci-fi: Multi author 5 book box set

## About The Author

Bringing their own experiences as a marginalized author to the page with flawed but genuine characters, O.E. Tearmann's work has been described as "Firefly for the dystopian genre." Publisher's Weekly called it "a lovely paean to the healing power of respectful personal connections among comrades, friends, and lovers."

Tearmann lives in Colorado with two cats, their partner, and the belief that individuals can make humanity better through small actions. They are a member of the Science Fiction Writers of America, the Rocky Mountain Fiction Writers, and the Queer Scifi group. In their spare time, they teach workshops on writing GLTBQ characters, plant gardens that showcase sustainable agricultural practices, and play too many video games.

Made in the USA
Middletown, DE
08 May 2023

30226333R00175